WHERE THE DAWN FINDS US

KATE HEWITT

Storm

This is a work of fiction. Names, characters, businesses, places, events and incidents are either the products of the author's imagination or used in a fictitious manner. Any resemblance to actual persons, living or dead, or actual events is purely coincidental.

Copyright © Kate Hewitt, 2026

The moral right of the author has been asserted.

All rights reserved. No part of this book may be reproduced or used in any manner without the prior written permission of the copyright owner. This prohibition includes, but is not limited to, any reproduction or use for the purpose of training artificial intelligence technologies or systems.

To request permissions, contact the publisher at rights@stormpublishing.co

Ebook ISBN: 978-1-83700-037-1
Paperback ISBN: 978-1-83700-039-5

Cover design: Eileen Carey
Cover images: iStock, Shutterstock

Published by Storm Publishing.
For further information, visit:
www.stormpublishing.co

ALSO BY KATE HEWITT

The Last Stars in the Sky
The Midnight Hour

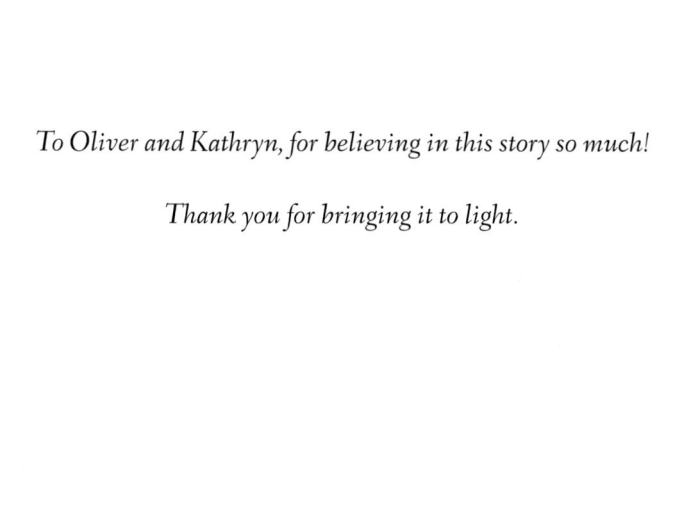

To Oliver and Kathryn, for believing in this story so much!

Thank you for bringing it to light.

ONE
ALEX

Our reception at the air base in North Dakota is something between a welcome-home party and a military parade. As I leave the plane, clutching my daughter Ruby's hand with my son Sam following behind, a ragtag band starts up an uneven version of "America the Beautiful" and someone throws confetti. It falls in a rainbow of paper pieces around us and I brush it out of my hair, like a bride. A cutting wind is coming off the plains, and it feels like we've landed at the very edge of the earth. Besides a few prefabricated metal-roofed sheds, all I can see in every direction is an endless stretch of brown, dirt and dead grass. Our new home.

Around fifty people have come with us on a military plane, to start life over in this square of land in the northwest corner of North Dakota that is now the entirety of the United States of America. Despite the music, the forced air of jollity, everyone is dazed and silent as they follow a man in combat fatigues onto the tarmac. The whole surreal scenario makes me want to laugh, and yet I am also so very close to crying, every emotion hovering near the surface, ready to break through and overwhelm.

It's taken far too much to get to this moment, this place, and in doing so I had to leave my older daughter behind, along with my husband's grave. I picture Mattie's pale face set in determined lines as we said goodbye; I was the one who clung, who didn't want to let go.

Now I squeeze Ruby's hand as we huddle with the other passengers on the airfield, waiting for directions. No one seems to know what to do, how to be, and as I tilt my head to the granite-colored sky I feel like it could swallow me whole. The open emptiness of the landscape makes me paradoxically feel both trapped and weightless, like I could free fall into an abyss.

"Welcome, welcome," the man in camo fatigues greets us, smiling widely while everyone stares blankly back. "Welcome to the United States of America!"

Or at least what's left of it. Eighteen months ago, nuclear bombs devastated most of the country's major cities, followed by radiation fallout and pollution from damaged factories and oil refineries. The last I heard, close to ninety-five percent of the population had died, including my mother, my siblings, my *husband*, as well as friends, colleagues, acquaintances... just about everyone I've ever known.

The only reason why I survived, along with my children, is because we were staying at my family's remote cottage in the Canadian wilderness, now nothing more than ashes and memories, a smoking ruin taken over by a roving gang.

I force those memories back as I board the bus. It's an old school bus with vinyl bench seats and a smell of stale sweat. Ruby and I slide into a seat in the middle, and Sam takes the one behind us.

I look around at my fellow passengers as they board; we all took the same two-hour flight from Mackinaw City, Michigan, to get here, but we barely spoke to each other along the way. Despite the hope we all want to feel, I think everyone is simply too burned out and broken to try to make pleasantries. And what pleasantries, really, can be made?

Not one of us has any idea what we're willingly walking into. Five months ago, I had escaped a settlement in North Bay, Ontario that kept us safe through barbed wire and intimidation, to live in a cooperative community on the shores of Red Cedar Lake, even further north. That was a needed respite, but it couldn't be the rest of my life, my children's lives, even if Mattie chose it for herself.

And yet is this—whatever this turns out to be—going to be any better? The question has been reverberating through me relentlessly since I first considered leaving everything I'd known to come here. I so want it to be better, and I know Ruby and Sam do, too. We've been given promises of education, opportunity, the kind of life we once took for granted, maybe even disdained a little. A house to live in, a yard, a car, an *internet connection*—all of them feel like miracles, or magic. It feels too good to be true, but maybe all we need to do is believe... and trust. Trust that this is a good future for us, that we can make it so.

"Welcome, welcome." This time it's a trim woman in her thirties, also in camo fatigues and sporting a neat dark-blond ponytail, who gives us the cheery hello. She stands at the front of the bus, a lanyard and whistle around her neck and a clipboard in her hand. I feel like we're going to summer camp.

Outside, the plains of northern North Dakota stretch on and on in a sea of deadened brown, towards the badlands twenty miles south, no more than hazy humps on the horizon. I think of the raggedy rendition of "America the Beautiful" that we just heard. *Amber waves of grain...* Right now it feels like a sea of nothing. The emptiness, the utter bleakness of it, unsettles me. I'm used to the thick pine forests and rushing rivers of northern Ontario, the smooth expanse of Red Cedar Lake, fringed by evergreens and birch. I want something to relieve my roving gaze, to settle on, but all I see is prairie.

"I know it's taken a lot for you all to be here," the woman resumes in a briskly cheerful voice. "And you'll probably have a lot of questions about what happens next. I'm here to tell you what those next steps are. First off, you'll be taken to an integration center in Watford City, where you'll spend three days in isolation." She holds up a hand to forestall any protests, although no one seems stirred to make any; we're all staring at her, slack-jawed, still too dazed to question or complain.

"I know that might seem a little alarming," she continues, "but it's simply a precaution to make sure our community is free of any communicable disease, infection, or, although this is less likely now, radiation."

She pauses, as if waiting for us to absorb the possibility that we're infectious, emanating toxins or radiation or who knows what else, before continuing in the same brisk voice, "From there, you'll be allocated housing and given information about education and employment. There are supports in place to help you integrate into this new life, which you will be able to learn more about during your time in isolation, through the information that will be provided."

Another pause, along with a sympathetic smile. "I know it won't be easy, but this is the beginning, and you are all part of creating the new United States of America." She says the last bit with a throb of emotion in her voice, and I suspect she wants us all to have a rush of noble patriotism, hands on hearts as we rise bravely to meet the future we will all forge together, this new class of patriots, but I can barely summon more than a flicker of feeling.

I glance again out the window and think of Mattie. I remember the feel of her thin arms wrapped around me as she'd promised me, fervent in her certainty, that she'd be okay.

How could I leave her? And not just her, but others we'd come to know and even love—Kyle, the kid we rescued who is now my daughter's boyfriend, something I admittedly feel decidedly ambivalent about, and Phoebe, the five-year-old whose mother lost her life when we were fleeing for our own. My friend Nicole too, and her teenaged son, Ben. I know Mattie is with people she knows and loves, but she's not with *me*. With us, her family.

I promised her I'd visit as soon as I can, but even as I said the words, I wondered if such a thing will even be possible in this new world whose limits and possibilities I have yet to fathom—or accept.

Before I left, we looked at a map and saw that Watford City is directly west of Red Cedar Lake, a distance of thirteen hundred miles, past the Great Lakes and across a country's border. It wasn't an easy journey even before the bombs, and in this brave new world where the only outpost of civilization is a few hundred square miles in North Dakota?

I just don't know.

On the way here, we saw encouraging signs—houses being repaired, medical stations offering services. The world, not as we once knew it but a faint approximation at least, was being rebuilt. But I still can't imagine how I or my children are going to exist in it.

"Look." Ruby tugs on my sleeve before pointing to the airfield outside. Some soldiers are loading our bags into another bus. We didn't have much—one duffel bag for the three of us, just our clothes and a few personal items. Judging by the bags they're throwing into the bus, most people are the same. We've all lost so much since the world caught fire. What are we going to gain here?

I twist around in my seat to smile at Sam. Nineteen years old, rescued by his father from college a month after the first bombs fell, it took them over four months to get back to us in Ontario, and I still don't know all that happened to them then, only that it haunted my husband, and my son, too, albeit in a different way. It's been a long time since he's been willing to look me in the eye.

"How are you doing, Sam?" I ask, and he hunches his shoulders, forces a smile.

"Okay, I guess. Where do you think they'll keep us in isolation?"

I shrug, managing a smile back. "I don't know." How could I? I don't know anything about Watford City, save that it's small and remote, a town of about six thousand, or at least it was. Who knows what the population is now, but it is the center of Western civilization.

The bus starts up and a ripple runs through the group, of anticipation and anxiety in what I think are equal amounts. *What are we heading into?*

I glance at a woman sitting across from me—middle-aged, haggard, her hair boasting a good four inches of steel-gray roots, the rest an artificial orange. I smile, and she smiles back, tremulously, before looking away.

The tiny airport is only a mile from the center of Watford City, such as it is, which seems far from an actual city, just a few streets, with only emptiness beyond. The buildings, many of brick, are all low, only one or two stories, and the town has an air of having been plunked down in the middle of nowhere, the wide sky above making it seem even smaller than it is.

I glance at some of the storefronts—Shooters Café, City Bar, the American Legion Club. New signs have been constructed in front—Integration Center, Employment Office, Medical Services. Most of the people walking down the street are in military uniform. It reminds me, weirdly, of the Old West, or at least what I imagine it must have been like—a feeling of optimism and expanse, of carving out the civilities in a land that is wild and untamed, and yet with a remoteness and sense of isolation that strikes an icy note in my soul.

The bus pulls into a Comfort Inn and Suites, a cluster of anodyne beige buildings surrounded by an expanse of concrete parking lot. More emptiness. I spy a welcome banner over the front doors.

"Please exit the bus and head towards the lobby," the woman who gave us the welcoming spiel instructs. "From there, you'll be allocated your room and given information about next steps."

Everyone starts shuffling off the bus; a few people whisper to each other, but it's still a muted, cautious crowd. Outside the cold air is like a slap to the face, a shock to my lungs; it's mid-April but in northern North Dakota there are not yet any signs of spring. The world, from the sky to the buildings to the stretch of prairies surrounding us, is a muted landscape of brown and gray in every direction.

We follow the others into the lobby, where several folding tables have been set up for registration, like we're at some corporate event where you mill around, chitchatting with strangers and sipping bad coffee.

Ruby slips her hand into mine.

At the first table, we're given lanyards with our names and birthdates on and instructed to put them on. At the next, an information packet in a plastic folder. At the third, a crate of dishes and utensils; we have a plate, bowl, cup, knife, fork, spoon each. Then we're told our room assignment, and finally everyone is ushered into a conference room with folding chairs, and we're given a rundown on what the next three days are going to look like.

"For the next seventy-two hours, you will need to remain in your hotel room," yet another member of military personnel states with firm precision. "I appreciate this might be frustrating for you, but I assure you it is a necessary precaution, to make sure that no infectious diseases are brought into our community. You have been given adequate food and water for this amount of time, and there are basic toiletries and other supplies in your hotel rooms. In emergencies, you may use the phone to call reception, but I repeat, that is only for emergencies. Any questions?"

A woman shakily raises her hand and the man nods, a permission to speak.

"I have asthma." Her voice trembles. "My last inhaler ran out two weeks ago..."

The man nods again, briskly accepting, unmoved and unfazed. "A medical officer will visit you in your room to assess any physical needs." He looks around the room without meeting any of our dazed gazes. "Any other questions?"

No one speaks or raises a hand. It's as if we've become passive participants, unable to summon either enthusiasm or objection. And yet, I reflect, what did it take for all of us to get to this point? I think of my own experience—fighting for my life, my family's life, my home. Going on the run more than once. I've killed at least two men. And yet here I sit, as docile and uncertain as a shy sixth-grader at middle-school orientation.

"Now you will be led to your rooms," the man says, and we all shuffle from our seats.

The group is divided by floor; Sam, Ruby and I are in room 324, and we follow a few others to the elevator, led by yet another person in uniform, this time a woman with short, steel-gray hair. Still nobody speaks. It's so *strange*, to be in a hotel, to have this illusion of normalcy, yet with everything feeling so unfamiliar. Even pushing an elevator button feels bizarre, watching it light up and hearing it ping like a tiny miracle. I am quietly amazed when we start soaring upwards.

We follow the woman to our room; she unlocks the door with a key card which she then pockets. She gestures to Sam, who opens the door, and we all step inside. It's a room just like any of the many other hotel rooms I've stayed in over the years—comfortably bland, some basic flower prints on the walls, scratchy, polyester comforters with a paisley pattern spread tightly across the two queen-sized beds, and from the picture window framed by beige curtains, a view of the parking lot, gray asphalt under a grayer sky.

It's not until the door closes and I hear the sound of a chain being slid across that I realize we've been locked inside.

TWO
ALEX

"Did they just *lock* us in here?" Sam demands, whirling around to face the bland, olive-green door that now looks and feels like the door of a prison cell, thick and impenetrable.

"It seems so." I let out a shaky laugh as I walk to the window to stare down at the empty parking lot. "I guess they don't trust us yet," I tell my son. It makes me wonder if we should be trusting *them*.

Ruby comes to stand beside me, and we both stare out at the uninspiring vista—parking lot in front of us and then the modest downtown of Watford City, its low brick buildings lining a grid of sleepy-looking streets. Brown fields stretch beyond, the browner badlands in the distance. I've never been somewhere that feels so *empty*. The view hurts my eyes; I can't find any comfort in it.

I turn around to look at our home for the next seventy-two hours. The two queen beds, a dresser, a desk, and a large flatscreen TV. Bemused, I pick up the remote control and dubiously press the power button. Amazingly, the TV turns on, a blue flicker before it settles on a home screen that welcomes us to Watford City.

When have I last watched TV? Back at the airbase in North Bay, where we lived for four months, I watched a movie they played in the gym like we were campers in need of entertainment

—some forgettable comedy from decades ago that had felt gratingly offensive in our current situation.

But as for TV... the last time I saw a screen come to life like this one just has, it was drone footage of the first bomb falling on New York City. I was only able to watch for a few stunned seconds before the camera cut out. Now I stare at the screen—besides the welcome message, there is an image of the Great Seal of the United States. I gaze at the familiar logo—the bald eagle, the olive branch and arrows, and the motto that every school child should know. *E pluribus unum.* Out of many, one.

Out of nothing, this.

"Is there actually TV?" Sam asks, a lilt of interest in his voice, the outrage gone. Who cares if we're locked inside if we have cable?

"Well, it seems there's something." I press a button and the screen changes to, of all things, an old episode of *Friends*.

"I know this one," Sam exclaims. "It's the one with all the cheesecakes."

Ruby comes to stand next to me as we watch—a cheesecake has mistakenly been delivered to Chandler's apartment, and he feels guilty for eating it. Then he gives some to Rachel, who eats it and also feels guilty. The hilarity continues, with them agreeing to give a second cheesecake back before fighting over it and dropping it and then deciding to eat it—off the floor. All of this is accompanied by a laugh track that grates on my ears.

It isn't until the credits roll that I realize we've watched the whole twenty-two-minute episode without any of us moving or speaking. I push power again, and the screen turns dark.

"Mom," Sam protests, and I turn to look at him. Under my gaze, he ducks his head, abashed, before raising it once more to gaze at me defiantly.

"What else are we going to do?" he asks, his tone aggressive, and I smile faintly.

"I didn't say anything."

"You didn't need to," he snaps, and I wonder where the

animosity is coming from, why he's angry with *me*. I suppose there's no one else to be angry with right now. I walk to the door and turn the handle, just to see, but I can only pull the door back an inch or two before the chain that's been bolted across it pulls tight. We really are locked in... something they didn't mention in their little welcoming spiel, when they talked about toiletries and making sure we had everything we need.

I release a shaky breath, determined not to panic. They're processing a lot of people here; obviously, they need an efficient system. One of the military guys on the plane said they were getting several hundred people arriving every day. In addition to Watford City, there are a dozen or so other towns in northern North Dakota that have been repurposed to be the birthplace of a new United States—Williston, sixty miles away and bigger than Watford City, and New Town, fifty miles away and smaller, are the ones I can recall. The whole area, of several thousand square miles, is patrolled, the guy told us, with manned checkpoint stations on all the roads. He told this to make us feel safer, but I'm not sure how reassured I am, now that I'm standing on the wrong side of a locked door.

I turn from the door. "Rubes, why don't we go through our supplies?" I nod to the two plastic crates on top of the dresser. "See what we've got."

"Okay." Ruby goes to the first crate, which is filled with freeze-dried meals—white chicken chili, morning oats, cheesy beef bowl, biscuits and gravy. Ruby goes through them all, counting each one. There are twenty-seven, enough for us to have three meals a day, such as they are. I remember buying meals like this for a camping trip Sam went on with the Scouts; it feels like a million years ago, otherworldly. Besides the meal packets, there are also thirty-six eight-ounce bottles of water and six bars of Hershey's chocolate. It feels like war rations, which in a way I suppose it is. It is certainly more food than we've been used to in the past.

For a second, I let myself remember those months at my parents' cottage—the woodsmoke from the fire, the stillness of the lake, the sense of peace we found there even as we were slowly starving.

Twenty-seven meal packets for three days is an absolute luxury. I need to remember that when I'm pacing this room, staring at that locked door.

"Well, we won't want for food," I say as cheerfully as I can, although I hear a tremble in my voice. I am thinking of Mattie this morning—her pale, strained face, Phoebe on her hip and holding hands with Kyle. My daughter is only sixteen and yet she has the toughened determination of a much older and battle-hardened woman.

We left her at Red Cedar Lake where she will act as mother to five-year-old Phoebe, a child we took in when her mother died, and wife—a thought I can hardly bear to articulate—to Kyle, the nineteen-year-old kid we took in out of pity more than anything else. This is not the future I wanted for my daughter—living in a commune, working herself to the bone just to eke out her survival, tied to a man she wouldn't have spared a second glance back in our old lives. If that makes me a snob, so be it. I want more for my daughter.

Why didn't she come with us?

And yet, looking at that locked door, I think I understand why.

"Is anyone hungry?" I ask. I have no idea what time it is; the day has passed in a blur of movement. We left just after dawn to drive five hours to Mackinaw City, leaving the car we'd taken from North Bay abandoned by the airstrip. Then we had two hours on the flight, and then who knows how long getting here, being *processed*. I glance at the gray sky, the sun no more than a brighter haze, but it's low in the sky, sinking toward the distant horizon. It must be nearing evening.

"What do you feel like, Sam?" I ask, my tone too jovial. "Pepperoni pizza bowl?" I sift through the packets. "Korean-inspired beef?" I turn to Ruby. "What about you, Rubes? Creamy mac and cheese? Homestyle chicken noodle casserole?"

It all sounds so delicious, until you realize it's nothing more than a dried powder with some boiled water to make it even remotely edible.

Ruby shrugs, seeming dismissive, but then, after a moment, she rallies and looks through the packets with some interest. "I'll have the biscuits and gravy."

That's a breakfast pouch, but I'm not about to argue the point. Fatigue is crashing over me, dragging me under. I want to curl up in a ball and forget everything, just for a few hours. Forget that my husband died just over a month ago, that I don't know when I'll see my daughter again, that this new world stretching in front of us feels frightening and, worse, maybe like a mistake.

Why did they lock us in?

I take a steadying breath and reach for the pouch Ruby selected. I know why they did. I understand it, even if I don't like it. It makes sense, or so I tell myself.

"Right, now we need some boiling water." I smile at my daughter, who smiles back uncertainly, doubt and fear lurking in her brown-eyed gaze. She is thirteen years old, and she has seen far too much suffering and strife for her young life. Since she was a toddler, Ruby has been selectively mute. I'm ashamed to say we didn't even notice at first; when you have a busy household with an eight-year-old boy and a five-year-old girl, you don't notice so much that your two-year-old isn't talking.

But then her preschool teacher mentioned it, her tone both sanctimonious and censorious, and I got all prickly and defensive, dragging Ruby to a specialist just to prove she really was fine, only to find out that while no diagnosis fit, she certainly had *something*. Enough, anyway, to have it noted to the school, so teachers can make allowances, and her friends can understand why Ruby might sometimes seem a little weird.

She has always been solitary, cautious, watchful. Eighteen months surviving a nuclear holocaust has, I fear, only exacerbated those qualities, and yet my youngest child is so sweet, so kind, paying attention to things no one else notices, diligent in her curiosity and care. My heart aches with love for her now.

We came here, in no small part, for her. For her and Sam to have at least a chance at a normal life—school, friends, happiness. I release a shaky breath.

"Is there a kettle around here?" I ask and Ruby points to one by the TV.

"Okay." I take it and head to the bathroom, a small, utilitarian room done all in white tile, to fill the kettle. As it fills, I stare at my reflection; it's been a while since I've looked in a mirror. I'm gaunt, gray-haired, wild-eyed. I look far older than forty-three. I flick my gaze away as the kettle overflows and lukewarm water splashes onto my hand.

"Okay," I say again as I head back into the bedroom. Sam is sprawled on the bed, moodily switching through channels. "It's all sitcoms," he informs me, "and nature shows."

"I wonder where they got them all," I remark as I plug in the kettle. I have no idea how the world is working anymore; how Watford City can have electricity and running water when most of the country lies in ruins. How we can be watching *Friends* and *Blue Planet* when New York City, Los Angeles, and at least two dozen other cities are nothing more than smoking ruins. When the entire east coast has become unlivable, thanks to both radiation and pollution from the factories and refineries that were blown up. When there are only about fifteen million people left in the entire US, eking out a living in remote communities and homesteads, and it feels like nothing *works* anymore.

I know from the guy on the plane that there's an air base about a hundred miles northeast from here. It's a headquarters for America's now nascent military... whatever that means.

The kettle boils and clicks off. I smile at Ruby.

And then someone knocks on the door.

THREE
MATTIE

Mattie wakes early when Phoebe tugs on her sleeve, silent and wide-eyed, standing by her bed, her thumb in her mouth. Outside the sun has only just risen, the shore of Red Cedar Lake lost in shadow as mist rises from its placid surface in ghostly shreds before evaporating into the pale blue sky. Her family left three days ago, for Watford City; Mattie hugged them in turn, stoical and determined, refusing to cry, wanting to be fierce. She chose to stay here. She wanted to; she really did.

It's the start of the rest of her life, but the trouble is, it doesn't *feel* like her life. Lately, more and more, Mattie has been feeling like a spectator to her own existence, as if she's watching it all unfold from the wings, or even from one of the cheap seats, high up in a darkened theater, wondering what's going to happen next, questioning whether any of it is believable, maybe even getting a little bored by the story. Maybe she'll just walk out, do something else, but of course she can't.

She keeps telling herself not to feel this way, yet she cannot shake the sense of surreality that this—*this*—is now her life. *Surely not*, some part of her whispers. *Surely this isn't it.* A fishing camp in northern Ontario, sweating six hours a day in the kitchen, a little girl she loves but isn't always sure how to mother, and Kyle.

"Are you hungry, Phoebe?" Mattie whispers, and the little girl nods. Mattie has known her for just over a year, has acted like her mother for the last few months. It is Mattie whom Phoebe comes to when she cries, when she's happy, when she wants something. Mattie who washes her hair and tickles her tummy, who cuts her food into tiny squares, who swings her up onto her hip where she settles comfortably, one skinny arm hooked around Mattie's neck.

Now Mattie takes the little girl by the hand and leads her out of the bedroom of the cabin she once shared with her parents and Ruby, Sam and Kyle next door, before her dad died and her mother and sister and brother left. The memory of them all causes an ache in her chest, like heartburn. Nothing will shift it.

She can't quite believe how alone she is, stuck in this tiny commune with no family whatsoever, nothing to truly tie her to this place or these people, and so she tries not to think about it too much.

In the living room, Mattie crouches to kindle the fire and then finds a granola bar for Phoebe from the stash that is running low. Vicky, who runs the community here, gave her a box last week, warned her that these kinds of items were becoming scarce, with no more Costco to dole out supplies. They need to be independent, Vicky told her, her tone both gentle and stern, her hazel eyes blazing with certainty. If they're going to make this community work, they need to eat only what they grow—vegetables from the greenhouses and garden, eggs from the chickens, fish from the lake. Next spring, there will be wheat and barley and corn. The granola bars, however, will soon be gone.

Phoebe nibbles hers quietly as Mattie grabs a cardigan from the bedroom—it belonged to her mother and still smells like her, of soap and sweat and some faint odor that Mattie can't identify but knows is her mom, a sort of musky sweetness that makes her think of impromptu hugs in the kitchen, or being sprawled together on the sofa in the family room, heads resting against the back, something mindless on TV. It was so very long ago, it feels like it never happened. Maybe it didn't.

Mattie pushes her arms into the sleeves, pulls it around her waist. Even though it's mid-April, there is still frost on the inside of the windowpanes, like an etching of lace. She can see the frosty puffs of her breath in the still air.

Mattie curls up on the sofa, Phoebe clambering onto her lap, her gaze on the flickering flames of the fire she kindled, something she didn't even know how to do a year ago and now is second nature, thoughtless. This moment, Mattie thinks, should be peaceful, full of beauty; through the picture window she can see the lake, now shimmering with dawn light, the last of the mist rising in the air, disappearing against the deepening blue sky.

Mattie presses a kiss to Phoebe's hair, her eyes closed. The little girl snuggles in closer, and something like peace tempts her, just out of reach, elusive as ever, a dream that dances away whenever she tries to reach for it. Her stomach is a knot of anxiety, her mind a haze of grief. She misses her mother. She misses her father, who died when it felt like she wasn't looking, slipping away before she'd barely been able to accept that he'd been sick at all.

Eighteen months ago, Mattie reflects, the thing she was angriest about was not having a signal on her phone. Who had aired her on Snapchat. Whether her pothead boyfriend was going to text her. Looking back on that girl is like looking back on some sad stranger, someone she doesn't like, and maybe even despises.

And yet the trouble is, she has no idea who she is now. She plays at being this badass teenager, like some defiant heroine of an angsty young-adult novel, hair blowing in the wind, hands on her slender hips as she strides her fantasy world, chin tilted in defiance.

But that's not, Mattie knows, who she really is. That's not who she feels like. Inside, she feels like the little girl who climbed into her mother's bed after she'd wet her own and begged her mom not to tell her big brother that she'd done it.

Tears crowd Mattie's eyes, and one trickles down her cheek before she dashes it away, angry with herself for giving in to such emotion. She kisses Phoebe's head again, swiftly, maybe a little too hard, and the little girl squirms away, bored with the quiet peace of the moment, such as it was. Mattie watches as Phoebe kneels on the floor to put together a puzzle. There are few toys at Red Cedar Lake; it used to be a fishing and hunting camp, with a dozen cabins and a dining hall, and now it's "an intentional community," at least that's what it might have been called in the old world, before the bombs.

Now, Mattie thinks, it's just people trying to survive.

Vicky dug out a few toys from some forgotten cupboard when they first arrived—the puzzle and a couple of books, a doll with no clothes, some Matchbox cars that were missing their wheels. It was the kind of stuff you might pay a quarter for at a garage sale, and yet it seems to be enough for Phoebe.

Mattie tucks her knees up to her chest and focuses on taking deep breaths. Sometimes doing that helps loosen the knot in the pit of her stomach, just a little. *Breathe*, she thinks. *Breathe, and maybe it will get better*. Or at least it will feel as if it does, for a little while.

The fire crackles and spits and Phoebe looks up, startled, before silently resuming her puzzle. Mattie closes her eyes.

She is picturing her father, the way she last saw him when he was lying in bed, so pale and weak he could barely lift his head from the pillow. And then she is picturing him as she remembers him from her childhood—whistling on the stairs, making blueberry pancakes on a Saturday morning, calling her Matilda—a name she's always hated, save for when her dad said it—in a fake British accent.

A wave of something like homesickness sweeps through her, although it can't really be homesickness because there's no more home to miss. This fishing camp on the shores of a lake she'd never heard of before is the closest thing she has to a home now.

She chose it, she reminds herself. She wanted this.

Phoebe rises from the half-finished puzzle and goes to stand before her, wide-eyed and solemn.

"I'm hungry."

Mattie startles from her reverie, lets out a sigh. "Want to go get some breakfast?" she asks.

Mattie gets their coats from the hook by the door, helps Phoebe into her boots. Outside it's still bitterly cold, the ground underfoot frozen hard. The ice covering the lake only broke up a few weeks ago, and the world is still firmly held in the barely loosened grip of winter. Spring, with its warm breezes and green grass and flowers, feels far away.

Mattie holds Phoebe's hand as they walk from their cabin to the main lodge, where the dining hall and kitchen are. On the still expanse of the lake, a loon makes an elegant landing, dark wings outstretched as it skates along the smooth water.

Inside the main cabin, Mattie breathes in the comforting smell of coffee and scrambled eggs. Sheryl, who ran this place before the bombs with her husband, Don, is in the kitchen, making breakfast. Nicole, who came with them from North Bay, is curled up on one of the sofas with a cup of coffee, looking pensively into the fire. She glances at Mattie as she comes in, offers a quick, guarded smile which Mattie returns.

Mattie does not know what to make of Nicole. She spent the first six months of the post-nuclear world in a bunker for billionaires with her annoyingly arrogant husband, William, whom she left behind at North Bay, and teenaged son, Ben. Ben is the same age as Mattie, but he has yet to shed the adolescent attitude of their old way of life, although he tries, at least a little. Both Nicole and Ben seem damaged and difficult, and Mattie has avoided them, which has been surprisingly easy in such a small place. Everyone is busy with their own chores, and Ben sticks with Kyle and Sam, at least he did before Sam left. Nicole seems to prefer being by herself, and that's fine by Mattie.

What, she wonders, is her family doing now? Is it safe in North Dakota? Is it *normal*? She has no idea if they're settled in a house, if her siblings will go to school, if it's going to be an army compound like North Bay was with all its restrictions and rules, or if it will be more like their old life, *real* life, albeit in a microcosm.

She misses Ruby's silent presence, even though her sister so often annoyed her, the way she stared at you with those big eyes, how she clung to their mom. She misses Sam's jokey attitude, even when she was frustrated by his bravado, how he could never be serious. She even misses her mom's constant, anxious frown, the furrow in the middle of her forehead that the last eighteen months has dug even deeper.

"Hey, Mattie. Phoebe." Sheryl is, as ever, friendly and warm as she slices bread for toast. "You guys hungry?"

"Phoebe is," Mattie tells her. "I'll just have coffee."

She puts a precious teaspoon of granules in the bottom of a cup; yesterday morning Vicky warned them all, in that same severe tone she'd used about the granola bars, that they were close to running out. The little luxuries and treats, like coffee and granola bars, are finally coming to an end, and after that they'll have to make do with whatever they can make themselves.

Mattie has been there before, the winter after the bombs, back at her family's cottage. They struggled through dwindling rations. They made coffee from cleaver seeds; they ate *beaver*. The feeling of hunger, that gnawing emptiness in her stomach, never truly went away. The setup here is better, but she does not want to go through that kind of frightening uncertainty again, and she doesn't want Phoebe to, either.

Doubt flickers at the edges of her mind and then darts away, like a minnow in the lake, a flash of silver before disappearing into the depths. Should she have gone with her family? Sometimes Mattie can't remember why she didn't. She likes it here, she does, but it's not *home*. Not yet, anyway. Maybe such a thing doesn't exist anymore and never will again. She can no longer imagine what it would feel like, to be that comfortable and at ease, sprawled somewhere without a single worry blighting the empty landscape of her mind.

Mattie settles Phoebe at a table with a piece of toast and a glass of milk, fresh from that morning's milking. She sits next to her, sipping her weak coffee, watching the sun rise higher in the pale blue sky, letting her mind empty out for just a few moments.

Then the door to the cabin opens and Vicky strides through,

looking as competent and determined as ever, like she's been up for hours. Vicky is Sheryl and Don's daughter; she spent her summers at the camp as a child and was a lawyer in Toronto before the bombs. Now she's the de facto leader of the place, kind but firm. Mattie likes her, but since her mom left she's felt a sternness from her, and a stronger sense of authority that would make her uneasy if she let it, but she chooses not to.

Now Vicky smiles at Nicole and then trains her gaze on Mattie.

"Mattie." Her voice is warm but Mattie prickles; there's a purpose to Vicky's tone that makes her tense. "How are you doing this morning?"

"I'm okay." Her voice comes out too thready, like she's holding back tears, and she isn't. She just feels so strange, like she's floating, apart from everyone and everything else. It's a feeling she's had since her family left that she hasn't been able to shake, despite Kyle's attentiveness, Phoebe's hugs, the warmth of the other people here, the beauty of the lake. All of it should ground her, and yet none of it does.

Vicky rests a hand on her shoulder, a solid, comforting touch and yet Mattie has to resist the urge to shrug it off. She knows Vicky is trying to be supportive; she just doesn't know how to accept that support, or even if she wants it.

"It's a lot to process," Vicky tells her. "I'm hoping we can arrange a call with your mom sometime soon, on the ham radio... I've heard that the systems are up and running again, although after everything, it's hard to believe." She speaks lightly but there is a hint of bitterness in her voice, like an aftertaste. Mattie knows from Sheryl that she lost her fiancé in the bombing of Toronto. Vicky never speaks of it but the grief is there, dark in her eyes, etched in the lines on her face.

"Yeah," she says in reply. "That would be good, to call." Although she's afraid if she hears her mother's voice on a crackly radio, she might fall apart completely, and she doesn't want that.

"In the meantime," Vicky says, and now she sounds purposeful, taking her hand from Mattie's shoulder and giving her a meaningful look that Mattie doesn't understand and isn't sure she likes. "There's something I need to talk to you about."

FOUR
ALEX

The knock sounds again, a light tapping. Sam, Ruby, and I all exchange uncertain looks.

"Hello?" a male voice calls, gravelly and humorous. "Anyone in there?"

"Umm..." I hurry to the door, open it the inch the chain allows me to. "Hello?"

A man, gray-haired with glasses, smiles at me, his eyes crinkling in a way that makes me want to trust him. "Hello, I'm Dr. Brian Westcott," he says. "I'm one of the medical officers here. May I come in?"

I gesture to the chain. "I think that's *your* call," I say. I meant to sound wry, but I sound angry instead. It's hard to stop feeling suspicious.

"True," Dr. Westcott replies easily, "but I still like to ask. This is your room, after all."

I step back as he undoes the chain and enters our hotel room. He looks to be in his mid-fifties, dressed in a plaid button-down shirt and jeans, carrying a canvas medical bag. He glances at all of us, smile still in place.

"Alexandra, Samuel, and Ruby Walker?" he asks.

"Yes," I say, my voice coming out a little too strident. "That's us."

"Good. Nice to meet you." He extends his hand, and one by one we shake it, Ruby last, looking timid. "I'm here to give you a quick checkup, just to make sure there aren't any pressing issues we need to deal with. And I'm also here to address any concerns you might have about your health—physical and mental. Wherever you've come from, I'm pretty sure you've gone through a lot." He puts his bag down on the dresser. "Any questions so far?"

"No, I don't think so," I reply. His friendly attitude feels both comforting and jarring. I don't know how to respond to it.

"Okay then, who would like to go first?" he asks, smiling at Ruby.

"I will," I say resolutely, and step forward.

Dr. Westcott turns his smile to me. "Great."

The medical exam is quick—he listens to my heart, checks my blood pressure, asks me to take deep breaths, examines my eyes and ears and teeth. I take it all stoically, like it hurts and I'm handling it when in fact he's incredibly gentle. "So, where did you all come from?" he asks as he rests two fingers against my wrist, checking his watch.

"Northern Ontario," Sam says. "A fishing camp there."

The doctor nods, his gaze still on his watch. "You guys like to go fishing?"

"A little," Sam allows. "I did there, anyway."

"Bet there were some serious trout. Walleye, too, in northern Ontario. Have you ever had pan-seared walleye with a little butter and lemon? Delicious." He smiles as he looks up from his watch. "Great. Looks good," he adds, nodding to my wrist. "I'd say, judging by your teeth and skin, you're a little malnourished, which is unsurprising, all things considered. I'll bring some multivitamins for you. Do you have any health concerns of your own?" He waits, his eyes crinkled, smile in place.

I have so many concerns, nameless, formless things swirling in my stomach and filling up my head, but none of them have to do with my body and I am not going to voice them to this man. "I don't think so," I tell him.

"Okay, then, next up."

"I'll go," Ruby says softly, and we go through the whole rigamarole again—heart, lungs, eyes, ears, teeth.

"You've got some twelve-year-old molars coming in, young lady," he tells Ruby after looking in her mouth. "I'm no dentist, though. Once you're out of isolation, we'll schedule you for a dentist appointment. All of you," he adds. "The last year certainly took a toll on our teeth."

I think of the molar I spat out a year ago, when malnutrition caused my teeth to rattle in my slack gums. The thought of going to a dentist now seems impossible, ludicrous somehow. I picture someone in scrubs, smiling down at my open mouth. *Raise your hand if anything hurts.*

Can things really be that normal?

"All right, young man," Dr. Westcott says to Sam.

He finishes the final physical check, pronouncing Sam fit although a little malnourished, the same as Ruby and me. "Multivitamins all around," he pronounces. "And it wouldn't hurt to take two a day. Now, Sam, do you have any concerns?"

"Umm... yeah." Sam ducks his head, deliberately not looking at me. "How would I know if I had, you know, radiation poisoning?"

Dr. Westcott's expression turns serious. "You said you all were in northern Ontario? I don't think you'd have much danger of fallout there."

"Yeah, but... I was in upstate New York before that, at college near Utica." He swallows, a gulping sound we can all hear. "My dad came and got me, and it took us four months to get up to Canada."

"Your dad?" Dr. Westcott turns to me, and now his expression is grave, and I think he must suspect what I'm about to tell him.

"My husband died a little over a month ago," I say stiffly. "He had a tumor in his stomach. From the radiation. At least, that's what we assumed."

Dr. Westcott nods slowly. "I'm very sorry to hear that," he tells me quietly. "Very sorry for your loss."

I give a jerky nod. I can't manage any words.

"Well, son," the doctor says, turning to Sam, "I understand your concern. At least ninety percent of the USA's former territory is unlivable at the moment, for a variety of reasons. There are pockets of safe areas, but they're hard to reach, and the east coast has pretty much been emptied out." He is silent, steepling his fingers together. "And I wish I had better news for you, that I could promise that you won't have any ongoing effects from your exposure." He falls silent again, and we wait for his verdict. "When did you get up to safety?" he finally asks.

"Last June," Sam says.

Dr. Westcott nods slowly. "Well, I can say this. If you'd had serious radiation exposure, it would most likely have manifested itself by now. The fact that it hasn't is good news for you."

"But some people... they can get cancer five years later or something?" Sam asks. My heart twists; he sounds so young. "Because of it? Could that happen to me?"

Slowly Dr. Westcott takes off his stethoscope, holds it in his hand like he's weighing it. "I wish I could tell you it couldn't," he says quietly, "but that's not a promise I can make, son. And the truth is, I can't make it for anyone, radiation or not. And with the way the world is right now..." He smiles sadly at each of us in turn. "Who knows what anyone or anything will be like in five years?"

After the doctor leaves, sliding the chain across with a clank, we are all silent, absorbing what he said, what it means. I wanted more optimism, more hope for the future, but five years out feels like a very long time. The last eighteen months have been endless.

"So, biscuits and gravy," I tell Ruby and reach for the kettle.

Sam takes the thick information packet and sprawls on one of the beds, flicking it open. Ruby stands next to me as I pour boiled water into the pouch and then, with a spoon from our crate of supplies, I prod the dried granules carefully. It does not look appetizing, and it doesn't smell it, either.

"When we get out of isolation," Sam announces, "we'll get given accommodation, like a *house*." He sounds incredulous, and I almost smile. Living in our own house feels like a luxury now. I think of the cabin we all shared back at Red Cedar Lake, its cozy wood burner, its gorgeous view. That was a pretty nice house, I acknowledge, and then I wonder again why we left.

"And," Sam adds, enthusiasm kindling in his voice, "there's going to be college at the Rough Rider Center just out of town. Classes start in May. They're offering degrees in business administration, computer science, and mechanical and civil engineering."

"Anything else?" I ask, thinking of my own degree in English.

Sam glances up from the folder, looking both amused and annoyed. "They've got to be practical, Mom."

"I suppose." I stir the biscuits and gravy again. "I think it's ready, Rubes," I tell her, and I pour the gray sludge into a bowl. Somehow it looks even less appetizing in a dish. "What do you think you want to study, Sam?" I ask, letting my voice lilt with interest. I want to be interested; I want to be excited. I want to let myself believe this is good and it will work, and yet all the emotions feel like they're at a distance, just out of reach, and all I can do is snatch at them.

"I don't know, maybe business administration." He studies the packet. "That's closest to what I was doing before."

A memory falls into my mind—talking to Sam on the phone a few weeks after he started college. His excitement about his classes, the pickup basketball games he was playing with friends, that he was thinking of studying economics.

"That sounds good," I tell him. "Now, what would you like?" I gesture to the pouches of dehydrated food. "Korean beef? Cheesy pepperoni bowl?"

Sam glances at them all with dubious disinterest. "I'm not hungry."

"Okay." I'm not either, even though I haven't eaten since breakfast just before dawn this morning—scrambled eggs and toast back at Red Cedar Lake. I'd gazed at the smooth expanse of the lake, silvered by pale moonlight, as the sky began to lighten on the horizon, and tried to hold on to my hope.

A wave of homesickness rolls over me, and once again I wonder why we didn't stay.

"What about school for Ruby?" I ask Sam. "Is there anything in there about that?"

"There's a high school here in Watford City," Sam tells us. "Seventh through twelfth grade. It's starting in May, too."

"Wow, isn't that great, Ruby?" I exclaim. My daughter is holding her untouched bowl of biscuits and gravy, looking uncertain about a lot of things in life, food and school included. I touch her shoulder. "It's going to take a while," I tell her, and then glance at Sam to include him in the conversation. "For us to adjust to this." Whatever this is.

"Yeah, well we have three days of nothing to try," Sam replies. He sounds jokey rather than bitter; I think reading about the college energized him, for which I'm glad. One of us needs to be excited about this new life, and right now I know it's not me.

I move to the window and gaze out at the gray parking lot and brown fields. The sun has set, and shadows are lengthening, the view of the distant badlands already lost in darkness. A few lights twinkle in the town, and they hearten me. Signs of life in this strange new world that I don't understand but need to accept.

I press one hand to the glass and think of Daniel, of Mattie, of everything and everyone I left behind, for this unknown reality.

Daniel... I promised him I'd take care of our children, that I'd carve a life for us all however I could. I'd convinced myself his legacy was us coming here, starting over, *building* something in a way we couldn't back at Red Cedar Lake, where everyone was hunkering down and just trying to survive for as long as they could.

Ruby comes to stand next to me, slipping her arm around my waist as she leans her head against my shoulder, her bowl of biscuits and gravy untouched and forgotten. Neither of us speaks as the last of the sun sinks behind the barren hills and darkness covers the world.

FIVE
ALEX

On the morning of the fourth day in our hotel room, the chain is slid across and our door is opened. It feels like a resurrection.

The last three days have been a slow descent into depression, a steady slide and then scramble as we tried to keep ourselves from it. Either Dr. Westcott or Diana, a cheerful nurse practitioner, came every day to check on us. We were given multivitamins; we ate our dehydrated meals. The Korean beef bowl wasn't too bad, but the cheesy pepperoni was terrible.

We watched sixty-five episodes of *Friends*, some of them more than once.

We stayed silent for hours at a time and then one of us would suddenly spark into fury. Sam stunk out the bathroom; Ruby burst into tears. I missed Mattie with an ache that was becoming too painful to bear, a constant throb that never abated. Gritting my teeth didn't work anymore, and I felt too empty for tears.

Occasionally, in a burst of determined optimism, we would talk about the future, shyly mentioning the things we were looking forward to, along with the things we weren't sure about. Would there be stores? Money? How big was the area we'd be allowed to be in, exactly? Could we get a dog? Plant a garden? Go to the movies? It was both fun and frightening to consider such questions, having no ideas of the answers because they weren't in the information packet, which we'd all read several times, so some sections were practically memorized.

You will be allocated accommodation in one of the twelve integration zones. Within three days of your resettlement, all those not in full-time education must report to the employment office.

I'll be working, I thought with a thrill of both anticipation and terror. I hadn't had a paying job since before I'd had Sam. Back in North Bay, I'd been assigned kitchen duty, but I was half-hopeful that there might be something better for me here. As soon as I think that, though, I feel guilty. Some part of me doesn't feel like I should look forward to anything, considering Daniel is dead and my daughter is over a thousand miles away, alone, and yet imagining myself in some useful and interesting work is just about the only thing that gives my spirit a little lift. Maybe I'll be a teacher, or work in an office and wear skirts and heels. It seems both absurd and wonderful.

Now, on our fourth morning, Ruby stays as close to me as my shadow as the door is opened. Our duffel bag is packed, along with the crate of leftover food and water. We've learned long ago to hold on to whatever you have.

"Everybody out, everybody out!" a man shouts in a drill sergeant's voice as he strides down the corridor. "Everybody downstairs to the reception room where you will receive your accommodation billeting."

Sam slings our duffel bag over one shoulder while I heft the crate of food, and the three of us edge out into the hallway. Everyone is emerging from their rooms, blinking like moles, expressions uncertain. We follow others who are trudging toward the bank of elevators; it takes several trips to get us all downstairs.

In the lobby, military personnel herd us toward the reception room, the kind of place that would have once been used for corporate functions, all beige walls and bland carpeting. Rows of folding chairs have been set out and we shuffle into our seats, still holding on to our bags. It takes about fifteen minutes to get everybody in—we weren't the only plane that landed three days ago, it seems. There has to be at least two hundred people here, of all shapes, sizes, colors, kinds.

There are grizzled old men and fresh-faced young women with infants in their arms. There are children, some kicking their legs against their chairs or looking around in eager curiosity, others pale and dazed, silent and still, clinging to the adults in their lives, whoever they are. There are people with piercings and tattoos and watchful expressions, and middle-aged moms like me who seem hassled and exhausted. All of us now refugees in this new, unexplored world.

Finally, a man, muscular and in his fifties, someone I've never seen before, although all the camo fatigues are blurring into one gray-green blob, comes to the front of the room to stand behind a podium.

"Thank you for all being here," he says, and someone a few rows behind us lets out a huff of disbelieving laughter, because really? We've all been locked in our rooms for three days. It's not like we had much of a choice about whether we wanted to *be here* or not. "I know it takes both courage and daring," he continues, his gaze moving around the room, "to be willing to venture somewhere new, especially when the old has been destroyed." He has a stentorian voice, the gift of oration. He doesn't need a microphone.

"Some of you might feel that you came here because you had no choice, because there was nowhere else for you to go," he tells us. "And I want to say now that you are brave, too, because it takes courage not to give up. It takes stamina. It takes *faith*."

Almost against my better judgement, I find myself feeling stirred. I think of the Bible verse Daniel clung to, in his last days. *Though the fig tree does not bud and there are no grapes on the vines...*

It takes faith, or maybe just folly, to believe things can get better when nothing looks as if it will. I want to believe it's faith, but I'm not sure I can.

"In a few minutes," the man continues, now addressing the practicalities, "you will all be allocated your accommodation either here in Watford City, or in one of the nearby settlements. We are continuing to expand our territory as land is cleared for habitation, but it takes time, and we need your patience and understanding. There is a great deal of rebuilding to do, and as we well know, Rome wasn't built in a day. Neither will be the new United States of America." He smiles, inviting us to share the vision as well as the joke. "In the meantime," he says more seriously, "we ask that you do not leave your allocated area without permission. It's imperative that we keep our communities safe and radiation-free."

It makes sense, and yet even so a heaviness settles inside me. More rules. More limitations. I am not surprised.

"All of you will be integrated into the communities here, with opportunities for education and employment," he continues. "Any medical needs have been and will continue to be assessed, and those of you with concerns will be issued an appointment at one of our medical facilities. Please wait for that notification unless there is a true emergency, and then you should take yourself to the medical facility in your allocated area." He gives a rueful grimace. "I'm afraid we can't have a designated emergency telephone number such as 911 or an ambulance service yet, but we are working on it, I promise you. Every day there are new developments, opportunities."

He pauses, taking the time to gaze around the room. "Until then, however, life might feel very regulated." He gives us a wry smile, his craggy face creasing in a way that makes him seem more likeable, despite the news he's giving us. "It's not the American way, to have so many rules and regulations," he adds, like we've pointed that out ourselves and he's just agreeing with us. "And as soon as we can lift any rule, any regulation, we will. That is absolutely our guarantee. We value the liberty of every person who has chosen to be part of the rebuilding of the United States of America."

He pauses, and I can't help but wonder who is the *our* that he's referring to. Who runs this country, such as it is? A corner of North Dakota no more, but still. The president of the United States hasn't been heard from for over a year. When they were on the road, Daniel and Sam heard on the radio that he was alive and well, in "an undisclosed location," but where is he now? Who, actually, is in charge of this whole place? I've seen a lot of military personnel around, but I have no idea who is giving them orders.

Who, actually, is giving *us* orders.

But do I even need to know? We're safe here, and more than that, we have—as this man has just told us—possibility, opportunity. Maybe I just need to stop being suspicious, let go of all my fears and regrets, and *believe.*

The man at the front has started talking again, directing us to a woman at a table on the side who has our billets. It feels like a cross between soldiering and summer camp, which I guess is about right. I take Ruby's hand, the crate balanced against my hip, as we head over, following Sam.

I still have a million questions—we may have a billet, but what about food? Pots, pans, sheets for our beds, toilet paper, soap, *everything*? It feels like a lot hasn't been covered. I still have no idea how this world actually *works.*

After waiting in line for about ten minutes, we are given an address, a photocopied map of the town, and a key to 306 Third Street, right here in Watford City. Those headed for other settlements will take a bus from the parking lot of the Comfort Inn, or rather the Integration Center, which seems like a bit of an ironic name considering we have yet to integrate into anything. We, however, can walk.

We step outside into a morning that feels caught between winter and spring—sunshine on our faces but a cold wind buffeting us, making us shiver. Sam takes charge of the map, peering at it for a few seconds before he announces, "So we head down Third

Avenue, turn left on Main Street, and then a right on Third Street. It shouldn't take too long." He glances up, his gaze scanning the street in front of us. "This town isn't all that big."

It really isn't, I can't help but silently agree as we start out of the Comfort Inn's parking lot. Watford City feels like no more than a couple of streets, all of them clean and neat and very structured, but also weirdly empty. Maybe it's the absolute hugeness of the pale blue sky above us, or the view of endless plains and hills that stretches out beyond the city limits, which are not all that far away. I can't shake the feeling that some giant hand has plucked us from Red Cedar Lake and plunked us down in the middle of nowhere.

We start walking, past shuttered storefronts, a few others open. The buildings are all low, most made of brick, and lamp posts line the wide, empty street. The flatness of the land and the wide sky above us make me feel like I'm viewing the world through a wide-angled lens.

As we walk, I notice that many of the stores and restaurants of Watford City's limited downtown have been renamed; they no longer operate as independent businesses but rather as government agencies—grocery store, pharmacy, clothing store, home goods, named for what they offer and nothing else, but I guess the new government doesn't have an ad agency or a marketing research team. In the window of the home goods store, I see a sign: *Flatscreen TV, only Five Hundred Tickets!*

I have no idea how much a ticket is worth or where we get them, but the weirdness of it still gives me a frisson of unease. *Tickets?*

"What is this?" Sam mutters, catching sight of the same sign. "The Soviet Union circa 1961?"

He took a Cold War class at college, I recall, and he's not wrong. It does feel a bit... communist. We keep walking.

We walk all the way down Main Street, a wide boulevard lined with stores, and then turn onto Third Street, which is a residential street with a lot of prefabricated ranch houses, all of them close together, modest and neat, with small backyards that look out onto the backyards of other similar houses. Like any normal neighborhood, but I'm still unsettled by the emptiness of everything. Maybe I just need a little time to get used to it, this big-sky country, the wide-open spaces. Some people love this sort of landscape, I tell myself. I can become one of them.

We find our house halfway down the street, olive green, with a front stoop of concrete and a deck out back, overlooking a small, square yard of scrubby grass. I stare at it for a few seconds, feeling completely discombobulated. Is this really going to be my home? Nothing about it is familiar, not even in a distant way.

Sam goes up the stoop and unlocks the door. I turn to Ruby, who is looking solemn but also wary.

"Home sweet home," I quip, and as soon as I say them I feel the words fall flat. This doesn't feel like home, and yet, for all our sakes, it needs to, preferably soon.

"It's pretty nice inside," Sam calls as he steps into the front hallway. "Come on in."

Ruby and I mount the stoop and step into the house. It smells of cleaning spray, like someone blitzed the house with bleach. The whole house is floored in gray laminate wood, with an open floor plan—living room, kitchen, laundry room, and a half bathroom downstairs. The living room has two gray sofas and a black laminate coffee table; the kitchen has a table with four chairs.

We walk through it all silently; it's like an Airbnb, everything pristine yet also soulless. Upstairs there are three bedrooms—a master and two small singles, and a full bathroom off the hallway, all in white. There are sheets and towels on all of the beds, also white and depressingly thin, and in the kitchen we find a box of dishes, another of pots and pans, a third of basic food items—UHT milk, powdered eggs, some cans of meat and vegetables.

None of us says anything as we stand in the kitchen, absorbing the sum total of our new lives. It's so much more than we've had in a long time, and yet it feels like so very little.

After a moment, Ruby goes to the sliding glass door that leads from the kitchen to the deck out back. I follow her, stepping outside to survey our tiny square of brown grass, surrounded by a high fence on three sides, houses beyond in every direction, just like ours. I turn my head and see the yards, one after the other, some fenced, some not. Some with decks or patios; one with a trampoline that lists to one side. I've lived in the wilderness for so long that this sight of suburban normality jars me. It feels constricting, even though it seems like we're the only ones on the street.

Really, I tell myself, *it's fine. It's nice. We can make a home here. We will.*

Ruby turns to me, her face an open question. "Where are they?" she asks, and I stare at her in confusion.

"Who, Ruby?"

"The people who lived here before." She looks around at the sterile, soulless house. "Where did they go?"

For a second, I see this house not as our new, empty abode, a blank slate upon which we will, hope-filled, write our new lives, but as someone else's home. I picture the rooms with throw pillows and piles of magazines, dirty dishes and cookbooks, trash and laundry.

Where *did* those people go?

SIX

MATTIE

"You want to talk to me?" Mattie looks uncertainly at Vicky, who has an expression she recognizes—of kindness but also quiet, steely determination. It either inspires or scares her, depending on how she feels, but right now her mood is definitely veering toward the latter. Without her mom she feels weak and scared, and as much as she hates that feeling, she can't shake it. "I mean, about what?" she asks, trying to moderate her tone.

"About you and Kyle," Vicky states calmly, and Mattie stiffens.

"Me and Kyle?" she repeats, a sharpness entering her voice. She knows there *is* a her and Kyle; they'd been spending more time together ever since they left the cottage back in June, and two weeks ago, Mattie dared him to kiss her, and he did. Clumsily, kind of wet, but she didn't really mind. There is something sweet about Kyle, something even weirdly pure or maybe just innocent, but also simple. Mattie has liked having him there, quietly adoring her, a sidekick she can command and depend upon when she chooses to, but she isn't sure how she feels about Vicky talking about *her and Kyle*. She isn't sure she wants anyone else thinking in those terms, even as she recognizes everyone does. Her mom thinks they're a serious couple. Mattie didn't dissuade her.

"Yes," Vicky replies patiently. "You and Kyle... and Phoebe."

She speaks like they are a unit of three, a family, but Mattie doesn't think that way. Not yet, and maybe not ever. It's her and Phoebe, not her and Phoebe and Kyle.

Mattie puts an arm around the little girl, who is still munching her toast. "What?" she asks, pulling Phoebe a little closer to her. "Why are you saying this? Is something wrong?"

"No, not at all," Vicky assures her with a smile. "Mattie, you don't need to look so worried, I promise!" she exclaims with a light laugh, but there is still something purposeful about her that Mattie doesn't like. "But you and Phoebe are staying in a three-bedroom cabin," she continues, "and now that Sam is gone, Kyle is staying in one by himself." She raises her eyebrows, as if she is inviting Mattie to share some kind of joke. "That's a lot of space for the three of you, don't you think?"

"Yeah, I guess, but... that doesn't really matter, does it?" Mattie asks uncertainly. There are fifteen cabins on the site, and only nine are now occupied. Mattie, Ruby, Phoebe, and her parents took up one, Sam and Kyle another. Nicole and Ben have a third, and Vicky a fourth. The Anglican minister, Stewart, has the fifth, and Rose and Winn, the hippy couple that Mattie secretly both envies and is intimidated by, the sixth. The seventh is taken by the Native American doctor Adam and his son, Jason, and the eighth by a middle-aged couple Patti and Jay and their two kids, Caden and Ella. They're nineteen and twenty-one, and Mattie hasn't gotten to know them very well. Vicky's parents, Sheryl and Don, have their own house, a little farther down the road.

With *six* empty cabins, why does it matter if she and Phoebe, and Kyle for that matter, have more space than they need? Why is Vicky so concerned?

"Well, it might not matter *now*," Vicky tells her, and now she sounds like a schoolteacher. Mattie has a sudden memory of Mrs. Robbins, her algebra teacher, telling her sternly that she must show *all* her work. "But it will eventually, when we have more people join us." She speaks as if people are lining up to be part of the community, bags in hand.

"More people are joining us?" Mattie asks. She has been at Red Cedar Lake for four months, and no one has joined them in all that time.

"Well, there are a few options," Vicky replies, and weirdly, her cheeks have gone pink and she sounds mysterious, like she's holding back a surprise. "From a community in Sudbury that's reached the end of its resources. Obviously we can't have a flood of refugees, or anything like that, but some people with useful skills, who can do manual labor and help us to defend this place... that would be good, don't you think?"

"Defend... from what?" Mattie asks, still sounding uncertain. "I mean, the world's getting back to normal, right?"

"It isn't back, though, is it? And meanwhile we need to have food to eat." Vicky speaks lightly, but her eyes have narrowed and Mattie has the sense she doesn't appreciate being questioned so much. "We have to have more people," Vicky states, "if we're going to be self-sustaining."

"But... more people here means we'll need to provide more food," Mattie points out. She is trying to sound reasonable but there is a fierce light in Vicky's eyes that is alarming her. She doesn't want more people to come here. There has been enough change already.

"Come here," Vicky says, and she holds out one hand. It takes Mattie a second to realize she is meant to take it, which she does, gingerly. Vicky pulls her along like a child, while Phoebe stays at the table and continues to eat her toast. Mattie gives her one panicked glance before Vicky pulls her into the kitchen, and then into the walk-in pantry.

"Look," she commands sternly, and Mattie does. The shelves are nearly bare; she sees one box of granola bars, two cans of coffee, a couple of boxes of chicken stock cubes, and not much else. It reminds her of back at the beginning, right after the bombs fell, and her mom insisted they make an inventory of everything they had at the cottage.

They went through the whole house, with Mattie counting and

calling stuff out, Ruby writing it down. It had felt like a game, but it had also been deadly serious. Mattie remembers feeling glad that they were actually *doing* something, even if it was just making a list, and that list didn't seem remotely long enough.

Now she glances at Vicky, who is staring at her hard, her hands on her hips, clearly expecting her to say something.

"We're running out of food," Mattie says, not quite a question.

"We are," Vicky confirms. "And we need to be self-sustaining, to be able to provide everything we need. It's what we've been working toward, what we all want, but now with these empty shelves, you can see that we're running out of time. We're going to have to work harder, longer, and for that we need more people. People to farm, to fish, to hunt, to grind grain into flour... there are so many things we need to do, Mattie." She gives her an encouraging smile, willing her to share the vision, and Mattie wants to, but...

Grind grain into flour? She may have learned a lot of new things these last eighteen months, but she has no idea how to do that. She swallows her unease, reminds herself that she's the kickass heroine who takes life by the horns, battles it—and wins. "Who are you thinking could join us?" she asks practically. "Just some people from Sudbury?" The few locals, she knows, have already been asked; those who wanted to have joined; those who didn't either remained on their own homesteads or left. Northern Ontario is not exactly a populous place. As far as Mattie knows, there aren't people lining up to become part of this small community.

"I've been speaking on the radio to someone from Sudbury," Vicky tells her, and again she has that mysterious tone, like she's keeping a secret. "He's going to come out here to visit, check things out. I think he'll really bring a lot to this community."

Okay, Mattie thinks, *but that's just one person. Even if this guy comes, it still leaves five cabins empty.*

"I need to reach out to some other people," Vicky continues, "groups that have formed or fallen apart. I have a few leads, and there are more people around than you think, but they're not always friendly." She pauses, her lips pursed. "But in the meantime, we need the space, to prepare for our future community members." She injects a note of playful enthusiasm into her voice as she continues, "So I thought you, Kyle, and Phoebe could share his cabin. It has two bedrooms."

Two bedrooms. Mattie is already shaking her head. "I don't think..." she begins, swallowing hard. "Kyle and I..." She stops. She does not want to have to explain to Vicky that the thought of sharing a bed with Kyle fills her with dread, that she might have kissed him and likes how much he likes her, but... she is not ready for that. She is not sure she ever will be, not with Kyle.

Vicky frowns, her eyes going soft. "I thought you were a couple," she says.

"We... we are," Mattie stammers, "but..." She wants to say she is only sixteen, that before the bombs, she'd only kissed one boy *twice* even though her mother feared she'd done so much more. She wants to cry that she's still little, but of course she can't. In this brave new world, she is an adult. Phoebe is practically her daughter, which makes Kyle...

"I'm not ready for that," she states firmly. "Phoebe and I can share a room, and we can move to a smaller cabin, but I don't want to live like... like that with Kyle."

Vicky stares at her for a moment, her lips pursed. "He adores you, you know," she says, and she sounds almost accusing, or maybe envious.

"I... I know," Mattie says. This whole conversation feels excruciating as well as confusing. Why does Vicky seem almost angry with her? "But I'm just not ready," she tells her, her tone one of finality. "I'm sorry, but I'm really not."

Vicky shakes her head, like she's disappointed in Mattie, which she doesn't understand. What does it matter to Vicky if she doesn't want to share a cabin—a *bed*—with her boyfriend? Even if more people come, and Mattie isn't sure they will, there is still plenty of space. Besides, no one is coming *today*, or even tomorrow. What's the rush?

"Is that... is that okay?" Mattie asks and then wishes she hadn't. She doesn't need Vicky's permission, surely, except maybe she does. Maybe, without her family, she's only here on sufferance. The thought causes fear to swirl in her stomach, bile to rise in her throat. She has to stay on Vicky's good side, she realizes, something she's never considered before, but... she still isn't going to move in with Kyle.

"Oh, Mattie." Vicky's frown clears, replaced by a warm and apologetic smile. She reaches over and squeezes her hand. "Of course it's okay! I'm sorry, I absolutely didn't mean to pressure you into anything. I would never want to do that." She lets out a rueful bark of laughter. "I really am sorry. I guess I just thought things were more serious between the two of you than they seem to you... something you might want to mention to Kyle." Her voice is gentle, but Mattie still feels accused.

She doesn't reply, because surely she doesn't need to explain anything about her personal relationships to Vicky.

"I thought you'd be pleased," Vicky continues. "And excited. After all, you chose to live here, didn't you? To be an adult here, without your family?"

Something in her tone rubs Mattie raw, but she's not sure what it is. She decides to focus on the immediate issue. "So I can stay in my own cabin?" she asks, and Vicky frowns again. "Or I'll move to a smaller one, like I said," she offers, but there is an edge to her voice, and Vicky tenses. The brief moment of warmth vanishes like the mist over the lake.

"Why don't you move in with Nicole," Vicky says, and it's far more a statement than a suggestion. "She and Ben are in a two-bedroom cabin. You can share with Phoebe, and Ben can move in with Kyle, since they're both single, or as good as." She rolls her eyes, and Mattie just stares at her. Was that meant to be some kind of criticism?

"Okay," she says, because the matter is clearly decided, and there's no point protesting.

When they first arrived, Vicky had said how this place was a cooperative, everything decided by group vote, but it certainly doesn't feel that way right now.

It feels like Vicky is making all the decisions, and Mattie has to go along with them... or else. Vicky turns and walks out of the pantry and Mattie follows her, feeling as if she's been scolded.

Phoebe has finished her toast, and she slides from her seat as Mattie comes toward her. She scoops the little girl up into her arms, burrowing her face in her hair to hide her expression. She feels angry, she realizes, but also near tears, and she can't really understand why everything happened the way it did.

From the sofa by the fireplace, Nicole is watching her with narrowed eyes. When Vicky goes back outside, Mattie walks slowly over to her and sinks down on the opposite sofa, Phoebe in her lap.

Nicole flicks her long, blond hair over one skinny shoulder. Eight months on from life in the billionaire bunker, and she still looks sophisticated and put together. *Did she bring tweezers*, Mattie wonders distantly. Her eyebrows look perfect.

"What was that all about?" Nicole asks.

Mattie's arms tighten around Phoebe. "I guess I'm going to be sharing your cabin," she answers shakily.

"What?" Nicole's voice is sharp with incredulity. "But we don't have room."

"Ben's moving in with Kyle."

"That's what Vicky said?"

"Yeah... and it didn't seem like it was up for discussion."

Nicole frowns but doesn't say anything more. Mattie presses her lips against Phoebe's hair as she closes her eyes. She wishes her mom were here. She wishes her mom could fight for her, face down Vicky and tell her that nobody is moving anywhere. But of course, if her mom were here, if she and Sam and Ruby hadn't left, this wouldn't have even been an issue.

Her throat aches with unshed tears, and she keeps her eyes closed as Phoebe squirms under her too-tight grip.

"So what Vicky says goes, hmm?" Nicole remarks thoughtfully, and Mattie opens her eyes to see the older woman gazing out at the lake, her forehead furrowed, her lips pursed in thought, her eyes narrowed in shrewd and calculating assessment.

"Are you okay with me and Phoebe moving in?" she asks uncertainly.

"It's not you two I'm worried about," Nicole replies cryptically. "But better you live with me than with Kyle. That was the other option, right?"

"Yes..." Mattie gulps, still feeling far too close to tears. "How did you know?"

"You guys were just over there." She nods toward the kitchen. "I could hear some of the conversation." Her lips curve in a cynical smile. "Sounds like Vicky's coming to like being the boss here."

Mattie swallows and says nothing. All she can think about is how much she misses her mom.

SEVEN

ALEX

I turn to Ruby, her question reverberating through me. *The people who lived here before... where did they go?*

I glance around our new home, everything so very clean and empty, *cleared out*, and I swallow hard. "I don't know where they went, Ruby," I finally say. "They must have just... left."

Sam props his shoulder against the doorway of the kitchen. "They might have died," he offers quietly.

"But there wasn't any radiation here." Ruby turns to him, her voice plaintive yet also firm, even defiant. "That's the whole point. That's why we're here. So nobody could have *died* from it here," she finishes. "Otherwise it wouldn't be safe."

For a few seconds, none of us speaks.

"Maybe they went to find family or... somewhere they felt was safer," I suggest. I feel as if I'm stumbling in the dark, trying to come up with some reason we can all accept. And really, that's probably what happened. There are empty houses and abandoned towns all over the country.

"Why don't we unpack," I say. I reach into the box and take out a can of black beans. "We can put all the food and dishes away."

Putting our meager supplies away takes all of ten minutes. It's only mid-morning, the day stretching emptily in front of us, along with every day after that. I feel like we're on some kind of stage, playacting at real life. At any moments the walls will crumble, the sets will fall, revealing the barren emptiness beneath these props, and how little life we have left to live.

Part of me just wants to scream.

"Mom, what's this?" Sam holds up an envelope lying on the counter that none of us had noticed. He opens it and takes out a bunch of blue rectangles made of laminated plastic. I stare at them blankly, as does Sam.

"Tickets," Ruby says quietly, and I remember the sign in the window. *Flatscreen TV, only Five Hundred Tickets!*

Sam gazes down at the tickets in his hand. "Is this like, *money?*" he asks, sounding incredulous. No one has used any kind of money in eighteen months. I can't even remember the last time I *saw* any —a crumpled bill, a shiny quarter. And now we have blue tickets.

"I suppose it is, or something like it," I reply. "Was there anything about tickets in the information packet?"

Sam shakes his head, and I wonder why I asked. I already knew there wasn't; we read that thing over and over again. Looking back, I can now see how much information it *didn't* give. How are we supposed to exist in this world, never mind thrive, when we don't know anything?

"There are some instructions," Sam says, taking a slip of paper out of the envelope. He reads out loud, "Tickets are used for payment and purchases of items available in various government-run stores. You have been given five hundred tickets for initial basic supplies and needs, and you will be paid in tickets when you begin your employment." He looks up, still baffled. "That's it."

"I guess it *is* like money," I say. "I suppose it makes sense, in a way. They can control it and keep track of these tickets, which they couldn't do with real money, not at this point."

"Still." Sam inspects one of the tickets. "It feels like something you'd get at a funfair, to trade for a teddy bear or something."

"Yeah." I laugh, because there is definitely something ridiculous about them. "I wonder who thought this up. And why are they blue?"

"They're not just blue," Ruby says, pointing to the back of the card Sam took out of the envelope. "Look."

He flips it over and reads out loud again. "Blue tickets are worth one hundred. Green fifty, red twenty, yellow ten."

"Well, now I know why we have five blue ones," I say, with another attempt at a laugh. This whole thing feels so bizarre, and yet I tell myself there's something good about it too. We are striving for normalcy in a way we haven't been able to for so long. Paying for something, even if it's with blue tickets, might feel satisfying.

"Should we go buy something?" Sam asks, a note of eagerness in his voice. "Check out some stores?"

"Those blue tickets burning a hole in your pocket?" I tease. "Sure, why not?" This house feels too empty and weird and very much not ours, and I am still thinking about Ruby's unanswered question. Where *did* all the former residents go? I don't even know who I would ask.

We gather our coats and head outside; the sun is warm, but the wind is chilly. Even so, I imagine I can feel the faintest breath of spring in the air. I glance up and down Third Street with its ranch houses one after the other, but the whole street seems empty. I can't tell if the houses look lived in or not; ours doesn't.

We start walking back toward Main Street and its modest array of government-sponsored stores. There are signs of the ravages of the past eighteen months, even though the radiation never got this far—empty storefronts, broken windows that have been boarded up, cracked pavement, abandoned cars here and there. There are also signs of life as it was—a poster under glass for a Rotary Club bingo, with a jackpot of four thousand dollars. Watford City's High School was putting on *Singin' in the Rain* two years ago, tickets five dollars at the door.

As we head toward the grocery store, a woman in a puffer coat passes us. Her cheeks are red with cold, her hair pulled back in a tight ponytail. She looks mid-thirties maybe, although it's hard to tell these days, since everyone seems older. She gives us a tight, uncertain smile before hurrying on. I don't even have time to smile back before she's gone. I wonder when people will stop seeming so suspicious, myself included.

Bells jingle as we open the door to the grocery store, a familiar and strangely comforting sound, another striving for normalcy.

"Good morning," the woman behind the counter greets us. She has a Midwestern twang and a friendly expression; I wonder if she's a local. Here might be someone who didn't leave Watford City. "You all new here?"

I smile back. "Just got out of isolation this morning."

She nods in understanding. "It's an adjustment, that's for certain. Have a look around. Everything's marked."

In truth, there is not much to look around at. Most of the shelves in the store are bare. I see a bunch of bananas, priced at fifty tickets, a couple of small, wrinkled tomatoes at ten. There are a few bags of flour, others of dried milk powder, and some off-brand Cheerios, and that's pretty much the store's entire stock.

"Sorry," the woman at the counter says. "I'm usually cleaned out by nine o'clock in the morning."

"Where does the food come from?" I ask her.

The woman does not seem surprised by the question; I'm guessing I'm not the only one asking this kind of thing, wondering how this new world works. "I get deliveries from the government every morning. They're controlling all the inventory at the moment, until supply chains can be restored."

"What inventory?" I ask. "Where are they getting..." I point to the off-brand Cheerios. "Oaty Hoops?"

She shrugs. "From their depots somewhere? I don't know, I just take it every morning."

"And supply chains..." I am so curious, but I try to moderate my tone. "From where?"

She shrugs again, spreads her hands. "I don't know exactly, but I've heard talk about places down south. You know, Chile, Argentina, Australia. They haven't been as affected down there.

And there are some other places in the US that are safe, pockets here and there." She smiles, her eyes crinkling in a friendly way. "They're clearing those out, reclaiming them, but it's hard. They have to do a lot of assessments, a lot of testing, and truth be told, there's just not much that's safe yet. Not just because of the radiation, but the ongoing pollution, too, from all the factory fires and so on." She grimaces. "I mean, at least the whole thing didn't plunge us into a nuclear winter, right? Thank goodness for small mercies."

"Right," I murmur. I pick up the bunch of bananas. I haven't eaten or even seen a banana in eighteen months. Now I think how strange they look, how very yellow. I don't even like bananas, but I decide I'm going to buy them, although fifty tickets feels like a lot. How much is one ticket supposed to be? Ten cents? A dollar? Or do we not even think that way anymore?

"Every week you'll get a box of basic staples delivered to your accommodation. They come from the military inventory and are free of charge," the woman tells me as I place the bananas by the cash register. She nods toward the bananas on the counter. "Then you can stock up with what you like here, using your tickets. Those come from greenhouses locally, which is why they're so expensive. Not many of them to be had. It's not like you can grow bananas all that easily in North Dakota!" She lets out a hearty laugh.

"Do you set the prices?" I ask, and she shakes her head.

"Oh no. I'm given a price list. But we'll be getting more in soon. In spring, they'll be planting grain, corn, potatoes... we'll get there." She sounds so sunnily optimistic, like all it's going to take is a little grit and elbow grease. I wonder if she lost anyone. Maybe here in Watford City, everyone was untouched... even if they're gone.

"What happened to all the people here?" I ask abruptly. "How come all these houses were empty? Where did they go?"

She stares at me like I'm stupid, and maybe I am. "They died," she says quietly, like it should have been obvious.

"But there was no radiation here—"

"Not from radiation," she interjects, her voice low. "From everything else. Illness. Untreated conditions. Cold. Starvation."

She pauses, her gaze back on the bananas between us. "My neighbor was a diabetic. She only lasted six weeks. And the people across the street died of cold. It was a hard winter, and not everyone had a fireplace, or wood to burn. And then the food ran out..." She shakes her head slowly. "It broke my heart, seeing the kids. Starving, they were, right in front of our eyes. Like we could actually *see* them disappearing."

My stomach clenches at the thought. I realize how lucky we are, to have survived this long.

"How come you survived?" Ruby asks the woman suddenly, surprising me, because she's not usually one to talk to strangers and the question sounds a little rude, even aggressive, which is so unlike her. I turn to her and see that her eyes are narrowed, her lips pursed. She almost looks angry.

"Luck?" the woman surmises, spreading her hands. "Providence? We had some food and supplies stored in the basement. My husband was a prepper, you know? He was ready for it, always thought something like this would happen, but he died over a year ago. Heart attack. Took him quickly." She falls silent for a moment. "I took in some of our neighbors for a while, a woman with two little kids, but they left a few months ago. Heard about a military base in Montana, near Great Falls, that was taking people in. A lot of people went together, to try to get there, although Billings was bombed, so I don't know... Never heard if they made it."

We are all quiet, absorbing this news. There are a thousand more stories like it, up and down this devastated country. Why did I think, even for a moment, that this woman might have emerged unscathed? That anyone might have?

"I'm sorry," I tell her, and she gives me a small smile, accepting. Ruby doesn't say anything.

"Everyone's lost somebody," she says, and I incline my head in acknowledgement. We certainly have. "That's fifty tickets," she tells me, and I hand over one blue ticket; we get a green one back.

"Do we get any more tickets?" I ask her. I am suddenly realizing how foolish it might have been, to spend ten percent of our tickets on a bunch of bananas I'm not sure any of us actually want.

The woman nods. "You'll get paid in tickets, once you get a job. Have you been to the employment center yet?"

"No, we just got out of isolation."

She nods again. "That's right, so you said. It's all pretty new, you know. Everything's just getting started, but you should head over to the employment center as soon as you can. Every week there's a reception for new arrivals, and you'll learn more there about how everything works here. They'll tell you when it is. They're still figuring it out, but we'll get there." Again I hear that airy confidence, but now I sense the sadness beneath. She needs to believe that this is going to work.

I know we do, too.

I take our bananas and we leave the store, walking down Main Street just to see what there is—a clothing store, a home-goods store, and a pharmacy are the only options, all of them advertising items for tickets. A pair of jeans is one hundred tickets. Boots one hundred and fifty. A throw pillow is twenty. A lamp fifty.

I glance around the empty street with its blank-looking buildings, the flat stretch of prairie beyond, wondering where everyone is. I suppose, with such slim offerings, there isn't much reason to be out and about. In the distance, a convoy of military trucks heads out of town, disappearing in a cloud of dust. The sight should inspire confidence, but it only makes me feel uneasy. I feel like we've landed on Mars, and we don't yet know if the aliens are friendly.

"Should we head back?" I ask Sam and Ruby, and they shrug their acceptance. I glance up and down the street, wondering what more there is to see. There's a playground in the distance, a towered structure with twisty green slides, like countless others I used to take the kids to, sitting on a bench scanning the tunnels and ramps or endlessly pushing a swing. They're too old for playgrounds now, though, and no one seems tempted to explore any further. Wordlessly we all turn to go back to Third Street.

As we walk, I notice that a few houses do look lived in—a trash can by the front door, a child's drawing taped to a window, a pink-seated bike in a yard. They hearten me, these little signs of life, of normalcy. They reassure me that life can happen here, that it can even be normal.

We are just approaching our house—our *home*, which is how I want to think of it even though it feels strange—when a woman comes out of the house next door. She's petite, with a raggedy brown bob, dressed in a turtleneck, fleece vest, and jeans. In our former lives, she might have been the classic soccer mom.

"Hi, are you our neighbors?" she asks. She has a Southern drawl, and I wonder how far she travelled to get here. What she might have endured. "We just arrived out of isolation this morning."

"So did we." Clumsily, the bananas cradled in my arm, I hold out a hand for her to shake. "I'm Alex."

"Chantelle." She smiles at Ruby. "My daughter Taylor is about your age. What are you, around twelve?"

Ruby nods, looking wary, and I put a hand on her shoulder, squeeze gentle encouragement. "Rubes," I say quietly, a prompt.

"I'm Ruby," she mutters reluctantly.

Chantelle's smile slips at my daughter's obvious reticence and then comes back, brighter than ever. "Well, you and Taylor will be in the same class, I guess, when they start up the school. Seventh grade?" Again Ruby nods, still looking reluctant. "Taylor, honey!" Chantelle calls into the house. "Come on out here and meet our new neighbors. There's a friend for you."

I cringe at this blatant social engineering, especially when I see Taylor. She has a high, blond ponytail and a slightly disdainful expression, her chin tilted upwards, her eyes narrowed. In our former lives, this kind of girl would have been Ruby's nemesis—the kind of girl who thinks Ruby is weird and tells everyone so, loudly, again and again.

I remind myself not to be so judgemental, just because a girl has a high ponytail and a frown.

"It's so nice to meet you, Taylor," I say, and she jerks her head in response. Her mother gives her a pointed look.

"Yeah, nice to meet you, too," she mumbles, with an eyeroll thrown in for good measure. Ruby does not reply.

As I stand there, I feel the familiar dread at having to help Ruby navigate social situations, and yet at the same time there's something wonderfully familiar about it. It reminds me of a time, a life, when my biggest problems were Ruby's social anxiety and helping her to make friends, not whether we'd have enough to eat or be attacked by a roving gang.

We really are striving for normalcy, I reflect as I squeeze Ruby's shoulder again, and she whispers, "Nice to meet you" while Taylor turns around and goes inside.

EIGHT
ALEX

The next morning I wake early, the backyard still shrouded in darkness. I make myself a cup of instant coffee with powdered milk and stand by the sliding door to the deck to watch the sky lighten above the sea of houses that surrounds me, all of them very nearly identical, as far as the eye can see.

I am thinking of Red Cedar Lake, and imagining Mattie standing in a similar place, watching the sun rise over the water and touching the trees with gold before she goes about her day. Is she happy? Determined? Missing me?

My daughter has grown so much in the last year and a half. Before the bombs, Mattie was the quintessential rebellious teenager—addicted to her phone, angry at us for depriving her of a social life. She'd been suspended from school for having cannabis in her locker, put there by her deadbeat seventeen-year-old boyfriend, Drew. Daniel and I had both been at our wits' end, and that was without considering the added stress of losing our house along with our life savings when Daniel lost his job and hid it from me for six months.

In light of what happened after, all that drama faded into insignificance. And I became so proud of Mattie, for the courage and determination she showed, the way she didn't let this frightening new life faze her. And yet underneath all that bravery, my little girl is only sixteen, and that sulky, rebellious teenager still lurks. She's not old enough to live by herself, in a community of people we'd only known for a few months, with a guy she insists she wants to be with even though I'm not entirely convinced he's the right choice for her.

I never should have let her stay.

Or maybe I never should have left.

But Mattie insisted she was basically an adult, and after everything we'd endured, I felt like I had to believe her. Trust her. I just wish she wasn't so far away.

Yesterday, after meeting Chantelle and Taylor, we trooped inside the house, but of course there was nothing to do. I made us lunch—canned hot dogs and black beans—and then we tried to walk over to the high school to register Ruby, but we learned from a passerby in the street that it was three miles away, next to the Rough Rider Center, where Sam would be going to college.

It felt too far to walk, especially with the wind being so cold and the landscape so bleak; there is nothing, not a hill, not a tree, to break the wind and keep it from slicing into you. We ended up going back inside and spent the rest of the afternoon feeling as trapped and bored as we had in our isolation unit in the hotel. At least there we'd had TV.

I missed Mattie with a fierce ache; if she'd been here, I'd thought, she would have cracked jokes and insisted we play games. She would have livened us up, but instead Ruby retreated into a morose silence and Sam studied the information packet again, as if it might offer something new.

Today, however, is a new day. We will register Sam and Ruby for school; I will go to the employment office. I am determined to make these strides, to start *living*, because that's why we came here.

That's why I left my daughter.

For breakfast, I make porridge with quick oats and water and top it with precious sliced bananas. Back at Red Cedar Lake, there were fresh eggs and milk, vegetables from their greenhouse. We ate better than we have here so far, but I tell myself not to make comparisons. Not yet, anyway. This life is just getting going.

"So, are we going to walk all the way to the high school?" Sam asks, sounding dubious. "It's pretty cold out there."

"It's only three miles," I reply bracingly. I am determined to be upbeat today, as well as unfazed. "In olden times, that would have been a Sunday stroll."

"Yeah, but... every day?" Sam looks even more dubious. "I mean, will they have buses or something?"

"I don't know, Sam. I guess they're still figuring it out." Already I can hear the tension in my voice, along with the uncertainty. My upbeat tone lasted all of ten seconds. "Rubes, you going to eat that?" I ask my daughter. She is staring at her untouched oatmeal, her forehead furrowed.

I take the chair opposite her and dip my spoon into my bowl. "Look, guys," I say in a confiding tone, "it's going to take a while to get used to this. And things here are just starting, you know? There are bound to be some growing pains as we all get adjusted, and the government figures out how to function successfully."

"Yeah, I know, thanks for the pep talk, Mom." Sam smiles wryly, and I feel better.

"Ruby?" I say, and she takes a bite of oatmeal, avoiding the banana. She doesn't like them, which makes me seriously question why I spent fifty tickets on them. Maybe because the tickets feel like Monopoly money, or maybe I was just so shocked at seeing the fruit that it felt like something I should want. Either way, I have a feeling they're going to go to waste, which seems like a tragedy.

"Picky eaters even in the apocalypse," I quip and am rewarded with a sudden, surprising scowl from Ruby, her brows drawing together, her eyes sparking with anger, startling me. I smile back, an apology, and she looks away. I need to be patient, I tell myself. Gentle.

We finish our oatmeal in silence, and then I tidy up while Sam and Ruby get dressed. Then we step outside into another brisk morning, the air sharp and pure, the world unfolding in every direction under an endlessly wide blue sky. I wonder if I'll ever get used to the sense of space here, and then I wonder why it makes me feel trapped rather than free.

Never mind, I tell myself. We're heading into the future, step by step down Third Street, past houses that still seem empty, although someone steps out of one and offers us an uncertain smile, which I return. Everyone is finding this strange, I think. We all need time to adjust.

We turn onto Fourth Avenue, or Route 23, a wider road with traffic lights that no longer work, but I suppose it doesn't matter because there isn't that much traffic. The road leads in a straight gray line toward the horizon, and we follow it out of town, toward the complex that houses both the high school and the Rough Rider Center.

A sidewalk runs along the road, brown fields stretching out in every direction, punctuated by the odd office building or apartment complex, most of them looking unused and empty. I am heartened when I see some kids kicking a ball in the parking lot of the apartment complex; their laughter carries on the cold wind.

We pass another bus coming from the airport; in its smeary windows I see pale faces, wide eyes. Across the street military personnel are unloading boxes into what used to be a bank. All signs of life, of progress, and yet somehow they both jar and reassure at the same time.

We continue to plod along, heads lowered against the wind, as the landscape empties out. In the distance a tall metal silo glints under the wintry sun, and I see a tractor cutting through a far field. More signs of life.

At the high school, however, we find the doors locked, the classrooms dark, with no signs of life at all. We walk over to the Rough Rider Center, a sprawling, modern-looking complex of concrete and glass where Sam is meant to be starting college in a couple of weeks, and find the same, everything locked and darkened. It's dispiriting, to have walked so far for no reason, and even worse, the rest of the day looms in front of us, utterly empty. I had been hoping that registering for school might take a while; maybe we'd even be offered a tour. I think about the playground again, and wonder if I could tempt my children to take a turn on the swings, for old times' sake.

"Now what?" Sam asks, which is exactly what I'm thinking.

"I guess they're not ready yet," I reply unnecessarily, and Sam gives me a classic "well duh" look that I am well used to as a parent. "I suppose we should walk back into town," I add. "Maybe some other things are open. We could look around a little more, anyway. We haven't seen all of Main Street."

Neither Sam nor Ruby look all that enthused by this prospect, but they shrug, which I take as acceptance. We are just starting back down toward the road when an army truck pulls up to where we're standing on the sidewalk. The driver rolls down the window, propping one arm on the door.

"Y'all need some help?" he asks us. He is maybe mid-thirties, tanned and muscular, with a buzz cut and a friendly expression, but he has the kind of fridge-like physique and matching manner that makes him a little scary.

"We were hoping to register for school," I tell him. "But everything's locked up."

"Registration starts Monday," he says, while I look blank because I have no idea what day it is. "In two days. You a new arrival?"

"Yes, just got out of isolation yesterday."

He sighs and shakes his head. "They're bringing 'em in too fast and we're not ready. We're still getting it all set up. You can't just move ten thousand people in like that." He snaps his fingers. "Anyway, they'll figure it out. You guys want a ride back into town?"

"Um, sure," I say, startled by the offer but also not wanting to schlep three miles down a straight road in this wind. "Thanks."

He leans over and opens the door and we all scramble in. "I'm Andy," the man says, giving each of our hands a firm shake. "Arrived here from Colorado six weeks ago. Where you all from?"

I think back to all the places we've been and let out a tired laugh. "Connecticut, originally, but we were in Canada when the first bombs fell. We've been up there, in various places, since the start, and we flew in from Mackinaw City four days ago."

Andy nods sympathetically. "Everyone's come from all over, some a real long way."

"How many people are here?" Sam asks.

He scratches his cheek, looking reflective. "I think we're coming on thirty thousand, across all the settlements? About twenty thousand in Williston, five in New Town, and five thousand here, plus a few more scattered around." He glances around the empty landscape. "I know you can't see many people out and about, but the ones who arrived a few weeks ago are working, and the new ones are probably all holed up in their houses for now. They're all still pretty cautious."

"Yes, I can understand that," I say. I gaze out the window at the fields flashing by, flat and brown, stretching to the sky. There's a beauty to the bleakness of the landscape, I decide, a sort of purity of line and color—brown field and blue sky, the horizon like the straight edge of a ruler.

Thirty thousand people seems like a lot, but according to reports I've heard, there are some fifteen million still alive in the United States alone. Where are they, and what are they all doing?

"What about everybody else?" I ask Andy. "I mean, the people who haven't made it to here yet, across America?"

He shrugs. "Who knows? They're holed up wherever they're holed up, I guess, doing their best to survive. There are groups that have taken over places—military bases, malls, that kind of thing. Some of them are peaceful, but there are a few militants and vigilantes around. I've heard about some group in Nevada that's taken over a golf club, set landmines all across the putting greens."

It's not really surprising, since we joined such a group back at North Bay, although as far as I know they didn't set any landmines. Still, the knowledge that there are countless more groups like that across the country makes me uneasy as well as exhausted. I want to be past that kind of existence, a fractured world of fortresses and fear.

"What about the friendly ones?" Sam asks. "Do you reach out to those?"

"We try," Andy replies. "We've got to find 'em first."

"And then what?" Sam asks, sounding genuinely curious. "Will you bring everybody here?"

Andy flexes his hands on the steering wheel. "I don't know about that. We haven't got room right now. But eventually we've got to be one country, you know? Under one government. We can't have all these isolated groups doing their own things, however they want to, because that just leads to anarchy. Chaos."

He makes it sound like such a reasonable proposition, and of course, on some level, it is. At some point, what is left of this country has to become unified. *Out of many, one.*

But as we drive the rest of the way into town in silence, I wonder just how that will happen.

NINE
MATTIE

Mattie is back in her cabin, packing her things to move to Nicole's while Phoebe does a wooden puzzle on the floor when Kyle strides in.

"What are you doing?" he asks, sounding hurt.

Kyle, Mattie has discovered, often sounds hurt. It made her feel protective of him at the start, and then proud when he rose above it and *did* things. He buried his aunt, Darlene, who had died of a heart attack back at the beginning. He skinned a beaver, and rescued Phoebe from the river when she'd been swept out, and learned how to fish and shoot a gun. All of these things gave Mattie glimpses of the man he one day could be, a man she could both like and admire.

But right now, when he is watching her pack with his shoulders slumped, his dark hair sliding into his eyes, looking like a hurt little boy, she finds she only feels annoyed and impatient.

"I'm packing," she informs him curtly. "Vicky has asked me to move in with Nicole."

"What..." Kyle lifts his head, his eyes widening. "Why? I thought... I thought you were moving in with me."

Mattie stills. "Why would you think that?" she asks quietly.

Kyle shrugs, shifting on the spot. "Vicky said."

"*Vicky* said?" So Vicky talked about her to Kyle? Mattie knows that's not unreasonable, yet she still feels annoyed by it, especially when she keeps going over in her mind the conversation she had with Vicky, wondering why it made her so uneasy. "You didn't think to ask me first?" she says to Kyle.

"Well..." He frowns, clearly unhappy. "I mean, why wouldn't you? We're together, aren't we?" He sounds even more like a little boy now, and Mattie is even more irritated.

She takes a deep breath, remembers that Kyle has kissed her twice, that they have spent a lot of time together, that she genuinely liked him, or at least convinced herself that she did. They have history together, a lot of history, and that counts for something.

It's only now that her family is gone and she's utterly on her own that she feels like maybe she doesn't like him, at least not nearly as much as she thought she did. Not *enough*.

"We're not *that* together, Kyle," Mattie says, unable to keep from sounding sharp. "I mean... I'm not ready to live with you. That's a big step, you know?"

"We wouldn't have to... you know..." he begins haltingly, and she wheels away to the bedroom to get the rest of her clothes. She does not want to have this conversation. Not even remotely. Her hands shake as she grabs a sweater from her drawer, one that Vicky gave her when she first arrived.

"Mattie." Kyle has followed her into the bedroom. He stands in the doorway, looking abject but also a little angry. "What's up with you? Have I done something wrong?"

"No." She breathes out. "You haven't." She folds the sweater, taking her time with it, her gaze fixed on the bright wool. "It's just me choosing to stay here wasn't... wasn't me choosing to be with you. Like that." It isn't until she says it that she realizes how awful it sounds. How cold.

Kyle is silent for a long moment. "I guess I sort of thought it was," he says finally, his voice small and sad. "I thought you and me and Phoebe... we were kind of like a family. That's how it felt to me."

He sounds so lost that Mattie feels even worse. They *were* like a family, swinging Phoebe between them by her hands, sharing a table at meals, curled up in front of the fire, her head on his shoulder, her mom watching them narrowly. She can't dismiss all that, even if part of her wants to.

It felt different when she had her family around. When she was trying to show her mom just how grownup she could be. Living her own life, choosing this, insisting she was an adult, independent, *badass*.

Now it feels like there's no one left to show.

"Mattie..." Kyle begins, and then stops, waiting for her to say something, but she can't. Her throat has thickened and her eyes are swimming with tears, and she just wants to be *little* again.

She wants to be little enough to clamber into her dad's lap, except her dad is dead. She thinks of when she used to stay home from school, sick with a cold or sore throat, and her mom would come in with a tray of chicken noodle soup and flat ginger ale, her hand cool against her forehead, her own forehead furrowed with concern. She's not sick now, but she wants that. She wants to be that little girl tucked safe in bed, knowing she is loved.

Mattie collapses onto the bed, her shoulders slumped, the sweater clutched in her hand. "I miss my mom," she gasps out. "I miss my *dad*. I miss my family." She wipes her eyes, ashamed of her own vulnerability.

"Oh, Mattie. Mats." Kyle comes to sit next to her on the bed, putting his arm around her. Mattie leans into him, the only comfort she can find right now, and she lets it be enough. She lets *him* be enough, because if he was yesterday, why can't he be now? It would be so much easier if he was.

"I'm here for you," Kyle says, his lips against her hair. "I want to be here for you, Mattie. Let me."

"I know you do." She presses her cheek against his shoulder as she squeezes her eyes shut, willing the tears back. She so wishes things were different, but she knows they can't be. If only her dad hadn't died. If only her mom and brother and sister hadn't left. If only she hadn't been so sure she knew what she wanted.

Mattie takes a deep breath and then pushes herself away from Kyle. She wipes her cheeks as she takes another deep breath. "I'm okay," she says, knowing she is trying to convince herself as much as Kyle. "I'm okay, I'm okay."

She drops her hands from her cheeks and sees Phoebe standing in the doorway of the bedroom, staring straight at her, blank-faced and wide-eyed.

"Phoebe..." she begins, but the little girl turns away, disappearing back into the living room.

***

Mattie moves into Nicole's cabin that afternoon. Kyle is put out; Mattie realizes he thought she'd changed her mind when she'd started to cry.

"I told you, it doesn't have to mean anything," he insists as she zips up a duffel bag.

"If it doesn't mean anything, why does it bother you?" Mattie tosses back.

Kyle crosses his arm over his chest, his face settled in discontented lines. "I don't want to live with *Ben*."

"You get along fine with Ben," Mattie replies dismissively. When her family first met Ben and Nicole, along with her showy, know-it-all husband, William, they'd all seemed insufferable, fresh from their billionaires' bunker, acting like they owned the world, such as it was. Nicole and Ben have gotten a little more bearable since then, and William is out of the picture, abandoned back at North Bay. Mattie's mom told her that he "wasn't a very nice man," which Mattie already knew but she guessed was code for being abusive. She avoided them both, discreetly, simply because it felt easier. But she can't avoid them now, at least not Nicole.

"If you're moving in with Nicole," Kyle says, "and Ben's moving in with me, who's moving into this cabin?"

Mattie glances around the three-bedroom cabin with its log burner and cathedral ceiling, the kitchenette and the picture window overlooking the lake. It's a nice cabin; it was starting to feel at least a little like home. Her dad *died* in this cabin. Maybe it is better to move somewhere else.

"I don't know who's moving in here," Mattie replies. She thinks of the guy coming to visit from Sudbury, and she wonders if Vicky does.

Nicole is waiting for her as she moves her and Phoebe's stuff across, Phoebe trotting quietly behind her. Nicole looks tentative but friendly, and Mattie wonders if she is looking forward to the company.

"I've changed the sheets in the bedroom," she tells her with a light laugh, "but there might still be a bit *eau de teenaged boy* about the place. Sorry about that. It will air out eventually, I hope."

Mattie doesn't like the thought that she's sleeping in Ben's old room, but she pushes it away as she dumps her stuff at the foot of the bed. There are two narrow beds, a tiny table between them, and not much else. She steps back into the living room, which is much like the one she's left, only not quite as big. Phoebe is curled up on the sofa with several picture books that Nicole has given her.

Looking at how snuggled in Phoebe seems, Mattie feels an unreasonable stab of jealousy. Nicole looks up at her and smiles.

"How are you doing?" she asks, her voice gentle in a way Mattie has never heard before, and as much as she craves some maternal kindness, it perversely makes her prickle. "I know it must be hard, having your mom and Sam and Ruby all leave like that."

"I could have gone with them," Mattie reminds her, her tone sharpening.

"I know." Nicole cocks her head. "That doesn't mean it isn't hard."

Mattie feels a pressure behind her lids, and she knows she doesn't want to cry in front of Nicole. She's being nice right now, but Mattie isn't sure she likes her. "I need to get to work," she tells Nicole. "Prepping dinner. Phoebe, come on."

"She can stay here," Nicole offers. "I'm just going to be darning sheets all afternoon. I can watch her." She smiles, looking hopeful, and again Mattie wonders if Nicole has been lonely. Maybe she's not as prickly as she has seemed.

Still, she wants to refuse, but she knows how ungracious it would seem. It's been challenging, to have Phoebe underfoot while she's been working in the kitchen with Sheryl and Patti, and yet she doesn't want to leave Phoebe with Nicole, and she isn't even sure why. It feels as if all her certainties are unraveling now that she's by herself, leaving her nothing but loose threads and tangles.

Isn't she better than this? Mattie tells herself. Stronger?

"Okay," she tells Nicole, and forces a smile. "Thanks."

Phoebe is happy enough to be left, which Mattie tries not to let sting. She walks down the path along the lake to the main cabin, her hands dug deep into the pockets of her parka, her head bent against the bitter wind.

In the kitchen, Sheryl is peeling potatoes and Patti is grating a turnip.

"Turnip and potato casserole for the third time this week," Sheryl says cheerfully, but Mattie thinks she looks strained; the smile slips off her face quickly. She remembers what Vicky was saying about how their food supplies were dwindling; having worked in the kitchen since she got here, she should have realized it herself, but somehow she's pushed the prospect away.

Since coming here, Red Cedar Lake had felt like a haven, a fortress. When Vicky first gave them the tour, Mattie was both amazed and comforted by the greenhouses, the barns, the chickens, the solar panels, all the signs of prosperity that felt like weapons against this new world. It had reminded her of the way they'd tried to make things, back in the beginning, at the cottage, before it burned down and they'd had to go on the run, but only better.

But now it all feels fragile, threatened, and Mattie's stomach seethes with anxiety at the thought. Her family is over a thousand miles away, across a hostile and unknown land. If Red Cedar Lake fails, where would she go? What would she have?

"Where's Vicky?" she asks Sheryl.

"She said she had to go out. She took the truck."

None of them have gone out very often; occasionally Adam would go on a medical visit to a neighbor, or someone would go out to look for supplies, but everyone mainly stayed put, working in the community. But now Vicky is going out, and Mattie doesn't know where. She thinks of the man from Sudbury she mentioned, and wonders if it has something to do with that.

She picks up a potato and starts peeling, telling herself not to worry. The only reason she is worrying at all, she thinks, is because her family has left. If they were here, everything would feel different. Safer. She wouldn't be worrying about nameless, formless possibilities. She wouldn't feel so paranoid.

She's gone through ten potatoes before she starts to feel a little better, the world returning to normal, and then the door to the kitchen opens.

"Mattie!" Vicky comes into the kitchen, smiling in her usual easy way, making Mattie forget how stern she'd seemed earlier. "All moved in?"

"I think so," Mattie replies.

"Good," Vicky says, and there is an excitement in her eyes, and an energy about her that's almost manic. She bounces on the back of her heels, her smile widening. "Because it turns out we need that cabin far sooner than I thought we would."

Out of the corner of her eye, Mattie sees Patti frown, Sheryl tense.

Vicky lets out a girlish giggle, a sound so unlike her. "We have a new resident," she announces, just as a man saunters into the kitchen, his thumbs hooked through his belt loops, and looks slowly, appraisingly, around.

TEN

ALEX

I stand on the threshold of the hotel ballroom, listening to sounds both familiar and so very strange—the murmur of conversation, the clink of glasses, *music*. How long has it been since I've heard the sorrowful strains of a violin?

It's amazing how much difference a single week makes. After those first few days in Watford City when we had to search for something to do, life suddenly got pleasingly busy. Buses and planeloads of people arrived, the government kicked into higher gear. Seemingly overnight, the little town was bustling with activity and purpose.

Sam and Ruby both registered for school, and I went to the employment center and filled out a long form about my education, skills, and interests while a woman behind the front desk chatted to me about where she'd been when the bombs fell—it seemed to have become lore, like asking where you were on 9/11 or, if you were old enough, when JFK was shot. I told her I was in Canada and left it at that; she'd been in Indiana, with her husband's family for Thanksgiving.

"As soon as it happened, we got in the car," she said, like she was telling a story. "Straight off. Needed to get back to Schererville to get our Schnauzers from the kennel. My in-laws refused to go with us. Said they were safer there." She was silent for a moment, her face drawn in reflective lines. "We never saw them again."

Everyone has a similar story, from the woman in the supermarket who has spent her whole life in Watford City, to Andy, the guy who drove us in the truck, who was in the military in Colorado; two-thirds of his unit deserted in the first few days. People share where they came from in a matter-of-fact way, without much emotion. We all know that everyone has history, painful and tragic. We can exchange information, compare notes, but no one is winning this contest.

Three days after we moved into our little house on Third Street, flatscreen TVs were delivered to every residence, and nobody needed five hundred tickets for them.

Now we can turn the TV on and get updates directly from the military headquarters at Minot Air Force Base just over one hundred miles away; so far it's only the weather or the store opening hours, but when Sam and Ruby start school, they will be able to access their homework assignments and message their teachers. Eventually all developments regarding this new country will be on there, although I can't help but think that it will be the developments those in authority *want* us to know. What might they be choosing not to tell us?

I am trying to shed my suspicion, however, little by little. Three days ago, a military plane arrived with dozens of crates of oranges from Argentina that were given out for free; it felt like a street party, everyone laughing in disbelief as their thumbnails bit into the peel.

We were told supply chains are being established, and the rest of the world is recovering, as we are. The mood felt hopeful and buoyant, even though there is still so much nobody knows, but I did learn just how sweet an orange tastes when you haven't had one in nearly two years.

Sam, Ruby, and I explored more of the town; we found the library, which had reopened, and got cards and took out some books in a way that felt reassuringly normal. We discovered a museum on the county's heritage and the history of North Dakota oil; really, the lady who ran it told us, it was amazing North Dakota wasn't bombed, considering the oil fields.

"But I guess they all just focused on cities," she finished sadly. "Worse damage, in a way. The human cost."

The human cost. Yes, we knew about that.

Yesterday Andy, the guy who drove us back from the Rough Rider Center, stopped by our house with a box of books and games for us to enjoy. They were all battered and well-used, Monopoly with some of the properties missing, some decks of cards and a couple of puzzles and crossword books. It made me wonder who they all belonged to before, but I appreciated his thoughtfulness. He also offered to take Sam out to Minot Air Force Base for a tour, which he agreed to with enthusiastic, maybe too much, alacrity. They haven't arranged a time yet.

Our neighbor, Chantelle, has been, in her determinedly friendly way, trying to push Taylor and Ruby together, assuming that, as two thirteen-year-old girls and neighbors, they will automatically be best friends. She has offered to have Ruby over, suggested they can take the bus together when school starts—we found out there *would* be a bus, much to Sam's relief—and she has asked Ruby, in that high-pitched, patronizing voice of an adult who doesn't truly understand a child, whether she likes shopping or music. She seems utterly determined to normalize our situation, neighbors in a small town, but I know we're not there yet, and considering the differences between Ruby and Taylor, maybe we never will be.

Ruby has answered Chantelle in barely heard monosyllables; she seems not only unenthusiastic but even a little hostile, especially for her, and so I've tried to politely put Chantelle off, telling her we need a little more time to adjust. I don't know what's happening to my shy, quiet daughter, but she seems far more intransigent than she ever has before, her silence more sullen than thoughtful, and it worries me.

I tell myself, just as I told Chantelle, that things will get better once we all feel more settled. Like me, I think Ruby misses Mattie. Despite all the positive steps we've taken here, I miss my oldest daughter with an ache in my middle that feels like I've swallowed a stone. Every morning, when I wake up and blink in the early-morning light, for a few futile seconds I forget—that Daniel is dead, that Mattie is over a thousand miles away. For a second or two, no more, my stomach doesn't seethe, and I enjoy the dawn light slanting through the window and creeping across the floor in pale, hesitant fingers. I even enjoy the view of sky and prairie; the openness doesn't unsettle me the way it used to. In some ways, it's nice to feel so small.

But then I always remember, and the truth slams into me like a sledgehammer, knocking me sideways and leaving me breathless. Daniel. *Mattie*. What is she doing? How can I reach her?

Why did I leave?

I've tried multiple times to find a way to call her on a radio or satellite phone. I've asked Andy, the lady at the employment center, the staff at the Rough Rider Center and the high school, just about *anyone* who might know, how I can get hold of some way to make a call, but so far I've been put off, told that radio or satellite calls aren't yet available for everyone, that I need to wait for protocols to be put in place. I am desperate to talk to my daughter, though, and so tonight I am determined to find *someone* who can make it happen.

"Are you coming in?" a woman asks me playfully, wine glass in hand, which still looks so jarring. How can I be at a *party*? I'm attending the welcome reception for new arrivals, and so I smile at her and nod as I step into the hotel ballroom and glance around at the motley crowd. Everyone has made something of an effort to dress up, but considering what we have to work with, the result is pretty mixed.

I'm wearing my best pair of jeans and a soft blue cashmere sweater Nicole gave me as a going-away present. I am conscious that my hair is raggedy, my skin is dry, and I'm still stringy from malnourishment, but I suppose despite all that or really because of it, I fit in. I asked Sam and Ruby if they wanted to come, but they both demurred. To be fair, it's an adult crowd here, but I could have used some backup and they might have enjoyed getting out.

"Get your wine before it runs out," the woman says, raising her glass in a toast. At the entrance, we were all given one ticket for a glass of wine. According to the message board on the TV, we are allowed only one glass each, since supplies are limited. Considering I haven't touched a drop of alcohol in over a year, I'm sure one will be enough.

I exchange my ticket for a glass of white, and for a second, as I take that first, crisp sip, I think back to those early days at the cottage, after the first bombs fell, when we were carving out a life for ourselves. Daniel had left to get Sam from college, and Kerry and Kyle were living with us after Darlene had died. It had felt so frightening and fraught, and yet I can't help but look back on that time with a weird nostalgia now—the way we worked together, building something good and even pure, if ultimately, tragically fragile.

I remember drinking our last bottle of wine with Kerry, curled up on the sofa after the kids had gone to bed, the only sound the comforting crackle of the fire, the deck outside heaped with snow in mounds that looked like whipped cream. We sipped Cabernet and reminisced about life as it was—takeout, reality TV, drycleaners, manicures. We missed a million little things.

Then we talked through the practicalities of our current life—whether we could trap a beaver, if the porridge oats would hold out another couple of weeks, what we could feasibly plant in spring. I miss that life, in a strange and confusing way, because it really was so hard and so frightening. I miss Kerry, who sacrificed herself for Mattie's sake in our escape. I haven't found a friend like her since.

"So when did you arrive?"

I turn to see a woman giving me a frank and appraising look. She's about my age, with short, spiky gray hair and a hardened expression that has, for the moment, morphed into something like friendliness. Still, I sense something about her that is tough, even aggressive, and as ever, I am instantly wary.

"A little over a week ago."

She nods. "Newbie, huh?"

Yes, I am, but the word still grates. "I suppose I am," I acknowledge with an attempt at a laugh. "What about you?"

"Got out of isolation this morning, so I'm even newer than you." She laughs, a hard sound, before gesturing to her glass. "Nice that they give us wine, anyway."

"Yes." A couple of sips and I already feel a little lightheaded, but maybe I'm just tired. This woman's manner, the aggression as well as the inexperience, jar me. "So where did you come from?" I ask, and her mouth hardens into a flat, uncompromising line.

"My husband and I had a farm in eastern Montana, near Jordan," she says. "Four hundred acres, grain and cattle." She is silent for a moment, seeming to work through some powerful emotion, and I take a sip of wine as I wait, steel myself for another sad story. "He died a year ago," she continues after a few seconds, her voice flat and hard. "Collapsed in the field, dead in an instant. I did my best to keep it going, but it was too much for me. Then the government came, told me I could come here and have a new life. A house, food, medical care... I have high blood pressure, and the medication ran out months ago. It seemed too good to be true."

I stare at her, caught between uncertainty and impatience. What is she trying to say, that it *is* too good to be true? "And then what happened?" I ask finally.

"I came and they locked me up for three days." She holds up a forestalling hand, and I realize I've already opened my mouth in protest. If she's out of isolation, then she must, like us, have a house, food. She'll have been given medication for her high blood pressure; I've *seen* the people lined up at the medical center. What is she complaining about exactly?

"I know, I know," she says. "They explained why, and I understand it, I do. And they did everything they promised." She pauses, her mouth hardening again. "But what happened to my farm in

Montana?" she demands. "Four hundred acres of good prime land. A farmhouse we built with our own hands. Tractors, trucks, forty head of cattle still there when I left..." She shakes her head slowly. "Where has it all gone?"

"Well, it's probably all still there," I say, although I imagine *someone* has made use of the cattle, and she looks at me hard.

"Did you see the news on the TV this morning? About 'reclaiming the land'?"

The last few days there have been updates about the reclamation of larger areas of North Dakota and Montana, northeast Wyoming, for the "new United States of America." It's all phrased as positive news, and it feels encouraging. As I joked to Sam, none of us want to live in North Dakota for the rest of our lives. Montana sounds a little better.

"Yes..." I tell this woman haltingly.

"They've reclaimed Jordan," she says, "or so they say, but nobody's asking me if I want to go back to my farm. Nobody told me it was safe there, that I could stay. Instead I'm living in a one-bedroom apartment on the outskirts of this one-horse town and eating black beans and rice three time a day." She sneers the words, her face full of pain, and then falls silent, waiting for my reply.

I stare at her for a moment without speaking, because I understand why she's upset but I also know I'm not about to enter into that spirit of suspicion and discontent any more than I already have, in the disquiet of my own mind. Every single one of us made a deal, I realize, in coming here. We agreed to sacrifice certain rights and principles in exchange for safety and opportunity. We did it with our eyes open, even if there was no real way to count the cost.

But surely we all had to know that some of that cost was giving up the life we once had—and yes, the freedom as well as the property. The cottage my parents built with their own hands is now nothing but ashes and ruin, and I doubt I'll ever be able to go back.

"I suppose," I tell her, "you could go back if you wanted to." My voice has the upward lilt of a question even though I meant it to sound like a statement, a *fact*, but already this woman is shaking her head.

"How would I get there? No one is allowed beyond Watford City without permission. We're *prisoners* here, don't you realize that?" She takes a menacing step toward me, and I hurriedly step back, nearly spilling my one precious glass of wine.

"We're not prisoners if you can get permission," I tell her primly. "And we chose to come. We weren't taken here forcibly." I sound sanctimonious, like an evangelist for this new country, and I realize in a startling moment of clarity that I don't want to be like this woman, angry and suspicious of everything and everyone.

I *chose* to come here, and I am going to choose to believe and trust, just as I told myself I would at the beginning. It's an act of will rather than a feeling, and I am putting it into practice right now.

The woman's lip curls as she glares at me, and then her gaze moves beyond me to the other side of the room. "Oh, look," she sneers. "The great man himself."

"What man?" I ask, turning out of instinct.

"Him." She points to a tall man who looks to be in his fifties; he has short gray hair and a craggy face, a kind expression, or so it seems from across the room. He's dressed in camo fatigues, like all the other military personnel, but they look worn-in and comfortable, and I decide they suit him. I have never seen him before.

"Who is that?" I ask.

"Major Jack Wyatt. He's in charge of Watford City. While I was in isolation, he was giving inspirational talks on the TV about how this was like the western frontier in the olden days; we're redefining manifest destiny for the twenty-first century." She rolls her eyes, her lip still curled, as I return my gaze to the man in question.

The man in charge of Watford City, who *does* seem kind, I decide, and who can help me find a way to contact my daughter.

ELEVEN
ALEX

It takes me twenty minutes to work my way across the room, mainly because it is crowded and everyone, it seems, is now eager to chat. The plug has finally been pulled, the dam has burst, and people want to spill their stories and share their pain. I listen to a dozen sorry tales more or less similar to my own before I am finally able to approach Major Jack Wyatt.

A woman trapped in an apartment building in South Bend, Indiana for six months before she escaped, living off bottled water and cat food.

A family who walked four hundred miles through the Midwest, trying to find shelter at Offutt Air Force Base, south of Omaha, only to find it had been bombed to a smoking ruin. Two of them died of radiation; only the mother and the baby were left, the mother shellshocked, walking as if she were in a dream—or a nightmare.

A man who escaped to his log cabin in central Wyoming, a one-room shelter with a self-composting toilet and no electricity. He lived there until a week ago, happy as a clam, save for the fact that he was from Denver, which was hit in the second wave of bombs, and every single friend and family member was dead.

As I listen to their stories, often told in dazed monotones, I nod, shake my head, smile, grimace, all of it in solidarity, because my story, in broad strokes, is painfully similar. I tell it just as tonelessly matter of fact, ignoring the welter of emotions and memories it stirs up in me as I skip some of the salient details.

We tried to wait it out at our cottage in Canada, I say, while my husband went to get my son from college. We were near starving, then we were attacked, my best friend died, my daughter nearly did. The radiation got my husband in the end. He died a little over a month ago. Now we're here, minus my daughter, who decided to stay in Ontario, and I'm not sure why I let her. I end with a feeble laugh that nobody returns.

I'm not asking for sympathy, and no one really gives it. It's just an exchange of information, the way to acceptance. This is who we are now. This is who we have become.

Finally, though, I make it to the side of the room where Major Jack Wyatt is chatting to a few people. His voice is low, well-modulated, without the grating jocularity I have noticed with so many people in power, especially in situations like this, when there is very little, if anything, to be jocular about. I hover uncertainly nearby, wanting to interrupt but feeling awkward about it. Even in the apocalypse, social niceties remain.

After a few minutes, though, the conversation peters out and Jack Wyatt turns to face me, like he knew I was there all along and was just waiting for the right moment to greet me.

"Hello," he says, sticking out a hand. "I'm Jack Wyatt."

I like that he drops the title and doesn't say he's the head of the whole outfit here. I take his hand, and his fingers, warm and dry, clasp over mine. It jolts me in a way I didn't expect and am not sure I like. I'm not ready to feel anything like that for anyone, not even remotely, not for a second.

When I pull my hand back he gives me the kind of sad smile that makes me feel like he knows my whole thought process and understands it.

"Alex Walker," I tell him. "I arrived here with two of my children about a week ago. I came from Canada, where my daughter still is. She's only sixteen, and I was hoping there was a way I could call her—on the radio or satellite phone or something." I say all this in an anxious rush and his patient smile doesn't slip.

"I'm sure there is," he tells me, and a wave of relief crashes over me, nearly making me stagger. *Finally* someone is telling me it's possible. I will be able to talk to Mattie.

"Thank you," I tell him, my voice heartfelt. "I would really, really like to talk to her."

He nods. "Of course you would. She's only sixteen, you say?"

"Yes..." There's no censure in his voice, but I still feel the need to explain. "We were staying in a community at a fishing camp up in northern Ontario. It's small and friendly, everyone working together, and she wanted to stay there rather than come here. My other children wanted to come here; my son was in college when the first bombs..." I trail off, abject, as I spread my hands. "I didn't know what to do."

"It sounds like it was a very difficult situation. Back in the day, getting your kids to agree on what fast food to have for takeout was hard enough, but this kind of life-changing stuff?" He laughs, but it sounds a little hollow, and I wonder what his story is. Where is his wife, his kids? I don't feel I can ask.

"So, do you know how I can be in touch with her?" I ask instead.

Jack Wyatt gives me a quietly considering look. "Why don't you meet me at headquarters tomorrow morning, at seven o'clock," he tells me. "It's in the old City Hall, on Second Street. They have a ham radio there that people have been using for personal communications."

For a second, I am gobsmacked. The head of this whole place is willing to meet me, to make a call? I think of the woman I met earlier, and how suspicious she was. I am choosing not to be suspicious now. I want to take Jack Wyatt at face value, and trust that he is a good guy.

"Thank you," I tell him. "Thank you so much. I'll be there."

TWELVE

MATTIE

"Hey, guys," Vicky says in that same too-cheerful voice. "This is Wade."

Out of the corner of her eye, Mattie sees Sheryl and Patti exchange a look, and then quickly glance away from each other as they go back to peeling potatoes, their heads bent. Meanwhile Mattie is both looking and trying not to seem as if she is looking at Wade.

He is maybe mid-twenties, although anyone over eighteen seems old to Mattie, so she can't be sure. He's wearing camo fatigues—pants and a field jacket, and she's pretty sure she sees the bulge of a pistol tucked into his waistband. His hair is dirty blond and pulled back in a messy ponytail, and he has a scraggly beard and moustache. His eyes are very green. Vicky is smiling at him as if he's a trophy she's showing off. She giggles again, a strange sound.

"Hey, Wade," Sheryl says, a beat too late, her voice a little too high. "Where do you come from?"

"He's from near Sudbury," Vicky answers in a proprietary way, while Wade continues to look around the kitchen like he's making a mental inventory. "But he's thinking of joining us here."

Again Sheryl and Patti exchange a look. Vicky speaks like it's

Wade's decision and no one else's whether he joins them at the camp, and a deep ripple of unease goes through Mattie. What happened to it being a cooperative, where everyone had a say, a vote? Then she tells herself not to overreact, that Vicky hasn't said Wade is definitely moving in. If he's thinking about it they'll be able to vote on it, just like they did when Mattie and her family, along with Nicole and Ben, wanted to stay. She remembers waiting outside the main cabin for the verdict, feeling the same kind of anxiety she felt in middle school, when team captains were picking kids for kickball.

Right now all of that feels like a very long time ago.

"Well, welcome, Wade," Patti says with a determined smile. "Do you have any family?"

His gaze moves slowly to her, lingers there as he waits a few seconds before he replies. "No."

"How did you hear about us?" Sheryl asks. She's looking at her daughter, whose smile has not slipped a millimeter. If anything, it's widened. She's shooting Wade sideways glances that seem strangely secretive, and which Wade completely ignores. Vicky is acting, Mattie realizes with a cold thrill of incredulity, like she has a *crush*. She reminds Mattie of the cheerleaders back at her old high school, getting giggly around the star quarterback. It sounds so ridiculous, and yet that is exactly how Vicky seems.

Once again, Wade waits before he speaks, glancing at Sheryl for several seconds before he deigns to reply. It's a power play, Mattie thinks, and a pretty petty one at that, not to mention cringingly obvious. Her suspicion hardens into dislike.

"From Vicky," he tells Sheryl, and does not elaborate.

"I'm going to show Wade the rest of the camp," Vicky says. Her voice is chirpily cheerful, her smile just as wide. "I just wanted to introduce you, say hello."

As she leaves the kitchen with Wade sauntering behind, a silence descends upon the three women. For a good five minutes, the only sound is the scritch-scratch of the potato peeler as the pile of spuds in the middle of the island grows.

"What do you think's going on there?" Patti asks at last, her voice low, as she puts down her peeler to dump five pounds of potatoes into a pot.

Sheryl presses her lips together. "Vicky will have some reason."

"Vicky's not in charge here," Mattie says, the words slipping out of her before she can consider whether they're the best ones. Sheryl frowns at her. "All I mean is," she persists, "everyone is meant to have a say about who joins. It's meant to be a community, a cooperative." She glances at them both, as much in fear as in challenge. "Right?"

"For someone who's been here two minutes, you have a lot of opinions," Sheryl replies tartly, and Mattie blinks, recoiling a little, because she's never heard the older woman speak to her like that before, but Sheryl is Vicky's mother, and maybe her remark came out like a criticism.

"Now, now," Patti interjects soothingly as she looks between them both. "Let's not get cross about it. He's just looking around. I'm sure we'll have a meeting about it later."

They don't talk about it again as they finish making dinner; when the casserole is in the oven, Mattie goes back to Nicole's cabin to check on Phoebe. Outside, the sky is darkening at the edges, mist rolling over the lake, which has gone still, the water looking greenish-black. On the far side of the lake, the evergreens look dark and impenetrable.

Mattie stands at the top of the hill that rolls down to the shore for a moment, breathing in the cold air, trying to talk herself down from this formless panic and dread she feels, swirling in her stomach, clutching at her heart.

Then she notices two figures out on the dock that stretches out over the placid water. It's Rose and Winn, the young couple who had been travelling across Canada, working odd jobs, before the world fell apart. Mattie doesn't know them very well; Winn has dreadlocks down to his waist and Rose has a piercing in her eyebrow, another in her lip. They seem impossibly cool to Mattie, and she is a little intimidated by them.

"Hey," she says as she steps onto the dock, the weathered wood creaking beneath her feet. They look up quickly, falling silent. Mattie has the feeling she has interrupted something. "How are you?" She doesn't wait for their answer before she continues, "Have you met Wade?"

"Yeah." Winn's voice gives nothing away. "Vicky's showing him around the whole place."

"Is he going to join us, do you think?" Mattie asks, and Rose shrugs.

"If we vote on it," Winn says. He still sounds guarded.

"Right..." She doesn't need to be worried, Mattie tells herself. Of course they're going to vote on it. And even if Vicky says they don't need to, there are plenty of other people here who might object to her making a unilateral decision, no matter that she's the de facto head of this place. Adam, the doctor, is quiet but confident, firm in his opinions. He won't let anyone walk over him. And Patti and Jay and their two kids are likely to be vocal, too. Patti didn't seem all that thrilled with Wade. And Nicole has certainly been unafraid to speak up in the past.

She's just feeling anxious, Mattie tells herself, because of that conversation with Vicky she had earlier about moving in with Kyle. It put her on edge, especially with her family gone. And Vicky has seemed a little different, but maybe she really does like Wade. Maybe there's more to Wade than Mattie saw in those few seconds.

In any case, she tells herself, she needs to remember that she's strong, that she can handle this. That she isn't going to let anyone walk over her.

"Okay," she tells Rose and Winn. "Well, I was just wondering what you thought about it."

They both shrug, seeming reluctant to say anything more, and Mattie wonders why they are being so cagey. But then they've always kept to themselves a little; Sam thought it was because they were stoners. Mattie wouldn't be surprised.

"Okay," she says again, and walks back down the dock and up

the hill to Nicole's cabin. Phoebe has fallen asleep on the sofa and Nicole is sewing with a brisk, grim-faced efficiency, her needle flying in and out of a tattered sheet.

"You've met Wade," Mattie states, and Nicole lets out a hard laugh.

"Oh, yes."

A wave of relief pulses through her; she can talk honestly with Nicole. Mattie hasn't always liked her; she's too hard and brittle for that, but right now she trusts her. "What did you think?" she asks quietly as she closes the door to the cabin.

"Well, he came in here with Vicky and strolled around like he was sizing up the windows for curtains," Nicole replies with a grimace. "Not that I think he has any interest in home decorating. But he's got enough ego to float this whole camp, so there's that."

"It's weird, isn't it?" Mattie agrees as she hugs herself. She suddenly feels cold, like an icy pit has opened up inside her, and she could tip right into it. "How Vicky just *brought* him here."

"Brought, or was compelled to bring?" Nicole asks with an arch of her eyebrow.

The coldness inside Mattie deepens, ripples out. "What do you mean?"

Nicole shrugs. "Like you said, it's weird. He just appears out of the woodwork? And why is a guy like him interested in this outfit, anyway?"

"What do you mean, a guy like him?"

Nicole snaps off a thread, her lips pressed together. "A prepper," she explains succinctly. "I've seen them before, although more the millionaire than the redneck variety, but they're essentially the same."

"A prepper," Mattie repeats slowly. She knows the word, of course. There have been plenty of preppers in this post-nuclear world—people, usually men, who have prepared for disaster and now exult in it, either by hunkering down, smugly complacent, or going on pillaging sprees, drunk on their newfound power. Mattie has seen both. Phoebe's mother, Justine, had a brother with an arsenal in his basement—assault rifles, pistols, even hand grenades. He killed himself before he could use any of it.

And then there was the gang that attacked them back at the cottage—wild-looking men with greasy baseball caps and long beards who seemed to get their thrills from terrorizing people—stealing, raping, killing. She's seen it all.

"But we're kind of past all that now," Mattie tells Nicole. "I mean, the world is rebuilding." On the radio they've heard about a medical center in North Bay that is offering vitamins and checkups. A military plane took her family to North Dakota from Michigan. Governments are finally starting to organize. Maybe there'll even be food deliveries at some point; Patti hopes so, anyway. They won't always be eating potatoes and swede casserole, eking out what little food they have to last another week or winter, no matter what Vicky said about their supplies dwindling.

Things are changing. They just have to hold out until the world gets back to normal. That, Mattie realizes, is what she's been hoping for—a world that feels familiar and safe, where she can stay at Red Cedar Lake and live without fear.

It didn't seem too much to ask... but now there's Wade.

"So, what do you mean exactly, he's a prepper?" she asks Nicole.

"I mean he has weapons and skills and a sense that the world has misjudged him," Nicole replies, and now she sounds tired. "Trust me, I've seen it before. Vicky was saying how he came out of Sudbury, had been running that place till it fell apart. Or they kicked him out. Who knows?" She sighs. "Wade has got all the equipment and ability, and now he just needs a place to use it and exercise it. My guess is he's sizing up the camp here to be that place."

"But why would Vicky allow that?" Mattie presses. It sounds alarmist, even to her. Vicky wouldn't just hand over control of the camp to *Wade*.

"Either because he's promising her something, or he's forcing her, or she's fallen in love with him," Nicole replies bluntly. "He's got nice eyes, I'll give him that."

"She did seem kind of giggly around him," Mattie says in a low voice. "It was weird."

"She's been without her fiancé for a while. She's probably lonely. And men like Wade... they can be weirdly charismatic, to some. Me, I don't buy it, but then I wouldn't." She lets out a hard laugh and Mattie suspects she's thinking of her husband.

"And you think Vicky would?" she asks.

"She certainly seemed pretty gassed about him being here," Nicole replies. "Giggly, like you said."

"I know, but..." Mattie thinks of how strong and capable Vicky has seemed from the beginning, a quiet, competent presence. "I didn't think she was like that."

"We can all be like that, with the right man, the right time," Nicole says. "And live to regret it." She pauses. "What about you and Kyle?"

Mattie immediately tenses. "What about him?"

"Well, you didn't move in with him," Nicole points out wryly. "Which I think was a good call, personally." She pauses. "You've been through a lot together, but that doesn't mean you have to love him. You aren't beholden to anyone, Mattie. I hope you realize that."

"I do," Mattie says, but her voice wavers. She is grateful for Nicole's understanding, but she doesn't know how to articulate it.

"Maybe you should talk to Vicky about it," Nicole suggests. "I'm a cynic, it's true. I could be way off base." She sighs as she folds up the sheet she was hemming. On the sofa, Phoebe starts to stir, lifting her dark head as she blinks sleepily at Mattie. "I hope I am," Nicole finishes quietly.

Mattie thinks of how she used to talk to Vicky before her family left, how Vicky seemed like she always listened. She remembers how she ran out of the cabin after her dad died, and Vicky found her and gave her a hug. No words, just that comforting presence. Maybe she should talk to Vicky. Maybe this is all in her mind, and it really will be okay. "I think I will," she tells Nicole.

She gets Phoebe a drink of water and some slices of apple and sets her up with a story book before she heads back outside to find Vicky. It's a little past five, a time when most people would be finishing work and heading to the main cabin for tea or coffee, a chance to catch up with one another at the end of the day, before dinner. Mattie has always enjoyed this time; she and Stewart have been playing a long-running game of chess, and Patti is teaching her how to crochet. Now, however, she sees that the main cabin is empty.

A lump forms in her throat and she swallows it down resolutely. She does not, she reminds herself, need to overreact. Everyone's probably just busy today. She heads for the small office behind the main cabin, where Vicky keeps her papers and the ham radio system that they used to contact the settlement in North Dakota.

Mattie knocks on the door; she can see Vicky through the glass pane, sitting at the desk, her long auburn braid resting over her shoulder.

"Come in," Vicky calls, and Mattie opens the door and steps inside. "Hey, Mattie." Vicky's voice is warm, and already Mattie feels better. This feels normal, the way it used to. Maybe she really has been paranoid. "What's up?" Vicky asks. "You're all moved in?"

"Yes, thanks." Vicky waits expectantly and Mattie wonders what to say. Already she feels foolish, like she's been imagining monsters hiding under beds or in closets. Wade might not even be a prepper, but if he is, it doesn't have to *mean* anything. Another healthy young man will surely be welcome when they start planting this spring, if he joins them at all. Maybe he won't. Maybe he won't want to, or maybe they won't vote him in. And why shouldn't Vicky be a little giggly around a guy she likes, with nice eyes? It's not a crime.

"Do you need something?" Vicky prompts gently. She is smiling, her head cocked. Right now she seems as warm and friendly as ever, and suddenly Mattie knows she cannot ask about Wade. She doesn't even want to; giving voice to her fears will only annoy or hurt Vicky, and right now that's all they seem like—nameless fears, easily dismissed.

"I was just wondering if I could use the radio to call my mom sometime," she says. "You've managed to reach Watford City before, right? I thought I could put a call in, just to find out if she's okay. How they've settled and everything."

"Of course," Vicky replies. "I should have thought of that myself. We can do it right now, if you like?"

Relief breaks over Mattie like sunlight from behind clouds, lighting up the whole world. She really was getting in a panic over nothing, she realizes, and almost laughs from the sheer joy of not feeling that swirling dread in her stomach anymore. She'd been so unsettled from her family leaving and then the whole thing with Kyle, but right now it seems obvious that there's really nothing to worry about.

"Okay, yeah, that would be great," she says. "Thanks."

She sits next to Vicky as the other woman slips on the radio headset and then speaks into the microphone. "CP ND 1," she says calmly, "this is VA3 RC, listening." She pauses and waits, and then repeats the call while Mattie sits with her hands clenched tightly in her lap. "CP ND 1," Vicky says for a third time. "This is VA3 RC, listening."

Mattie knows she won't be able to hear anything since Vicky has headphones on, but she strains to listen anyway—the static and crackle of the radio, the tinny sound of a distant voice. *Come in, VA3 RC. This is CP ND 1, listening. We hear you.*

Vicky tries again, and then again, waiting a minute or two each time, before she slips off the headphones and shakes her head. "I'm sorry, Mattie," she says, sounding genuinely regretful. "Nobody's answering."

"But don't they have the radio manned all the time there?" Mattie asks a bit desperately. "It's the headquarters of the *entire* us right now." It seems absurd to think they would not have someone on radio communications twenty-four hours a day.

Vicky shrugs as she switches off the radio. "I'm sorry, I don't know what to tell you. Maybe they're on a different frequency now or have an encrypted signal. They're also probably getting dozens of calls all the time and can't respond to every single one right away. We can try again later."

Mattie nods, swallowing the acidic taste of disappointment. She realizes just how much she wanted to be in touch with her mom. She'd been half-hoping she might even hear her voice, although she realizes that would have been unlikely. Still, she imagines it.

Mattie! It's so, so good to hear you, sweetheart.

Mattie blinks rapidly as she slips off the stool. "Thanks for trying, anyway," she says, and Vicky nods.

"We'll try again later," she tells her. "I promise."

"Okay." Mattie hesitates and then blurts, "What about Wade?"

Vicky cocks her head, her body going still. "What about him?"

"Is he thinking of joining us here?"

"Maybe," Vicky replies lightly. "Like I said this morning, it would be good to have some more help, and Wade has a lot of skills. I think I mentioned before that he was working on a farm near Sudbury before, and if we want to have a significant crop this summer, we could use his expertise." Her eyes narrow slightly. "Is there a problem?" she asks, sounding more confused than accusing, and Mattie immediately backs down.

"No, no," she says hurriedly. "I was just wondering."

Vicky nods slowly. "Okay."

They stare at each other for another few seconds before Mattie turns toward the door. "It's going to be time for dinner soon," she mumbles. "I should go help."

"All right, I'll see you in a bit." Vicky sounds friendly again, as warm as she's always been, and yet as Mattie slips through the door and heads back to the main cabin, the lake now shrouded in darkness, she feels more alone than ever.

THIRTEEN
ALEX

Sam and Ruby are both sleeping when I slip out of the house at six forty-five the next morning, my parka zipped up to my chin and my hat pulled down to my ears. It's mid-April, but there's frost on the ground and at this time of the morning, the temperature is still well below freezing, and as ever, the wind blows in from the prairies, relentless and becoming familiar. I almost welcome its cold, cleansing sweep as I walk briskly toward the old City Hall on Second Street, feeling determinedly buoyant with optimism. Today I am going to talk to my daughter. I choose to believe that, just as I've chosen to believe that this new country has good intentions and acts in good faith, that they're here to help us, including Jack Wyatt.

I think of the old quote, by Ronald Reagan maybe, that the most terrifying words ever spoken are *I'm from the government and I'm here to help*.

Once upon a time, such a quip would have made me smile. Now I choose—*choose*—to believe those words aren't terrifying but affirming. Hopeful and necessary, because God knows we all need someone to help us right now.

Jack Wyatt is waiting outside the military headquarters,

dressed in his usual army fatigues, and holding two thermoses of what I hope is coffee.

"It's only instant," he greets me as he hands me one of them. "But it's hot."

"Thank you." I unscrew the thermos and breathe in the familiar, comforting smell. "That's really very kind of you."

"Well, it is early, and I appreciate you coming out."

I can't help but let out an uncertain laugh. "I'm the one who appreciates *you*," I tell him. "I've been asking everyone I can how I can contact my daughter. You're the first person who offered a solution."

His eyes crinkle as he smiles. He has very nice eyes, a warm golden-green hazel, with deep crows' feet fanning out on either side in a suntanned and weatherbeaten face. "Well, that's what I'm here for," he quips. He gestures to the front door. "Shall we?"

The City Hall still bears some resemblance to what it once was —a small municipal building that offered tax help and free rabies shots for your pets. Some of the posters are still on the wall, faded and forgotten; a US flag hangs down between them, looking faded and a little tattered. Inside, rooms have been cleared for military apparatus; there is a whole bank of radio receivers and transmitters, black boxes with dozens of switches and flashing lights. There are a handful of people on duty even at this hour, sitting in front of the machines with headphones and expressions of fierce concentration.

"They're monitoring all the chatter," Jack explains. "As we continue to rebuild, and others are doing the same, we're in increasing contact with various settlements around the country."

"And what about other countries?" I ask, curious to discover more about how this brave new world works.

"Ah, that happens somewhere else. We're fairly small potatoes here. Minot Air Base is where a lot of the international communication takes place. I don't have much to do with that."

We walk past the radio room to a small room with a far humbler ham radio, similar to the set I'd seen at Red Cedar Lake.

"This is used for personal communications," Jack explains. "Everybody's got someone they want to try to contact, it seems." He holds the door open for me and I step inside; the room is no bigger than a booth and our shoulders brush before Jack murmurs an apology and eases a few inches away.

"Now, I hope you know the call signal of the place you're trying to contact?" he asks as he pulls out a chair.

"Yes, VA3 RC."

"Ontario, right? All their signals begin with VA or VE 3." He reaches for the headphones. "You want to put these on?" He smiles wryly. "You've done this before, right?"

"A little." Back at Red Cedar Lake, I briefly spoke to the military staff in charge of the transport from Mackinaw City, but I'm far from an expert.

"Well, it's pretty easy." He pulls the microphone toward me. "You speak into the microphone, and then you listen for a response. It might take a while. Is the radio where your daughter is generally manned?"

I think of Vicky's little office, empty whenever she was working, which was most of the day. "Sometimes," I allow. "I think she'd check it in the morning."

"Your daughter?"

"Vicky, the woman who runs the camp." Although it's technically meant to be a cooperative, it has been obvious from the start that Vicky is in charge, in her quiet, competent way.

"Okay, well, we can give it a try. The call signal here is CP ND 1."

I slip on the headphones and Jack reaches for the transmitter while I speak into the microphone. "VA3 RC, VA3 RC," I call, my voice quavering with nerves. "This is CP ND 1, listening." I hear static and silence, and I count to thirty slowly before I start again. "VA3 RC, VA3 RC, this is CP ND 1, listening." I go through the whole process again, and then a fourth time, counting to sixty this time.

There's no response.

I know I shouldn't be surprised; Vicky doesn't listen to the radio all that often, but I did tell her I was hoping to make contact after I arrived and part of me expected her to be on the front foot, checking in regularly. I don't know how difficult it will be to try again. Jack has been very kind, but he is the commanding officer here. I can't expect him to drop everything again and again just so I have a chance to talk to Mattie, and I don't know if he would, anyway. This feels like a one-time favor, maybe even a chance to show what a nice guy he is, or maybe that's me being cynical. There's something affable about Jack Wyatt, as well as trustworthy, and perversely that makes me wonder if I should trust him, as nice as he's being.

I try again, and there's still no reply. "I guess no one's listening right now," I say as I slip off the headphones. My voice is thick with disappointment. I so wanted to talk to Mattie, or at least *someone* at Red Cedar Lake.

"You could try again at the third hour," Jack offers. I must look blank because he continues, "You know the three-three-three rule with ham radio? You listen for three minutes at the top of every third hour, on channel three. It's a way to make an emergency contact. I'm sure this Vicky, if she operates a radio, knows about it." He gives a slight grimace. "I would have suggested we meet at nine so we could take advantage of that, but it gets pretty busy here then. Still, if you want to come back later and see if someone can help, you're more than welcome to."

"Thank you, you've been so kind." Maybe too kind. Why is he being so nice to me? Is it stupid to feel suspicious? I swallow past the lump that has formed in my throat as I reach for my thermos of coffee.

"You must be worried about her," Jack remarks quietly. "You said she's sixteen?"

I nod. "We were all staying at this fishing camp up past North Bay—they're pretty well set-up there, with solar panels and an artesian well and some farming, chickens, that kind of thing..." A sigh escapes me. I miss the little community at Red Cedar Lake, its coziness and comfort. "But it didn't feel like a life with a future," I tell Jack, "and so my son and younger daughter and I came here. Mattie insisted she wanted to stay."

Jack frowns and I continue, feeling compelled to explain. "I understand why she did, in a way. We've moved around a lot—we were at my family cottage first, and then it got taken over by a gang. Burned to the ground." Even if that was my choice, rather than let those marauders have it free and clear. "We were on the run, pretty much, for a while, and we camped out in a provincial park for a few weeks before we ended up at the settlement in North Bay—the old NORAD complex?"

"Yeah, I know it."

I sigh. "That didn't work out so well."

"I've heard about that," he says. "They can be a little controlling."

"Yeah." I take a sip of coffee. "So we ended up at Red Cedar Lake, and for the first time in a long while we all felt safe. I guess Mattie doesn't want to give that up."

"That's understandable."

"What about you?" I ask. "How did you end up here?" Belatedly I realize the question might seem nosy, and also I'm aware how much time I'm taking of someone who has to be a very busy man. Maybe it's the close quarters of this little booth, the sense of intimacy it creates, but I want to know Jack Wyatt's story.

"Well..." He releases a long, low breath. "I was stationed out in Colorado. When the first nukes hit, I was put on active duty, but frankly it was chaos from the get-go. We were deployed first to control rioting, and then to deal with a factory fire, and then we were going to be offering relief aid... but when more and more bombs fell, it all just fell apart. We were disbanded about three weeks after the first hit. My family had already gone up to a little cabin we have, in the Rockies. I joined them there. We thought we'd wait it out—I'd made sure there was plenty of bottled water and dehydrated meals there years ago. I wasn't a prepper, per se, but I liked to be prepared."

His eyes crease again as he smiles, this time the curve of his mouth touched with sadness. "But there's prepared and then there's *prepared*, you know?" he continues. "We didn't have enough for a year, a year and a half. We held out for six months, through that first winter. I hunted and fished, and in the spring my wife had a little garden, but it was hard going. Makes me think that those first pioneers were made of some seriously tough stuff."

I smile at that. "For sure."

"When the weather turned in the fall," Jack continues in a quieter voice, "we were coming up on a year... my daughter got a cough. Just a cough, nothing to worry about in the real world, the old one, but... it got worse. She'd had asthma as a kid, but we thought she'd grown out of it. And then we ran out of firewood, even though my son and I had blistered our hands practically to the bone chopping all summer. It was so cold in the cabin, and that made her cough worse. It turned to pneumonia, and she struggled to breathe. Sometimes I can still hear her gasps." He falls silent for a few moments. "She died in January."

"I'm so sorry," I whisper. I know from experience there's nothing more I can say.

Jack nods in acceptance. "My wife died three weeks after. She wasn't even sick, not like that. She just wasted away. Malnutrition or a broken heart? Probably both." He shakes his head as a sigh escapes him.

"And your son?" I ask, because now I am seeing how alone Jack seems, despite the smile, the good humor.

"My son survived. We had a radio like this one, so we were able to get some news, and when we heard about this place, my military unit getting recalled... I wanted to go. But by that point, Josh didn't want to have anything to do with it. He was angry, maybe at me, for not keeping everybody safe. I understood it. When I came here, he went south. He'd heard about some people who had some kind of community in the Rio Grande National Forest, near Telluride. He decided to try to find them." He pauses. "I haven't seen or heard from him since February, but every so often I try to call them, just as you did your daughter."

"Oh, Jack." The words slip out of me, far too familiar, and yet somehow appropriate for this moment. I understand now why he was so willing to help me. "I hope you hear from him."

"And I hope you hear from your daughter." He sighs again before tipping back the thermos to drink the last of his coffee. "Have you been assigned a job yet?" he asks, and it feels right to talk about the future.

"Not yet, but I filled out a very long form."

He smiles at that. "We're trying to match people to their interests. We're not meant to be a colony of mindless worker bees. What did you do, before everything?"

"Classic stay-at-home mom," I admit with a grimace. "Laundry, book club, class mom... I'm sure you get the picture. I thought about going back into publishing—I worked as an editorial assistant for about thirty seconds before I had kids. But I never did, and so now..." I shrug before admitting, "I don't know what I'm good at anymore."

"Well, you're obviously good at surviving," Jack replies after a moment. "And raising resilient kids."

I feel a warm glow at the compliment, which seems sincere. "Thanks," I tell him, "but I'm not sure what that translates to career-wise."

"We'll see." We both stand, once again aware of just how small this booth is. "I hope you settle in well here, Alex, and that you find a fulfilling job and make contact with your daughter." Very briefly, he rests one hand on my shoulder. "Please do keep trying. Follow the three-three-three rule and come back here at nine, noon, three p.m. ... whenever you can make it. You'll reach her eventually, and in any case, it sounds like she's in a good place. A safe place."

"Yes, I think she is." I feel comforted, and less bereft at not having been able to talk to Mattie. "Thank you."

"You're welcome." He smiles at me before holding open the door, and I slip out. As we part ways outside of the building, I feel a strange and unsettling sweep of loss. I'm not likely to spend much time with Jack Wyatt again, and I realize I'm disappointed. The knowledge unsettles me, and I feel a pang of guilt. My husband died little more than a *month* ago. I can hardly be thinking about another man like that.

And yet... it had felt nice, talking to another adult. Feeling less alone, just for a few minutes. Outside, the sky is a pearly pink at its edges, and the sun touches every building, bathing each one in gold. For a second, this bleak new world seems beautiful—the air sharp and clear, the sun so bright. For a second, I let it feel like home.

I walk down the street, tilting my face to the sky, and I don't look back.

FOURTEEN
ALEX

Four days after my attempt to contact Mattie, there is a summons on my screen, right below the weather—high of fifty-five and sunny. The message says I am to report to work at 109 Main Street at nine o'clock that morning. No other information is given.

I am intrigued as well as apprehensive; I am ready to work but I wish I knew what I was doing. Am I going to be paid in tickets, like the woman at the store said? There's no mention of a salary, and I have no idea what is at 109 Main Street. It's not an address I've been aware of, even though I've walked down Main Street many times, have been in every store it offers. I guess I'll find out now.

Sam and Ruby start school next week, and I leave them eating their oatmeal, with Sam promising to keep an eye on his sister all day, to walk toward Main Street. Spring is finally in the air; the buds on the admittedly few trees in the town are unfurling, tight, tiny green nubs unclenching into blossom, the fields in the distance slowly becoming more green than brown, bringing a sense of freshness to the landscape that seemed so barren. The sun is warm on my face as I turn down Main Street. Other people are going to work as well, and the town is coming to life, a mini rush-hour of pedestrians looking, or at least feeling, important. It all almost seems normal, a day in the life of anyone.

Over the last four days, I've gone back to City Hall several times to follow Jack's recommended three-three-three rule. Twice I waited for over an hour for a chance to use the radio only to have no response from Red Cedar Lake; another time I waited for even longer to no avail, being finally told to come back later. Yesterday afternoon, on my fourth try, I finally made contact.

"CP ND 1, this is VA3 RC," came Vicky's disembodied voice over the line. "Listening."

"*Vicky!*" My voice exploded with relief. "This is Alex. I wanted to talk to Mattie... is she there? Can I talk to her?" In my eagerness and desperation, I tripped over the words.

"Alex." Vicky's voice was warm, if a little reserved; I've always felt like she holds something back, maybe because of her fiancé dying when Toronto was bombed. Maybe she just can't help it. "It's good to hear from you," she said. "How is North Dakota?"

"It's good, it's coming along, but Vicky... can I talk to Mattie?"

Vicky let out a little sigh. "Sorry, Alex, but she's out right now. She left a little while ago."

"Out?" I was confused, maybe even a little alarmed. In the four months I was at Red Cedar Lake, no one in my family left the camp even once. And now Mattie is *out*, the minute I call? "Where has she gone?" I asked.

"We've been scoping out some local fields for farming," Vicky explained. "Mattie wanted to go along. We're trying to expand, you know, so we can be completely self-sustaining. Plant a lot more—wheat, barley, corn. But I'll tell her you were in touch, Alex. She'll be so glad to know you got there safely."

I was swamped with disappointment, even though I'd tried to mentally prepare myself for not being able to speak to her right then. "Okay, well, can we arrange a time to talk?" I asked. "Maybe tonight, at six, after you've had dinner?" I knew I'd move heaven and earth to be in this booth at that time.

"Maybe not tonight," Vicky replied, and I had to tamp down

my frustration. Why not tonight? Didn't she realize how important this was to me? "We have a few things going on, a community meeting," she explained. "But tomorrow night?" Her voice softened with sympathy as she added, "I'm sorry you have to wait. I know it's hard, but everything's fine here. Mattie is fine."

"That's good to hear," I said. I couldn't help but think that Vicky didn't seem *that* sorry. Not sorry enough to let Mattie duck out of a simple community meeting. But then I told myself that I was overreacting; that since Mattie and I were both safe, there was no real rush, and maybe the meeting was important. I knew Vicky set great store by the cooperative nature of the community there, which was a good thing.

"Okay, sure," I finally said. "Tomorrow at six. Make sure she's there, Vicky, please. I really want to talk to her."

"Of course," Vicky said with her usual warmth. "I promise."

I'm thinking of that promise now as I head down Main Street this following morning. I'll talk to Mattie *tonight*. It's basically guaranteed. The thought lifts my heart and puts a spring in my step. I find I'm looking forward to whatever my job is. At least, I'm curious.

Five minutes later, as I'm standing in front of the office of the *McKenzie County Farmer*, I find out. It is apparently the county's "premier newspaper." And only newspaper, I imagine, but my curiosity is well and truly piqued as I open the door.

It's a small building, with a little lobby area and some office space behind; on the walls are framed front pages of the newspaper through the years. According to a banner on the wall, the *McKenzie County Farmer* was founded in 1908. I step closer to one of the older framed front pages to read the headline from 1953:

President Eisenhower Makes Dedication Speech at Opening of Garrison Dam; Estimated Twenty-Five Thousand People Attend.

My gaze moves to the next one, from 1920.

Influenza Hits McKenzie County; Death Tolls Rises.

I am just studying the third, about the local oil industry in the 1970s, when the door to the office opens and a man strides out. He's in his fifties, with a head of curly gray hair and a tanned, weathered face.

"Are you Alex Walker?" he barks, and I nod, a little taken aback by his brusqueness.

"Yes, and you are...?"

"Bruce Tyson." He sticks out a hand. "Newly appointed editor of the *Watford City News*." There is a wryness to his tone that I like, an affability beneath the bark. As I shake his hand, I find myself smiling.

"And who am I?" I ask.

He grins. "Newly appointed feature writer. Right now, we're the only two employees."

"Excellent."

We smile at each other, and I experience a lick of excitement, of *ambition*, something I haven't felt in a very long time. I have a job, and I think I'm going to like it. "So what now?" I ask.

Bruce spreads his hands. "Your guess is as good as mine. Before all this, I was an English teacher. I helped out with the school newspaper, but I was only an assistant. To say I'm in over my head is an understatement, but I guess we all are here."

"Well, I don't have any experience of newspapers besides doing the crossword," I tell him. "So you beat me by a mile."

He laughs at that. "I guess we're the best they've got. Come on back and I'll show you what we're working with."

I follow him back to the office space, which feels a little bit like a time warp, both from before the bombs and even decades before that. Everything looks old and worn and at least twenty years old. There are half a dozen desks in the open plan area, and battered metal filing cabinets line the walls. A window looks into what I assume was the senior editor's office, a small room with a desk, a chair, and a view of the parking lot.

"The printing press is downstairs," Bruce tells me. "The computers work, but they're basically just glorified typewriters. There's no internet to speak of, as I'm sure you know. We'll have to get the news from the ground."

"And what's the brief here?" I ask. I sound responsible and serious; I feel like I'm playacting. I could be watching a sitcom about a serious journalist, or a sitcom about a woman *pretending* to be a serious journalist. Laughs every minute as she bumbles her way through various comic scenarios, betraying her ignorance at every turn and yet somehow managing to write a Pulitzer-Prize-winning article, of course. Who knows, I think, maybe that can be me.

"The brief?" Bruce sighs. "Beats me. The CO said he wanted a newspaper for local residents, something to lift people's spirits, make them feel like things are happening here."

"But things *are* happening, right?" I half-joke, and he raises his eyebrows.

"Well, they must be, if you read it in the news." He sounds too cheerful to be cynical, and I choose to take the joke at face value.

"Okay," I tell him. "And is this a digital newspaper, to be published on the information system?"

"Digital and paper. The CO wants paper copies on every street corner, or just about. Says he's old school that way."

Something about the way he speaks about the commanding officer strikes a chord. "The CO..." I prompt. "Of the newspaper, or...?"

"Major Wyatt. He's running Watford City."

I avert my face to hide my expression, although in truth I'm not even sure what that expression is. I haven't seen Jack Wyatt since I said goodbye to him four days ago, and I don't expect to, considering how busy he must be, how unimportant I am. Knowing that he was the one who must have arranged for me to have this position gives me a warm, jumpy sort of feeling inside, and I do my best to ignore it. I need to focus on the job, which is what I want to do. I want to succeed at this.

"Okay," I say again. "So how do we find this news? Go out on the street? Interview people, or..."

"We're not quite that desperate," Bruce assures me. "Not yet, anyway. We're going to be given a sheet every morning, by Command, of news items and various developments they want us to cover. We turn them into articles, with a definite upbeat spin, and we add a puzzle page, a humor section, a little bit of lifestyle..." He lifts his gaze to the ceiling. "'Ten ways to use dried milk powder that you never thought of.' That kind of thing."

It feels like wartime; all we need is a bit of Blitz spirit and some gumption, gosh darn it. "Sounds great," I say, and Bruce arches a skeptical eyebrow.

"We'll see," he replies. "The printing press is in the basement, and I have absolutely no idea how to work that behemoth, but I guess we'll figure it out. Major Wyatt wants the first paper printed and distributed by Friday."

Again I feel that lick of excitement, of ambition. I am so ready, I realize, to *do* something... and I'm very grateful to Jack Wyatt for giving me this chance.

Bruce and I spend the next few hours going through the office. We read old newspapers and organize desks; I insist he takes the editor's office while I make myself at home at a corner desk in the main office, with a view of the street. After we have our lunch—rehydrated chicken stew for me, some kind of soup for Bruce—we head downstairs to examine the printing press, which indeed is a behemoth, filling up most of the room. There are stacks of newspaper sheets that go between massive metal rollers, but neither of us has a clue about any of it.

"I could really use the power of Google right now," Bruce muses, his hands on his hips.

"There must be an instruction manual," I offer, and he arches an eyebrow: his classic response, as I'm starting to discover.

"Be my guest and have a look," he replies, throwing an arm out.

I hunt through a few drawers, but nothing jumps out. Bruce is examining some of the printing plates, clearly having no idea what to do with them.

"We need an expert," he announces. "I'll mention it to Major Wyatt."

"You sound like you're friendly with him," I remark, and he shrugs.

"He's a friendly guy, I guess." There is a note of reserve in his voice that I can't help but notice.

"You guess?" I repeat, my eyebrows raised.

"Well, he's part of the system. There's no getting away from that."

"And you're suspicious of the system?"

Bruce shrugs. "It just seems a bit... opaque. I mean, who even is in charge? I heard the president died months ago."

"He did?" I am jolted; I hadn't heard that, but it feels like something I should have known. Something I should have been told.

"And who's running the military? Keeping them all together? When the bombs first fell, they were nowhere to be seen, I know that much." His face darkens with what I suspect is a memory.

"I guess it took some time to organize," I remark uncertainly. I feel Bruce Tyson is someone I could like, but I don't want him asking these kinds of questions. I don't need any more doubts. "Major Wyatt helped me try to get in touch with my daughter," I tell him. "I really appreciated that."

"Well, like I said, he seems like a good guy." Bruce glances at the massive printing press. "Why don't we leave this," he suggests, "and brainstorm some articles based on the sheet they gave us? We can get writing, at least, and figure out the printing later."

We head back upstairs and sit at the table in the tiny conference room, to look over the sheet Bruce was given. There are four points on it, each one briefly summarized. *Full-time education begins for those aged 6–20* reads the first one, with a few statistics underneath. There are one hundred and twenty students enrolled at the elementary school, three hundred students currently enrolled at the high school, and four hundred and fifty at the college. The numbers are encouraging.

The second item is *Contact made with South American countries, more imports expected soon.* In addition to the oranges, we can expect bananas and mangoes in the next few weeks.

"A mango..." Bruce murmurs with longing. "I haven't had fresh fruit besides that one orange in months."

"Do you know what's happening in the rest of the world?" I ask him. "We're in touch with Argentina, but what about Australia? Or China? Or, I don't know, France?"

He shakes his head. "I only know what they tell us, same as everybody else." He points to the sheet. "And that's our job, to spread the news so people feel informed."

"Feel informed, even if they're not?"

He smiles and shakes his head. "You said it, not me."

The third item is about parcels of summer clothing being available for pick-up from the Comfort Inn; the fourth is about land clearances: *One thousand square miles cleared for habitation.*

I think of the woman at the welcome reception, her face twisted with bitterness. What *did* happen to her farm, I wonder?

"You want to take the first point and write something up?" Bruce asks. "You can walk over to the school for more information and a quote. No phones working yet, but soon, I hope. That might be one of next week's items."

"Okay." I feel rejuvenated, both by the work and the prospect of talking to Mattie later. "I'll walk over there now."

Life is *happening*, and it energizes me. As I walk along Main Street, out toward Route 23 and the high school, I am humming under my breath. I imagine the articles I'll write, seeing them in print, being paid, even in tickets, for work I want to do that encourages other people. It all feels good.

The future finally, *finally* looks bright.

FIFTEEN

MATTIE

"Are we good?"

Mattie looks up from the laundry she is folding, instantly wary. Kyle is standing in the doorway of her and Nicole's cabin, looking aggrieved. Outside the sun sparkles on the ruffled surface of the lake, and the first buds are coming out on the trees. The world is waking up, and Wade has been at Red Cedar Lake for a week.

"Why wouldn't we be good?" Mattie asks. She knows she sounds a little petulant, but she doesn't care. The relief she felt when she spoke to Vicky and they tried to reach her mom has trickled away, replaced by an ever-deepening unease.

She tells herself she's being stupid, paranoid, but she still can't shake the feeling. Living with Nicole's cynicism doesn't help either; Nicole clearly doesn't like Wade, doesn't trust him, and she bitches about him and the way Vicky cozies up to him just about every night.

"I thought Vicky was better than that," she said last night, shaking her head, "but I guess she was lonely." She gave Mattie a suddenly stern look. "Don't ever let loneliness guide your decisions. Trust me on that one."

Mattie is thinking of that advice now as Kyle says, "It feels like you're avoiding me." The words seem to hang in the air and then settle.

"I'm busy," Mattie finally says. She folds another towel, hard and scratchy from being dried in the fresh air. "As are you," she adds. "What have you been doing with Wade?" She can't keep an edge from her voice. Wade hasn't *done* anything, but he still makes her feel afraid. Maybe it's his presence, the way he strides into a room, looking around like he's taking stock. Or maybe it's how he always waits before answering a question in his laconic, self-assured way, giving out as little information as possible. Or maybe it's the way everyone else seems to edge around him, like they're afraid, as she is, but nobody wants to say anything. Vicky always asks his opinion, breathlessly, her eyes wide. Mattie can't tell if she adores him the way Nicole seems to think she does, or if, like the rest of them, she's afraid. Maybe it's both.

There has been no vote. Two days ago, Mattie finally worked up the nerve to confront Vicky. "Is Wade staying?" she asked. "How come we haven't voted on it?"

A decided coolness came over Vicky as she gazed steadily back. "He's only been here a few days," she told Mattie. "He's still checking things out. Just as you and your family did, not that long ago." She folded her arms, staring Mattie down so she felt defensive. "Why are you so prickly about him?" Vicky asked. "He's here to help us, Mattie. When you and your family rocked up here unannounced, just striding into the camp and making yourselves comfortable, nobody made a thing about it. No, we rolled out the red carpet for you, Red Cedar Lake style. So why aren't you doing that for Wade?"

Because you're doing that enough for all of us, Mattie almost snapped, with some of her old spirit. "I'd just like to know what's going on," she said instead.

"What's going on is that someone with a lot of experience, equipment, and ability is willing to join our community to help make it more viable." Vicky shook her head, looking both disapproving and disappointed. "Why can't you understand that?"

Mattie had felt she'd had no choice but to drop the matter, and she hadn't spoken of it since—not to Vicky and not to anyone else, not even Nicole, whose dark predictions made her feel even uneasier. A few days ago, she asked Adam what he thought about Wade, and he eyed her coolly.

"I think he could be a big help," he said, and Mattie realized she, along with Nicole, really was in the minority. It was time to shut up... but that didn't keep her from worrying.

"What do you mean, what am I doing with Wade?" Kyle asks now. "Working. What's the big deal?"

"What kind of work? Where do you go? He's always driving out somewhere." Wade had arrived in a big, souped-up pickup truck with Monster-style wheels. Mattie can hear the sound of the engine revving all the way from the far side of camp.

Kyle shrugs. "We're just scoping out some fields around here, for planting. Vicky wants to plant wheat, barley, oats... you know, really get things going."

"You don't know how to farm," Mattie replies, and Kyle looks hurt.

"I know more than you," he shoots back. "You grew up in the suburbs. And anyway, we're just looking. When the time comes, we're going to need all the willing workers we can get. But I wasn't talking about all that," he adds, and now he's the one who sounds petulant. "I was talking about *us*."

Mattie sits on the bed, slumped, a towel still clutched in her arms. She knows she owes Kyle a real answer. They've been through too much, but like Nicole said, that doesn't mean they're in love. She doesn't owe him anything but her honesty. "I don't know, Kyle," she says quietly.

"You don't know *what?*"

"I've been thinking..." She hesitates, lets the idea unfurl inside her. "I've been thinking about joining my family in North Dakota," she says, trying out the words, and Kyle's eyes widen.

"*What?*"

"I miss them, and I want to be with them," she says more staunchly. "That's understandable, isn't it—"

"But you don't even know if they've made it," Kyle exclaims, and Mattie flinches. "Or what it's like," he amends, seeming to regret sounding so cavalier about her family's fate. "I mean, it could be like North Bay, but a thousand times worse."

"It could be," she allows, "but—"

"Wouldn't your mom have been in touch if everything's okay?" Kyle presses. "Why hasn't she been?"

"So what are you saying?" Mattie demands. She rises from the bed, tossing the towel aside. "That my mom is dead or in *prison* or something?"

Kyle flings his hands up in defense. "I'm just saying you don't know. Until you hear from her, you should think twice about heading all the way to North Dakota."

"I don't think I want to stay here," Mattie says quietly, and Kyle frowns, lowering his hands.

"Mattie, babe, what's wrong?" He comes forward and puts his arms around her, and Mattie lets him. It feels good to be touched. "What are you scared of?" he asks gently.

"I don't know." She leans her forehead against his wiry shoulder. "I don't know," she says again.

"Is it Wade?" Kyle asks. He's rubbing her back in rhythmic circles in a way that Mattie both craves and despises. She knows she has always been this way with Kyle; their relationship has never been as straightforward as she made out to her mother. "I know he's kind of a badass," Kyle continues, "but he's cool, you know?"

"Is he?" Mattie closes her eyes. She wants to stop fighting; more importantly, she wants to stop feeling so afraid.

"You don't need to worry, babe," Kyle says. "It's all good."

Mattie opens her eyes and steps back, forcing Kyle to drop his hands. "Yeah," she says. "You're probably right." She stares at him for a moment before turning back to the towels. After a few more seconds, Kyle leaves the cabin.

. . .

That afternoon, Vicky informs her she'll be going out with Wade. Mattie stares at her silently, wide-eyed with dread.

"I'm going with... with Wade?" she finally manages. "But why? And where?"

"Don't you want to get out, see a little bit of the world?" Vicky asks playfully, and instinctively Mattie shakes her head. "You've had some concerns about Wade," Vicky continues in a brisker voice, "and this is the best way to deal with them. We're looking at cultivating some fields nearby. I'm sure he'd appreciate your opinion."

What, Mattie wonders with something close to panic, does she know about cultivating fields? And she's pretty sure, really, absolutely *positive* that Wade will not appreciate or be interested in her opinion. She also knows she can't refuse.

Half an hour later, she's sliding into the passenger seat of Wade's souped-up truck. It smells of cigarettes and stale sweat and she breathes carefully through her mouth, turning her head to look out the window as Wade reverses quickly down the rutted dirt drive. It is only the two of them in the truck, and Mattie's heart pounds, her hand slippery on the handle as Wade revs the engine and roars out onto the empty road.

"Where..." Mattie's voice is thin and papery, and she clears her throat before trying again. "Where are we going?"

Wade glances at her, amused. He knows she's nervous, and Mattie suspects he likes it. "Farm near here, a couple of miles away," he says, drumming his fingers on the wheel. "Going to see if anyone's using the land, the house."

"I thought most of the people here were self-sufficient already," Mattie ventures. "Won't they be farming their own land?"

"Well, some people have upped and left, haven't they?" Wade drawls. He glances at her, his voice dropping in a suggestive way that makes her skin crawl. "You a city girl, Mattie?" he asks. "You all sophisticated?" He draws out every syllable of the word in a way that feels mocking.

Mattie turns back to the window. "Not really."

"You like them city boys?" Wade continues in the same low, drawling voice. "Because I reckon you could do much better than that little runt Kyle." He lets out a bark of laughter while Mattie keeps her gaze trained on the empty fields blurring by. "That's his name, isn't it?" Wade asks. "Kyle?"

Wordlessly she nods, her gaze still fixed out the window. A startled gasp escapes her as she suddenly feels Wade's fingers on her jaw, digging in, hard enough to hurt.

"You want to look at me while I'm talking to you?" he asks quietly, his fingers still digging in, making her wince. "Because I find it kinda rude for you not to." He squeezes her jaw even harder and Mattie has to suppress a whimper as she forces herself to turn her head to face him.

"I'm looking at you," she whispers through her squeezed lips, his fingers still grasping her as they rattle along at at least sixty miles an hour. Wade isn't even looking at the road, and Mattie is as afraid of crashing as she is of what he might do to her.

Finally, after what feels like an age, he releases her jaw. Mattie lets out an audible breath, determined not to raise her hands to her face and massage her aching jaw.

"That's good," Wade says in approval as his gaze returns to the road. "That's very good."

Abruptly, he jerks the wheel hard to turn off the road, the back wheels lifting with a squeal as he does a sharp 180. Mattie is flung against the door, bruising her shoulder.

"Where... where are we going?" she cries.

"I think we can head back now," Wade tells her. "I think you've learned your lesson."

Mattie stares straight ahead, her throbbing jaw clenched. She does not speak as they drive back to Red Cedar Lake.

Vicky comes out of her office as Wade pulls up in the truck.

Mattie has a sudden and desperate urge to burst into tears, but she keeps herself from it. Vicky is smiling.

"That was quick," she says with a questioning glance at Wade. "Did you go to the Bryces' farm?"

"Yep, all clear," he replies easily. "They left months ago, I'd say."

"They have forty acres," Vicky says, sounding pleased. "And it's only a couple of miles away."

"All we have to do is clear it," Wade replies. He slings an arm around Vicky's shoulders in a way that makes Mattie think he's done it many times before. Her sense of fear is coalescing into a dark dread, fast turning into despair. Vicky is like a different person when she's with Wade. Whether it's out of love or fear or both doesn't matter; the result is the same. Wade is running the camp.

How is she going to get out of here? Because now she realizes, more than ever, that she needs to. She needs to go to North Dakota, whatever it's like there, and be with her family.

"Mattie, good news," Vicky says. "Your mom's been in touch."

Mattie nearly sobs with relief. "She has?"

"Yes, while you were out. We arranged to have her radio back tomorrow at six."

Tomorrow... it feels like ages away, and yet Mattie clings to the hope. Tomorrow she'll talk to her mom. Tomorrow she'll ask her about coming to North Dakota.

Vicky smiles as she rests a hand on Mattie's shoulder. "I'm sure she'll want to hear about how well you're doing," she tells her. "And you can tell her about the community meeting we're having."

"Community meeting?" It's the first Mattie has heard about it.

"Yes, tonight. We're voting on Wade joining the community."

Mattie swallows hard as her gaze moves inexorably to Wade, who smiles back at her, a hint of mockery glinting in his eyes.

"Should I be worried?" he teases Vicky while looking straight at Mattie.

Vicky only laughs in reply, the question clearly so absurd it doesn't need an answer.

SIXTEEN

ALEX

At five fifty-five that evening, I am in the radio booth, headphones on, hand on the microphone eager and so very ready to talk to my daughter. I cleared the timing yesterday with the radio personnel, so I was able to walk right into the booth. Now I just need to call her.

I press the headphones against my ears as I lean over the microphone, breathless with both anxiety and excitement. "VA3 RC, this is CP ND 1," I say, and my voice trembles. "I'm calling for Mattie X. Mattie X, VA3 RC, do you read me?"

I hear static, silence, and then, like a miracle, a *triumph*, a wavery voice. "CP ND 1, this is VA3 RC, listening."

"*Mattie.*" A sob escapes me, and I press my hand to my mouth, afraid I might lose it completely. "Oh, Mattie, Mattie, it's so good to hear your voice." I close my eyes, my heart aching with love for my daughter over a thousand miles away.

"It's good to hear yours too, Mom." My daughter sounds tearful, and I hope it's just the same kind of emotion I'm feeling, and not something else. Something more. There is so much I want to say, to ask; the words feel like marbles in my mouth, and I can hardly get them out.

"Mattie, oh Mattie, are you okay? Are you good?" I ask in a

rush. "How are Phoebe and Nicole? And Kyle too, of course..." I don't want her to be mad that I forgot to ask about her boyfriend. "How are things there? Is it warm yet? I miss you so much."

"I'm good, Mom," Mattie says. It's hard to hear her tone on the radio, but I sense she's missing some of her usual sassy spark. "Everything's fine here. You know, the same." A pause, a crackle. "More importantly," she asks, "how are *you*? How is North Dakota?"

"It's good. Really good." I let out a trembling laugh. "I have a job, working on a newspaper. Today was my first day."

"A newspaper?" She sounds incredulous. "Wow."

"I know, crazy, right? Everything's just starting up, but it feels hopeful. Good." I pause, wanting to ask her if she'll reconsider, but knowing I have to respect her decision to stay. "I miss you," I say instead.

"I miss you too," she says, and her voice catches. "A lot."

"Oh Mattie—"

"I mean, things are good here," she continues in a rush. "Really good. You... you don't need to worry about me. We're going to start planting soon, I think..."

"I'm always going to worry about you," I protest. "That's my job."

"I know, but..." She hesitates and then says resolutely, "You don't have to."

I try not to let her determination sting. Mattie is, I already know, trying to prove she's a grownup, a woman capable of making her own choices. Considering all she's endured these last eighteen months, I know I have to let her... but it's hard. I hate having her so far away. I hate not knowing what's going on in her life.

"I'm going to try to arrange a visit," I tell her, making sure to keep my tone briskly upbeat. "To see you. I don't know how or when, but I'm going to figure it out. Maybe on a military truck or something. I can catch a ride." Even if we're not yet allowed to leave the Watford City limits.

There is a staticky silence, and I think Mattie hasn't heard me. "Mats, did you hear what I said? I'm going to visit—"

"I heard," she cuts across me. "That... that would be great, Mom. But... don't rush. I mean, you've got your whole life to figure out there, and you know, things are pretty busy here, so..." She trails off, and again I try not to feel stung. It's harder this time.

Mattie doesn't seem thrilled by the idea of a visit, but I know how proud my daughter can be. She won't want me to visit until she's got her own life figured out, until she can show me how well she's done on her own, just like she said she would. I understand that, but it still hurts.

"Okay, well," I reply, clinging to my upbeat tone, if only just, "it will probably be a while before I can figure out a way to get there, anyway."

"Yeah," she agrees, and we both lapse into a silence that is made a thousand times worse by every mile between us. I feel like she's already bored by the conversation, and that hurts too. Typical teenager, even in an apocalypse. The next thing she's going to say is *Well, I'll let you go...*

And sure enough, that's pretty much what happens.

"I have to go, Mom," Mattie says abruptly. "Phoebe needs me. But let's talk again soon, okay? Maybe next week?"

Next *week*? "Okay," I say, because I don't feel like I have a choice. She sounds like she's about to hang up. "Same time, same day?"

"Sure." She sounds hurried, a little hassled, like she can't wait to be doing something else. "Okay, bye, Mom. Love you."

And then she's gone.

I sit there, still holding the microphone, the headphones clamped on my ears, listening to nothing but silence. I'm relieved, *so* relieved, to have finally connected with my daughter, but I'm also disappointed.

That was it?

Apparently it was.

I sift over the conversation in my mind, trying to remember

exactly what Mattie said, the timbre of her voice, the choice of words. It was hard, on the radio, when I was straining to listen, but I can't tell if she's experiencing the kind of homesickness I'd expect, mixed with her usual insistence on proving to me she can manage. Or is something else going on?

But what would that be? I tell myself not to be so suspicious—not about her, and not about there. Everyone at Red Cedar Lake has been lovely and supportive; the community had such a nice feel when we were there, welcoming and warm.

Is it Kyle? I wonder with a pang. Maybe Mattie is regretting casting her lot with him. When we first came across Kyle, he was hiding in his crappy apartment, completely helpless and frankly pathetic. He's grown a lot since then, but Mattie could do better, and I don't think I feel that way just because I'm her mother. I feel affection for Kyle, but not much more than that.

Someone raps on the door, clearly impatient to have their turn on the radio, and with a sigh I rise from the chair. Next week, I tell myself, I'll get more out of her. I'll come with questions; I'll gently press for answers. At least I know she's healthy and safe.

I'm just heading out of City Hall, my thoughts still on Mattie, when I hear someone call my name.

"Alex! I hope you got in touch with Mattie?"

I blink Jack Wyatt into focus, more pleased than I should be to see him. "Yes, I just spoke with her now." My voice wobbles betrayingly. "Sorry," I tell him, and I have to brush at my eyes. "I'm a little emotional."

"Completely get it," Jack assures me. "How is she?"

"She's good... I think." I hesitate before admitting, "She didn't say much, just that she was fine, everything was fine... typical teenager, right? You'd think a nuclear holocaust might give them a little more emotional sensitivity, but..." I try to laugh, but the sound is raggedy, subsiding into an even more raggedy sigh. "Sorry," I say again. "I don't really know what I'm feeling. Relieved, mostly, that she's okay."

"Yes." Jack looks serious, and I think about his son somewhere in Telluride; that is, if he made it through the Rockies in February. It's not a given.

"Have you heard from your son?" I ask.

He shakes his head. "Not yet."

We both fall silent, and after a few seconds I rouse myself. "Thank you for putting me forward for the newspaper job," I tell him. "I'm assuming it was you?"

He smiles, his eyes creasing in a way that is already starting to feel familiar. "It was."

"Well, thank you. I'm enjoying it so far, but actually... I might need to interview you?" The idea comes to me as I say the words. "I interviewed the secretary at the high school this afternoon and got hold of a few facts to round out that article, but the piece about the thousand square miles cleared for habitation? Would you be able to give some detail on that? Not now, of course," I say quickly. "If we could set a time..." Belatedly, I wonder if I'm asking too much. But it was Jack who wanted the newspaper in the first place, and I want to write a good article, one backed up by facts.

"That sounds great," he tells me in his easy way. He's always so affable and agreeable, it almost makes me suspicious, but I choose not to let it. "When were you thinking?"

"The paper is meant to be printed on Friday... about that," I add. "Neither Bruce nor I know how to operate a printing press, and I have a feeling it's not intuitive, or at least not intuitive enough."

Jack nods. "Bruce mentioned that to me. I'll get someone on it."

"Thanks." I am amazed that Jack can be so competent and efficient, and all with such good humor. He lost his wife around the same time I lost Daniel. How can he smile so much? Does he feel the kind of grief I feel, that rushes in the minute you give it space, like cold air through cracks? When he told me about his family the other day, it seemed as if he did.

"In terms of an interview," Jack says, glancing at his watch, a rugged-looking thing that should belong to a scuba diver or a helicopter pilot, "my days are a little busy..."

"Evenings are fine, if you're free," I say, and then will myself not to blush, because of course there is absolutely no reason to blush about anything.

"Tomorrow night?" he suggests. "You could come by my condo if you like. I live on the Strata Estates, south of downtown. 505 Creekside. Say, seven?"

"Okay, sounds good." I feel a ripple of something—anticipation mixed with anxiety—and I smile in farewell before heading outside for the walk home through a deepening twilight, the prairie touched with violet and indigo, the first stars glimmering on the horizon.

I'm just heading into the house when I see my neighbor Chantelle appear on her front stoop, scowl at me, and then turn to go back inside.

I falter in my step, calling out, "Hey, Chantelle—" as the door closes with something close to a slam.

What was *that* about? I have a feeling it involves Ruby, who has still not warmed to Taylor even though they'll be in the same class starting Monday. I know I need to get to the bottom of what is going on with my usually mellow if quiet daughter, but it's hard to work up the will when there are so many other things competing for my time—and my mental energy.

Sam is getting ready to go out as I come into the kitchen. "Where are you off to?" I ask as he zips up his coat.

"Andy's opening the high school for some guys to play basketball," he says. Andy, the guy who first gave us a ride, has remained a presence in my son's life, for which I'm grateful. "He's picking me up in a couple of minutes."

"Sam, that's great." Something that would have been unremarkable in our old, pre-holocaust lives feels like an unimaginable gift now, both a blessing and a luxury. "That's really nice of him."

"Yeah." Just like Mattie, Sam doesn't want to waste time on conversation with his mother. He grabs a granola bar from our weekly food parcel while I wonder what to make for dinner. Although we all got to taste an orange, the food available is still bland and minimal—beans, rice, powdered eggs, dehydrated meals. This week we got a tiny, precious jar of raspberry jam and a canister of freeze-dried hard tack; apparently you just add water, knead and bake it into bread. I haven't braved it yet, but maybe I should.

"Where's Ruby?" I ask my son, who is already headed toward the door.

"Up in her room. She seemed mad about something." And then Sam is gone, and with a sigh I head upstairs to talk to my daughter.

Ruby is lying on her bed, staring at the ceiling, her hands folded on her chest so she looks, unsettlingly, a little like a corpse.

"Rubes." I perch on the edge of the bed. "How are you?"

No reply. I'm well used to Ruby's silences, but lately her lack of response has felt different. Angrier, but also more despairing. I reach over to touch her hand, but she shifts away.

"Ruby?" I ask gently. "Is everything okay?"

She doesn't reply, simply stares at the ceiling. "I can't help you if you don't tell me," I say.

"You can't help me at all," Ruby replies flatly. The words jolt me, because they're so unlike her. Ruby has always been my gentle spirit, and even though I've often worried about her, she's been my easiest kid, the one who gets along with everybody, who watches the world with wide eyes as she slips her hand in mine.

This Ruby feels different, like she's hiding herself from me on purpose. I remind myself that she's thirteen, that teenaged moods kick in hard around then, no matter what's going on in the world. Haven't I seen that just today, with both Mattie and Sam? Why should Ruby be any different?

"Okay," I tell her, trying to sound like I'm not bothered. "Chantelle seemed kind of annoyed when I came home. Do you know what that's about?"

"I don't care," Ruby replies in the same flat voice, and she rolls over onto her side so her narrow back faces me. "She thinks Taylor and I are going to be best friends, and we *never* are."

I decide now is not the time to press the matter. I wait a few seconds, just in case she might say something else, but Ruby, of all people, knows how to maintain a silence, and so finally I pat her back and then rise from the bed.

I go into my own room, intending to change into pajamas even though it's only a little past seven. It's getting dark out and I'm tired, and I feel like being cozy, even though the hours of the evening stretch in front of me, lonely and empty.

For a moment, I can almost hear Daniel's voice.

Seven o'clock? It must be jammy time! His eyes glinting into mine as he hands me a glass of wine, a joke between us that, come evening, I was likely to change into my pajamas as soon as possible.

The ache of missing him leaves me breathless for a minute, the grief I keep at bay for most of the day now rushing in, overwhelming me. I sink onto the bed, my head bowed, my shoulders slumped, and simply let the sorrow rush through me, an unrelenting river that carries me in its current.

All the hope and optimism I'd been feeling for this new life of ours—the house, the job, Sam playing basketball and Ruby going to school—feels pointless now. I don't want any of it.

I just want my husband back.

SEVENTEEN
ALEX

Jack's home is a modest townhouse in a sea of similar townhouses on Strata Estates, a development on the edge of town that looks very new, its single-story houses all connected and fronted by tiny lawns. Considering he's the commanding officer of this whole operation, I'm surprised at how small it is.

Something of that must show in my face because as Jack opens the door he jokes, "Welcome to my castle."

"There wasn't some splashy McMansion you wanted to move into?" I ask as I step straight into the living room, a narrow rectangle of a room that feels a little claustrophobic. It has a sofa, a coffee table, and a TV and that's it.

"Why bother?" Jack replies with a shrug. "I'm only one person."

The way he says it reminds me of the loneliness I felt last night. This morning, like a tide, it has receded, but I know from experience it's only a matter of time until it comes back, maybe even stronger than before.

"Your role should come with some perks," I protest, and he smiles.

"It does. I have beer." He says this so proudly that I don't have the heart to tell him I don't like beer.

"Impressive," I say instead. "Is that like, military rations? A tot of rum for the sailor?"

"Pretty much. I get one six pack a week, all for me." He speaks lightly but I still ache for him, the loneliness so evident in his life, as it is in mine. "It's only Miller Lite," he warns me as he heads to the kitchen. "No IPAs or anything like that."

"Miller Lite sounds great." I shed my coat, conscious that this is feeling a little more like a date than I expected it to. I came here with questions for an interview, but right now it feels like we're just going to hang out.

"How are your kids?" Jack asks as he returns to the living room with two cans of beer. "I don't think you told me their names."

"Sam and Ruby." I take the offered can with murmured thanks. "They're doing okay. Excited to start school on Monday." Sam is, anyway. Ruby is still being angrily monosyllabic, a change I'm struggling to get used to. "Thank you, by the way," I add, "for sending someone to look at the printing press. Bruce had a crash course in how to operate it, and I think with a little trial and error, we might get there."

I sit on one end of the sofa, and Jack takes the other.

"I'm looking forward to the first issue," he says, and raises his beer can in a toast before taking a sip.

I take a sip of mine, trying not to wince at the taste. Why am I so nervous? Jack is being friendly, but he's not being weird. I'm pretty sure all the awkward vibes are on my side, because I haven't been alone with a man like this besides my husband for far too long. I feel like a teenager, trying to seem normal.

"So, the one thousand square miles of area cleared for habitation," I state, my voice coming out a little too loud. I pull out my notebook and pen, every inch the avid reporter, or at least trying to be. "Talk me through that. Where is it?"

"I can show you," Jack replies. "I have a map." He rises from the sofa and heads to the kitchen, returning with a rolled-up map that he unfolds on the coffee table. It's a topographical line map of the state of Montana that shows elevations and rivers, but no cities or towns, so it feels like a blank canvas, like he's Lewis and Clark, exploring a wide-open country that's completely untouched, save, I suppose, for those pesky Native Americans that got in the way.

Again I think of the woman at the welcome reception, her forgotten—or not—farm. What is the US government doing with all the people and homes in these supposedly cleared areas? And how can I ask Jack in a way that won't seem suspicious or give offense?

"So the area cleared for habitation is here," he says, running a line down the map with one lean finger. "Eastern Montana, running from Glasgow, just north of the Missouri River, to Sidney, on the North Dakota border, and then south to Jordan." He runs his finger south, tapping the map a couple of times. "It's good, open farmland, so the hope is within the next planting season, we'll be able to grow enough to sustain our current population. We're looking at wheat, oats, barley, lentils, and flaxseed, all already local to the areas in question."

"And how is it cleared exactly?" I ask as I take another sip of beer. The taste is growing on me.

Jack settles back in his seat. "Well, it happens in stages. First, we scope out the area with nuclear scout drones, to detect any radiation. If the levels are low enough, we go in with teams who sweep the area on the ground and do some soil testing. We have a relief aid team to deal with anyone in the area who might be suffering—emergency medics who can offer some basic care. Usually it's a question of dehydration or malnourishment, but a lot of the people have already left—or died."

"Okay," I say. So far this sounds very reasonable, which is reassuring.

"Then another team comes in to assess what's needed for next steps. We have some satellite images from before the bombs, but nothing current." He smiles wryly. "The satellites are still functioning in orbit, but the infrastructure to access their information and images is no longer in place. That's something we're working on, too."

"So you need to see what it's really like on the ground?"

"Basically, yes. We have teams that do an inventory of what's there—both in terms of populations and infrastructure. For example, there's a minerals manufacturing plant near Sidney that's undamaged, so that's promising. But you might not know that Billings, Montana was hit in the third wave of strikes." He pauses, as if to give that information the gravity it deserves. I had no idea that Billings was hit. It had a population of... what? Maybe one hundred thousand? Everyone just *gone*, and so many other places, places I don't even know of, as well.

"Most of Montana's manufacturing was located in Billings, Bozeman, and Missoula," Jack continues. "Unfortunately, we can't yet get across to Bozeman to assess what's happened there." He shifts in his seat as he takes another swallow of beer. "I don't know how much you know about nuclear fallout, but most of the initial radiation from the blast zones dissipates within just a few weeks, so that's not really the issue."

I nod; I remember Daniel telling me something similar. At the time, I wondered how much it mattered, when it had still felt like the whole world was on fire.

"If it had just been one bomb," Jack continues, "or even ten or twenty bombs, we'd probably be back to normal by now, or as much as we could be, all things considered. But there were so many strikes, timed and positioned to create maximum devastation, not just with radiation, but with ongoing pollution and firestorms. We haven't gone into full nuclear winter, thank God, but the growing seasons are considerably reduced, and in certain areas the radiation has seeped into the groundwater. So there's a lot of different things we're dealing with, and there are large areas of the country we still can't access and probably won't be able to for years or even decades to come."

"I heard ninety-five percent of the US population has died," I say quietly.

"That's the current assessment," Jack replies in the same grave tone. "Give or take a few."

"But that still leaves around fifteen million or so, right?" I press. "And that's a lot of people, considering the North Dakota settlement is only... what?"

"Currently? About one hundred and twenty-five thousand."

"So... what about the rest of the country?" I ask. "Where are they and what are they doing?"

Jack shrugs. "In a way, your guess is as good as mine. There are probably hundreds of settlements across the country where people are hunkering down, still trying to survive as best they can. We know of some communities, like the one my son joined near Telluride. And some military bases have been taken over, like what you experienced at North Bay. The challenge is trying to unite these communities under one government, especially when they're in pockets all over the country that are otherwise inaccessible, thanks to the radiation and pollution."

I nod slowly. "Right."

Jack lowers the beer can from his lips as he gives me a frank look. "You don't sound convinced," he remarks mildly, but with a slight edge to his voice that makes me stiffen.

"Convinced?" I repeat. "Of what?"

"I don't know. The truth of what I'm saying?" The edge is more audible now, and for a second, the silence between us feels strained as I struggle to think of a reply. "You know, I understand about being suspicious," he tells me. "After that first wave, I felt completely let down. My unit disbanding, everybody out for themselves, running for the hills? That's not what I joined the Army for. And I saw a lot of stuff I wish I hadn't, on my way to our cabin in the Rockies. A lot of dog-eat-dog mentality, and worse." He falls silent, seemingly lost in memory, and I can't help but think of some of the things I've seen... and done.

When we first fled the cottage, I killed a man in cold blood. I thought it was the right thing to do, that he was a threat to my family, but I've wondered ever since. It's far too easy to become hardened without even realizing it's happening. It's something I've struggled with, my children have struggled with, seeing me like that. It changes a person, maybe forever.

"I can believe that," I say quietly, and Jack nods somberly.

"I bet you can. On the run, moving from place to place... you probably saw a lot of stuff."

"My husband saw more," I blurt out. "He drove from our cottage in Ontario all the way to my son's college, near Utica. Around three hundred miles, maybe. It took him four months to get there and back." Jack nods, waiting for more, and I continue hesitantly, unsure if I really want to share all this. "When he came back... he wasn't the same. It wasn't just what he'd seen, I think, but what he'd done. And he wouldn't tell me what it was. I never found out." And now I never will.

"Maybe that was for the best," Jack suggests gently.

"He died in March. A tumor, from the radiation. He sacrificed himself for my son." Suddenly, with no warning, my eyes fill with tears, and I turn my head, embarrassed. My throat feels too thick to speak, and I can't keep the tears from spilling over, trickling down my cheeks.

"Alex..." Jack leans over and rests his hand on my arm, a comforting weight that I feel I should shrug off, but I don't. "I'm so sorry."

"You know what it's like," I force out, my voice thick and garbled with tears. My nose is running too, and I run my wrist under it, wincing at what a mess I must seem, especially to someone who seems fully able to keep his emotions in check.

"I do." He's silent for a moment and I struggle desperately to get myself under control. I'm far too close to breaking down completely, and I really don't want to. "I thought I could handle it," Jack says after a moment. His hand is still on my arm. "Being in the Army, thinking I was made of tougher stuff... I thought the loneliness, the grief... I could deal with it." He falls silent again, his throat working, his fingers tensing on my arm. "But I can't," he admits, his voice catching. "I wish I could, but I can't."

I make the mistake of looking up at him, shocked to see tears of his own pooling in his eyes, the look of desperation on his face that I know is mirrored on my own. For a second, no more, with both of us caught in the wild maelstrom of our grief, it feels like this moment could tip over into something else.

I want to be comforted. I want to be *touched*. And I think Jack does too. We stare at each other, neither of us moving or even breathing.

Then, with a feeling like a thunderclap, sanity returns; I ease back, and Jack removes his hand from my arm. He gives me an apologetic smile as I wipe my eyes. A few moments pass, both of us cringingly awkward as we try to recover our equilibrium. Neither of us mentions what just didn't happen, and I begin to wonder if I imagined it.

"So, any more questions?" Jack finally asks, and I think about how many I have, and none of them have to do with the land cleared for habitation.

EIGHTEEN

MATTIE

There is a bruise along Mattie's jawline, faint and purplish, that sprouted this morning. Gently she runs her fingers along it as she stares at her reflection in the mirror, two days after her outing with Wade, and then the community vote that night, which was unanimous, just as Mattie knew it would be. She wonders how many of them have had a similar outing with Wade.

At the meeting, Vicky spoke enthusiastically about how Wade could help them farm; how he brought "security," which Mattie supposed was code for guns; how he could help "protect" them, which was code for prison. No one said a single word in response.

Looking around at all the deliberately blank faces, Mattie couldn't tell who was a true convert and who was just frightened. When she and Nicole got back to their cabin, Mattie tried to talk to her about it, but Nicole was just as negative—but also alarmingly dismissive.

"It's too late, Mattie," she said flatly. "Trust me, I know how this goes. He's here to stay and we just have to figure out how to deal with it, whatever that looks like." She gave Mattie a sympathetic smile. "I know you want to come out swinging, but sometimes you just can't. And who knows, maybe Wade won't be so bad. I've been burned once by a guy like him, so I'm cynical." She let out a shudder. "I'm glad I'm not Vicky."

Mattie was glad she wasn't Vicky either; the way Wade had manhandled her had deeply frightened her, but that hadn't been as bad as the radio call with her mom last night.

Even now, the morning after, Mattie has to close her eyes against the painful memory. She'd been so excited to talk to her mom; she had resolved to ask her to help her get to North Dakota. She'd believed, like a little kid, that her mommy could make it all better. But her *mommy* hadn't had a clue what was really going on.

Wade had been in the room with her, sprawled in a chair, his knee nudging hers, his legs spread obscenely wide as he'd listened to every word of her conversation. As Mattie had spoken to her mom, her gaze trained on Wade like a frightened rabbit, he'd lifted his field jacket to show the pistol tucked into his waistband. And as he'd watched her talk to her mom, he'd caressed the gun in a way that had made Mattie's skin crawl. There had been something almost sexual about it that she couldn't bear to think about, even now.

Mattie meets her tired gaze in the mirror as she drops her fingers from her jaw. She thinks of Nicole's words—*he's here to stay and we just have to figure out how to deal with it*—and she knows she doesn't want to accept that. *Live* like that, always terrified of what Wade might do. Somehow, she has to find a way to get to North Dakota—and really, why should it be so hard? Why should Vicky or even Wade *want* her to stay, if she doesn't want to be here? It doesn't make sense. They should just let her go. And so, Mattie resolves, she's going to talk to Vicky about it today... and do her utmost to avoid Wade completely. That's her plan, and she's going to make sure it works.

As she steps into the living area, where Nicole is curled up in front of the fire, her housemate does a doubletake.

"What the hell happened to your jaw?" Nicole demands. She looks almost angry.

Mattie glances at Phoebe, who is curled up next to Nicole. "Wade," she says quietly.

"Wade?" Nicole sounds incredulous, which surprises Mattie. Did she not realize what he is capable of? "Wade, what, *punched* you in the jaw?" she demands.

"Nicole." Mattie nods meaningfully to Phoebe, but Nicole has worked herself up into a temper. "I knew the guy was an ass," she declares, "but I didn't think he was *abusive*. Not like that." She shakes her head, her mouth tight with self-disgust. "When will I learn?"

"It happened when I went out with him, to look at some fields." Mattie's mouth twists. "We didn't look at them."

"Mattie..." Nicole's expression becomes troubled, her forehead puckered. "You should have told me."

"I thought I did," Mattie returns with some heat. "I told you I was worried about him—" She stops abruptly, remembering Wade last night, his hand caressing his gun. Maybe she shouldn't even be having this conversation. What if Nicole does something stupid? What if Wade finds out? It won't be good for her, she knows that much. "Never mind," she says abruptly. "It happened. It's over."

Mattie turns away, reaching for her coat. Part of her is dreading showing up at the main cabin, having to see everyone, and especially Wade. Will other people notice the bruise? Will they say anything? Mattie thinks they probably won't, and the knowledge fills her with despair. She *has* to get out of here. She has to get back to her family, her mom... She thinks of her mother's voice, full of tearful relief on the radio, and she wants to drop to her knees and howl. She wants to be held and rocked like a baby and told in a comforting murmur, the voice of ultimate assurance, that everything is going to be all right.

She wants, she *needs* her mom.

"Come on, Phoebe," she says in as cheerful a voice as she can manage. "Let's get some breakfast."

"Have you talked to Vicky?" Nicole asks. "Have you told her?"

She nods meaningfully towards Mattie's mouth. "It might make a difference."

"No." Mattie isn't sure she wants to mention Wade's manhandling to Vicky. She looked up to her, before all this, counted her a friend and maybe even a mentor. The thought that Vicky might justify or approve of Wade's actions, or even worse, have suggested them herself... well, it's information Mattie knows she can't deal with just now.

"I'm going to talk to Vicky," she tells Nicole. "But not about that." She glances pointedly at Phoebe; she doesn't want to discuss her plans in front of the little girl. Phoebe is pretty quiet, but the last thing Mattie needs is for her to blurt out something. There's no one she can trust, maybe not even Nicole.

"Okay," Nicole says at last, relenting. "But Mattie, please. Take care of yourself."

As much as Mattie appreciates Nicole's concern, it feels pretty pointless. She wants someone to help her, not offer platitudes. Without replying, hand in hand with Phoebe, Mattie steps out into the brisk spring morning. She wishes she could enjoy the view of the lake—its smooth surface, the dense evergreens on the other side, the sense of spring in the air, that promising hint of warmth. Just a few weeks ago she would have taken a deep breath and let the air fill her lungs and feel like she'd finally arrived at a place where she could be happy. Where she could feel both safe and free.

Now she trudges to the main cabin, determined to find her moment with Vicky.

Rose and Winn are eating breakfast at one of the tables, their heads bent close together. They look up at Mattie and then away again as she comes into the cabin. Adam is at another table with his son, Jason, who is only a little older than Phoebe, and almost as serious. Adam gives Mattie a nod, but he doesn't say hello. Mattie wonders if she is imagining the coolness she feels from him and the others. She's barely said anything, but she feels as if she's become the community's problem, because they know she doesn't like Wade.

Breakfast is scrambled eggs and apple compote, and Mattie doles both out on two plates before she and Phoebe retreat to the far side of Adam's table. She gives him an uncertain smile, and his eyes narrow as he looks at her.

"Banged yourself up there, it looks like," he remarks quietly.

"Yeah, I walked into a door," Mattie says, her tone too full of irony; she knows it's a bad idea, but sometimes she simply can't help herself.

Adam frowns. "Well, then, I guess you need to be more careful," he replies, and then rises from the table, motioning to Jason to follow.

Mattie absorbs the sting of that statement, trying not to let it hurt. She's pretty sure Adam has guessed that Wade is the cause of her bruised jaw; she's also pretty sure he is choosing not to care. What she doesn't understand is how swiftly people's attitudes have changed from friendly community to this dark, cold-eyed suspicion. It can't just be Wade; he's only been here a little over a week. Is fear that powerful a motivator, or were the people here hiding their true natures all along?

Mattie and Phoebe eat their breakfasts quietly, keeping their heads down. As Mattie goes into the kitchen with their dirty dishes, Patti presses a dishcloth into her hand. It's cold, and when Mattie opens it, she sees it holds a block of ice. She glances at Patti, whose face is full of sympathy, and wordlessly Mattie presses the ice to her jaw.

It's this small, simple act of kindness that gives her the courage to find Vicky. She leaves Phoebe with Patti, who is always happy to keep an eye on the little girl, and heads to the office behind the main cabin.

The little room is empty, the door locked, which gives Mattie pause. She doesn't remember the door ever being locked before.

"Are you looking for something?"

Mattie whirls around to see Vicky standing there, dressed in a parka, jeans, and fur-lined boots, her arms folded and her face set in a frown. It doesn't feel like a good start, but Mattie still lifts her chin.

"Yes," she says. "I was looking for you. I wanted to talk to you about something."

Vicky nods to the cloth-covered block of ice Mattie is still holding; it's now dripping onto the ground. "You might need to deal with that first." She doesn't ask why Mattie has it, and she doesn't mention Mattie's jaw.

"Okay. I'll be right back." Mattie hurries to the kitchen where she dumps the ice in the sink before running back to the office. Vicky has gone inside, her back to Mattie as she organizes some papers.

"I think I want to join my family in North Dakota," Mattie blurts out, wishing immediately that she sounded more decisive. Her tone made it sound like she was asking Vicky for permission.

"You do?" Slowly Vicky turns around, her expression impassive. She doesn't say anything more.

"Yes," Mattie replies, and now she sounds firmer. "I do."

Vicky cocks her head. "You think it's going to be better in North Dakota?" she asks, sounding skeptical, maybe even a little sneering.

"I just miss my mom," Mattie whispers. "And my family. I want to be with them."

Vicky nods. "Okay," she says. "That's understandable."

For a second Mattie forgets to breathe. Is it really going to be that simple? Once again, she has that sense she's being ridiculous, a whiny little girl complaining about nothing, but then she remembers Wade's fingers on her jaw, the bruise that Vicky can surely see, and she knows she's doing the right thing.

"Will Kyle go with you?" Vicky asks, like it doesn't matter to her whether he does or not.

"I... I don't think so." Until Vicky asked the question, Mattie hadn't realized she knew the answer. She doesn't want Kyle to come. She'll miss him, she knows she will, but she needs to do this on her own, and in any case, Kyle seems happy enough here, under Wade's wing.

Vicky nods slowly. "And Phoebe?"

"Yes, Phoebe will come," Mattie says quickly. Of that there is no doubt. Phoebe goes where she goes; they are a unit and have been for a long time.

"And Nicole?" Vicky presses. "And Ben?"

Mattie has barely spoken to Ben in all the time she's known him. As for Nicole... she has no idea what she wants. She's not sure Nicole does either, but if Nicole wants to go with her, she wouldn't mind.

"I don't know," she says after a moment. "I can ask her, but... this is really about me wanting to be with my family."

Vicky doesn't reply, merely gives her a considering look. "You're kind of fickle, Mattie," she finally remarks as she turns back to her desk, lifts a piece of paper, studies it, and then puts it down again. "Aren't you?"

"I..." Fickle? Mattie has no idea what she means. "I don't know what you—"

"What I mean is," Vicky cuts across her, her voice hardening, "you come here, accept all we have to give, even if it costs us, and then decide to go on your merry way with no thought as to any obligation you might owe us. Your mother was the same."

Mattie opens her mouth, shuts it. Even with Wade's arrival, she has never heard Vicky talk like this, her tone hard, even cruel.

"I've worked hard here," she says unevenly. "In the kitchen, and the greenhouse—"

"You think peeling a few potatoes makes up for the food we've had to give you? The clothes? The firewood? The medicine Phoebe had when she had a fever—do you think we have an endless supply of ibuprofen? Or what about your dad?" The sudden sneer in her voice makes Mattie blink, shocked. She hates anyone talking about her dad, and certainly not like this. "Adam gave up the last of his morphine to comfort your dad in his dying days," Vicky tells her. "You didn't even think about that, did you? None of you did." She shakes her head, a gesture of disgust.

"Vicky..." Mattie has no idea what to say. "When you voted us to be part of the community here, that's what you were voting for," she says finally, a wobble in her voice before she regathers her conviction. "You can't be mad that we ate food and used firewood when we were *part* of this place. That's not what this camp was about. At least," she adds, her voice rising, "that's not what you *said* it was about."

"It wasn't about freeloaders who scrounge off us and then walk away when they feel like it," Vicky retorts. "I gave your mother fifteen *gallons* of gas to get to Mackinaw City. She didn't even think about it, just accepted it as her due."

Mattie shakes her head slowly. She has never heard this kind of thing from Vicky before. "Why did you give it to her, then?" she asks.

"Because I was trying to be nice," Vicky snaps back. "And because she, and the rest of your family, weren't pulling their weight. Frankly, I'd rather you'd all gone."

"What..." Mattie stares at her, shocked. She had no idea Vicky felt this way. She wonders if she really does, or whether it's down to Wade's influence. Has he been whispering these things into Vicky's ear, telling her what a saint she is for putting up with the American freeloaders? "If you felt that way all this time," Mattie protests quietly, "you should have just said. If you didn't want us here, we wouldn't have stayed." She can't help but feel Vicky is lying, or at least rewriting history, perhaps even in her own mind and her own memories, thanks to Wade. Her welcome and warmth over the last four months felt sincere. Mattie believed in it.

But maybe she, and her mom, and her whole family, had just been fooled. Or maybe Wade has even more power than she's realized, manipulating Vicky in all kinds of ways.

"You think I could kick you all out just like that, without everyone else condemning me?" Vicky asks, and now she sounds weary. "A family, children, including a *toddler*, and a dying man?"

At Mattie's look of surprise, she says flatly, "I knew your dad was dying the second I saw him. I'm amazed none of you saw it. I guess you didn't want to."

Mattie feels as if she is spinning. She'd trusted Vicky, and now she wonders if she ever should have. Or has Vicky herself changed, beaten down by the disappointments of life, the stress of having to provide for all these people, the presence of Wade? Either way, the result is the same—this.

"I guess you really won't mind if I leave, then," she tells Vicky. She doesn't understand why she feels so hurt by everything that Vicky has said, considering her current predicament. Maybe it's better this way. Easier, even if it hurts. She'll walk away without a backward glance.

"I won't," Vicky confirms. For a second, she looks as if she's sorry and wants to say something more. Mattie waits, hopeful, even now wanting somehow to reconcile. But then Vicky shakes her head. "Good luck getting to North Dakota," she tells Mattie. "Because I'll tell you right now we won't be giving you anything—not a car, not a gallon of gas, not a granola bar. We can't afford it, not for someone who's just walking away after taking so much from us." She levels Mattie with a flat, merciless stare. "However you try to get there, it will have to be entirely on your own."

NINETEEN
ALEX

On Monday morning, I pack lunches for Ruby and Sam, just as I did so many other mornings, back in my old life. This time there are no lunchboxes, no single-serve yoghurts or silver foil pouches of juice, no morning TV droning in the background as I try to find a banana that isn't too brown.

This time I've made a big batch of rice and beans, and I dollop some of it into two thermoses that I bought for fifty tickets at the home-goods store. I wonder how long the ticket economy will last. Some of the new arrivals can't keep from treating the tickets like Monopoly money; one guy blew his whole first packet on a games console. Sam doubted whether it even worked. Others of us hoard the tickets carefully, saving them for something special, like a thermos.

Considering we get food rations from the government every week, and parcels of clothing are available on a rotating basis, it feels like we don't really *need* the tickets. Maybe it's just a way to give us some control... or at least feel like we have it.

On Friday, the first issue of *Watford City News* came out, all four pages of it. Bruce and I had worked nearly through the night to get it done, and I was rather ridiculously proud of it. It felt good to work hard, to produce something, even if Bruce's slight cynicism about it all frustrated me. I wanted him to be as positive as I was; his mocking jibe that it was one step up from a nursing-home newsletter stung maybe more than it should have.

In any case, it seemed other people didn't think I should be proud of it either. When we started distributing it around town, more than one person scanned the headlines, shook their head, and then threw the paper in the trash.

"People want the truth," Bruce said with a shrug when we passed another paper that had been thrown away. "And they're pretty sure this isn't it."

"Is that what you think?" I demanded. "Why work on it at all, if you think it's just propaganda?"

"I don't know what I think," Bruce admitted. "I want to believe in this world, Alex, just like you do. After all I've seen, though, I just don't know if I can."

All of it was dispiriting, to say the least. It was also worrying. Was "upbeat" a code word for propaganda? I thought back to what Jack had told me, about the reclamation efforts. The way he'd described how they reclaim the land; I'd believed him. I'd trusted in the government's good intentions. And I still do, considering the fact that I have a house, a job, and my kids are starting school again.

What is there not to like? Not to trust?

But then I think about the woman whose lip curled as she read the headline I'd so carefully crafted—*Government Reclaims One Thousand Square Miles of Prime Farmland. "We'll feed the nation," says Commanding Officer Jack Wyatt*—and I feel a flicker of unease, even of shame. I tell myself that nameless woman's response is not my problem, but I can't help but wonder if it points to something that is, or at least might be.

"Okay," I tell Sam as he comes downstairs. "I've packed your lunch."

"Mom, I'm not, like, six." He rolls his eyes, smiling; he's in a good mood, excited to start. Yesterday, Andy took Sam and a bunch of other young guys all the way out to Minot Air Base for a tour.

They were gone all day, and Sam came back buoyant. It's good to see him so happy.

"Well, were *you* going to pack it?" I retort good-naturedly. Impulsively, I loop my arm around his neck and bend him over so I can kiss his head. He lets me, briefly, before squirming away, shaking his head.

"*Mom.*"

"I'm excited for you," I tell him before adding more quietly, "Really."

Sam's expression turns serious. "I know." He pauses before adding, "I wish Dad could have come here. I wish he could have been part of the rebuilding."

Just like that, the grief rushes in again. It's like I've turned on a tap and am filling up with cold water. "I know," I tell Sam. "Me too."

Ruby comes downstairs, slouching into the room, her face set into discontented lines. Yesterday, while Sam was away, I'd suggested we walk to the children's park on Main Street that has a small playground; she'd refused, simply shaking her head. She'd spent the entire day in her room, doing I don't even know what. Probably nothing, which also made me sad.

Back at Red Cedar Lake, Ruby had pursued the passion she'd discovered during our time at the cottage of using plants and herbs for both food and medicine. She'd gleaned her learning from books, had shown me how to make porridge from cattail tubers and grind up willow bark for pain relief. She'd been so quietly, happily confident, and right now it feels like that girl is gone. I want her back. I hope going to school might help, but I'm afraid that it won't, that it might even make things worse.

"Hey, Rubes." My voice comes out a little manic. "I've got lunch here for you." I hold out the thermos and she takes it silently. "Breakfast," I tell her, but she ignores me. I glance at Sam, who shrugs.

"Mattie was like this," he whispers. "Remember?"

I nod, trying not to look as hurt as I feel by Ruby's rudeness.

Yes, I remember, but Mattie didn't turn thirteen in a post-apocalyptic world. *Mattie...* I'm going to talk to her tomorrow night, and I'm going to ask her a lot more questions. Maybe I'll even ask her advice about Ruby.

Just then there's a knock on the door, and I hurry to open it. Chantelle is standing there with Taylor, looking resolute. "I just wondered," she says stiffly, "if Sam and Ruby wanted to wait for the bus with Taylor."

I haven't yet gotten to the bottom of whatever made my neighbor mad the other day, but I appreciate the effort she's making now. Students will be picked up for school from the bus stop at the corner of Third and Fourth Avenue.

"That would be great, thanks," I say, only to have Ruby push past me, her shoulder knocking into Taylor's hard enough to make her stumble, the brand-new backpack I saw in the home-goods store for one hundred tickets sliding off her shoulder.

"Ruby!" I gasp in outrage, while Chantelle's mouth thins.

"Your daughter has a problem," she tells me. "I've been trying to be understanding, because God knows we've all gone through a lot, but she has a *problem*." With that, she turns around and marches off our front stoop with Taylor.

"Sam," I say to my son, and he nods in understanding.

"I'll stay with her."

I watch him go, shaking my head at what just happened. I don't even *know* what all that was about. And I don't know how I can reach Ruby to talk to her about it. Every single conversation we've had she has comprehensively shut down. I drift back inside, mindlessly tidy up, my mind still on Ruby. I want her first day of school to be a success, but already I feel like it's a failure.

I don't have a lot of time to dwell on it, though, because I have to get ready for work myself. I trudge down Main Street, barely aware of the tulips pushing up in the flower beds by the park, a reminder that the world renews, even in the apocalypse.

. . .

When I get to the office of *McKenzie County Farmer*, now *Watford City News*, I am surprised to see Bruce cleaning a crusty yellow mess off the glass of the front door.

"What happened?" I exclaim and he turns to give me a wry smile.

"Powdered egg," he explains succinctly. "I guess they didn't have real eggs, so points for ingenuity." He nods toward the caked-on mess. "This is the mend-and-make-do spirit of the Depression, right here."

"But why?" I ask as I drop my bag to help him clean it off. He hands me a rag with a shrug.

"They didn't like our newspaper?" Bruce surmises, seeming undaunted by the possibility. "You saw how they were putting it straight in the trash. Or it could have been kids with nothing better to do, breaking the curfew."

According to the news on our TV screen, last week a nine p.m. curfew was implemented for all children under eighteen. I understood it, but I could also see why it made people uneasy. And it wasn't mentioned in our newspaper.

"Do you think people are actually protesting the news?" I ask as I start to scrub. The stuff has dried on hard.

"That's certainly one conclusion I could draw from this occurrence," Bruce says dryly. "People have been suspicious for a long time. Selling them our Pollyanna version of this new world might not be as welcome as we want it to be."

"This feels aggressive, though. I mean... it's one thing to throw the paper away. It's another to egg our front door." The difference, I think, between indifference and anger.

"I guess some people have strong feelings."

I glance at Bruce, his usual expression of wry cynicism on his face, the expression of a crotchety guy you can't help but love. But is that who he really is? I might have worked side by side with him for the last week, but I realize I don't actually *know* the man. "What about you, Bruce?" I ask quietly. "Do you have strong feelings? About this world, the way it's run?"

He is silent for a long time, scrubbing away. "I'm too tired for that," he finally says. "And too worn out. So I shoot my mouth off to you and that's about it." He sighs, shaking his head, and I see a glimpse of the man beneath the rueful exterior—someone who has been broken, just as we all have.

"Jack said the same thing, you know, about people being suspicious," I tell him. He said it about *me* being suspicious. But like Bruce, I feel too tired to keep up the pretense that I'm strong enough to do something about it.

Bruce cocks an eyebrow. "Jack, huh?" he says, and stupidly, I blush. Bruce, I think, pretends not to notice.

"Well, it's Jack who thought a Pollyanna paper would be a good idea," he says as he continues to scrub. "So while I generally think he's a pretty switched-on guy, he might have been wrong there. Maybe people need a more honest version of what's happening here."

"Maybe." I think of my coverage of the reclaimed land. I was so excited to write something, to feel important, but if I'd been more courageous, more willing to risk this newfound fragile stability that I crave, I might have presented a more balanced and nuanced view of the issue. Tracked down the woman from the welcome reception and gotten her side of the story. But I didn't. I wasn't, I'm forced to admit, even tempted to. I just wanted to do something and have it feel good and easy. The realization shames me. The next article I write, I resolve, I'll do better. I'll be more honest.

"So what do we do now?" I ask once we've managed to scrub off most of the powdered egg paste from the door.

Bruce sighs. "Write the next paper? I don't know what else we can do. I'm not a revolutionary, Alex. I'm not a rebel." He drops his dirty rag into the bucket. "I'll show you the brief I was given from HQ."

Once we've finished cleaning up, we settle down in the conference room. Silently he hands me the single typed sheet.

1. *School Officially Starts! Over 700 students were welcomed to Watford City High School and Rough Rider College this week in a successful launch of the city's educational program.*
2. *Planting in the Montana farmlands begins the first week of May, with experts predicting that there will be enough grain to sustain two hundred thousand people through the winter.*
3. *Cellphone service will resume in the next few months. As the electrical grid is restored, all residents will be given a cellphone for personal and professional use.*
4. *Watford City's first city-wide social event, held in the Comfort Inn on the first Saturday in May. Come hear The Bluegrass Boys. All attendees over twenty-one will be entitled to one glass of wine or beer, subject to the presentation of a ticket.*

I lower the paper. "Well, it all sounds positive," I remark with a rueful smile.

"It does, doesn't it," Bruce agrees, with the same cynical undercurrent to his tone that is starting to annoy me.

"If you can't be a revolutionary or a rebel," I tell him, "why do you keep acting so suspicious? What's the point?"

He laughs. "Now *that's* honest. There is no point. It just makes me feel like I'm doing something when I'm actually not." He holds up his hands in a gesture of helplessness. "I'm the apocalyptic version of a keyboard warrior."

I shake my head, still annoyed. "Either we get on board with this, or we don't," I tell him. "Instead of just low-key bitching about it all the time."

Bruce makes a face. "Fair," he says. "But like I said, I'm not a firebrand. Not anymore."

"It doesn't seem like anyone is," I reply tartly. "Civil unrest is reduced to hurling some powdered egg at a door." I lean back in my chair as I trawl through all the suspicions I've had, formless but persistent. "I don't even know if there's anything to find out," I tell him. "And I get that this newspaper was meant to be more of a folksy newsletter than something setting the gold standard of investigative journalism. But..." I swivel to face him. "It feels like there are a lot of unanswered questions, and maybe our job should be to find the answers."

He stares at me for a moment, a small, wry smile twitching his lips. "Questions such as?" he finally asks.

"Such as," I say slowly, "what about everyone else in this country? What's happening to them?"

"You know as well as I do that a lot of those people are in inaccessible places. They can't be rescued, not yet." He drums his fingers against the table. "But a lot of them are in *inconvenient* places," he adds quietly. "Like the six thousand Native Americans who were holed up on the Fort Peck Indian Reservation in northeastern Montana."

Shock ripples coldly through me. Six *thousand*? Jack definitely didn't mention anything about *that*. "Do you know what happened to them?" I ask, and Bruce shrugs as he spreads his hands.

"Who really knows? Assiniboine and Sioux tribes, and they're gone. Just... disappeared. Fort Peck is part of the reclamation project you wrote about last week. The reservation is over two million acres."

I gape at him, feeling betrayed. "And you didn't think to tell me about that when I was writing up the article? You might not want to challenge the status quo, Bruce, but maybe I do."

"Do you?" he asks, and the words hang there, in the air. I can tell from Bruce's face that he knows I'm just as cautious and cowardly as he is when it comes to questioning our nascent government, and once again I feel ashamed. It's easier to question and complain than to *do* anything about it. "I didn't tell you about it because you weren't going to write about it," he says after a moment. "Like you said, we're a folksy newsletter, Alex, and eviscerating exposés are not in our brief."

"How did you even find out about it?" I ask.

"I talked to a guy who was part of the reclamation effort. He had a couple of beers and his reservations about the reservation came out." Bruce smiles wryly at the pun, but the bleak expression in his eyes chills me.

"But why?" I ask helplessly. "Space surely isn't the issue. This country is *empty* now. Why would they have to kick people out of anywhere?"

"Empty and unusable," he reminds me. "That may change in time, as the land recovers, but for now... this area is all they've got. And they want it all."

I shake my head, still not wanting to believe what Bruce seems to be implying. "So what are you saying, they *murdered* six thousand Native Americans?"

"No," he replies reflectively. "I wouldn't go that far. At least, I don't think I would. But they're not there now, and they haven't shown up here, have they?"

"Maybe they're in one of the other towns." There are over twenty new settlements now, scattered across northwest North Dakota and northeast Montana, accepting new residents just about every day, including, maybe, the Native Americans from Fort Peck.

"Maybe," Bruce allows, but he sounds far from convinced, and as much as I talk a big game about challenging the status quo, we both know neither of us are going to do anything about it, and so I deflect, and I know Bruce knows that's what I'm doing.

"You're starting to sound like a conspiracy theorist," I tell him with an attempt at a laugh, and he gives a small smile of acknowledgement back. "Six thousand people just disappear? I don't think so." He smiles and shrugs, and I continue more forcefully, "I'll ask Jack about it."

Bruce raises both eyebrows. "I didn't realize you were so close to him."

"I'm not," I say quickly. "But... I trust him to tell me the truth."

Bruce makes no reply to that, and I wonder if I really do trust Jack that much, or even if I should.

TWENTY

ALEX

I'm so consumed with my conversation with Bruce that, incredibly, I almost forget about my radio call with Mattie. Fortunately I remember at a quarter to six, and I hurry to the radio booth. Sam and Ruby finished school several hours ago, and I'm eager to know how their day went, especially since Ruby was so difficult this morning, but first I need to talk to Mattie.

I'd told Sam and Ruby they could meet me at the town hall to join the call, but when I arrive I find neither of them there, and I fight both frustration and disappointment. Don't they want to talk to their sister?

In any case, when I make the call to VA3 RC, there's no answer. I try five, six times, frustrated because we'd agreed on a date and time. Never mind Sam and Ruby, *Mattie* should be there. The answering silence is far more unnerving than before, and I am reminded of how tearful Mattie seemed at the beginning of our earlier call, how quickly she tried to end the conversation. Is something going on up there, or am *I* the conspiracy theorist now?

Someone taps on the booth door, and I leave with a murmur of apology to head home to Ruby and Sam.

. . .

"How was school?" I ask Sam as I come into the house. He's sitting at the kitchen table, a textbook in front of him, which seems like a good sign.

"Yeah, it was good." He lifts his head to smile at me. "I had Intro to Computer Science and Macroeconomics today."

"I thought you were going to meet me in town to call Mattie," I remind him, trying not to sound too censorious, and Sam makes a face.

"Sorry, with everything starting today, I forgot. How was she?"

"She didn't answer."

Sam shrugs, unfazed. "I guess she's busy too."

"I suppose." Looking at Sam now, bent over his books, I can't believe it was only a little over a year and a half ago that we were moving him into his freshman dorm, hefting a futon and a minifridge in the humid mid-August heat as he looked forward to the rest of his life. And now we're here again, and it feels like a miracle, but just like I intimated to Bruce, I still don't know if I can trust it.

I turn to gaze out our little patch of yard; the grass is finally starting to turn green. Maybe I'll plant something out there, now that spring is almost here. Vegetables to augment our weekly food parcel if I can find seeds, or maybe even flowers. Flowers, *beauty*, would be welcome, a luxury we've had to learn to live without.

"And Ruby?" I ask as I turn back to Sam. "How did she do?" In response he simply shakes his head, and my stomach cramps with anxiety. "Sam—"

"I don't know how she did, good or bad," he says quickly. "She wouldn't talk to me on the bus this morning. Or after. As soon as we got home, she just went up to her room."

Ruby has spent a lot of time in her tiny box of a room. I let out a low breath as I steel myself to confront my daughter, *again*. I still can't quite believe, never mind understand, the hostility emanating from my once so easy child. Why is she so angry? And why does it feel like it's aimed at everyone, not just at me?

I mount the steps slowly, gearing myself up for some kind of confrontation. I know I can't let Ruby stonewall me with silence forever. It's at moments like these—and really, every moment—that I miss Daniel. In the past, when I became soul-weary with the relentless slog of parenting, he would step in with the light touch, the easy tone. I'm sure the kids realized we were tag-teaming, but it still worked. Sometimes you just need to hear a different voice.

But now there's only me, and my voice, and I'm tired of the whiny, fearful sound of it, never mind Ruby. I take a deep breath, throw my shoulders back, and open the door to Ruby's bedroom.

The room is empty.

I look around the small space as if she might be hiding somewhere in it, but of course she isn't, because there is no place to hide. I duck into Sam's bedroom and survey its typical teenaged-boy mess, and then mine, the bed rumpled on only one side, its lopsidedness giving me a pang—and then finally the bathroom, which is also empty.

I thunder downstairs, and Sam looks up from his textbook, bemused. "What?"

"Ruby's not upstairs."

"What—"

"Did you hear her go out?"

"No—"

I wrench open the door to our little patio, but it's empty out there, as is the yard. Ruby must have left the house. She's *run away*, and while I tell myself I don't need to be so scared, that Watford City is small and safe as well as patrolled by the military, the truth is, I'm terrified.

Something about this doesn't feel right. At all.

"Sam," I practically plead, "what happened today?"

He shrugs, mystified, already a little impatient. "Mom, I told you, I don't know. Ruby's just been in a mood."

"Yes, but..." It's been more than that, I realize. I've been so fixated on Mattie and the newspaper and just wanting *something* in life to be simple. I told myself she'd adjust. That she was still my easy child, even if she seemed so difficult.

But right now it feels as if something might be really, really wrong.

"I'm going out to look for her—"

"Mom, maybe she's just hanging out with friends," Sam suggests. I give him a look, and he falls silent, repentant. Ruby has never hung out with friends.

"Do you want me to come with you?" he asks, and I shake my head.

"You stay here, in case she comes back." I try to swallow my fear; my mouth tastes metallic. Maybe she just needed some space, some silence. Maybe it's all going to be okay. And really, there's hardly anywhere for her to go. Watford City is small, and teenagers have the nine p.m. curfew. I really shouldn't be as worried as I am.

I keep telling myself that as I head out into the darkening night.

"You're overreacting," I mutter under my breath, and I think how, if Daniel were here, he'd ask me, in his serious, reasonable way, what exactly it is that I'm afraid of. And then I realize that I'm not afraid Ruby's in trouble or danger; I do believe Watford City is a safe place, powdered egg on doors aside.

No, I'm afraid of what brought Ruby to this moment, that she wants to wander out into a chilly, twilit night on her own without telling anyone, that she seems angry about everything, that she refuses to speak in a way that feels hostile rather than sorrowful or simply a choice to be quiet.

My daughter is *different*.

I'm turning down Main Street, scanning the empty road, when I hear someone call my name.

"Alex!"

I turn to see Jack striding toward me with a smile that slides off his face when he sees how anxious I look.

"Alex... what's wrong?"

"It's my daughter, Ruby," I blurt. "She left the house without telling anyone and I don't know where she is." I realize how ridiculous I sound. Ruby is thirteen, not six. "It's just so unlike her," I try to explain, my voice catching. "Really unlike her." I don't know how else to explain it without launching into the kind of lengthy description of who Ruby is that Jack really does not need to hear.

He frowns, his lips pursed in thought. "Did something happen at school?"

"I don't know," I admit. "I don't know anything because she refuses to speak. She's been so angry lately, aggressive, and that's also unlike her. It's scaring me. Sorry," I add. "This isn't your problem. You probably have somewhere to go."

"Actually, I was glad to run into you. I had a proposal to run by you, but that can wait for now."

A *proposal?* I have no idea what he means, and so I just shake my head helplessly.

"Do you want me to help look for your daughter?" Jack asks, and after a second, I nod. I don't have Daniel, who is the person I really want, but I know I don't want to do this on my own. I'm too tired and too scared, and I still don't know if I can trust Jack, but at least he seems to want to help me now.

We fall into step as we continue down Main Street, the stores now dark and shuttered, the streets empty even though it's only a little past six o'clock.

"Any ideas where she might go?" Jack asks, and I shake my head.

"Pretty much none. I mean, where is there around here for a kid to go?"

"Well, we are working on that," Jack says with a smile in his voice, although his tone is still serious. "There's a possibility of opening up the library in the evenings for kids to hang out in. I know they need social opportunities."

"Ruby's not even social," I tell him bleakly. "She's been selectively mute since she was five years old, which basically means she only talks when she chooses to. The more stressed she is, the less she talks, and she's been virtually silent since we came to Watford City." The truth of my words thuds through me. "I don't think I fully realized that until recently," I admit to Jack. "Because I normally take her quietness for granted. But the last few days, it's really gotten bad. And the *anger*... she's never, ever been an angry child. She's the meekest, mildest..." I trail off, knowing I sound like I'm exaggerating, and maybe I am. I just don't understand what is going on with my daughter.

"She's gone through a lot," Jack says, "just to get here."

"I know, and I told myself she just needs to adjust, but she's been on a downward trajectory since we arrived." Again the words thud through me. "I don't think I've fully realized that, either," I admit with an unhappy smile. I am starting to feel like the world's worst mother, and I am still so scared for Ruby.

"We'll find her," Jack says, and I don't miss the *we*. It doesn't make me feel any better, even though I want it to.

We walk in silence for another few minutes, scanning storefronts and parking lots, the night sky wide above us like an endless canvas of unrelenting black. I still haven't got used to how big the sky is out here, how empty the world, stretching on endlessly in every direction. We're in the middle of downtown and yet it feels like we could be out on the prairie, and while I sometimes enjoy the sense of space, right now it just makes me feel far too small.

Then, as we pass the children's park, just across from a wooden building in the style of an old-fashioned general store that used to sell ice cream and trinkets and is now shuttered and empty, I see a shadowy figure hunched on a swing, barely more than a hump in the darkness, legs halfheartedly pushing against the earth. The creak of the swing's chain punctuates the still night, and I catch my breath sharply.

"Ruby...?" I call, and a pale face looks up, barely visible in the dusky darkness. Still, I recognize that face, the slumped shoulders of that woebegone figure. "Ruby!" I call again, and then I start running toward her.

I drop onto my knees in front of my daughter and reach for her, so glad she's safe. But Ruby doesn't cling to me the way she once would have. Instead she stiffens inside my embrace, and then, in one short, sharp movement, shoves both my shoulders so that I fall back, sprawled onto the dusty ground, too surprised and winded to utter more than a shocked "oof."

"Are you all right?" Jack asks, reaching out to help me up as I scramble to my hands and knees, and Ruby takes off, sprinting out of the park and down the street, until she's no more than a shadow, disappearing into the dark.

TWENTY-ONE

MATTIE

"So, basically, we're screwed."

The dry, humorous note in Nicole's voice makes Mattie grit her teeth and clench her hands into fists. The other woman's cheerful fatalism is not what she needs right now.

No, what she needs right now is a plan, a *solution*. Vicky might have told her she won't help her get to North Dakota, but that doesn't mean she can't go. There has to be a way to get there. She just needs to figure out what it is.

"We're not screwed," Mattie says as she paces their cabin. It's evening, Phoebe is tucked up in bed, the sky above the lake scattered with glittering pinpricks of stars. It's been three days since she confronted Vicky, and each one has felt endless, and yet at the same time, they have gone by far too fast. Time is running out, and if they don't make a move soon, Mattie fears they never will.

Yesterday, she went to Vicky's office at the time she and her mom had agreed, for the radio call she'd desperately been looking forward to all week. She'd been really hoping Wade wouldn't be there, but it turned out Vicky had been bad enough. When Mattie had asked to use the radio, Vicky had said she would make the call, and from her tone it was clear she would brook no argument.

Vicky had slipped on the headphones, twiddled a dial, pursing her lips while Mattie had ground her teeth in frustration, because something about the smug way Vicky glanced at her as she continued to give out their call name made Mattie think she'd done something to the radio, or *wasn't* doing something, so the call couldn't go through, and the whole thing was an insulting charade.

Unfortunately, she didn't know enough about radios to be sure, and she knew any accusation would only make things worse.

"Try again next week, maybe," Vicky said coolly, slipping the headphones off her ears, and Mattie had wanted to scream.

"But I *said* I'd be here," she told Vicky, trying to keep the tears from her voice. "My mom would have done whatever she could to make sure she was there to pick up." Mattie knew that absolutely; her mom would have moved heaven and earth if she had to, to be on the radio when she'd said she would be.

"I don't know what to tell you," Vicky had replied. "Maybe she's busy, Mattie." There was no pretense of friendly concern now, no hint of warmth in her eyes. Somehow, by questioning Wade and wanting to leave, Mattie had become Vicky's enemy, and she feared there was no going back from that.

She considered trying to get into the office another time to use the radio on her own, but Vicky keeps the door locked and her mom most likely won't be on the radio herself if it isn't at an agreed time. She also doesn't want to get caught, especially by Wade.

How is it possible to feel so *trapped*?

"We're not screwed," Mattie states again, more forcefully, and Nicole, sprawled on the sofa, merely raises her eyebrows. "We just need to find a way to get to North Dakota."

"Which is thirteen hundred miles away," Nicole reminds her matter of factly. "And we have no car, no gas, no *food*—"

"We don't need to go the full thirteen hundred miles on our own," Mattie protests, her hands clenched at her sides, her voice rising shrilly. "We just need to find someone who's willing to help us. There are people out there who are working toward making the world more normal. Someone nearby will have a radio, and we could call—" She stops abruptly because, to her annoyance, Nicole is shaking her head, a slow but certain back and forth. "What? Why is that so unreasonable?" she demands, a tremble to her voice. She wants Nicole to be on her side, to help her brainstorm, but since she started this conversation, she's just been the rueful voice of doom.

"Mattie, think," Nicole says, and now she sounds tired, any pretense at cheerfulness gone. "What do you think Wade has been doing every time he heads out in that stupid truck of his?"

"Checking out fields—"

"Fields?" Nicole scoffs. "Really? And that takes so much time and effort? They're *fields*."

Mattie stares at her, feeling stupid. "Then what..."

"He's getting rid of all the people around here," Nicole replies quickly. "That would be my guess, anyway. He's intimidating them into leaving... or worse."

Mattie thinks of Wade's fingers on her jaw, the way he told Vicky the Bryces' farmhouse was empty. *They left months ago*, he'd said, but what if they hadn't? "You don't think he's... *killing* them," she whispers. Despite her fear, she almost wants to laugh. It sounds so melodramatic, the stuff of horror movies and urban legends. Surely it can't be true?

"I don't know what he's doing," Nicole replies wearily. She leans her head back against the sofa. "The people around here are made of tough stuff, so I can't imagine they'd leave easily. But he's doing *something*, I know that much." She shakes her head, the words subsiding on a sigh of resignation.

"But..." Mattie sits heavily on the sofa as she drops her head into her hands. She feels as if she can't make sense of anything. Why won't Vicky help them, even if it's just to let Mattie contact her mom? Why doesn't she want them to leave, if they're not happy to stay? And why as good as imprison people when the world is meant to be waking up and returning at least a *little* to the way it used to be? "I don't understand," she whispers.

"I'm not saying I know for sure," Nicole tells her after a moment, "but I told you I've seen guys like Wade before. For people like that, nuclear bombs were what they'd been waiting for. A chance to have power, to build their own little kingdom. The fact that things might be getting better on the outside isn't good news for them. Pretty much the opposite."

"But Vicky..." Mattie protests. She can understand that about Wade, but Vicky was never like that. Vicky was her mentor, her friend.

"Vicky lost everything when Toronto was bombed," Nicole reminds her quietly. "Her home, her job, her fiancé. Maybe this feels like the only thing she has left, and if everyone leaves, if the world becomes normal again, she loses it." She falls into a reflective silence. "Maybe she's convinced herself this is the only way she can protect it. I wouldn't be surprised."

"That's so messed up!" Mattie exclaims, and Nicole's mouth twitches in a smile.

"Agreed."

Mattie shakes her head and rises from the sofa. "We still have to try," she insists. "If we don't..." She doesn't want to think about what might happen if they don't. She knows she doesn't want to be alone with Wade ever again.

"And if we do and fail?" Nicole asks quietly. "Sweetheart, I know you don't want to hear this, but that's going to be worse."

"So you think we should just stay here and take it?" Mattie demands as she whirls around, her voice and body shaking, her hands clenched into fists so tight, her nails are digging half-moons into her palms. "Wait for Wade to build his... his *harem*?"

Nicole goes still. "Has he touched you?" she demands in a low, dangerous voice, her eyes flashing. "Besides the jaw thing, I mean?"

"No," Mattie admits, "but I feel like he could. He *will*." As she says it, she's afraid it's true. She does not feel safe with Wade at Red Cedar Lake... in all sorts of ways.

Briefly Nicole closes her eyes. "I really thought this kind of thing was over," she mutters, as if to herself. "You don't know how much I wanted it to be over. How much I want to be *past* this."

"Nicole, it *can* be over." Mattie rushes over to the older woman and grabs both her hands, seized by a wild sense of both possibility and resolve. "It can be over *if* we get out of here. Right now, Vicky has said we're free to go, so let's *go*. We're not escaping, we're just leaving. They'll let us—"

Nicole opens her eyes to subject Mattie to a flat stare. "So they say."

"What do you think will happen? They'll chain us up to stop us from leaving?" A visceral shudder goes through her at the thought; sometimes it doesn't feel so outside the realm of possibility. "They wouldn't," she states, firming her voice, needing to believe it.

"I don't know if they would or not," Nicole replies. "But they might. And even if they did let us go, without any supplies or provisions? What would we do? Where would we go, Mattie?" Nicole's voice is gentle now, and that feels worse. "We just walk out of here... and what?" she presses. "We're miles from anyone."

"Not that many miles," Mattie insists. She doesn't actually know what settlements, if any, are around the camp; she vaguely remembers Vicky once talking about going to the Costco in Sudbury, some eighty miles away. Can they walk eighty miles?

It might be spring, but the nights are still well below freezing and it's too early to find anything to forage; Mattie isn't confident enough to hunt or fish, even if they had a gun or fishing rod. It feels hopeless, but it can't be. She won't let it.

"The first house we come to," she tells Nicole, "we ask for help."

"And they're friendly and have a radio," Nicole replies, nodding along. "Right. Because that always happens."

Mattie drops her hands and shakes her head, fighting a sense of confusion as well as disappointment. Why is Nicole so resistant?

"So what's the alternative?" she asks. "Seriously, what? Because all you're doing is shooting every suggestion down."

Nicole lets her head hang low, her dark-blond hair falling in a golden sheet to obscure her face. "We wait it out," she whispers. "Like you said, the world is getting back to normal. At some point the police or the Army or someone comes and tells us we need to fall in line. We wait for that, and then when there is somewhere else to go, we go."

Mattie stares at her, an improbable hope warring with even deeper disappointment. Could it really just be a matter of time? "That's all you've got?" she finally demands.

Nicole looks up, looking guilty but also defiant. "Yes," she retorts. "I'm sorry, Mattie, but I'm tired and I've been through a hell of a lot already. I don't know what your mom has told you, but..." Her voice wobbles and she tucks her knees up to her chest, wrapping her thin arms around them. "I can't risk going through that kind of stuff again. All I want to do is lie low. All I *can* do... because that's all I've got." She glares at Mattie, but there is a pleading look in her eyes, as if she is asking for understanding or maybe even forgiveness. "That is literally *all I've got*."

In that moment, Mattie realizes Nicole, despite her feisty, bitchy persona, is not nearly as strong as she seems. She's not strong enough to make a break for it, and Mattie isn't strong enough to go it alone.

She straightens, walks to the sliding glass door that leads out to the path down to the lake. The moon has slid behind a cloud and she can't see the water, only the expanse of darkness where she knows it is. She leans her head against the cold glass and closes her eyes.

It's only just beginning, and yet she feels it's already too late.

TWENTY-TWO

ALEX

"A *mission?*"

I stare at Jack in surprise, my pen forgotten between my fingers. I'm sitting at my desk at the office of *Watford City News*, thinking up copy for our next edition, and Jack Wyatt has just told me he wants me to accompany a military unit on a mission to southern Montana to observe the "reclamation process" firsthand.

"It will inspire confidence," he tells me with a crooked smile. "I'm trying for transparency. Restoring trust."

He sounds so earnest, and I feel so jaded. It's been three days since Ruby ran out of the park, not coming home until after curfew, causing me hours of worry, even more after she'd returned, silent and seemingly still furious. I have a bruise on my shoulder from where she pushed me. She has refused to say so much as a word.

"When is this mission?" I ask.

"Next week. It's about one hundred and fifty miles away, maybe six hours round trip. You might have to stay overnight, depending on how things go."

"Overnight..." Can I leave Ruby alone with Sam for a night? I feel like my head is too full of fears—not just Ruby, but Mattie, whom I still haven't heard from even though I've attempted to contact her twice. It seems strange to me that no one has ever been on the radio, but I tell myself I'm being paranoid. There's no reason to think anything is going wrong at Red Cedar Lake. The days are getting warmer, the nights longer; they're probably just busy.

And now, as Jack talks about a mission, I think of Bruce's intimations about the Native Americans, how they apparently disappeared from the Fort Peck Reservation. I don't want to believe him, but I also know that part of me does. It's a hard place to be in, especially with everything else jostling for space in my tired, anxious brain.

And now I'm meant to go on a *mission*.

"Is it... is it dangerous?" I ask, and then immediately feel like a wimp.

"You'll be well protected," he assures me. "And I don't think it's *particularly* dangerous, as you won't be one of the first teams going in." He hesitates, his eyes crinkling in concern. "I hope you know I would never knowingly put you in a situation that I considered dangerous."

Something about his tone makes me blush and look away. It doesn't feel right for him to talk that way, to intimate, no matter how obliquely, that we have some kind of relationship, because we don't.

The night before last, entirely unexpectedly, Jack showed up at my house. After I'd opened the door, I'd simply stared at him for a few seconds, totally shocked. I didn't even think he knew where I lived, although I realized, as the CO of this whole place, of course he could find out. Still, his presence was jarring, even as part of me reluctantly welcomed it.

"I'm sorry, I see I've surprised you," he said. "I just wanted to see how Ruby was doing."

"Oh..." I glanced over my shoulder toward the kitchen, where Ruby and Sam were eating dinner in silence. It was kind of him to inquire, but it also felt a little presumptuous. Nosy. "She's the same, really," I told him in a low voice.

After she'd run out of the park, Ruby had headed home and locked herself in her bedroom. While I was grateful she wasn't still wandering on her own in the dark, she'd felt as far away from me as ever.

Since then, I still hadn't managed to get more than a few syllables from her, and most of those had been demanding to be left alone. And now Jack was there, and Ruby and Sam were both craning their necks, trying to figure out who had come to our door.

"I'm sorry," Jack said, and I realized I'd left him on the front stoop like a beggar.

"Do you... do you want to come in?" I asked, stepping aside so he could, although I wasn't sure I wanted him to. He came inside, seeming to fill up the small space of the front hallway. I could feel Sam and Ruby's curiosity like a palpable force emanating from the kitchen.

"I don't think you've actually met my kids," I remarked awkwardly. "Come on in." I must have sounded as halfhearted as I felt because Jack gave me an uncertain smile.

"I don't want to intrude..."

"It's fine," I said quickly. I was embarrassed by my own obvious reluctance. "Sam, Ruby?" I called as I beckoned Jack backward toward the kitchen. "Meet Major Jack Wyatt." I made him sound a little bit like a superhero, and Jack winced ruefully.

"Wyatt...?" Sam asked, standing up quickly from the table. "Isn't that—"

"The commanding officer of Watford City?" I filled in. "Yes."

"And only of Watford City," Jack added. "Small potatoes, really." He stepped forward to shake Sam's hand. "Glad to meet you, Sam."

Ruby stared at him balefully, refusing to rise from the table, and Jack smiled at her. "And you too, Ruby." He turned back to me. "Were you able to talk to Mattie again?"

"No," I admitted. When we'd been looking for Ruby, I hadn't had a chance to tell him that Mattie didn't make our planned radio call. "She didn't show, as it were..."

"Why do you think she didn't?" Sam asked, sounding more concerned than when I'd first told him.

"Things were a little crazy that night," I reminded him quickly, not wanting to get into the whole Ruby thing again. "Anyway, I'm sure she's just busy. I'm not worried." At least, I was *trying* not to be that worried. I've reminded myself a thousand times that I trust Vicky and everyone else in the community at Red Cedar Lake, that Mattie is among friends, even if I hadn't known any of them for very long. That missing our radio call is just a typical teenaged thoughtlessness, not a sign of some kind of trouble or danger. *I* was the one who had moved somewhere, not Mattie.

"What's the name of the place where she is?" Jack asked. "I could ask the comms guys if anyone has heard anything. They're keeping on top of all the chatter. You know some of these places can get a little..." He paused as he glanced at Sam and Ruby. "Intense."

I thought of North Bay, and how controlling that situation became, forcing us to conduct what was essentially a prison break. But Red Cedar Lake wasn't remotely like that, and I wasn't sure I wanted the *comms guys* looking into the community there. I thought of Bruce's ominous words about Fort Peck, and I was pretty sure I wanted to keep Red Cedar Lake below the radar, at least for now, even from Jack.

"That's very kind of you," I told him. "But I really don't think it's anything like that. I'm sure Mattie will remember to call next week." I turned to Sam and Ruby. "You guys should definitely come with me next time."

Jack, maybe sensing a rebuff in my words, left soon after, and after Ruby had gone upstairs, Sam stood in the kitchen as I started to wash the dishes.

"Why didn't you want to tell Major Wyatt where Mattie is?" he asked after about a minute of quiet, the only sound the clink of the dishes in the sink as I started to scrub. Of course my son had picked up on my reluctance.

"It's not that I didn't want to tell him," I said carefully. "I'm just not sure I want the whole military getting involved."

Sam leaned his shoulder against the doorframe. "Why do you think Mattie wasn't on the radio when you told her to be?"

I shrugged, wanting to keep it light, needing it to be. "Like I said, she's probably just busy, you know, with Phoebe, Kyle..."

"She doesn't even like Kyle," Sam said dismissively, and I stilled, a soapy plate in my hands.

"*What?*"

"Mom, get real. Remember Drew?" Of course I remembered Drew, the seventeen-year-old pothead my daughter had been dating at only fourteen. My hair had started to turn gray when I found out about the relationship we'd expressly forbidden. "Mattie just likes to yank your chain with the guys she likes," Sam said. "I mean, *Kyle?*" He rolled his eyes.

"Kyle's grown a lot in the last year," I protested, half-amazed that I was defending him, because while I admittedly did have some affection for him, I'd been harder on him than most.

"Not that much," Sam stated definitively. "Mattie didn't stay at Red Cedar Lake because of Kyle, I'll tell you that much for free."

"Then why?" I demanded helplessly. Why would my daughter choose not to go with her family, if there was no one to stay for?

Sam was silent for a moment. "I don't know," he said finally. "But Mattie always liked to be different, you know? If you said red, she said blue. Always. It was pretty annoying."

"Yeah." I managed a chuckle even though his words tore at me. Mattie had always been headstrong, even difficult. I just thought she'd outgrown that kind of petulance, but maybe old habits, old *natures*, die harder than I thought. Maybe it takes more than a nuclear apocalypse to change our very selves.

"Do you really think the government here might do something bad?" Sam asked. "I mean, that's why you didn't tell Major Wyatt about Red Cedar Lake, right?"

"I don't know what they'd do," I admitted heavily. "And maybe I'm just being super paranoid, but that's not information I want to reveal just yet. To anyone." Not even Jack.

"Okay." Sam nodded slowly. "But Mom... maybe you should

be a little more paranoid about what might be happening at Red Cedar Lake."

I gave an instinctive snort of disbelief, shaking my head. "Sam, everyone there was so kind to us. I don't think they've all changed somehow, in a matter of *weeks*."

"I don't know," Sam said. "I mean, I liked it there, and they were nice, but didn't it feel a little... clubby?"

I stared at him. "Clubby?"

"Like, culty, but not totally."

"*Culty?*" Now I was really dismissive. "No way. They were just a close-knit community helping each other out. You've watched too much TV, Sam—"

"Not lately," he replied dryly, and I laughed.

"I'm sure it's fine," I told him firmly, doing my best to quench the flicker of doubt his words had caused me. "I'll call Mattie again the same time next week and talk to her then." I felt better just saying the words; the sound of my own certainty reassured me.

And now, the next morning, Jack is here, asking me to go on a *mission*, to promote transparency and restore trust, and I don't know whether I care about either. It feels like there is too much going on, so much battling in my brain. I long to stop being afraid, but just like the grief, the fear keeps creeping in, whenever I let it.

"You know about the powdered egg on the door, I guess," I remark wryly, "if you're talking about transparency and trust right now."

"I do," he confirms. "And frankly, that's just the tip of the iceberg. Over the last eighteen months, people have learned, rightly, to be suspicious. I'm trying to be as open and honest as I can and having a reporter go on one of our missions is part of that."

He holds my stare, unblinking, in what first seems guileless but then starts to feel like a challenge. *Trust me... or else.*

For a second, I think of asking him about Fort Peck, but then I push the notion away. I don't want to seem as suspicious as everyone else, even if I am. Jack is offering me an opportunity—to experience firsthand what I've been wondering about. I need to go on this mission, not just for the sake of trust or transparency, but to allay my own formless fears and also do my job, which I genuinely care about.

"So?" Jack asks. "What do you say?"

I nod slowly, my stomach swirling as I consider the implications—leaving Ruby and Sam, potentially overnight, going on something that very well might, no matter what Jack said, be dangerous. Seeing more of this strange new world we're forming.

"Okay," I tell Jack, my voice firming with decision. "I'll go."

TWENTY-THREE
ALEX

The Bluegrass Boys are striking up a soulful yet upbeat tune as I step into the ballroom of the Comfort Inn and Suites, wearing my best jeans and the cashmere sweater from Nicole. It's basically my only nice outfit, and this is the second time it's getting an outing. Ruby and Sam stand behind me, looking around uncertainly. I had to cajole Ruby to come to this city-wide social tonight. I couldn't leave her at home alone, not with the way she's been—still surly, still silent, still scaring me.

I'm trying not to think of that as I clutch my ticket for my much-needed glass of wine. Sam is looking around for his friends; since starting college almost a week ago, he's become enthusiastic and invigorated about everything, which has been wonderful to see. At least I have one child I'm not worried about.

I'm both glad and grateful that this new world, this new life, is working out for Sam. He's taking classes he enjoys, he's made friends he likes, and Andy has taken him and some other guys under his wing; he's opened the gym several nights so they can play basketball, and he's offered to take them out in a military Humvee. For Sam, life is good.

As for Ruby... she's had one week of school and all I can say is, at least she's gone. She does her homework methodically, angrily even, refusing to talk about it or anything. Sometimes when I look at her, I feel like I don't even recognize my daughter. Sometimes she practically *vibrates* with fury, and when she doesn't, she's silent and sullen, which is both a relief from the rage and yet another worry.

Where, oh where, did my Ruby go?

I glance back at her now, and see she's looking around with reluctant interest, and my heart lifts with improbable, even impossible hope. In the last week, there have been the briefest of glimpses that have reminded me of who my daughter truly is. One morning, before breakfast, she came up to me and put her arms around me. We didn't speak; I knew instinctively that words would have broken that precious spell. We just hugged, for a few seconds only, and then she slipped away again, but it's a memory I cling to.

Another time, walking down Main Street, I pointed to some dandelions growing in the sidewalk cracks. "Pick a few of those and you could make some tea," I said. "Didn't you tell me that dandelion promotes digestion?"

Before we'd come to Watford City, Ruby had been something of a budding herbalist. It feels like a long time ago now, but my mention of dandelions had brought a shy smile to her face before it slid off and she looked away.

Still, it was another glimpse, a potential victory.

"Rubes," I say now as lightly as I can, "do you want to get a drink? I think they have sodas." I give Sam as discreet a pointed look as I can, and he loops a friendly arm around his sister's shoulders.

"Come on, Rubes. Maybe there's even Dr. Pepper."

Back in our lives, in what feels like a million years ago, Ruby loved Dr. Pepper. I allowed her one a week—back then I was that kind of mom—and she would deliberate and deliberate about when she should crack that can open.

Oh, those memories. So bittersweet, so painful, and also so surreal, like they happened to someone else, or even not at all.

As Sam and Ruby head over to the sodas, I look around for the wine. The music is thumping, and plenty of people are clapping or stomping along; the mood is so different from a few weeks ago at the welcome reception, when we all seemed shellshocked, looking around dazedly at what this world had to offer us.

No matter what Jack or Bruce have said about suspicion, right now it feels like everyone is eager to celebrate.

"Hey, I remember you."

I turn, and my heart sinks, because it's the angry woman from the welcome reception who once had a farm in eastern Montana. She's pretty much the last person I want to see right now, because I just want to enjoy my evening. I want to be happy, even if just for a night, free from the usual cares and worries.

"And I remember you," I tell her in a jovial tone. "You've been out of isolation for a while now. How's it going?"

I already know from her stony expression that it's not going well, and my heart sinks further. Whatever she's about to tell me, I already know I don't want to hear it. I look around once more for the wine.

"I asked about my farm," she tells me grimly. "And guess what they said?"

"What?" I reply in a dutiful murmur.

"That I can't go back. That all reclaimed land belongs to the government, and my farm is part of their 'regeneration program' and is 'earmarked for other purposes.'" She makes claw-like quotation marks in the air with her fingers, her face twisted with scorn and rage. "So here I am, living in a studio apartment that's smaller than my kitchen back home, eating dehydrated goop for every meal and working in a warehouse ten hours a day, packing food parcels, which isn't doing wonders for my back." She lets out a snort of disgust. "So how is this a better life? You tell me."

I don't reply, because I have no idea what to say to her. At least she's not starving, but I doubt that's what she wants to hear right now. And as for the farm... the government taking ownership feels wrong, deeply so. This is *America*, the land of opportunity, of the free. Whatever problems the United States had as a country, at least the government allowed you to own your own land. Live your own life. And yet... it doesn't feel like my fight.

"I'm sorry," I finally say, inadequately, and she snorts again, seeming almost as disgusted with me as she is with our government. Part of me doesn't blame her. I wonder if I look as spoiled as I feel, with my cushy journalist job, my three-bedroom house, the access I have to the radio and who knows what else through my friendship with Major Jack Wyatt.

I have, entirely unexpectedly, ended up in a very privileged place in this new world, and I am more aware of it than ever as I stare into this woman's angry face.

"Alex!" Jack's voice is full of warmth as he comes toward us, and I immediately tense. I already know his presence is not going to make anything easier.

At his arrival, the woman looks startled, and then incredulous, and then sneering. I see her evolving mood like the changes of the seasons, and I know whatever happens next is not going to be good.

"I don't think we've met," Jack says, the perfect gentleman. "I'm Jack Wy—"

"I know who you are," the woman spits, and then she turns on her heel and stalks off. Jack stares after her, his mouth tightening for a second before he shrugs, seemingly unsurprised.

"Sorry about that," I tell him with an uncertain laugh. "She cornered me."

He takes a sip from his glass of wine. "It happens." He doesn't ask what we were talking about, and I don't feel like enlightening him. I didn't come here tonight to rehash all those fears. Then he gestures toward the ticket I'm still holding. "You want to trade that in?"

"Absolutely," I reply, my tone so heartfelt that Jack laughs. He puts his hand under my elbow as he guides me toward a waiter with a tray of half-filled glasses, all one ticket is worth, apparently. The crowd parts before us like the Red Sea, and I feel the speculative glances aimed our way. Jack is a public figure, and I am... nobody. Until now.

I am both shy and embarrassed at the attention, and yet at the same time, to my shock and even dismay, some small, feminine part of me craves it. The speculative glances. The envious ones, too. Jack takes two glasses from the tray, even though my ticket only entitles me to one.

"They're small," he mouths, and I smile, although I can't help but feel uncomfortable. I don't want special treatment... even if I sort of do. With wine glasses in hand, Jack leads me to a quiet alcove off the main ballroom. I know I should keep tabs on Ruby, but I also know Sam won't leave her alone, and I crave a moment of quiet conversation, of feeling light and free and also interesting to somebody, even Jack. *Especially* Jack. Because I can tell by the way he looks at me that he finds me interesting, and that is both dangerous and headily addictive.

"Sorry," he tells me as he turns to me. "The music was a little loud."

"Nice to hear it, though," I venture as I lean against the wall and sip my wine. Jack is standing close to me, his shoulder nearly brushing me, his hand bracing the wall by my head in a way that makes me feel both pleased and nervous. "I remember thinking at the night of the welcome reception," I remark, my voice wavering with nerves, "that I couldn't remember the last time I'd heard a live instrument. I don't think I realized how much I'd missed it until I heard it again."

"I wonder how many things there are like that," Jack muses. "Things we don't even realize we miss."

I feel like it's the start of a game, and so I lean my head back against the wall as I look up at him. "Summer barbecues," I say. "With burgers and ribs and sodas in the cooler, nestled in the melting ice." I am picturing Daniel in his silly *Kiss the Cook* apron, and it makes me ache.

He nods slowly, a small smile quirking his mouth. "Driving in the car on a Sunday afternoon, with the sunroof open and the windows down."

"Hanging our stockings on Christmas Eve. Even though my

kids didn't believe in him anymore, they still used to put out a snack for Santa." We haven't really celebrated Christmas for the last two years. The day has passed almost like any other.

"Planting our vegetable garden every May. We had a pretty big one." A small sigh escapes him, and I'm pretty sure he's thinking of his wife.

We're both in danger of slipping into sadness, and so I decide to change the mood. "Muzak when you're put on hold. The same cheesy tune, over and over again, in your ears. And all the while you're trying not to *scream* with rage at being put off by some anonymous person in a call center thousands of miles away."

He laughs softly, shaking his head. The funny thing is, I *do* miss things like that, the utter *luxury* of being annoyed at something so trivial.

"Sausage and egg McMuffins that taste so delicious when you're eating them," he says, "even though you feel nauseous ten minutes later and seriously regret your choice."

I laugh back at him. "So true."

We subside into silence again, but this time it feels different. Jack is looking at me intently. My heart skips a beat and then starts beating double time, and it's not necessarily with anticipation. I'm not ready for this. Not remotely.

"Alex..." he says, his voice lowering.

"I need to check on Ruby," I blurt. I slip out from under his arm and hurry back to the ballroom. I don't look back.

TWENTY-FOUR
MATTIE

Mattie wakes, sensing something is different. Wrong. She sits up in bed, pushing her hair out of her face, willing her heartbeat to slow. Next to her Phoebe breathes evenly, deep in sleep. Outside the window, the light from a full moon burnishes the lake in silver, so it looks like a metal plate.

It's been a week since her showdown with Vicky, and each day has felt like a minefield she has to tiptoe through, wincing with every step. It's abundantly clear to everyone at the camp that Wade is now in charge of things, although Vicky still pretends to be.

It is Wade who orders people around, who put Kyle and Ben and Caden on weapons training, who inspects the kitchen and the cabins like they're in the military and he's the drill sergeant. Mattie isn't bothered by the way he'd put them into traditional roles—women and girls on cooking and cleaning, men on hunting and fishing. She was in the kitchen anyway, but she still resents the tradwife box Wade has smirkingly dropped her into.

And he *does* smirk, alarmingly often, his gaze lingering on her in a way Mattie both hates and fears. The bruise has faded from her face, but she still remembers the feel of his fingers clamping on her jaw all too well.

Two days ago, she should have had her radio call with her

mom. Mattie went up to Vicky to ask her to open the office so she could get on the radio, and to both her shock and complete lack of surprise, Vicky refused.

"I don't think that's a good idea right now," Vicky said with the kindly firmness of a parent telling their kid to get off social media.

Mattie strove to keep her voice level as she replied, "What do you mean? I need to talk to my mom about how I can get to North Dakota. Since *you* won't help me, maybe she will."

Vicky's eyes flashed at that, and Mattie knew she'd made a mistake. "You seem to take help as your due," she snapped, "no matter the cost to us. And I don't trust you or your mom. I've heard on the radio that the forces in North Dakota are monitoring communities. Sometimes they go in and try to take them over. So, no, I don't want you talking to your mom and alerting her to anything *you* think is going on here." She spoke definitively, the subject closed.

"But she's expecting me," Mattie protested, caught, as she so often felt she was, between anger and fear. The anger, at least, felt stronger. "If I don't show up for that call, she'll think something's wrong," she continued, her voice rising. "That will alert North Dakota to what's going on here more than me talking to her ever will."

For a second, no more, Vicky looked hesitant, and Mattie thought she would relent. Then her expression hardened. "You can talk to her next week," she said brusquely, and started to turn away.

"Vicky..." Mattie threw an arm out to catch the other woman's sleeve, but she was already too far away. "Why are you doing this?" she asked in a whisper. "What happened to community spirit and cooperative living and everyone having a say?"

"I'm not the one who changed, Mattie," Vicky fired back. "I'm not the one who started challenging everyone about every little thing."

"What's the point of cooperative living if you can't challenge anything?" Mattie cried. "It's cooperative in name only then—"

"You're the only one here acting like this," Vicky cut across her.

"No one else has a problem. This is your issue, not mine, not Wade's, not anyone else's here."

"But you're not letting me go!" Mattie cried.

Vicky flung an arm wide. "You can walk out of here anytime," she stated coolly. "You just can't take any of *our* supplies with you."

Mattie stared at her in frustration, knowing there was no use in laboring the point that without supplies, she could hardly travel thirteen hundred miles on her own. And after talking to Nicole, she knew she wasn't strong or brave enough to venture out on her own in such conditions. A sixteen-year-old girl alone, defenseless, unprepared... it was a recipe for disaster, even tragedy.

Which is why she needs to talk to her mom, but Mattie isn't holding her breath for Vicky to let her next week, no matter what she's said.

And now it is the middle of the night, and something is wrong. Mattie isn't sure what, but the back of her neck prickles and her eyes strain the darkness. Then she hears it—a motorized sound in the distance, some kind of intermittent mechanical whirring. She glances at Phoebe, still asleep, and then slips out of her bed and into the living room. She considers waking Nicole, but Nicole has not been very helpful lately.

Mattie grabs her coat and stuffs her feet into her fur-lined boots —boots Vicky generously gave her, back at the beginning. Sometimes Mattie wonders if Vicky has a point about her accepting so much help, but if so, she's made it abundantly clear already.

She steps outside into the clear night; the air freezes in her lungs as she tilts her head to the star-spangled sky. She breathes in deeply as she hears the same mechanized sound, punctuated by silence, then starting up again, coming from behind the main cabin. Slowly, keeping to the shadows, she heads down the path. Her boots crunch on the gravel but besides that and the sound of what Mattie is pretty sure is some kind of tractor or tool, the night is still, silent.

At the main cabin she hesitates, and then creeps around the

side, pressing close to the wall. Whatever is happening, she's pretty sure she doesn't want to be seen.

There, behind Vicky's office, she sees figures. Someone is operating some kind of drill or machine, and another person is standing nearby, directing a few others who are carrying what looks like lumber. What, Mattie wonders, could half a dozen people in this community be doing under the cover of night?

Holding her breath, crouching low, she creeps closer. She recognizes Kyle operating what she suspects is an auger post-hole digger, Ben holding what she soon realizes is a fence post. Caden is stringing what looks like wire from post to post.

Barbed wire, Mattie realizes as the moonlight glints on one of the metal thorns. They are building a fence. A barbed-wire fence.

For a second, her mind freezes, blanks. A *fence*. A fence to keep people out… or to keep them in? Why else would they be doing it in the middle of the night?

Mattie watches them for a few minutes. They work quietly, efficiently, without speaking, putting in the posts and then stringing the barbed wire, everyone operating in silent sync. The moonlight catches Ben's face; he looks brutally determined, older than his sixteen years, his hands covered in thick work gloves as he fixes the wire to the next post. Mattie suddenly feels deeply afraid, even more so than when Wade grabbed her jaw.

She tells herself she's overreacting, that a fence could be a good idea, if there are dangerous forces out there, marauders and renegades and vigilantes. But… the world is supposed to be getting *better*. Safer. And this fence feels like a secret kept from the people stuck behind it, not from those on the other side.

She keeps watching, trying not to panic. Vicky told her she could leave whenever she chose. A fence doesn't change that… does it?

A sliver of moonlight catches Wade's face as he turns from the barbed wire. He's smirking, the way he always does, and in the still night air, Mattie hears his rejoinder to one of the other guys.

"No one's getting through this sucker," he declares. "Not without my say-so." They high five, and Mattie's stomach churns.

In that moment she knows, absolutely, that once this fence is built there will be no way out of here, not without Wade's permission. She could leave now, gather her things, grab Phoebe, and *run*. But how far would she get? The nights are still freezing. She has no food, no water, and there is no one outside of Red Cedar Lake that she can trust.

There is, Mattie fears, no one inside she can trust either. Maybe not even Nicole, who seems so spent.

What on earth is she going to do?

Another few minutes pass as the men continue to work. Mattie creeps back around the corner, afraid of being seen. She considers waking up Nicole, but she can't bear the thought of having to listen to more of her fatalism. *What's the big deal about a fence, Mattie? At least it will keep us safe.* She can hear Nicole's tired tone, imagine the weary shake of her head.

What she has to do, Mattie realizes, is contact her mother. Or maybe not even her mother, but North Dakota. Vicky said they were listening to the "chatter," and so they must have someone on the radio at all times. If she can radio North Dakota, she might be able to get help. She has to alert *someone* to what's going on here, before it's too late.

She is seized by sudden, desperate determination. Why didn't she think of this before? Why did she wait so long, dithering and dithering because she felt like such a little girl? What happened to her strength, her defiance? It's almost too late to do anything; whatever she does, she has to do it now.

Mattie runs quietly along the side of the building to Vicky's office, which is locked, as it always is these days. She doesn't hesitate as she searches the ground for a rock, finding a small one along the side of the cabin. She grabs it and smashes one of the panes in the door, closest to the knob.

The crash of the rock hitting the glass sounds far too loud, and

Mattie holds her breath for a few seconds, waiting for a response. If they heard, she'll run, she thinks, but no one comes.

As carefully as she can she sticks her arm through the shattered pane; broken glass sprinkles the ground but there are still some shards stuck to the window, gaping like broken teeth. She tries to reach down to flip the lock, but it's difficult and the inside of her wrist catches on a shard of glass. She lets out a gasp and withdraws her arm; blood runs down her wrist.

She tries again, closing her eyes against the pain, doing her best to ignore the trickle of blood from her wrist to her hand, making her palm slick and her fingers sticky. Finally she manages to flip the lock, and she opens the door.

Knowing she probably only has a few minutes, if that, Mattie studies the radio's transmitter as she cradles her injured arm. She's never operated it before; Vicky has always turned it on, set things up, but surely, *surely* it can't be that hard. She flips a switch, and the transmitter lights up. Then she grabs the headphones and presses the button on the side of the microphone.

"This is VA3 RC," she says, her voice trembling. "VA3 RC, is anyone listening? I'm at Red Cedar Lake and I... I think we might be in danger here; the people at the camp have built a fence and I don't think they're going to let us out. I'm only sixteen and I'm really scared..." Her voice trails off in a tearful tremble, and she takes a breath, tries again. "This is VA3 RC," she states more firmly. "Is anyone listening? I need to reach North Dakota, CP ND 1; I'm looking for Alex Walker... please send help to Red Cedar Lake, Ontario, immediately. The community here, it's—it's been taken over, and people are in danger." She pauses, desperately hoping for some response.

Roger that, VA3 RC. We're listening and we're sending help. Hold tight.

It feels like something out of an action movie, and it doesn't happen. There is only silence. Mattie isn't even sure if she's operating the radio properly. The futility of the whole situation brings tears to her eyes, and she blinks them back furiously.

"This is VA3 RC," she tries again. "Red Cedar Lake, please send help. May Day, May Day, *please send help*." Her voice rises on a strangled cry as panic crashes over her and she closes her eyes and mouths a prayer.

Please. Please, someone...

More silence.

She is just about to try a third time when a heavy hand clamps down on her shoulder and wrenches it back. With a cry, Mattie stumbles backward, the microphone falling from her hand with a clatter as the headphones slide back on her head.

"What the hell," Wade demands in a low, savage voice, "do you think you're doing?"

TWENTY-FIVE
ALEX

I'm sitting in an army Humvee, dressed in camo fatigues, sporting aviator sunglasses and hiking boots, and feeling pretty badass. I know it's ridiculous to feel this way when Jack has just given me some clothes, but I experience a kick of adrenalin as we roll out of Watford City in a long convoy of army vehicles—in addition to Humvees, there are MRAPs, or Mine Resistant Ambush Protected vehicles, and armored combat earthmovers.

I'm doing my best to hold on to my excitement and not be alarmed that the convoy feels like the moving frontline of a war, rather than a jaunt out into the countryside. This is serious.

I knew it was serious, of course; I've lived in this world long enough to know that when you leave any kind of secure settlement, you're putting your life in danger, no matter what Jack said about it being safe. At least being in an armored Humvee in a convoy of similarly tricked-out vehicles is better than rattling along alone in my dad's old truck, like I was back at my family's cottage.

The sky is a bright, hard blue as we drive southwest toward the state border. The driver of the Humvee is Eric, a young guy with a blond brush cut and a reddened, windburned face; judging from his terse manner, I get the sense that he's not thrilled I'm along for the ride. I can't really blame him. I'm a clueless civilian gawping at whatever military maneuvers they're going to make.

My mind is full of questions and rumors—is the area we're going to empty? And if so, where did all the people *go*? And what exactly am I meant to be documenting—the Army's efficient and kindly organization? Part of me is worried this is no more than a propaganda exercise, and even worse, that's the only reason Jack asked me to go. The only reason he's been so charming and solicitous and interested.

We drive south on Route 7, empty fields just starting to turn green on either side of us. Occasionally, in the distance, I glimpse the glinting metal roof of a barn or a silo, a tractor moving through a freshly plowed field—heartening signs of life—but the farther we drive, the more I realize how remote a location we're in. Would North Dakota look like this *anyway*, I wonder, or has the world really emptied out?

"Have you done many of these missions before?" I ask my companion. He slides me a brief sideways glance before returning his gaze to the road.

"A few."

Clearly we're not going to have a conversation.

I try to relax, resting my head against the back of the seat. I offer up a silent prayer that Ruby will have a good day at school. Sam assured me that he'd take care of her; I'll be back tomorrow afternoon, but it feels like a long time away, especially with Ruby the way she is.

This morning, as dawn light crept across the floor of my bedroom, she appeared by my bed, silent, a question in her eyes. I moved over and she snuggled in with me, and my heart ached with relief and gratitude that my gentle daughter was still in there somewhere, underneath all the anger. I wrapped my arm around her waist and we snuggled close, falling into a doze until we had to get up at seven.

As encouraged as I am by that moment we shared, I can't help but worry about the day and night ahead, with Sam managing

Ruby on his own. I know Sam will do his best, but he views Ruby's mood as akin to Mattie's, and my fear is that he's wrong. Something else, something bigger, is going on, and I don't know how to deal with it.

We drive for two hours without speaking, down straight, empty roads through flat fields punctuated only very occasionally by the odd farmhouse, too far in the distance to discern whether it's occupied or not. The fields are freshly tilled, the earth a rich, dark brown rather than the deadened brown of the prairie just a few weeks ago. The emptiness feels encouraging; it's going to be filled.

"Are we going to a particular location?" I finally ask, just to break the silence, and Eric gives me a look like I'm stupid, which I suppose I am. Of course we're going to a particular location. "I mean, *what* particular location?" I clarify. "No one told me."

Eric flexes his hands on the steering wheel, his lips pressed together in apparent disapproval. "Ekalaka," he tells me. "A small town in southern Montana. It's got about two hundred houses and a couple of stores and cafés as well as two schools, so it's one of the bigger settlements in the area, although it only had about four hundred people, back in the day."

It's the most this guy has spoken since I met him, and I appreciate the information, even if I don't feel that much wiser. What are we going to do once we get to Ekalaka? And what happened to the four hundred people who once lived there?

It occurs to me that I really should be getting into journalist mode, asking questions, pressing for answers, but I'm reluctant to, and it doesn't have to do with Eric's obvious reticence... but mine.

As much as I want to do my job and do it well, I'm scared of changing the status quo. I'm afraid to learn uncomfortable truths that I then have to *do* something with. I like my job, our little house, the small but comfortable life we're starting to build. Even Ruby's anger feels like something that can be managed, with time and patience, but if I start to poke at the cracks I'm starting to see in the very foundations of this life, what then? What happens? What do I choose?

Where do we go?

And so I stay silent, and I don't ask Eric the pressing questions I know I should. I don't ask him where the people went, or why this corner of southeast Montana seems so empty, when it's far enough from the radiation that people shouldn't have had to leave. We pass a sign for the Crow Reservation, and I don't ask about that, either.

Maybe I'm a coward, even the worst kind, but I just don't want to know. I *can't* know. I'm simply not strong enough. And so I'll go on this mission, and I'll see what Eric and even Jack wants me to see, because while I wouldn't go so far as to say this whole thing is staged, I suspect it might be curated.

And I'm okay with that. Sort of. In any case, I tell myself, I can always ask the questions later.

We drive for another hour; the flat, freshly tilled fields turn to gently rolling hills of bright green grass, the badlands of the Dakotas left behind for the foothills of what Eric tells me are the Big Sheep Mountains. It's beautiful country, especially in early spring, when the whole world is coming into bud under a vast, blue, wide-open sky.

As we pass into Montana we go through a border checkpoint—two armed guards and a little booth, nothing more, but I notice a barbed-wire fence running in either direction, cutting across the prairie in a savage line, and shock jolts through me, even though I know it probably shouldn't.

"Is there a *wall?*" I ask Eric, my voice sharp, and he glances at me, already irritated.

"It's a fence, not a wall."

"But a border," I press. "Is there a border all around the reclaimed areas?"

"Of course there is," he tells me. "That's kind of the point of the reclamation. Securing areas and incorporating them into what is the current USA."

"Yes, but..." I don't know why the sight of that fence jolts me. It should be reassuring, I think, because it's keeping us safe. It should also be unsurprising, because I knew something must be doing that job, but I'd just never seen it before. It might be more than one hundred miles from Watford City, but it's still there, and I don't know if I need to let that trouble me or not.

We slow down at the checkpoint, and Eric explains who I am. I smile at the guard, who looks back at me, unsmiling and seemingly unimpressed, before waving us through.

"If I was on my own," I ask Eric, "would I be able to get through?"

He looks incredulous. "Of course not. You couldn't even go past the limits of Watford City. Right now, everyone needs to stay in their assigned zones."

It feels like postwar Berlin, a world carved up into pieces, and I'm only allowed in one. I look out the window at the rippling grass, the blue sky, the rolling hills stretching to mountains that are no more than blurred violet shapes on the horizon, and in some strange way all this wide-open beauty feels farther away than it ever has.

"What if someone wanted to leave?" I ask Eric. "Like, for good?"

He is silent for a few seconds, clenching and unclenching his hands on the steering wheel. "I'm not really the one to ask," he finally says, "but it's not as if people are *prisoners*. They chose to come here for safety and opportunity. If you really wanted to leave, I think you could, but you might not be able to come back."

When we finally get to Ekalaka, all one square mile of it, I am ready to get out and stretch my legs, breathe deep under that big sky, and forget Eric's answers to my questions.

The convoy of vehicles stops in front of what was once some kind of courthouse or town hall, a squat rectangle of a building set a little bit apart from the few others. Ekalaka looks like no more than a junction of two streets, the few buildings lining them seeming very small amidst all the emptiness.

I see a library, a saloon, a couple of storefronts, a few streets of houses beyond… it's like a modern version of an old west cowboy town, with nothing else there at all. As I step out of the Humvee, I imagine I can hear the eerie whistle that accompanies every western I've ever seen—which admittedly are few—and picture the tumbleweed bowling dustily down the street, toward the endless horizon.

I try to stay out of the way, clearly ignored, as the military team gets to work. They go into every building, armed and resolute, calling out, checking it's clear, shouldering their way in to examine what's there. Other people are taking soil samples, consulting maps, discussing, I suppose, what this settlement is going to become, another cog in the machine that is the new United States of America.

I'm caught between unease and hope, excitement and fear. After watching the different groups go about their business, clearly intent on what they're doing, I realize I really do need to get into some kind of journalist mode, and so I approach a couple of men in military fatigues deep in discussion in front of an empty Stompin' Grounds Coffee Shop.

"Hi!" My voice wavers as I greet them and they pause in their conversation, clearly trying to hide their annoyance and not succeeding very well.

"As you probably know," I continue in a firmer tone, "I'm with the *Watford City News*." They don't roll their eyes, but it feels as if they do. "Major Wyatt asked me to accompany you today so we could see how the reclamation process works. Do you think you could talk me through some of what you're doing?"

One of the men, older and grizzled, with a nose that looks like it has been broken more than once, sighs. "We're discussing how best to utilize these spaces," he informs me briskly. "Every time we incorporate a new area into the secure zone, we need to discuss the logistics of the settlement and how it will augment those we already have. We have eleven thousand people who are currently waiting for housing, so we also need to make sure that each settlement is operating at maximum capacity and effectiveness, with enough on-site resources for the incoming population." He nods toward the coffee shop. "We're considering whether this should become a food distribution center."

"Eleven thousand people are waiting for housing?" I exclaim. I had no idea.

Some emotion passes across the man's face, a mix of irritation and pity. "That we know of," he replies with emphasis. "There are many more who want to be housed but have no way of contacting us. We have teams going out regularly on sweep missions to pick up those people, sometimes hundreds at a time."

"And where do you house them until you have a settlement prepared?" I ask.

Before the man can reply, I hear a sound like popping corn and dust flies in my face, stinging my eyes. The man grabs my elbow, wrenching it as he pushes me to the ground, hard enough that my cheek hits the dirt and my ears ring.

"We're under fire!" I hear someone shout, and it takes me a dazed few seconds to realize we're being shot at.

TWENTY-SIX
ALEX

My cheek is stinging and I can taste blood in my mouth as I stay on the ground, my belly pressed to the bare earth, while around me soldiers get in place to return fire. I've been in some pretty dangerous situations before, including exchanges of gunfire, and yet this still feels shocking to me, because I really thought I was safe. I thought my enemy, if I had one, was the faceless bureaucracy that was making all these decisions—and is now trying to protect me, because, I realize, I am completely defenseless and exposed.

The man who I was talking to is also belly-flat on the ground, his head raised and his eyes narrowed against the metallic glint of the sun as he surveys the wide-open space for signs of whoever has been shooting at us.

My whole body thrums with adrenalin, every muscle painfully tense as I brace myself for a bullet. Right now it feels like we're all open targets, and I'm the only one without a weapon.

"You," the man says, nodding at me. "Start crawling toward that door." He jerks his head toward the door of the coffee shop. "*Slowly*; you don't want to attract attention. Stay on your stomach, and commando crawl if you can."

I nod jerkily back. When our cottage was attacked nearly a

year ago, I commando crawled out of it as it caught fire, forced to leave everything behind, fleeing with the people I loved. Being in that kind of situation again is bringing back the memories thick and fast—the terror, along with the ice-cold resolution. Kerry being shot in front of my eyes, gasping out that she'd rather go quickly this way. Smoke spiraling into the sky as my parents' home burned to the ground.

Slowly I lift my head a millimeter from the ground. I hear gunfire again, but this time they're shooting somewhere else. In the distance, someone cries out. I force myself onto my elbows, even though part of me doesn't want to move at all. I drag myself forward, digging my elbows into the ground, my whole body feeling as if it is vibrating with tension. At any moment, any *millisecond*, I could be shot...

I manage to move forward a couple of inches, and then a few more. I hear another spatter of gunfire, and then one of the soldiers shouting to another, although their words are like white noise to me. My world has shrunk to the dirt-and-gravel parking lot right in front of my nose, the blood trickling from my cheekbone and my lip, the door to the coffee shop an endless twenty feet away. It feels like an unfathomable distance; I might as well be crossing the Sahara.

I keep moving forward. Time slows, each second seeming to take an age. My elbows dig into the dirt and my right cheek throbs. I hear more gunfire, more shouts, but I try to tune it out. I'm maybe fifteen feet away, twelve, *ten*...

A bullet shatters the glass of the door right in front of me; a shard flies out and hits me in the other cheek. When I instinctively raise my hand to my face, it comes away wet with blood. I drop my hand back to the dirt and keep crawling.

Finally, *finally*, I get to the door and with a gasp I reach up, my blood-smeared hand shaking, and turn the knob. The door swings inward and I heave myself across the threshold, managing to crawl around the corner before I collapse onto the floor.

The room spins and I close my eyes, everything in me throbbing with pain. I must have passed out, because the next thing I know someone is shaking my shoulder.

"Miss... miss... we need to get that cheek stitched up."

I blink blearily at the man in front of me, someone I don't recognize, but I see from the insignia stitched onto his field jacket that he's a medic.

"My *cheek*..."

"Looks like a piece of glass flew at you and cut you up pretty good," he says with a small, sympathetic smile. "You're going to need a couple of stitches."

Still in a daze, I let him help me up and then to an unoccupied building that has been set up as a temporary headquarters, with folding tables and chairs. A few others are being tended to, including a soldier who looks Sam's age who has been shot in the leg; another medic is cutting away the blood-soaked cotton of his pants and I look away quickly.

I am guided to a chair and as the medic starts dabbing my cut with antiseptic, causing it to sting, my brain finally kicks in. "Who shot at us?" I ask, and he shrugs.

"They didn't leave a calling card, but it looked like it was just a couple of vigilantes. They shot a few rounds and then disappeared."

"Does that happen often?" I think of Jack, assuring me this mission would be safe... and I realize that despite my cynicism, I really did believe him. Maybe I shouldn't have.

"Often enough," the medic replies grimly. "Sometimes it can be a full-out assault by an armed group. This time it wasn't so bad."

"But why?" I press. "What's the point of attacking us?" Belatedly I register my use of "*us*." I was suspicious and unwelcome, but I feel part of this now. Nothing like some stranger spraying bullets to give you some community feeling.

"Not everyone likes the government coming in," the medic replies. "Some people prefer it the way it was before." His mouth twists. "Lawless anarchy works for some, you know?"

"I guess." I don't have the opportunity to say anything more, because he's taking out a needle and thread and suddenly I feel queasy. How bad is my cheek? I thought he might slap on a Steri-Strip or something, but this looks serious.

"I've put on some numbing cream," he tells me, "But you might feel a little tugging. And you might end up with a cool-looking scar, depending on how it heals."

I don't particularly want a scar on my cheek, cool or otherwise, but I nod dumbly as he starts to stitch.

A few minutes later, he's done. He tidies up the sutures, snipping the ends, and then hands me a bottle of water and a couple of pills.

"Take these for the pain," he advises. "You can visit the medical center back in Watford to have the stitches removed in ten days or so." He moves on to another patient before I can thank him.

I sit there for a few moments, staring blankly into space, before I unscrew the cap of my water bottle and take a long swallow. I toss back the pills, crunching them between my teeth so their bitter taste floods my mouth. How close, I wonder, did I come to dying today?

I try to untangle my emotions, whether I am simply thankful to be alive, angry at Jack for putting me in this situation, or ashamed that I suspected this was just a propaganda exercise when obviously the situation is a lot more complicated than I'd thought. In the end, I realize I don't feel anything; I'm just numb.

I drink the rest of the water while people move around me, briskly efficient and admirably capable. I am humbled by the way they handle the situation, without fanfare or fuss; it looks like the vigilantes, whoever they were, managed to hit at least half a dozen people before they were driven off.

After a few minutes, or maybe an hour, I'm not sure, Eric comes to stand in front of me. He surveys my face dispassionately.

"I'm sorry you got hurt," he tells me stiffly. "I have orders to take you back tonight."

"I thought we were camping—"

"The orders changed, because of the danger," he cuts across

me. I can tell from his tone as well as his disgruntled expression that he's not pleased at being my escort back to Watford City and de facto babysitter when everyone else is staying here.

"Okay, thank you," I say humbly. "When do we go?"

"Now, so we can get back before dark. We'll be taking an MRAP."

I follow him to a vehicle that looks like a cross between an armored truck and a tank. Eric helps me up into the passenger seat before going round to the driver's side. I still feel numb, barely able to comprehend what happened, or how quickly.

Eric starts the truck, and we drive down the dusty road, away from Ekalaka. As I glance out at the rolling hills, I no longer see their spring beauty, but rather the danger that could be hiding behind every innocent-looking crest.

It takes us just over three hours to return to Watford City, and they pass in a daze that is thankfully uneventful. We are not attacked, and Eric doesn't speak. I stare out the window as the scenery rolls by in one brown-green blur, hills rolling out to flat fields, and then the endless prairie, my mind as empty as the barren landscape all around me.

It isn't until we pull onto Main Street and Eric stops in front of City Hall that the shock suddenly kicks in, like an icy wave crashing over and drenching me. As I clamber out of the MRAP, my knees buckle. I throw out one hand toward the side of the truck to steady myself, and then, to my surprise, I feel arms around me.

"*Alex.*"

It's Jack, and too surprised to resist, I hug him back numbly, registering the feel of his arms pulling me close, the comfort as well as the strangeness of them. Then my damaged cheek hits his collarbone, and I let out a little cry and ease back.

"I'm sorry," he says, his hands on my shoulders, steadying me. "Look at your poor cheek." He shakes his head and I glance up at him, see his face full of recrimination. "When I heard about the attack, I couldn't believe it. It's almost always the first teams that get attacked... if I'd known you'd be in such danger, I never would have suggested it, I swear—"

"It's okay, Jack." I speak slowly, like I have to find the words at the bottom of a well. I feel so cold, and also so exhausted, and I can't believe that Jack didn't know this would be a risk. I don't trust him to tell the truth about this, I realize, and the thought makes me feel sad more than angry.

"Alex, you're shaking," Jack says, and to my surprise I realize I am. My teeth are chattering, my knees knocking. "It's shock," he explains gently. "Come with me."

He takes my hand, and after a second's hesitation I follow him into City Hall, too tired to resist. He leads me to his office, which looks like it once belonged to the mayor of Watford City. Jack sits me in a chair, then pulls out the bottom drawer of his desk and takes out a bottle of bourbon.

"For the shock," he says, and pours me a generous two fingers' worth.

I've never liked whiskey and I don't think I'm about to start, but I toss it back without a qualm and barely a cough. Jack smiles briefly before shaking his head.

"I'm so sorry," he says quietly. "I hate the thought that I put you in danger."

"You couldn't have known," I reply, as if by rote, but as I think about the events of the day and how they unfolded, the lack of surprise from the medic or anyone else... part of me thinks Jack must have known, or at least suspected, and maybe that was the point.

Wouldn't that be the best way to get me firmly onside, writing firsthand about the dangers that our military faces, the dangers our boys are protecting us from, and turn everyone, myself included, into a glowing patriot?

What, I wonder numbly, if that was the plan the whole time?

TWENTY-SEVEN
MATTIE

Mattie wakes up to bright morning sunlight and a head that feels too heavy to lift from her pillow. She's in her own bed, she realizes with some surprise. The last thing she remembers is Wade coming into Vicky's office while she was trying to contact someone on the radio, to no avail. He grabbed her and threw her to the floor; Mattie remembers hitting her head before everything went black.

But if all that happened, how is it that she's here, tucked up like a child? Was it all a *dream*? For a second, relief floods through her at the thought. How wonderful it would be, she thinks, if it had all been no more than a dream. The barbed-wire fence, Wade saying how no one would ever get out, the attack, or even everything before that.

She closes her eyes, determined to believe in the fantasy, if only for a few moments. It's a sleepy Saturday morning and she's in her bedroom back in Connecticut, in the house they had to sell because her dad hadn't been paying the mortgage.

Her parents believed they'd managed to keep the news from her and Ruby, but sometimes Mattie had sat on the stairs, listening to them argue. She knew her dad had lost his job and lied to her mom about it. She knew he'd used all their savings and remortgaged the house without telling her. She knew it was his fault they were about to lose their house, but when she'd heard her dad fight back tears one night while her mother sounded so hard and cold, Mattie's heart had felt as if it had crumbled into pieces. From then on, she'd been angry at her mother.

It occurs to her now, with her eyes still closed, that she has often picked the wrong person to be angry with. Her mother, back then, and now, Vicky. Vicky, Mattie realizes, is no longer running Red Cedar Lake. She's as much a prisoner as Mattie is, even if she likes to act like she's in charge, even if she likes being dazzled by Wade.

Because Wade, Mattie knows, is in charge here now. Wade, who built the fence and came into Vicky's office and stood over her, leering, after he'd thrown her to the ground. She remembers *that*.

But, Mattie reminds herself, she doesn't want to think about that now. With her eyes still closed, she wants to hold on to the fantasy that she's in her bedroom with the purple walls and the leather beanbag, that her dad is making his Saturday special of blueberry pancakes, that her mom is drinking coffee and waiting for her to come downstairs so she can tell her to "make a start" on her homework. She wants to believe Ruby is curled up on the family-room sofa reading a book, and that when she unplugs her phone from the charger in the kitchen—no phones upstairs has been a longstanding family rule—there will be messages and texts from her friends as well as her stupid boyfriend, Drew.

Drew. She was so obsessed with him, Mattie recalls, and it was so pointless. She knows he's most likely dead now, along with all her friends, almost everyone she ever knew. The whole world has changed, and she can't hold on to the fantasy any longer; it's already evaporating like mist, leaving her with the cold, hard reality of her present.

She opens her eyes and blinks her room into focus. She sees, to her surprise, that the wrist she cut on the broken glass has been bandaged with gauze. Outside the sky is a bright, fierce blue. Who brought her back here? Who bandaged her, took care of her?

The door opens, and Vicky stands there, looking the same as always in a cable-knit sweater and jeans, her long brown hair in its usual braid. She seems tired but composed and she surveys Mattie for a moment before she says, "Good, you're awake."

Mattie has no idea what to say. She wonders if she should try to apologize, or explain, or beg Vicky to let her leave. She'd go now, Mattie thinks, if Vicky would let her, even if she couldn't take so much as a granola bar. Right now, she rates her chances out there better than here at Red Cedar Lake.

Vicky walks toward her, her hand raised. Mattie shrinks back against the bed, bracing herself; Vicky looks as if she is going to slap her across the face.

She doesn't, though; she just rests the back of her hand against Mattie's forehead, a motherly kind of touch that some part of Mattie craves, and she feels herself softening, yearning.

"No fever," Vicky remarks, before she pulls a chair up to the side of Mattie's bed and sits down, her hands clasped between her knees. "Mattie," she says after a moment, her tone gentle, "I know this is hard for you, without your family here."

Mattie stares at her uncertainly, still having no idea what to say. Wanting to believe in her kindness, maybe too much. "I'm sorry if I've seemed a little... harsh," Vicky continues in the same gentle voice. "I know we've had a few arguments in the last few weeks, and I really am sorry for them. I guess I felt a little... *hurt* that you were so willing to leave." She gives a rueful little grimace. "The same with your mom, too, if I'm honest, and I know that's on me. You guys have every right to live your lives."

"But it was your idea," Mattie protests, her voice scratchy, like she hasn't spoken for a while, which she supposes she hasn't. "With my mom. You *told* her about North Dakota."

"I know." Vicky nods, accepting, her expression calm and thoughtful. "I've thought about that, and I think maybe part of me didn't believe she'd actually do it, you know? That her loyalty was to the community here, who helped you and your family so much."

There's no recrimination in Vicky's voice, just a simple statement of fact, but it feels unyielding, implacable.

Once again, Mattie has no idea what to say. She can understand Vicky's sentiments, sort of, but her behavior has gone beyond a little *hurt*. She's been so spellbound by Wade, so in his thrall. Does Vicky know how Wade has treated her? Did she *sanction* it? And how was her mom supposed to have known that Vicky hadn't meant any of the stuff she'd said?

"Listen, Mattie," Vicky says, and now she sounds regretful, a little sad. A sense of anticipatory dread creeps coldly along Mattie's skin. She feels as if everything is leading up to this. "I haven't wanted to scare you, especially as you're so young and your family isn't here, but... no matter what you think you know, or hear from anyone else, it's still not safe out there." She nods to the window, her serious, earnest gaze encompassing the whole world. "In some ways, it's more dangerous than it's ever been."

"What... what do you mean?" Mattie asks when it seems as if Vicky isn't going to say anything more.

"I mean instead of just roving gangs, there are *militias*," Vicky states, her voice rising with the force of her emotions. "People who haven't just grouped together but have formed armies. They've taken possession of abandoned military vehicles, weapons... they're a *threat*, Mattie. A threat to us. That's why we built the fence. To keep everyone here safe."

"In the middle of the night?" Mattie dares to ask and Vicky lets out a little, impatient sigh.

"Yes, because we didn't want to draw attention to ourselves, give anyone any encouragement to attack. The truth is..." She pauses and then says in such a deliberate, dramatic way that Mattie almost wants to laugh, "we're being watched."

"*Watched...*"

Vicky nods solemnly. "I heard it on the radio. Lots of people have, all over the country. The US as well as Canada." She leans forward. "The government operating out of North Dakota is clearing out communities like ours, even up here in Canada. The

Canadian government is working with them, and they're not giving anyone a choice whether to go or to stay. Sometimes, if they anticipate trouble, they go in with guns blazing. There have been *casualties*, Mattie. Deaths."

Mattie blinks, absorbing this. "But only if they resist..." she finally protests weakly, and Vicky lets out a huff of disbelief.

"So you think it's okay for the US government to take over your land, your *life*, and tell you what to do, where to go? To arrest or imprison you, even *shoot* you, if you dare to disagree?" she demands. "Is that what you think?"

Mattie stares at her, at the fierce light firing her eyes, and doesn't know what to think. She's so tired, and her head hurts, and she wants to go back to sleep and dream of her mom and blueberry pancakes.

"I don't know," she whispers, only because she can tell Vicky is waiting for an answer.

"Wade was in one of those communities," Vicky tells her. "Everyone minding their own business, just like we are, and the government came in—the US government no less, on *Canadian* soil—and disbanded them. Some of their members were killed. Wade's lucky he got out alive." She sits back as if satisfied, waiting for Mattie's humble apology, but Mattie doesn't even know what she's meant to be sorry for. So much, and yet nothing at all.

"You said there were militias," she replies after a moment. Her head feels fuzzy, and it hurts to keep all her thoughts separate and clear. "If there are, then the government has to use some force to deal with them... right?"

"That's their *excuse*, Mattie, don't you see?" Vicky exclaims, as if she's being dense, and maybe she is. She feels dense, like her head is stuffed with cotton. "They *claim* a group has weapons, is violent, and then they go in and start shooting and people *die*, all because they want their land. Habitable land is scarce these days, and the US government will stop at nothing to get it. Don't you understand?"

Mattie starts to shake her head, but that hurts, and so she stops.

"But if you build a fence..." she says haltingly, "and have Kyle and Ben and Caden practice weapons training... and don't let me talk to my mom or anyone in North Dakota... all these things will draw attention to us. Don't *you* understand?" she cries, briefly lifting her head from the pillow as her temples pulse with pain. "You're practically inviting the Army here with all the stuff you're doing, or not doing."

Which, she acknowledges dully, might be for the best. Maybe then she could be rescued from what is starting to feel like an endless nightmare, but maybe that's just because her head hurts so much. Maybe she's read it all wrong—Vicky, and even Wade—and overreacted about everything. Right now, when she feels so tired and thick-headed, she's not sure.

Vicky lets out a long-suffering sigh. "You're tired," she says after a moment, her tone gentle, "and you're probably confused. What I'm trying to explain to you, Mattie, is that we need to be prepared, both for the militias that are forming in response to what the US government is doing, *and* the government itself. We're not violent, but if they come to us, we need to be prepared to fight for what we've built here."

"Fight the *government?*" Mattie whispers. She's pretty sure that never ends well.

"If we have to," Vicky replies staunchly. "If that's what it takes. We can't roll over and let them take our land, our very selves. 'When tyranny becomes law,'" she quotes, her voice thrumming with conviction, "'then rebellion becomes duty.'" She leans forward, reaching for Mattie's hand. "We *have* to resist."

Mattie stays silent, letting Vicky hold her hand, too tired to do anything. *Feel* anything. Vicky might have to resist, but she knows she doesn't have the strength. Not to resist Vicky, or especially Wade. How would she ever get all the way to North Dakota anyway? And if there's any chance the government there *is* tyrannical, like Vicky said...

Mattie closes her eyes. It would be so much easier, she thinks sleepily, to simply *believe* Vicky and stop questioning everything she says or does. Maybe she doesn't even need to. Fighting has got her nothing but hurt.

Gently Vicky squeezes her fingers. "You understand what I'm saying, don't you, Mattie?" she asks, and her voice is gentle, the way it used to be when Mattie looked up to her and called her a friend.

"Kind of," she whispers, her eyes still closed.

Vicky squeezes her fingers again. "I know this is hard, but we really do want the best for you. To keep you safe... and keep everyone in this community safe."

"I know," Mattie whispers. She feels as if she's floating away on a river of sleep, to dreams of her mother and Saturday mornings, Ruby on the sofa, her dad flipping pancakes too high, joking about how they'll stick on the ceiling...

She wants to live in that world. Why can't she live in that world?

"I know," she says again as she drifts off on the pleasant current of memories.

"Good girl," Vicky says, and then lets go of her hand.

TWENTY-EIGHT

ALEX

Jack drives me back home after comforting me with a hug and another healthy shot of bourbon. I feel exhausted but also wired, my mind racing with thoughts and yet all I want is sleep. That numbness back, even. I'm still shaking, but it feels more internal, like there are a bunch of marbles rattling around inside of me.

I don't know what to think about anything anymore. Including Jack.

"Mom," Sam exclaims, his jaw dropping at the sight of me. I haven't looked in a mirror since this morning but judging from the horrified expression on my son's face, I must look pretty awful.

"I'm okay," I tell him as I give him a one-armed hug. "Just a cut on my cheek, that's all."

Ruby appears behind him, looking even more horrified, her eyes wide and her face pale.

"I'm okay," I assure her, and she rushes toward me, wrapping her arms around my waist as she hugs me tightly. I return the hug, just as tight, grateful for my girl. If this whole incident brings Ruby a little closer to me, it will have been worth it... even if I don't know how to make sense of what happened today.

"What happened?" Sam asks as Ruby eases away from me. He

directs the question as much at Jack as at me, and it is Jack who answers.

"There were some vigilantes out where your mom was going with our second team," he explains. "We usually have good information on any hostile operations in the area, but this was just a couple of lone wolves. Hard to predict, and I'm very grateful she's safe." He gives me a warm, almost possessive look that neither of my kids miss, which annoys me, because it feels like too much, especially when I'm not sure I can trust him.

"Thank you for taking me home," I tell Jack, a little formally. "I think I'm going to clean myself up." It's clearly a dismissal and he looks a little stung, but I can't worry about his feelings right now. I have too much other stuff to be dealing with.

After Jack leaves, I again reassure Sam and Ruby that I'm okay, and then I head upstairs to assess the damage. The sight of my face in the bathroom mirror is a shock. My eyes are still wide and dazed, my hair a snarled mess, and the stitches on my cheek run from the corner of my eye nearly to my jawbone and make me look like Frankenstein's monster. Purplish bruises bloom on either side of them, and there is another bruise on my other cheek from when that soldier pushed me to the ground.

No wonder the kids looked so horrified. *I'm* horrified, and the medic's remark about a cool scar comes back to me, less of a joke than I'd thought. This scar will not be cool.

Gently I run my fingers down the stitches, wincing at how sensitive they feel. I touch the bruise on the other side of my face, and wince again. I decide to forego washing my face and simply brush my hair and change into pajamas, even though it's only dinnertime. I'm exhausted.

I open my bedroom door and give an inadvertent little gasp as I see Sam standing right in front of me, his arms folded.

"Mom... was it really vigilantes?" he asks in a low voice, no doubt not wanting Ruby to overhear us.

"As far as I know, Sam." I move past him to go downstairs.

"Who else would it be?" Our food parcel isn't due for another two days, and there isn't a lot to choose from for dinner.

Sam follows me all the way to the fridge. "What if it was more than that?" he asks. "A militia or private army or something? Andy was telling us there are a lot of rebels out there, forming into groups. You know, some crazy people who don't want the country to get back to the way it once was. They all want their own little kingdoms."

"That may be," I allow, "but I think some people are genuinely worried about what getting the country back will look like... or how it will happen." I pause, my hand on the fridge door. "I mean right now, the government is exerting a lot of control over our lives. They tell us where to live, where to work, even what food to eat." I nod at the mostly empty fridge before taking out a single shriveled tomato. "After the relative freedom of the last few years, that might feel unnatural to people. Wrong."

He stares at me hard. "Does it feel wrong to you?"

"Sometimes," I admit. "When we drove to Montana, we had to go through an armed checkpoint. That felt weird."

"All countries have borders," Sam points out reasonably. "It's just that the USA's borders have shrunk. For now."

"For now," I agree quietly. I take a can of beans out of the cupboard. Another bean stir fry it is. I wonder when the military will use up its supply of beans; the cans must be from before the bombs. I think of Bruce mentioning mangoes, and Jack telling me how we will be self-sustaining within the next year. Right now it all feels far away.

"Why are you so skeptical?" Sam demands as I open the can of beans and pour its fairly unappetizing contents into a pan. "Do you know how hard everyone in the government is working to keep us fed and safe?"

I think back to Sam in his high-school days, when he was passionate about every conspiracy theory—Area 51, JFK's assassination, the moon landing... he would have questioned and debated every point. Now he's a patriot.

"Do *you* know?" I ask mildly, and Sam presses his lips together.

"Andy tells me things," he says, somewhat repressively, like he's got secrets he can't share with me. "Actually..." He pauses, and I tense. *What now?* "Andy's asked me and a couple of the other guys at college to do some premilitary training. You know, like being in ROTC, kind of."

"Premilitary training?" I am instantly wary, picturing, rather ridiculously, something like teens in Hitler Youth outfits goosestepping down Watford City's Main Street. "What kind of stuff?"

Sam shrugs. "Some weapons training, stuff like that."

"Weapons training..." I really don't like the sound of that.

"Mom, this is our *country*," Sam says with passionate emphasis. His face is flushed, his eyes bright. "We have to defend it. Stand by it. After what happened... don't you want to safeguard what's left?" Before I can answer that, he continues swiftly, "We can't ask the government to do everything. We have to take responsibility ourselves, step up, show them we mean it..."

I'm pretty sure Sam is parroting what Andy has said, and I'm trying to decide if I mind. Patriotism is no bad thing, surely, especially when it is, as Sam said, so sorely needed.

And yet... I still have so many questions. I want to know what happened to the people in all those empty towns. I want to know where six thousand Assiniboine and Sioux went. I also want to know why Jack assured me it would be totally safe to travel with a military operation when it obviously wasn't.

But I also want to stop being so suspicious. The thought of letting the questions slip away, drifting on a breeze of well-intentioned indifference, never letting them needle me in a dozen different ways...

It's very appealing. I don't want to be like that woman who keeps accosting me, angry about her farm. I have a *life* here now, and I think I could learn to be happy with it if I let myself.

"The training would be at Minot Air Force Base," Sam says, and I am jolted out of my wistful reverie.

"Minot? Isn't that over a hundred miles away?"

Sam nods. "Andy would take a few of us there on weekends. We'd stay overnight."

I swallow hard. "Sam... are you sure about this? I mean, *weapons* training... it's still dangerous out there." I think of this morning, crawling on my belly as bullets spattered around.

Sam straightens, a look of pride flashing in his eyes. "I know it's dangerous out there, Mom," he says. "That's why I want to do it."

"So I heard you nearly got killed," Bruce remarks the next morning when I head into work. He raises his eyebrows as he nods toward my face. "That's some souvenir."

"I know, right?" I try to keep it light. I'm exhausted from yesterday, as well as from another morning of Ruby's sullen silence. She stormed out of the house without saying goodbye or waiting for Sam.

Bruce eyes me appraisingly, his eyebrows still raised, clearly waiting for more.

"What?" I ask in good-natured exasperation. At least I hope I sound good-natured.

"Are you convinced by our great nation's display of mercy and might?" he asks with a wry twist of his lips. His tone is sharper than I've ever heard before. "Now that you've seen them in action, saving your life, driving off the faceless bad guys?"

I shake my head slowly. I don't want to have this conversation, the same one that's been happening in my head, but I know I have to. Need to, maybe.

"I'd like to be convinced," I tell him honestly. "Even if I'm not, and it's obvious *you're* not, whether you're willing to do anything about it or not."

His eyebrows inch higher. "Oh, now *I'm* under the microscope?"

"No," I say quickly. "I just want to know why you're so suspicious. I know you've heard rumors, but... is there more to it than that? Do you know something I don't? I mean, besides Fort Peck—"

"Six thousand Sioux isn't enough to cause alarm?"

"Don't," I say quietly. "I just mean something personal. Besides a rumor."

He sighs, raking his hands through his curly hair as he pushes himself away from his desk. "You know where I was when the first bombs fell?" he asks, and I shake my head. Surprisingly, I haven't heard his story, besides that he was a high-school teacher. "New York," he tells me, and I can't help from giving a soft gasp of surprise. New York City was more or less incinerated; I saw the footage on the TV at the very beginning, nothing but smoke and flames.

"How..."

"I was teaching uptown, near Columbia. The bomb fell in midtown, so I was about three and a half miles away. We all went into the basement of the school—twenty teachers, over one hundred kids. We locked the door, hunkered down. A science teacher said most of the radiation would dissipate from the atmosphere within three days. We just had to hold on for that long. We had some food and water, although not a lot." He shakes his head slowly. "Of course, he was wrong. The pollution from the factory fires, the exploded oil refineries... the contaminated soil and groundwater... the whole tri-state area was a write-off. Of course nobody knew that when we were down in that basement."

He lapses into silence, his face drawn in sorrowfully reflective lines. "I volunteered to go up for a recce after three days. By that point, everyone was at the end of their rope... kids crying, people falling apart..." He sighs. "When I did go up... well." His expression is so grim, I practically wince. I've seen a lot of things since the world fell apart, but I'm pretty sure Bruce saw worse in Manhattan.

"The world was a totally different place," he says quietly. "It was *gone*." He falls silent again, seemingly gripped by a powerful emotion, before resuming. "We were trapped on Manhattan Island. The bridges were down because of structural damage from the bombs, the tunnels weren't safe, and the island was on *fire*.

Buildings collapsed, whole blocks turned to rubble, the air thick with smoke and pollution, and of course most of Manhattan just *gone*... I kept waiting to wake up, but I never did."

For a second he looks so bleak I almost want to give him a hug. Then he turns to look at me, his expression turning fierce. "And do you know where the military was, or the firemen, or our glorious boys in blue?" I stare at him in silence and he finishes flatly, "Nowhere. Nowhere to be seen. They didn't show up for anyone stuck on Manhattan, even though there were *millions* of us in need of help, who had survived, who had to get out. They didn't even *try*. And when I finally made it out the other side, on a *rowboat* across the Hudson, the only military I saw were waving their weapons around and looting for themselves. Everything official had been disbanded. They were as bad as any other gang." His tone is one of finality, like he's had the last word.

I wait a few moments before I speak, giving his story the solemnity it deserves. "I'm sorry about that," I say quietly. "Truly. But Bruce... you know as well as I do that doesn't mean that everyone is like that. Every police officer, or fireman, or military personnel. There are good guys too."

"And the good guys are the ones who made it here?" he fills in. "Who build the new world while the bad guys just disappear into the distance?"

"Bruce..." I try for a smile. "Do you really think the people here are that... *nefarious*? I mean, they've housed us, given us jobs, fed us... I think they're trying to do something good here."

"Maybe," he allows. "I'm not a conspiracy theorist. At least I don't think I am." He manages a wry smile. "I don't think there's some grand evil plan they're secretly enacting. But are they the *good* guys?" He shakes his head. "That I don't know. Maybe nobody is, not in this new world. We've all had to compromise... and we're all too broken."

I am about to reply when we are both startled at the sound of someone hammering at the door. For a second I see a look of fear pass across Bruce's face, and I wonder if he's worried the not-so-good guys are on his case.

But it's not the military, or the government, or anyone official at all.

It's Sam.

"Mom..." he says breathlessly when I run to open the door. "You need to come. It's Ruby."

TWENTY-NINE
ALEX

The Watford City High School smells like gym socks and brown-bag lunches; it seems some things never change. I stride down the hall, toward the principal's office. I feel both numb and angry; all I know is that as they were arriving at school, Sam saw Ruby get angry at someone before being hustled away by a teacher. When he went to ask about it, he was told she was in isolation. When he pressed, he discovered she'd been restrained.

Words and actions I never would have associated with my daughter. Now the principal has agreed to see me, and I have no idea what I'm going to say to her, never mind what she might say to me.

"Mrs. Walker." The principal, Mrs. Weeks, is a neat woman in her forties with a blond bob, standing behind her desk with a calm yet steely expression on her face. As I enter her office, I feel as if I could be back in Connecticut, summoned to Mattie's school when cannabis was found in her locker.

Mattie. Tomorrow night is our planned radio call, and I'm desperately hoping she'll be on it. But as for now, I need to think about Ruby.

"Mrs. Weeks," I greet her. She gestures for me to sit down but I stay standing. "My son told me Ruby has been restrained and put in isolation." My voice rings with accusation.

"Yes, we felt that was best, considering the level of disruption she's been causing," Mrs. Weeks replies without a flicker of remorse. "Your daughter has been very aggressive toward her classmates."

"Aggressive..." Even having borne the brunt of Ruby's anger, I still struggle to believe such a thing. My shy, quiet, gentle daughter being *aggressive*? "She's normally a very compliant girl," I tell Mrs. Weeks, who looks understandably skeptical. "Since we've come to North Dakota, things have changed. I don't know why." I lower myself into the chair. "What happened this morning?"

"She attacked another student," Mrs. Weeks tells me flatly. "Throttled her, in fact. It took two teachers to pull her off the poor girl."

"What..." I feel faint with shock as I try to picture the scene. "I can't... I don't..." I shake my head. "Were they arguing?" I ask, a little desperately. "Did the other girl say something..." I need to find some way for this to make sense.

Mrs. Weeks gives me a severe look, worthy of any principal. "Do you honestly think anything that girl might have done justified that kind of attack? Ruby was *choking* her."

I swallow the taste of bile in my mouth. "Okay." I nod, accepting, even though everything in me resists. "And what happened to Ruby then?"

"She was restrained by two teachers, who sustained some injuries in the process," Mrs. Weeks informs me, and I gape.

"What kind of injuries?"

"One was scratched across the face; another was slapped." Mrs. Weeks' voice is decidedly cool. "Considering how much Ruby was resisting them, they felt the need to restrain her, which they did." She pauses. "We have plastic handcuffs for that purpose, which they used on your daughter before isolating her in a classroom that was not in use."

"*Handcuffs?*" I am appalled at the thought of thirteen-year-old

Ruby being treated in such a way, at *school*. What kind of school has handcuffs anyway? "That seems unnecessary—"

"Trust me," Mrs. Weeks interjects crisply, "it was not. Considering the severity of the situation, I am suspending Ruby from school for two weeks and advising you to have her psychologically tested at the medical center. Her behavior is not normal." She glances away, and I realize the conversation is over.

"I'd like to see my daughter," I say stiffly.

"You can see her and take her home," the principal replies. "And I hope you are able to find some treatment that helps her." She moves around her desk. "I'll take you to her myself."

Silently I follow Mrs. Weeks down a hall lined with lockers and posters advertising healthy eating and digital safety—bygones from another, easier age. She arrives at a classroom at the end of the hall; through the pane of glass I see Ruby sitting in a chair, still handcuffed, and my chest burns with outrage.

"Did she really need to be handcuffed while sitting in an empty classroom?" I ask as the principal unlocks the door; she gives me an opaque look, saying nothing. As soon as she opens the door I rush toward my daughter. Ruby glares at me mutely, her eyes like burning holes. I take a step back.

"Ruby..."

"Ruby, your mother is going to take you home now," Mrs. Weeks says, as if talking to a dangerous animal and trying not to reveal her fear. "I'm going to take off the ties on your wrists so you can leave. I hope you'll behave sensibly."

Ruby raises her hands in response as the principal carefully unclips the plastic handcuffs. I hold my breath as my daughter is freed, and Mrs. Weeks steps smartly back. Ruby doesn't say a word as she rises from the chair and then walks out of the classroom.

I glance at Mrs. Weeks, trying to form some apology, but nothing comes to mind. "Thank you," I mutter, and then I hurry after my daughter.

I catch up with her at the front doors, putting my hand on her shoulder, hard enough that she tries to squirm away. "No," I hiss.

"No more, Ruby." I realize I'm furious, but I'm also afraid. I don't understand what's going on, but I know my daughter needs help. Whether we can find it here is another question altogether.

We walk out of the high school and start back down the road toward Watford City, a three-mile trip that I hope will give us both time to compose ourselves. It's a beautiful spring day, the air warmer than it has been in recent weeks, the sun shining, the fields rolling out in a carpet of green. The endless open sky still overwhelms me, but I can find a beauty to it all—more than I could before, anyway.

After a few minutes, Ruby jerks away from my grasp and keeps marching down the road.

"Ruby..." I trail after her, a helpless supplicant now. "Talk to me. What's going on? Why are you so angry all the time?" Admittedly it's not the most neutral question, but I'm at a total loss. Why has my daughter changed so much? Is it just from the trauma of everything that has happened to us, or is it something more sinister than that? Has something happened *here* that she won't talk about?

My steps slow as I consider the question and its possible answer. Ruby seemed to become angry as soon as we were out of isolation. I think back, try to pinpoint the moment when I knew something had changed, but I can't.

"*Ruby...*" I say again, but she just keeps walking.

We walk all the way back into town, the fields stretching out on either side interspersed with the odd empty-looking building, without exchanging so much as a word. A bus rattles by with another load of new residents; behind the tinted glass I see their wary, wide-eyed stares. A man's haggard face catches my glance and I think I see a spark of recognition in his eyes, his hand pressed to the window, before the bus rumbles on.

I slow down, trying to think who it was as Ruby just carries on walking. I'm sure I recognized that face... Ruby has gotten about thirty feet ahead of me and I hurry to catch up with her, exasperated and anxious all over again. What am I even going to do with her for the next two weeks?

We're walking by the Comfort Inn, the bus I saw earlier being unloaded, when it hits me.

"Ruby, wait." When I grab her arm she tries to shake it off, but I hold on tight. *"Wait,"* I say again, a command, as I watch the rest of the refugees come off the bus. They look exhausted, shocked, some of them clearly terrified. Where have they come from, and why do they seem so scared?

Then I see him—the man I recognized, walking with a limp, his shoulders slumped, everything about him dejected, defeated. I squeeze Ruby's arm as I lurch forward, pulling her along.

"Tom!" I call and the man turns, surprise rippling across his weary features. It *is* Tom, I realize with a jolt of shock. Tom, my husband's friend, who helped him back in Utica and was reunited with him in North Bay.

Why is he now here?

THIRTY
MATTIE

When Mattie awakes it's late afternoon, judging by the light, the sun's low, golden rays slanting across the floor. Her head still feels heavy but it's clearer, and she doesn't feel as out of it as she did before. Was she *drugged*? Mattie wonders. She wouldn't put it past Vicky, although why she would bother, Mattie can't begin to think. She's already trapped here. She knows that full well. That fence isn't just to keep people *out*. Mattie is almost certain of that.

Taking a deep breath, she sits up and swings her legs over the side of the bed. Her head swims and her stomach rolls. When she puts a hand to her head, she feels a bump like a goose egg on the back of her skull. She wonders if she got a concussion when Wade knocked her to the floor.

Mattie is about to rise from the bed when she hears movement from the living room, and she stills. It doesn't sound like Nicole; the footsteps are too heavy, the movements too loud. Carefully she edges off the bed and cracks the door open a half-inch. A gasp escapes her, and she opens the door all the way.

"What are *you* doing here?" she asks Kyle.

Kyle sniffs as he slings a duffel bag onto the sofa. "I'm moving in."

"What—"

"Don't worry, I'll take the other bedroom," Kyle assures her, unable to keep the bitterness from his voice.

"But Nicole—"

"Vicky wants Nicole and Ben to be together," he cuts across her. "Keep everyone in families, she said."

"You're not my family," Mattie shoots back, and Kyle looks hurt.

"Why have you gone against me so much?" he asks in the woebegone voice of a little boy that annoys Mattie more than anything else. It's how Kyle used to sound, before he got stronger. Before she paid him some attention and decided she cared. "What have I done?" he asks plaintively.

"Nothing," Mattie admits. "I'm just... I'm not in a good place right now." She wraps her arms around herself as she steps into the living room. Why would Vicky want Nicole to move out? She must have suspected they were talking, maybe even making plans. She's trying, Mattie realizes, to separate them. And is Kyle here to keep an eye on her? He's clearly in Wade's pocket, with all the weapons training, belly laughs, and bro slaps on the shoulder.

Mattie sinks into a chair, resting her pounding head on her knees. Does any of it even matter? she wonders. She can't leave. She won't be able to use the radio again, not in a way that would be helpful to her. Vicky and Wade will both make sure of that. Maybe the best thing she can do is accept the fact that this is her life... and just like she told her mom, she chose it.

Tears sting her eyes and she blinks them back, determined not to feel sorry for herself. She knows there's no point. She raises her head to look up at Kyle, who is gazing back at her in concern.

"Mattie... I don't know what's going on, but I want to help," he says unevenly. "I want to be there for you."

"You know Wade caused this," she says, angling her head and pulling back her hair so he can see the bump on her head. "He threw me to the floor."

Kyle looks solemn. "I know," he says, and Mattie twists back to gape at him.

"You *know*? And you don't care?"

"I care," he replies, his voice rising, "but Mattie... you put the whole camp in danger, going on the radio like that. The US is coming into places, taking them over. Do you really want that here?"

"I don't want Wade," she flashes back, and Kyle sighs.

"Is he really that bad? Look, I know he can be a little tough, and he's full of himself, but... he's got this place in shape. We can defend ourselves, and we'll be self-sustaining by the fall. Those are good things."

"Are they?" Mattie raises her fists to her eyes, presses them into her sockets until she sees flashing lights. Sometimes she wonders if she's crazy, if she just needs to fall in line the way Kyle is doing. The way it feels like *everybody* is doing, even Nicole. Then she thinks of Wade sitting next to her as she called her mom, the look on his face close to a leer, and she knows she's not overreacting. She's not making a mistake. She drops her fists from her eyes.

"Where's Phoebe?" she demands.

Kyle shrugs. "I don't know; I think Vicky might be watching her."

"Vicky...?" Vicky hasn't shown all that much interest in children, and Phoebe doesn't have a special bond with her. An icy finger of unease trails along Mattie's spine. She wants Phoebe with her. Safe, or as safe as she can possibly be in this place. How did Red Cedar Lake, once such a haven, become as good as a prison? She still can't understand how it happened so fast. It's only been a month, and yet everything has changed.

Although, she acknowledges, maybe it hasn't changed as much as she feels it has. Maybe it was like this all along, and she never wanted to see it.

Does it even matter now? She has to find a way forward.

"I'll go get her," Mattie says and Kyle shrugs, seemingly indifferent. He never cared about Phoebe the way she does, Mattie knows, no matter what anyone has said about them being like a family.

Outside Mattie tilts her face to the sun's gentle warmth, taking a deep breath to steady herself. The sky is pale blue, the lake smooth and still beneath it. As she walks along the path at the top of the lake to the main cabin, she notices how quiet it seems. Where is everybody? In the distance, the barbs of the fence glint under the late afternoon sunlight.

In the main cabin she finds only Patti, doggedly peeling potatoes in the kitchen.

"*Mattie.*" She puts down her peeler and comes around the kitchen island to give her a gentle and unexpected hug. Mattie returns it gingerly, grateful for the touch. Maybe she has one friend here after all. "I'm so sorry," Patti whispers as she releases her, her voice hushed. She looks around the kitchen as if expecting eavesdroppers. "How's your head?"

"It still hurts." Mattie can't tell what Patti is sorry about, what she knows. "What did Vicky tell you happened?" she asks.

Patti hesitates, returning to the other side of the island and picking up her peeler. She peels two whole potatoes before she finally replies. "Just that you fell." Her voice is careful, toneless.

"Fell?" Mattie repeats. "And you believe that?"

Patti sighs and puts down the peeler. "No," she admits. "I imagine you had a run-in with… with Wade. Vicky told us you were trying to use the radio." Her voice is so low Mattie can barely hear it.

"A run-in," she repeats with a huff of disbelief. "That's one way of putting it."

"Mattie…" Patti shakes her head in warning. "Don't," she advises. "Kicking against the goads won't help you here."

"Kicking against the *goads*?" Mattie doesn't even know what that means. "Patti, you must know what Wade is like," she says, dropping her voice as she takes a step closer. "Why does everyone just go along with it? With him?"

"It's not like we have a lot of choice," Patti whispers, her voice coming out in a low hiss.

"He's one man—"

"With an arsenal. And some people like having him here, you know? It makes them feel safe." She pauses, her head bent over the pile of potatoes. "And maybe we are safe. Maybe it's better this way." She pauses again and then says in an even lower voice, "Rose and Winn are gone."

"Gone?" Mattie blinks. If they could go, why can't she? "When? How?"

"They left in the night, when the fence was being built. No one saw them go, as far as I know."

"So you mean they escaped," Mattie says bitterly.

Patti sighs. "It could be worse."

"Could it?" she demands, her voice rising so the older woman's eyes widen in alarm. "I'm *trapped* here, Patti. Vicky won't let me contact my family. Now there's a fence, she won't let me leave. I might never see my mom or my brother or sister again." To her shame, Mattie starts to cry, big gulping sounds like she's five years old and scared of the dark.

"Oh, Mattie. Mattie, honey." Patti comes around the island again, putting her arms around Mattie. This time she leans into her, craving the comfort. She misses her mom so much. "I don't know what to do," Patti whispers against her hair. "I can't... Wade..." She gulps. "Can't you make the best of it, honey? You've got Phoebe and Kyle..."

Mattie pulls away, disgusted now. "I don't want to make the best of it," she hisses. "I want to get *out* of here." Even as she says the words, she feels their futility. No one is going to help her. Not Patti, not Nicole, not anyone. "Do you really believe," she asks Patti, and now she sounds despairing, "that it's okay for Wade and Vicky to keep me here like a prisoner?"

Patti sighs. "I'm not sure it's really like that—"

"Isn't it?" Mattie demands, and Patti just shakes her head. She doesn't want to argue, Mattie knows, and she doesn't want to believe. Just like that, her fiery fury goes out, leaving her feeling flat and hopeless. One thing at a time, she tells herself. She needs to find Phoebe. Once she has her back, she can figure out a way to get out of here... without anyone else's help.

She heads out to the living area of the main cabin, checking herself when she sees Vicky striding in.

"Where's Phoebe?" she asks, too aggressively. Vicky frowns in response.

"She's sleeping," she says coldly. "I'm glad you're feeling better."

"It's a little late for her to be sleeping," Mattie says firmly. "I'll wake her up and bring her back to my cabin."

Vicky smiles in a way that makes Mattie grit her teeth. "Mattie, she's fine," she says, as if placating someone who is clearly overreacting. "I've realized how unfair we've been to you," she adds, and Mattie can only blink, bracing herself for what's coming next, because she's pretty sure it's not *so we're going to figure out a way to get you to North Dakota.*

"Really unfair," Vicky continues, clearly warming to her theme. "You're all of sixteen, and we've burdened you with the care of a child?" She shakes her head sorrowfully. "We never should have allowed that. You're far too young to act like a mother."

"What..." *Allowed?* What is Vicky talking about? Phoebe came with them. With *her*. Vicky has nothing to do with Phoebe, should have absolutely no say in her care. "Where's Phoebe?" she asks again, her voice a low throb of fury.

"I told you, she's sleeping. And from now on she can stay with Wade and me." Vicky's voice is kind but firm, a tone Mattie used to love but which she now realizes is Vicky's way of steamrolling over any objections. She smiles, folding her arms, and Mattie imagines the three of them all cozy in their cabin, a *family*.

"So you and Wade are living together now?" she jeers, too angry and afraid to moderate her tone.

"Do you have a problem with that?" Vicky asks coolly.

"No, why should I?" Mattie throws at her. "I hate Wade. He's *vile.*"

Vicky's face darkens, and Mattie knows she's gone too far. "He told me I could do better than Kyle, you know?" she adds recklessly, her voice high and thin. She wants to hurt Vicky, even though she knows she will hurt herself in the process. "He meant *him*, just so you're clear. Not that I'm interested at all, so you don't need to worry on that score, because I know how much you like him. He's got you wrapped around his finger, has from the beginning—"

"Mattie. Stop." Vicky's voice is lethal, her face composed but her eyes narrowed to dangerous slits. She is furious; Mattie knows she has said far too much. "You're just embarrassing yourself," Vicky states coldly. "I can understand why you have a crush on Wade, but—"

Mattie chokes at that, so angry she can't even get the words out. "I... would *never*..." she finally manages to gasp.

"This kind of petty point-scoring is low, even for someone your age." Vicky talks over her sternly. "I think this is a good place to end the discussion." She walks away without another word, leaving Mattie pulsing with pointless fury... and no closer to getting Phoebe back.

A jagged cry escapes her as Vicky closes the door, and she whirls back to the kitchen, already knowing she won't find an ally in Patti...

"Vicky won't let Phoebe back to live with me," she declares, and Patti's face is suffused with sympathy but not surprise.

"You're a little young to have the full care of a child, honey," she says.

Mattie takes a menacing step toward her, her fists clenched at her sides. "Phoebe came with us," she states furiously. "She's known me like a mother for a *year*. Vicky has no right."

Patti falls silent, seemingly chastened but unwilling to help in any way. Mattie whirls around, disgusted, helpless, everything in her pulsing with rage. Vicky has found just about the only way to keep her here forever. Without Phoebe, she realizes hollowly, she'll never leave. For a second, she considers it—

escaping on her own, alerting the US government, coming back to get Phoebe.

But no. Mattie knows she can't risk leaving Phoebe here on her own... not for weeks or months, even forever if she can't find a way back. Something Vicky has undoubtedly thought of.

Still, Mattie tells herself, Vicky can't keep the little girl prisoner forever. Somehow, she will find a way to get Phoebe and leave this place for good.

She doesn't know how, but she's determined to do it. No matter the cost.

THIRTY-ONE
ALEX

"*Tom.*"

In my disbelief and joy at seeing someone I know, I grab him by both shoulders, which are painfully thin under my clutching hands. "It's Alex, Daniel's wife. You remember Daniel—"

"Of course I remember Daniel." Tom's tired face creases into a smile as he glances around. "Where is he?"

I shake my head, and Tom's smile fades. "I knew he was sick," he murmurs. "I'm so sorry. I guess... I guess it was quick?"

"Kind of." Those last few weeks of watching my husband waste away felt endless, and yet they were far too short. I shake my head slowly. "But Tom... what are you doing here? Are there others from North Bay here?"

Daniel first met Tom on the road to Utica; he took him in, fed him, and helped him on his way. Later, Daniel told me, he went back to Tom's farmhouse with Sam for help, but the place was abandoned, and he'd feared the worst. Then their paths crossed again at North Bay, and I often saw them deep in discussion. I don't know what they talked about, but I know from Daniel that Tom helped him to forgive himself for whatever he'd done. I still don't know what that is and have made peace with the fact that I most likely never will.

But now I want to know why Tom is here.

I drop my hands from his shoulders as he glances around with rueful weariness. "Everyone from North Bay is here, or somewhere," he says. "They cleared the place out."

"*Cleared...*" That doesn't sound good. "What do you mean?"

He shrugs. "You know how it was. Leadership getting a little too full of themselves, I guess. They had access to weapons, planes even... and they weren't giving any of it up. The government came in pretty hard, a full-on military operation. It... it wasn't pretty." He falls silent, and I swallow hard.

"Did... did people *die*?" Having escaped from the place myself, I can understand why the government would want to take it over. But the use of force, of violence, doesn't sit easily with me, especially when my daughter had been handcuffed earlier today. What is this new world we're supposed to be creating?

Tom nods soberly. "Like I said, it wasn't pretty."

"But North Bay was just doing its own thing," I argue. "They were keeping to themselves, weren't they? They weren't *attacking* anybody."

"I guess you can't have civilians in charge of military-grade weapons," Tom replies practically. "And truth was, nobody was negotiating on either side. They made sure we wouldn't go down without a fight... every man had to have a weapon. I didn't want to, but..." He trails off, shaking his head. "I had no choice."

"And your family?" I whisper.

Tom's face crumples suddenly and his eyes fill with tears. "I don't know where they've gone," he admits, wiping his eyes with a grimy sleeve. "They took all the women and children away when they took over and rounded up the men to come here. I asked when I could see my family again, but no one would tell me." He clutches at my sleeve, the pleading of a desperate man. "Do you know? Can you find out?"

"I... I'll try," I tell him. "Of course I will. But Tom... they'll let you know where they are, won't they? I mean..." I don't know what I mean. I don't want to believe a gentle and kind man like Tom could be separated from his family for no reason. I don't want to believe that's the kind of world we live in now, the kind of world we *have* to live in.

"I don't know," he says, looking defeated as he drops his hand from my sleeve. "They've said we might be prosecuted."

"Prosecuted..." I am horrified. "You mean, put in *jail*?"

He shrugs, seeming too weary and heartsore to care about his own fate. "Maybe? Who knows? They handcuffed us all, back at North Bay, and loaded us onto a military plane. They won't tell us anything."

I think about asking about Nicole's husband, who was the second in command at North Bay, but I'm not sure I want to know, and I don't think she'd care anyway. Still, I am deeply uneasy about it all. Shooting... rounding up...handcuffs and *prison*... I swallow hard.

This sounds like the kind of thing Bruce was talking about, except I haven't wanted to believe it. Now I might not have a choice.

"Hey! You!" A man in uniform, shouldering a military rifle, shouts over to us with a nod at Tom. "Get a move on. Now."

Tom gives me an apologetic grimace. "I have to go."

"Tom..." Now I'm the one clutching at his sleeve. "I'm so sorry," I tell him. "I'll try to find out what happened to your wife, I promise."

"Abby," he tells me before he turns away to follow the others into the hotel. "Her name is Abby."

Ruby and I are both silent as we watch the soldiers herd the men into the hotel, all of them looking as tired and defeated as Tom. The same guy who shouted at Tom gives us a forbidding glare.

"You should get a move on too," he says meaningfully, and so we do.

. . .

We stay silent as we head back home—Tom's words, his resigned expression, the prospect that the entirety of North Bay, over five hundred people, has been *cleared out*...

It's a lot to take in.

Back at home, I realize I have more pressing matters to deal with. "Ruby," I say, pitching my voice somewhere between gentle and stern, "we need to talk."

Her expression turns obdurate and she folds her arms, but at least she doesn't stomp upstairs.

"Come on," I say, more gently. With one hand on her shoulder, I guide her to the sofa. "What's going on?" I ask. "What happened today? Mrs. Weeks said you *attacked* someone." Ruby subjects me to a flat stare and says nothing. "I know you can stay silent for a long time," I warn her, "but I'm pretty good at waiting, too. And you're not in trouble," I assure her, even though I think maybe she should be, "but it's clear you're having a hard time, and I want to help you. That's all this is about, Ruby. Trying to help you."

More silence. I am not surprised.

"Moving here has been hard," I tell her quietly. I feel as if I'm fumbling through the dark, with no idea what the right words to reach her might be. "Adjusting to a new way of life. Leaving Mattie behind... and Dad." My throat thickens and I have to blink hard. "Ruby—"

Before I can say anything more, my daughter's face screws up and suddenly she starts screaming—a loud, keening wail that makes me want to clap my hands over my ears. "Ruby... *Ruby!*" I try to reach her but she pulls away, stumbling up from the sofa, her hands clutching at her head as if she's in pain. "Ruby, please," I beg her. She's still screeching, her eyes wild as she blunders around the living room as if looking for an escape.

I watch her helplessly, then let out a shriek of my own as she starts hitting her head against the wall.

"*Ruby!*" I run over to her, trying to pull her away from the wall, but she shrugs me off with enough force to send me stumbling back and then keeps hitting her head against the wall—*thunk, thunk,*

thunk—each time I feel the jarring pain of it myself and I realize I'm crying, just as Ruby is, because this is far too much pain for a thirteen-year-old girl to bear.

"Ruby, *please*." I crouch near her, the stitches in my cheek throbbing with the effort as I pull at her arm to no avail. Already I can see a bruise flowering on her forehead. "Whatever it is, whatever... Ruby, let me help you—" She pushes me away hard and I fall back, one hand to my pulsing cheek, just as the front door is thrown open.

"Ruby!" Sam stands there, looking horrified. Then he strides over and kneels down next to his sister, putting his arms around her in a bear hug, forcing her to the floor with gentle strength.

Her body, vibrating with tension before, goes boneless, and she crumples inside Sam's arms as she starts to sob, the small, mewling sounds of total despair tearing at my heart.

"It's okay, Rubes," Sam murmurs as he continues to hold her. "It's okay, it's okay. It's going to be okay."

Ruby doesn't reply, but neither does she resist his constraining embrace.

I don't know how long we all lie there on the floor, stunned and reeling, Sam's arms around Ruby, but at some point she stops crying; her eyes are open, but she looks as if she's asleep. Eventually, Sam picks her up and carries her upstairs; she is as docile as a baby in his arms, her eyes already fluttering closed.

By the time he comes back downstairs I have composed myself, wiped my face and checked my stitches, and am in the kitchen making coffee. Sam stands in the doorway, looking tired.

"She's asleep."

I nod jerkily; I may look more composed, but I still feel deeply shaken inside. "Good."

"She needs help, Mom." Sam's voice is sad and I nod again, even more jerkily.

"I know," I whisper.

"I think she misses Dad," Sam says quietly. "One night I heard her crying in her bed. She kept saying his name. I went in to say something, but she just got angry with me."

I close my eyes briefly. In another world, Ruby would have had grief counseling, support groups, friends, or at least distractions from all the sorrow and fear. She's had none of that here.

"Did you ever find out what happened today?" I ask Sam.

He shrugs. "It's that girl Taylor. She's kind of a... well, sorry, but a bitch. You know the type. She teases Ruby and then acts all innocent, like she was just being nice." He widens his eyes in a parody of what Taylor probably looked like. "I feel like, once, Ruby would have just ignored it, but now..." He shakes his head. "I just don't think she can take any more. Of anything."

I nod slowly. It's time to get Ruby some medical help, but considering she was handcuffed at school, I don't even know what that would look like, or if it's even possible. I could ask Jack for help, and I probably will, but after talking to Tom I'm not sure how that conversation would go, or what he would advise. Maybe he'd support the kind of discipline she faced at school. He's in charge here, after all.

"Are you going to be okay on your own this weekend?" Sam asks, and I look at him blankly.

"What..."

"I'm training at Minot," he tells me. "Remember?"

No, I didn't remember. And in any case, I thought that was more of a theoretical thing, not something that was actually happening this weekend. "Okay," I say, although I don't like the idea of my son doing some kind of military training. I picture him shouldering his way into a place like North Bay, assault rifle at the ready, and I have to suppress a shudder.

Sam comes over to put a hand on my shoulder. "It's going to be okay, Mom," he says.

"You know I saw Tom from North Bay? Dad's friend? He's just arrived."

"He has?" Sam doesn't sound all that interested. "I guess more and more people will be showing up here, now that we're really getting going."

"They cleared North Bay out," I tell Sam flatly. "People *died*."

Sam blinks, unfazed. "Well, you know what that place was like," he says after a moment.

"Yes, but the *government*—"

"Mom, when we were trying to get out of there, they *shot* at us." Sam shakes his head, sounding disapproving, maybe even disappointed. "Why are you so suspicious of the government?" he demands. "You *know* what it was like at North Bay. You chose to escape. And now you're blaming the government just because they dealt with the mess—"

"They went in with guns blazing—" I protest, but Sam cuts me off.

"So you've heard," he scoffs. "They needed to use reasonable force, *obviously*." He shakes his head again. "I don't think this is even about North Bay," he tells me. "Or Ekalaka, or wherever else you're worried about. I don't even think this is about the government."

Now I'm the one trying not to scoff. "Then what is it about?"

"It's about *you*," Sam states flatly. "You know how they made a little kingdom of North Bay? Well, you did the same at the cottage." He holds up a hand to stem my understandable outrage. "I'm not saying you abused your power or whatever, I know you didn't, but you had something there that you wanted to keep. And ever since you lost it, you've been second guessing everything, suspicious of everyone. It's like you don't want to trust it here, because what you really want is to go back... and you can't."

I blink, feeling more exposed by his assessment than I wanted or even expected. I thought I was trying to trust this new world, but maybe Sam is right, and I've never really succeeded.

Maybe he's right too: that just like Ruby, and maybe even Mattie, all I want to do is go back.

THIRTY-TWO

ALEX

The next morning I walk with Ruby to City Hall. I'm afraid to leave her alone at home, but she's as docile as a lamb as she walks beside me through a beautiful spring morning. Flowers are coming up everywhere, like harbingers of the future, bright yellow daffodils and slender-stemmed tulips, and even though the beauty should gladden my heart, for some reason it only makes me feel sad.

I think, like Sam said, I really do just want to go back. Back to the way things were... and yet I know I can't—to Connecticut, to the cottage, to a life when I had a husband and a home and hope for the future. All of that is gone, gone forever, and somehow I have to find a way to forge a future—here, or at least *somewhere*. For the first time since arriving in Watford City, I let myself think of somewhere else. Could we go back to Red Cedar Lake? Do I really want to? And will moving really accomplish anything?

I think of Sam now at Minot, learning how to shoot a gun, and Mattie back at Red Cedar Lake, so strangely silent, and Ruby next to me, even more so, and part of me just wants to either crumple or howl. But I don't, I can't, and so I head to City Hall and tell the officious-looking woman at the reception desk that I need to speak to Jack Wyatt.

"He's very busy," she says, sounding as officious as she looks, and I give her a gimlet stare.

"He'll speak to me." I realize I am certain of that—and also what a privilege it is, and one I'll trade in on any day, anytime, for the sake of my family.

The woman glares at me, her lips pursed, before she says briskly, "I'll see if he's available."

I wait, holding Ruby's hand, as the woman heads back to Jack's office. Just a few minutes later Jack himself comes to greet me.

"Alex!" He smiles at Ruby, his eyes crinkling with concern. "And Ruby. How are you both?"

Predictably, Ruby doesn't reply. "Could I talk to you for a minute?" I ask. "Privately?" I rest my hand on Ruby's shoulder. "You can wait here for a few minutes, Rubes, okay?"

She nods silently, which is more than she's done in the past, and I let myself be heartened. Jack looks quizzically between us as Ruby drops into a chair, and I turn to him with an air of expectation.

"Okay," he says, still with that quizzical smile, and then turns back to his office, gesturing for me to follow him.

I step inside, releasing a shaky breath as Jack turns to me, his smile morphing into a frown of concern. "Alex," he says, "is everything okay?"

"Yes..." I begin, only to realize how much it's not. "No," I admit, and to my shame my voice trembles and I have to blink hard.

"Oh, Alex..." Jack steps closer to me and then, gently, as if asking for permission, pulls me into a hug. As my arms surround him almost of their own accord, I realize that I didn't come here for Jack's advice or authority; if I wanted a diagnosis or treatment for Ruby, I could have just gone to the medical center myself.

No, I came here for this. For comfort, for compassion, for the simple feel of another person's arms around me, even someone I don't entirely trust. I don't feel strong enough to keep handling everything on my own—Ruby's rage, Mattie's silence, Sam's leaning towards a military-driven life... and then there are the farther-ranging worries about Watford City, this country we're building, and what I'm doing it all for.

But beyond all these worries that on an average day I feel I could still handle, there is the tiredness—physical, mental, emotional. Just like Ruby, I've been through a lot. Every single person here has, so I'm far from unique, but that doesn't make any of it easier to bear.

"Has something happened?" Jack asks. He's still holding me, one hand rubbing my back in a way that feels comforting but far too intimate—because the truth is, as much as I *thought* I wanted a hug, I'm not sure I wanted one from Jack Wyatt.

He feels too different from Daniel, taller and wirier and with a smell of leather and fresh air that is not unpleasant, but neither is it familiar. Hugging him feels wrong, and so I step back with a sniff, wiping my eyes as I say, "Sorry about that. It's just been a difficult few days."

"It's okay," Jack replies, seemingly unfazed both by the hug and me ending it. "What's been going on? Can I help?"

"It's Ruby, mainly," I admit. "She's been acting out, as I told you before, and at school yesterday she... she attacked a girl. The principal put her in *handcuffs*." I'm hoping for some outrage on Jack's part but he just nods, accepting, and I realize I'm not surprised. "She's also been suspended for two weeks," I continue. "I think she has some kind of PTSD—I mean, doesn't everyone these days?" I try for a laugh but only manage a raggedy huff. "I don't know what to do."

"Have you taken her to the medical center?" Jack asks, and of course that's what I *should* have done, but I came here instead.

"I thought about it... but what could they really do? It's not like she needs antibiotics or a Band-Aid."

"Alex, the medical center is very well resourced, all things considered," Jack says in a voice that sounds both gentle and stern. "And there are several esteemed psychologists on hand to help people with their trauma. I really think Ruby could benefit from some therapy. Unless you think something specific has set her off?" He frowns. "Nothing's happened that you don't know of?"

I don't know if he's talking of some kind of abuse or assault, but Ruby has hardly been out of my or Sam's sight since we came to Watford City. "I don't think so," I tell him. "But I suppose I can't be one hundred percent sure."

"Well, I think the best thing to do is have her evaluated," Jack tells me briskly. "I'll put in a word for you, if you like. It may get her seen sooner."

"Thank you." I'm not above accepting such privilege, especially for my daughter's sake.

Jack regards me for a moment, his head tilted to one side. "Was there something else?" he asks quietly, and I'm about to say no, because I've presumed enough and everything I'm worried about feels so nebulous, but then I hear myself blurt out instead, "What happened to the Native Americans at Fort Peck?"

Jack's eyes widen. "What do you think happened to them?" he asks after a moment. I hear a mildness in his voice that feels like it's being stretched over something else, something darker.

"And all the people who lived in places like Ekalaka or Jordan or wherever else you've reclaimed... there *were* people there, weren't there?"

"Some," he allows. "As I think I told you before, we have a medical team going in to assess needs."

"And what about North Bay?" I burst out. "I was there before, you know. Yesterday I saw someone I knew from there—he'd been arrested. Separated from his wife and family..." I trail off because for the first time since I met him, Major Jack Wyatt looks angry. His eyebrows are pulled together in a ferocious line, his lips thinned, color high on his lean cheeks, and right now he scares me a little.

"Alex," he says, and the mildness is stretched even tighter, like an elastic band about to snap, "why are you asking me these questions?"

"Because I want to *know*," I cry. "And at the same time, I *don't* want to know. I wanted to be part of something bigger. I wanted to help rebuild this country, but... I keep hearing things. Seeing things. *Feeling* things." I shake my head helplessly. "A woman in Montana wants to go back to her farm and she's not allowed. Six thousand Native Americans just disappear from a reservation? And what about the people who were living in Ekalaka? And as for North Bay—"

"If you really were at North Bay," Jack cuts across me, his voice hard, "then you know any force used was warranted."

"My friend told me people died," I state quietly. "Is *that* kind of force warranted?"

"If people have AK-47s pointed at you, then yes," Jack snaps. He takes a deep breath and then lets it out slowly. "I'm sorry, but what's going on here?" he asks as he rakes a hand through his hair. "I thought you came here for my help, but it now sounds like you're accusing me. What do you want, Alex?"

It's a fair point, and an even fairer question. What *do* I want? I think again of what Sam said—to go back. Poking holes in our life here won't accomplish that, though, so why keep doing it? Are all my doubts and fears no more than a form of self-sabotage, because for some twisted reason I can't accept this new life? Can't let myself believe in it, because I feel guilty or weak or undeserving? Daniel wasn't the only one to struggle with guilt. I did too, for the death of a man I never even spoke to. I killed him in cold blood. It's not something you ever forget—or forgive.

And yet would my perverse brain really sabotage our life here because of that?

The psychological self-analysis is too much for me now, and I slump into a chair. "I'm sorry," I tell Jack. "I don't mean to accuse you of anything. I'm just... afraid. Of so many things."

Jack sits down opposite me, the flash of anger replaced by simple weariness. "What things?" he asks gently.

I shake my head as a tired sigh escapes me. "Ruby... how angry she is. And Sam... he's at Minot for some kind of military training, and I just don't know if that's what I want for him. And Mattie...

she hasn't shown up for our radio calls, and part of me thinks I must be crazy because the people at Red Cedar Lake are some of the kindest I've ever met, but I'm worried about her. And..." I hesitate before the words, the loss, tumble from my lips. "I miss Daniel. My husband. I'm *tired* of doing life without him. And sometimes..." My voice subsides into a shamed whisper. "Sometimes I just don't want to anymore."

While Jack gazes at me with so much sympathy, I give in and start to cry, the hiccuppy sobs of a hurt child, but I can't even be embarrassed because the relief of letting my grief escape is too great. I don't think I realized just how much I'd bottled inside until I started to sob.

"Alex." Jack doesn't hug me this time, for which I'm grateful. "I know what you're feeling," he says. "I feel it too." He pats my hand just once before sitting back in his chair. "I don't have any answers," he says. "God knows I wish I did. But unfortunately, I think it's just something you have to walk through, day by day and step by step."

"I know." I wipe my eyes as I try to get my crying under control. "I know," I say again. "Thank you." I still don't feel embarrassed, but the relief isn't as acute. The comfort Jack offers me feels impersonal, the kindness he shows the same he'd show to anyone. Maybe I'm not special to him, or maybe he's not special to me. Either way, I feel disappointed in a way I can't explain.

"So you'll get Ruby evaluated?" he asks, and I have the uncomfortable suspicion that I have taken up too much of his time.

"Yes, I'll go there now."

"And when is your next scheduled call to Mattie?"

"Tonight at six."

"Why don't I come with you? If you can't get through on the ham radio, maybe we can try the official communications." I hesitate, thinking of North Bay, and Jack reads my reluctance perfectly. "Alex, we're not some authoritarian dictatorship here," he tells me, an edge of irritation to his voice. "I know you've seen some things that seem questionable, and in reality nothing is as black and white as any of us would like it to be. Do we use force sometimes? Yes. Not by choice but by accident, because no one wants to wind up dead. And do we remove people from their homes? Sometimes, yes, for the greater good, for *now*. Because whenever we reclaim an area, we have to test the soil, the groundwater, go through every square inch with a fine-toothed comb essentially, and we can't have people in our way, protesting their rights. Besides, the people we've encountered have been in need of medical attention, nutrition, *care*. We're trying to help them."

He blows out a breath before admitting, "But there is some self-interest as well. You remember getting shot at?" He nods toward my stitched-up cheek. "The guys in the field face that and worse every day. The people who choose not to go tend to be suspicious, sometimes violent. It's easier on everybody if we just have a completely clear policy. No one stays on reclaimed land. That's it." He shrugs as he spreads his hands. "Is it fair? Maybe not. But it's what we have to do for now, if we're going to rebuild this country from the ground up. Compromises have to be made, by everyone. In the long term, things will be different. Our hope is that if people want to, they'll be able to go back, but not yet."

Go back. The words feel like both a promise and a lie. "I understand that," I whisper. I don't disagree with anything he's saying, but his pragmatism borders on ruthlessness and it doesn't make me feel much better. I wanted to be part of something bigger, but life in Watford City still feels very small, and I'm not sure it's what I want for myself—or my children.

"I should go," I tell him as I rise unsteadily from the chair. "Thank you. And I'm sorry for offloading on you the way I did."

My tone is formal, and Jack frowns. "You know I don't mind that," he says quietly, and I look away. The silence stretches for a second or two, and then Jack rises from his seat. "I'll see you at six," he says.

THIRTY-THREE
MATTIE

Over the next few days Mattie does her best to do everything right. She accepts the mundanity of her chores without a murmur; she pretends to ignore Wade's knowing smirks and even the occasional pat on her back that strays a little too close to her butt. She speaks in a low, submissive voice, and nods in agreement whenever anybody speaks. She is a model member of this community, or so it seems.

In reality, every second Mattie spends in submission, she is considering how to get away. She has walked the perimeter of the fence that now surrounds the entire camp, all the way to the lake. She has gone down to the dock and wondered if she could steal a canoe and paddle across to the other side, but the day after, padlocks appeared on all the boats' chains.

Mattie did not question it; she didn't even mention it, but she could tell from the way Vicky glanced at her that her captors knew she'd noticed. She was being watched, every second of every day.

And she was watching too, everyone around her—Patti and her family, who seemed unhappy but had accepted their lot, and Sheryl, who was protective and defensive of her daughter, her spark-filled gaze brooking no arguments. She observed Jason, his dark head bent as he conferred with Wade. Stewart seemed troubled but was adopting a pastoral stance, murmuring words of bland encouragement, offering tepid smiles. Ben, Mattie saw, had become Wade's acolyte, and Kyle wasn't far behind. Although she and Kyle were sharing the same cabin, Mattie did her best to ignore him without being rude about it. At this stage in the game, she wasn't going to antagonize *anyone*.

And then there was Nicole, who Mattie couldn't figure out at all. Nicole understood what was happening there and didn't like it, but neither did she seem at all moved to do a single thing about it. She darned sheets and listened to muted conversations about planting and, eyes narrowed and lips pursed, she watched her son swagger about. She ignored Mattie completely, which stung, even though Mattie returned the favor and ignored her. Maybe it was safer that way; Vicky had separated them after all, and probably for a reason.

And so the days passed, and Mattie did her best to battle a swamping sense of despair. She had come to accept that she could not escape on her own. She could not climb the fence; she had no tool to cut through the wire. And in any case, she was being watched nearly every moment of the day; Vicky or Wade were never far from her. At least, not far enough for Mattie to attempt escape. She wouldn't leave without Phoebe anyway, and Vicky was still doing her best to keep the little girl from her.

Mattie had had it to her back teeth with Vicky's thoughtful murmurs about how much she'd had to deal with, that she was too young to act like a mother. Vicky hadn't thought she was too young to move in with Kyle, she'd wanted to snap, but as with so many other things, she kept herself from it.

She was going to be good, because good behavior was going to get her what she wanted. Since she couldn't escape, Mattie had come to realize, she had to be rescued. And to be rescued, she had to be allowed to use the radio.

And for that, she had to convince Vicky she needed to contact her mother—not for her own sake, but the sake of the camp. And, Mattie knew, that realization could not come from her.

It took three days of drip-feeding Patti and Sheryl shy, hesitant remarks about how she hadn't spoken to her mom in over two weeks, and how she might get worried, which could cause trouble for the camp. All said with a screwed-up face and a halting manner before shrugging like there was nothing she could do about it and letting the matter drop, forcing herself not to push it too far in case anyone got suspicious.

Finally, the morning of her scheduled call with her mom, Vicky approaches her after breakfast, unsmiling and determined.

"Mattie, I think it would be a good idea if you called your mom on the radio tonight. She's expecting you at six?"

With effort, Mattie keeps her expression hesitant, humble. "I think so," she says, her voice wavering in a way that is all too real. She knows she cannot mess this up.

"I hope you'll remember what I said about not endangering what we're trying to accomplish here," Vicky tells her meaningfully. "You know the US government came and cleared out North Bay? I heard on the radio that over twenty people died."

"What?" Mattie's mouth drops open. She'd convinced herself that Vicky's scaremongering was just that, but now she sounds certain, even a little smug, as if she knew how much this information would shock her.

"Came in with a team of Marines, assault rifles and submachine guns. They even had a grenade launcher." Her eyes narrow as she takes a purposeful step toward Mattie. "You see what we're up against? So please don't get any ideas of telling your mom you're not happy here."

"I won't," Mattie says meekly, although she feels like she's swallowing her tongue. She longs to snap that she wouldn't need to tell her mom anything if Vicky would just let her go. She knows there's no point, and she can't risk making Vicky angry.

Besides, she does understand, at least a little, where Vicky is coming from. She has had hours to think about Vicky and how she's changed, and she accepts that Nicole's cynical version of events is probably true—Red Cedar Lake is all Vicky has left. She isn't going to lose it to the new world that's forming, especially if that new world seems suspicious and violent. And then of course there is Wade... wrapping Vicky around his finger, promising her he can keep her camp safe, and probably a lot more besides.

While what might have happened at North Bay gives Mattie pause, it's not enough to deviate her from her plan. North Dakota might not be the perfect place, far from it, but it's got to be better than here.

Just after dinner, a little before six, Vicky nods to Mattie and she rises from the table to a host of speculative gazes and follows Vicky out of the dining hall to the office behind. As she steps inside the little room her heart starts to pound and her palms turn slick. The last time she was in here she was desperately trying to get help, and Wade found her.

She still remembers the feel of his fingers clamping around her arm, the way he flung her to the floor. The pane of glass she broke has been covered with a piece of cardboard and duct tape.

Vicky foregoes the headphones and has the radio on speaker. She pulls the microphone toward her, her gaze steady on Mattie, as she speaks. "CP ND 1, this is VA3 RC listening. I'm looking for Alex Walker; her daughter Mattie is waiting."

Mattie holds her breath, her hands clenched together in her lap.

"CP ND 1," Vicky tries again, "this is—"

"VA3 RC, this is CP ND 1," her mother's breathless voice cuts across the line and Mattie has to bite her lips to prevent a sob of relief. "Is this Vicky?" her mom asks. "Is Mattie okay?"

"Yes, Mattie's right here, she's been doing fine," Vicky says in her calm, sure voice. "Sorry, things have been a little busy lately, but we're all good here." She glances again at Mattie, her eyebrows raised.

"Hey, Mom." Mattie's voice wavers and Vicky frowns.

"Mattie." Her mother sobs with relief. "I was so worried when you didn't show up the last few weeks—"

"I know, I'm sorry about that," Mattie says, and now her voice sounds stronger. "Like Vicky said, things have just been really busy, but everything is fine here."

"Oh, good—"

"How are you?" Mattie asks. "How is North Dakota?"

"Oh, well." Her mom's voice wavers. "Pretty good," she says, and her tone makes Mattie wonder if there's more truth to what Vicky has been saying than she wants there to be. "How is Kyle? And Phoebe? And Nicole—"

"Good, good," Mattie says quickly. "Phoebe's learning to read. And Kyle is..." She searches for something positive to say about Kyle; they barely speak now. "Getting really into the community," she says at last. "And Nicole is sewing, like, constantly. It's really spring now—the lake is so beautiful, and the leaves are just starting to come out. But tell me what's going on there," she finishes in a rush. "How is Sam? And Ruby?"

"Oh..." Again her mom's voice wavers, and Mattie starts to feel afraid. "They're good," she says. "I mean... it's an adjustment, you know? It was always going to be an adjustment. I'll get them on the radio next week so you can hear for yourself. But Mattie, are you happy there? Because I can always—"

"I'm happy," Mattie cuts across her quickly, sensing that Vicky is seconds away from ending the call. "It's all good, Mom, you don't need to worry at all."

"Oh... okay," her mom says after a slightly startled pause. She sounds both relieved and hurt, and it makes Mattie ache.

Vicky runs a finger across her throat, a sign to end the call that feels chilling. Mattie only has seconds left.

"Well, say hi to everyone for me," she says in as jovial a tone as she can manage. "Sam and Ruby..." She glances at Vicky, who is looking impatient. "And Kerry," she says quickly. "Say hi to Kerry for me, Mom, okay?"

A second passes that feels endless and then she hears her

mom's voice, just as jovial. "Of course I will, Matts," she says. "I'll say hi to everyone."

Mattie releases a long, slow breath, and then before she can say goodbye, Vicky ends the call.

"Who," she demands in a voice like iron, "is Kerry?"

THIRTY-FOUR
ALEX

For a second after the call ends, I simply sit there, staring into space, my mind whirling. *Say hi to Kerry for me, Mom...*

But Kerry is dead. Kerry died saving Mattie's life nearly a year ago, which Mattie knows full well; I have seen how she has struggled to work through the guilt and grief her death caused.

"She sounds like she's doing well," Jack says, his tone upbeat, and I turn to stare at him in disbelief. Of course he doesn't know who Kerry is. He doesn't know that Kerry is dead, or that my daughter knows that, *lived* it, more than anyone.

"She's not," I state flatly. Realization is creeping up on me like a cold mist, ready to crash over me. "She's not doing well at all," I say numbly, because as I replay the stilted conversation in my head, I know unreservedly that that is true.

"Alex," Jack protests, now sounding as jovial as I was pretending to be, "she might have sounded a little emotional, but—"

"*No.*" I slap my hand on the table to silence him, my fear and fury coalescing into a hard, hot ball inside me. What is happening at Red Cedar Lake that my sixteen-year-old daughter has to speak to me in *code*? "She asked me to say hi to Kerry," I tell him, "and Kerry is *dead*. Kerry died saving Mattie's life." My voice throbs with memory. "The only reason Mattie would say her name is if she was trying to tell me that something was wrong."

Jack stares at me, his forehead crinkled, his eyes creased, as if he's trying to figure me out. As if he thinks I'm being ridiculous, hysterical, and meanwhile my certainty is growing.

My daughter is in danger.

"Okay," Jack says at last, still sounding irritatingly skeptical. "You think she's being held there against her will?"

"I don't know." I shake my head, a violent back and forth. "I don't know. But something is wrong, I know that much, and she needs me—she needs me to go to her."

"Alex, it's over a thousand miles," Jack protests, and now he's sounding frustratingly reasonable. "You can't go that kind of distance on your own."

"You can't stop me," I fire back instantly. "I don't care if there are borders and checkpoints and I'm not meant to leave this stupid little town. I'm *going*!" My voice rises in a shriek, my fists balled; I am ready to fight.

Jack takes me by the shoulders. "Okay," he says gently. "Okay. We'll get you there."

A shudder escapes me, and I bow my head. "I'm sorry," I tell him. "I'm sorry..." My mind is racing with ways to get to Mattie. I left Ruby at home alone for this call, promising her she could speak next time; I think some part of me knew there might be a problem, and I didn't want to set Ruby off. And Sam is at Minot until tomorrow, but I need to leave now.

I need to save my daughter *now*.

"What can I do?" I ask Jack. "I don't know what to do. Ruby—"

"We'll find a way to take care of Ruby. When is Sam back?"

"Tomorrow." My voice vibrates with frustration. "If someone was forcing her to say all those things..." I think of the way Mattie insisted I not come, that everything was fine. How *stupid* could I be, feeling hurt instead of suspicious? A ragged cry escapes me, torn from my lips. If something happens to Mattie, it will absolutely be all my fault.

And yet at the same time, I can hardly believe that something *could*. I left Mattie in hands I trusted... I remember how Vicky hugged me goodbye, how she promised me she'd take care of my daughter. But what if something has happened to Vicky? Instantly I picture Red Cedar Lake being taken over by the kind of wild-eyed renegades that attacked the cottage. Vicky insisted they were safe, I saw myself how the world was getting back to normal, but... what if something has happened?

And then I remember that something already has. It must have, for Mattie to mention Kerry like that.

"Okay," Jack says, his voice steady. "I can send a small detachment there—"

"No." I'm thinking of North Bay, and I can't stand for Mattie to be in that situation—guns blazing, people dying. "No, Jack," I insist, "this can't be anything official."

"I wasn't thinking *official*," he says. "To be honest, I can't do anything official without the Canadian government's say-so, and it's not my call anyway. I'm not that important." He smiles wryly, although his hazel eyes are troubled. "But I could rustle up a few guys, at least."

A few guys. But how would that go? If there's going to be some kind of stand-off... but why am I thinking this way? I feel paranoid and ridiculous, until I remember Mattie's deliberately offhand comment. *Say hi to Kerry for me...*

There's no way I could have misinterpreted that. No way at all.

"No," I state definitively. "I can't risk it, Jack. If something happens, if there's some kind of shoot-out..." I can't keep from shuddering. "I can't risk that, with my daughter."

"Then what, Alex?" Jack asks, the voice of reason. "You go by yourself—and do what? If something is going on, you need backup. Trust me." His voice drops to a low, grim note. "I've seen these types of operations before. They're all over the country, like gangrene. Some little community gets taken over, usually by some guy who's been waiting for this opportunity all his life—"

I let out a whimper. "Jack, *please*. Don't."

"I'm sorry." He shakes his head. "I'm not trying to scare you, but it happens."

I'm so scared for Mattie—all of sixteen, alone in a strange place, *vulnerable*... and I left her there. How could I have possibly? I resisted the idea at the time, but not nearly enough. I should have put my foot down and forced her to come with us, and Kyle and Phoebe too...

"Listen," Jack says calmly. "I'll radio Minot and get Sam back. Then I'll see if I can mobilize a helicopter to get a few guys to Mackinaw. From there they can go check out the camp. They'll be discreet, Alex. No one goes in with guns blazing if it's not warranted."

"But I don't want them to go in with guns blazing *at all*," I cry.

"I know," he replies, "but what else can we do? If she's in trouble, you can't handle it by yourself."

I know he's right, even though I resist it. I need support, backup. I need *a few guys*, whatever that looks like. The thought is as terrifying as it is reassuring. I don't want to do this alone, but neither do I want to relinquish control—or put my daughter in danger.

"Okay," I tell him. I sniff and then nod. "Okay, thank you."

"Why don't you head back to Ruby?" Jack suggests. "I'll make some calls and then let you know."

It feels wrong to walk home like I've had a normal chat with Mattie, but that's what I do. As I walk, my mind races and reels through all the possibilities, each one as unwelcome as the next. The fishing camp has been taken over by renegades who are now controlling everyone, including my daughter. It's better than having it burned to the ground, or everyone attacked and killed, and yet... *what is happening to Mattie?*

And if the camp *hasn't* been taken over... is there another possibility? I recall the people I knew there—Vicky and Sheryl and Don, Patti and her family, Stewart, the kindly minister, Adam and Jason, Rose and Winn... they all seemed benevolent, but did I really know them all that well? And what about Nicole and her son, Ben? I thought I knew her well, but I'm not sure I could have ever truly called her my friend.

When I get home, Ruby must see something of what I'm fearing in my face, because she rises from the table, her face pale, her eyes wide.

"Did you talk to Mattie?"

I nod. "Yes..." My instinct is to shield my youngest child from what I know or at least fear; I've always felt that Ruby was too sensitive to bear the weight of anyone else's anxieties, but maybe that's where I've gone wrong. Maybe I should have included Ruby more, and then she might have been able to share her anxiety and anger in return. As it is, Ruby's evaluation, diagnosis, and treatment will all have to wait until I return: I pray, with Mattie.

"But something's wrong," Ruby states, not a question, and I take a deep breath.

"I think something might be," I admit. "When I was on the radio to Mattie, she asked me to say hello to Kerry."

Ruby's forehead furrows. "*Kerry...*"

"I think she was trying to tell me something, to warn me," I explain while Ruby continues to stare at me hard. "That something is wrong there."

"So what are you going to do?" Ruby's tone has turned belligerent, like she's daring me to act, because she suspects I won't do anything; it feels unfair but also reminds me how much Ruby's silence has hidden, and how much I need to untangle and understand.

But for now... I have to focus on Mattie. Mattie, whose life might be in danger. "Sam is coming back from Minot," I tell Ruby. "He'll take care of you while I'm gone."

"I don't need anyone to take care of me," she snaps, and I look at her pleadingly.

"Ruby, you know what I mean. I just want you—all of you—to be safe."

Ruby shrugs angrily away, and I suppress a shuddery sigh.

How long till Sam is back, and we can go? Two, three hours? That's probably the minimum.

Only an hour later, however, Jack appears at my door. I have a backpack with a change of clothes and some bottled water and beef jerky, and I've laid out meals for Ruby and Sam for the next twenty-four hours. There wasn't much more I could do besides wait, while Ruby curled up in a corner of the sofa, sullen and silent.

"I'm sorry," Jack says as he steps into the house. Those were not the first words I wanted him to say, and my stomach dips.

"Why are you sorry?"

"I've been told I can't mobilize anyone. After what happened at North Bay, HQ is reluctant to get involved in any more incidents, especially in Canada. And we need all our manpower for some civil unrest that's been happening in South Dakota." He shrugs, accepting, resigned. "I'm sorry, Alex."

I stare at him for a second as I absorb the fact that there will not be *a few guys* after all. There will be only me. And how can I get to Red Cedar Lake on my own?

"I'm still going," I tell him. "Don't say that I can't."

"I wouldn't say that," he replies. "I understand you need to go."

"But how?" I don't have a car. I don't have gas. I don't even have permission to leave Watford City.

Jack smiles faintly, although his eyes droop sorrowfully. "I'll take you," he says.

THIRTY-FIVE
ALEX

Jack might have been forbidden from using any human or weapon support, but he does have access to an SUV with a full tank of gas, another twenty-five gallons in the trunk. I don't ask him where he got it, or if he's allowed to have it, I just climb into the passenger seat.

Sam arrived back from Minot Air Base around midnight, equal parts annoyed and alarmed, and I made him promise he wouldn't leave Ruby alone for a second. She might not need anyone to take care of her, but I still need her to be safe.

"Mom, let *me* go," Sam said. "I have experience, if there really is a threat."

I knew after being at Minot, firing at targets and commando crawling through barbed wire, he'd be eager to do something real, but I was not about to endanger another of my children. "I need you to stay with Ruby," I said firmly. "Jack and I will go, and if it looks like there's a threat, we'll call in support locally." At least that's what Jack said we would do. Whether that local support would materialize is another matter.

We have plenty of time to think of a plan, because it will take at least twenty hours of driving to get to Red Cedar Lake, all the way across North Dakota and Minnesota and then into Ontario. As we head out into the night, I can think only of Mattie.

"Thank you," I tell Jack after we've been driving for a few minutes, having left Watford City behind us for the endless plains, now shrouded in darkness that is unrelieved by any light at all, the moon sliding behind a bank of clouds. "I know you didn't have to do this. It was very generous of you."

"I'm glad to do it," he replies. "I'd do it for my son, if I could."

"Do you know for sure he's in Telluride?"

"I've had confirmation he's there, but he's not interested in making contact and the community is peaceable, so there's no need to go in with, as you say, guns blazing." He sighs. "Sometimes I'm tempted to do just that, just to get him back. But even if I dragged him back to North Dakota, I don't think it would change how he feels. How he blames me for Susan and Rachel's deaths." He presses his lips together as he stares straight ahead.

Susan and Rachel. He's never told me their names before, and it gives them a reality, a humanity, that I didn't feel for them when they were just stories, especially as I've heard so many stories like Jack's.

"I'm sorry," I say quietly, and Jack shrugs.

"It's the same story as so many other parents, isn't it?" he remarks with an attempt at wryness. "Estranged parents, angry child. It just happens that this time it's during a nuclear apocalypse."

"I've thought that," I tell him with a small, answering smile. "Teenage attitude is amplified rather than eliminated by a nuclear disaster."

He laughs softly. "I know, right? And as a parent you want to just be like, 'don't you realize what's going on? I don't have *time* for this!'"

This time we both laugh, a soft sound in the dark that eases my anxiety just a little.

Jack reaches over and covers my hand with his own. "It's going to be all right, Alex," he tells me. "It really is."

"But you can't know that for certain," I tell him shakily. "You can't make that a promise."

"True." His hand is still covering my own and I find I don't mind. The warm, dry heaviness of it is comforting. "But I can promise that I will do whatever I can, whatever it takes, to make sure Mattie is safe." His fingers squeeze mine. "That *is* a promise."

There is a throb of emotion to his voice that makes me suspect this is about more than just Jack helping me out because he's that kind of guy. Maybe he's trying to make up for the guilt of letting his own daughter die, even though we both know he couldn't have saved her. Or maybe it's the unspoken implication, heavy between us, that our relationship is teetering between professionalism, friendship, and maybe even something more, which panics me if I think about it too much.

I don't say anything in reply; I just smile and then slide my hand from his.

At the checkpoint, Jack explains he's on official business and we're let through without comment. A shiver of apprehension goes through me; we're in wild, open territory now, where anything could happen, the flat prairies rolling onto hills, no more than mounds in the darkness, under the endless night sky.

I think of the vigilantes who shot at us at Ekalaka, of the renegades roaming through Ontario I've encountered myself, of who knows how many communities tucked away in the plains and hills all around us. The road we're on is empty and quiet, cutting across the state, with only a few potholes after a year and a half with no maintenance. We're driving well north of any potential radiation sites; Milwaukee and Detroit were both hit, but Jack has assured me we shouldn't be in danger, at least not from nuclear fallout.

Despite this, the emptiness of the landscape is disconcerting, even after all this time; we pass a truck stop that advertises showers, a laundromat, and free Wi-Fi, but the complex is dark and empty, with weeds growing through the broken windows.

After three hours, we change drivers and Jack cracks open a thermos of coffee he brought, which we pass back and forth. The silence between us feels comfortable enough, and driving takes all my focus and at least distracts me from worrying about Mattie.

"We should sleep," Jack says after another hour or two. "We can pull off, or if you think you're okay at the wheel without me to keep you awake, we can take turns sleeping and driving."

I have a sudden memory, clear and sharp, of Daniel and I driving across country to see his sister when Sam was a toddler, Mattie a baby. We drove all night while they slept, having decided that was easier than trying to entertain two fractious children for hours on end in the car.

"Let's keep driving," I say, and Jack puts the seat back and settles more comfortably against it, closing his eyes. Maybe it's a military thing, but he manages to fall asleep in what feels like a few seconds, while I drive and drink coffee, my entire focus on the empty road in front of me.

Occasionally there are signs of life—a farmhouse in the distance that looks lived in, a hand-painted sign staked to the ground advising people that it's private property. At one point, a truck passes me in the left lane, zooming by before being swallowed up in the darkness. I start to relax; the emptiness of this world feels less frightening, and there is something almost normal about driving along a road in the dark. I only wish I had the radio to keep me alert.

Invariably, my mind turns to Mattie. What will we do when we get to Red Cedar Lake? Will there be signs of danger, or will we walk into a trap? I trust Jack to be able to assess the situation, but it's still only the two of us. I really could have used a few guys to help rescue my daughter.

Because I can't bear thinking for too long about Mattie and the danger she might be in, my thoughts drift to Daniel. In a strange way, having Jack lying in the seat next to me makes me feel closer to my husband, as if I can pretend he's there rather than this man I'm forced to depend on but don't fully know.

I imagine Daniel starting to snore, and how I would poke him in the shoulder, gently at first, and then a little harder. How he would startle awake, and then good-naturedly grimace as he rubbed his shoulder while I rolled my eyes, and then we'd both burst into laughter.

The memory makes me ache, but not in a bad way. I still miss my husband desperately, but just imagining how it would be between us, realizing I knew him as well as I know myself, makes me smile, even now.

After a couple of hours Jack wakes up, and we swap positions. We're in the middle of Minnesota now, and besides that one truck we haven't seen anyone. Jack refills the gas tank while I settle into the passenger seat and then we're off again, toward the south side of Lake Superior.

I doze for a little while but I can't sleep properly, and eventually I give up and stare gritty-eyed out the window. I'm not sure how much time has passed when Jack suddenly speaks.

"I want you to know," he says, his gaze on the road ahead, "that I may not have agreed with everything the government has done, but I still support it. That's a choice I made, when I came to Watford City. I believe in my country, I believe in what we're trying to accomplish, and I accept that compromises need to be made... but it's a trade-off, and it's not one that everyone agrees with." He flexes his hands on the wheel. "But I do, and I'd do it all again, even with the losses we've suffered, the mistakes we've made." He glances at me, his expression opaque in the darkness. "Maybe that makes you feel differently about me."

"I don't know how I feel about you," I say honestly, and Jack grimaces. "The thing is," I explain slowly, "I understand what you're saying, but... I'm not sure I want to be a part of it. Not in the way that I am now, anyway." The words settle between us, and I realize how much I mean them.

"So what are you saying?" Jack asks, sounding both curious and belligerent. "Would you leave Watford City?"

"I don't know." I rub my temple. I'm tired enough now to feel almost as if I'm existing outside of my body, even as everything in me aches with exhaustion.

"If you did," Jack presses, "where would you go?"

Home. The word comes to me unbidden as well as pointless, because there is no more home to go to. There is nothing left for me in Connecticut, and the cottage is a ruin. And yet, I think, doesn't everyone in this new world want to go home? Yes, like Jack, I'd like to build something better, but deep down, I just want to go back to a place I've known and loved and *been* known and loved.

"I don't know," I tell Jack. "I don't know if there's anywhere *to* go." I glance at him. "How long is the country going to be nothing more than North Dakota and a little bit of Montana?"

"We're reclaiming more land every day," he says, "however you feel about that. In six months, a year, I'd say most of what's reclaimable will be reclaimed—maybe ten to fifteen percent of the total landmass of the US. And in a year, maybe two, life will be back to normal… or as normal as it can be. There are parts of Europe and Asia that are existing normally already, you know. Life *will* return to the way it was." He sounds so certain, strident even, but I can't help but think he's wrong.

Life *can't* return to what it was, because every single person will have lost someone. And what about all the people who, like Daniel, might have been exposed to more radiation than they realized? In a year or two or five, there might be an epidemic of cancers. Even more people might die. But I know Jack needs to believe in a bright future; I understand and even admire it… but I'm not sure I share it. Not entirely, or maybe just not yet.

"Alex…" Jack says and then stops. I tense, already suspecting what he might be going to say, and I don't want him to say it. The silence stretches on and neither of us dares to break it. "I hope you stay in Watford City," he says at last, and we leave it at that. Anything more remains unspoken, which is a relief.

Fourteen hours later, having driven through the night and day and then into night again, we arrive at Red Cedar Lake, having followed the crumpled map across 94 East, then Route 34 to Route

2 to Route 28 to, finally, Route 64 into Nipissing and Red Cedar Lake itself.

Jack cuts the engine when we're a quarter mile from the entrance to the camp. "Just in case," he says, and I watch, my heart in my mouth, as he gets his gear from the trunk—a backpack with provisions, bullet-proof jackets for the both of us, and a wicked-looking rifle, which he straps across his chest.

I am both heartened and frightened by all these preparations; I knew Jack was a career soldier, but I didn't truly *see* it until now, as he becomes grim-faced and, holding up a pair of night goggles to his eyes, he scans the darkened landscape with a professional, dispassionate air.

"Do you see anything?" I ask in a whisper. The woods rustle in the darkness all around us, a sound that feels ominous even though I know it's just the wind. The air is chilly even though it's nearly May, and high above the sky is dark and clear, pin-pricked with stars.

"No," Jack says as he lowers the goggles. "Let's walk along the road but keep well to the side in case there's a patrol."

A *patrol*? I know it's possible, but the prospect still terrifies me.

We walk in silence all the way to the entrance to the fishing camp. When I left just a little over a month ago, it was a friendly-looking gate made of red cedar logs with "Red Cedar Lake Fishing Camp" carved into the wood on an archway above. Now there is a forbidding five-bar iron gate stretching across, topped with barbed wire, and a barbed-wire fence, over six feet high, runs along either side.

I stop and stare at the gate, the fence, as the reality of what we're facing reverberates through me. My daughter, I realize, is trapped, and I have no idea how we're going to get her out.

THIRTY-SIX
MATTIE

"Who is Kerry?" Vicky demands again, her gaze hard as she glares at Mattie. "Why did you mention her?"

"She's just a family friend." Mattie is amazed at how she sounds—surprised, even bewildered, a little hurt, like she's the little child Vicky keeps treating her as. "My mom reconnected with her in Watford City. I haven't seen her since before the bombs."

"*Kerry...*" Vicky still looks suspicious, and Mattie holds her gaze in a way she hopes isn't challenging.

"She mentioned Kerry the last time we spoke," she tells Vicky, like it's no big deal. "Ask Wade. He was here. He heard the whole conversation." She is counting on Vicky *not* asking Wade, because of course her mother did not mention Kerry, because Kerry is dead. Or if Vicky does ask him, she prays that Wade won't remember or care. If Vicky knows she was trying to warn her mom...

Mattie does not want to consider that possibility.

Vicky continues to stare at her while Mattie shifts in her seat, trying to look innocent but not *too* innocent and then giving the game away. "Should we go back?" she asks Vicky. "I'd like to see Phoebe."

Vicky's frown deepens as her stare turns into a suspicious glare. Mattie spreads her hand in an appeal. "Vicky... what?" she asks, trying to sound plaintive but also a little annoyed and afraid. "Why are you looking like you're mad at me? I'm trying to do what you wanted. I'm trying to make it work here." She lets her voice waver, and in truth it isn't too hard. None of this is as much of an act as she wishes it was. She's trying to be the badass *playing* at being a little girl, but she really just feels like the latter.

"I don't trust you, Mattie," Vicky says at last. "Because you haven't proven yourself trustworthy. I don't think you believe what we've told you. How dangerous the world is. How safe you are here." She cocks her head. "Maybe we need to show you."

Mattie's heart stills and her eyes widen. "*Show* me...?" She has no idea what Vicky means, but it feels like a threat.

"Yes, show you," Vicky repeats with a decisive nod. "Make you realize just how dangerous the world still is. Maybe then you'll finally appreciate us." There is a light in Vicky's eyes that scares her, because it looks a little wild. Mattie has always understood that Vicky is in thrall to Wade, to preserving the community here, but right now she looks a little crazy.

"Yes," Vicky says, rising from her chair. "Wade will show you."

"*Wade...*" Mattie is instantly alarmed. She does not want to be shown anything by Wade.

"You know he's been going out on expeditions," Vicky says, sounding like a schoolteacher. "He knows what it's like out there."

"And you don't?" Mattie says before she can think better of it; she has dropped her meek persona for a brief moment, but Vicky notices.

"I've gone out too, of course," she says severely. "But I trust Wade."

Mattie does not trust Wade. Mattie does not trust Wade *at all*. "Vicky," she calls in a high, thin voice, as the older woman moves to the door of her little office. "Vicky, I don't want to go anywhere with Wade." She sounds like a child, begging not to be left alone in the dark.

Vicky turns to her, scowling. "What," she demands, "do you

have against him? You've always misjudged him, Mattie." She shakes her head, derisive, dismissive.

"*Vicky...*" Mattie knows she cannot tell Vicky that Wade hurt her. She won't believe her; Vicky does not *want* to believe her. Or, even worse, she already knows and doesn't care. Either option is frightening, and Mattie knows, instinctively, viscerally, that to go outside the camp with Wade will be the end of her. She cannot allow it to happen.

"*Please,*" she calls as Vicky opens the door. She hates that she is begging, but she has to. Vicky walks out without another word.

Mattie lurches up from her chair, her heart like a trapped bird inside her chest, beating desperate, futile wings. She *has* to get out of here... and yet she can't. And even if her mother has somehow managed to get help, it still won't arrive for hours, if at all. She's on her own, and she has no idea what to do.

She looks around wildly, and her fear-filled gaze falls on the radio transmitter. Maybe if she calls someone, anyone... but she wasn't able to before and she only has minutes, maybe seconds... but what else can she do?

Her breath comes in ragged bursts as she reaches for the radio, but then a sudden terror overtakes her. Calling someone won't work; it will be too late. She flings the microphone away from her and bolts out of the room.

She sprints down the path past the main cabin. Her only thought is to hide until this blows over, if it ever will, but as she rounds the corner, Wade saunters out of the dining hall, followed by Vicky.

Mattie skids to a stop. Wade grins slowly, knowingly. "Where do you think you're going?" he drawls.

"Nowhere with you," Mattie retorts. Her voice is shaking. She can see Nicole, Ben, and Adam all watching from the big picture window. Not one of them moves, although Nicole looks alert, tense. Mattie thinks about calling out to her, but what could she do? She hasn't done anything so far.

"Now, now, Mattie," Wade says, and his tone is that of a parent placating a child. "Let's just take a deep breath here, okay?" He takes a step toward her, his hands outstretched. "I don't know what's got you so spooked." Another step, and Mattie backs away, stumbling in her haste.

"I don't want to go anywhere with you," she says.

"*Mattie.*" Vicky's voice is firm as she stands behind Wade. "You need to think about the community as a whole, and not just yourself. Do you know how much trouble you've caused us these last few weeks?" she demands, her voice rising. "How much stress and anxiety? We took you in out of the goodness of our hearts and you've repaid us with nothing but hostility and suspicion. All Wade wants is to show you what's going on out there, so you might stop resisting every single damned thing!" Her face twists with sudden fury as Wade takes another step nearer.

For a second, Mattie falters, and that is a mistake. Wade reaches out and clamps his hands on her shoulders. Mattie twists, trying to get away, but his hands are vise-like and she can barely move. She screams, a loud, unholy shriek, and she catches a glimpse of Nicole's white face in the window.

"I... don't... want to go... *anywhere* with you!" she gasps out as she continues to struggle. She manages to free a hand and rakes her nails across Wade's cheek, drawing blood. He swears and the hands on her shoulders clamp harder, squeezing her very bones.

"Mattie, what is *wrong* with you?" Vicky asks, shaking her head. "We're trying to help you. Why can't you see that?" In response Mattie struggles harder, and Wade lifts her right off her feet.

"You can't take her out like this," Vicky says. "Let's just contain her." She gives Mattie a stern look. "Mattie, this is for your own good."

Wade carries her in a fireman's lift, one arm pressed across her back to keep her from struggling, to one of the empty cabins. She continues to struggle and kick as Wade dumps her on a bed.

Mattie sits up with a gasp, but Wade has already left her and locked the door. Her breath comes out in a rush as she looks around the bare room. There are worse things, far worse things, than being locked in a room alone, but she fears those things might be yet to come.

In the meantime, she realizes there's no escape. The door is locked, and even if she could break the glass, the one window has shutters on the outside.

Exhausted, overwhelmed, Mattie sits back on the bed and hugs her knees to her chest. She closes her eyes and longs for her mother.

Night falls and no one comes. Sometimes she hears muted sounds in the distance, but she can't tell what they are. At one point she falls into a doze. She's hungry and thirsty, but no one brings food or water, and she doesn't think she could manage to eat anyway. Mattie tries to stay alert, but she is so very tired.

Dawn breaks, the light filtering from underneath the shutters, and still she's left alone. She wonders if they'll leave her here forever, if someone in the distant future will come upon her curled-up skeleton, tucked up on the bed.

Hours pass. Mattie tells herself to be hopeful, that the longer she's left alone, the more time her mom has to summon help. Sometimes she starts to doubt herself, to wonder if she really has got everything wrong, if she's ungrateful and more trouble than she's worth, if the reason she feels so alone is because she's being unreasonable.

Then she doubts her mother; did her mom even understand what she was trying to communicate? And does she have the power to do anything about it, so far away? When someone finally opens the door, what is going to happen to her?

And then someone does. Mattie hears the click of the lock, and her heart feels as if it has stopped, suspended in her chest, everything in her icy and still. The door opens and Wade stands there, smirking. There is nobody else with him.

Mattie's heart now begins to beat harder than ever, as if it could pulse right out of her chest.

"Well, hello there," he drawls. "Feeling a little nicer now, Mattie, honey? Maybe a little more... compliant?" He starts to close the door behind him while Mattie simply stares at him, wordless with terror. Wade smiles, his eyes glinting, making her skin crawl with the smug certainty she sees in his gaze.

Then a foot nudges the door, swings it back open.

"Not so fast, you son of a bitch," Nicole says. She's pointing a small, pearl-handled pistol right at his chest.

THIRTY-SEVEN
ALEX

The sound of a gunshot reverberates through the stillness of the night. Jack and I stare at each other in the dark, wordless with shock, the barbed-wire fence glinting in the moonlight.

"*Mattie...*" I whisper.

The harsh planes of Jack's face are gilded in moonlight; I've never seen him look so fierce, and yet also strangely detached. It's chilling and comforting at the same time, because I'm pretty sure he can handle this situation much better than me.

Sure enough, he slips his backpack off his shoulder and takes out a pair of slim bolt cutters, clipping the fence with brisk precision. I am both gratified and impressed; I wouldn't have even thought of bringing bolt cutters, not that I had any to bring.

He clips the barbed wire to make a rectangle big enough for us to climb through, carefully; I can't believe it's been that easy so far, but of course getting into the camp is only the beginning.

Jack takes my hand as I gingerly climb through the fence, the gunshot still reverberating through me.

What is happening here? Where is my daughter?

Once we're through the fence we stand there together, still holding hands, getting our bearings.

"The gunshot came from over there," Jack murmurs with a nod of his head. "Alex... I think it's better if I go alone."

"No," I say instantly, and he talks over me.

"I'm experienced, I'm armed, I won't react emotionally—"

"*Jack.*" I turn to face him. "This is my daughter. You don't even know what she looks like. If she saw you, she wouldn't know you or trust you. I'm going."

He is silent for a minute, studying me in the moonlight. "Fine," he says. "But take this." He hands me a pistol. "I'm guessing you know how to use a gun?"

I swallow hard; in an instant I'm remembering Daniel teaching me how to use a rifle, back when the first bombs fell. How I tried to hit a tin can and failed, time and time again. And then, just a few months later, I shot a man right in the chest. A few months after that, I did it again.

"I do," I tell Jack.

He nods briskly. "Good."

And then he turns and walks silently down the road toward the camp, as quiet as a cat. I do my best to follow just as quietly. I have no idea what we'll find, and I'm praying that gun hadn't been aimed at my daughter. I force myself not to think about it; I need to focus on this moment, and the next, when it comes to finding Mattie.

We walk along the road to the main cabin, everything still and dark, the moon a sickle of silver high above in a midnight-dark sky. It all feels weirdly familiar, and yet also so strange—why is there a *fence*? Have there been new dangers—and from within or outside? There was certainly no fence back when Daniel and I first drove up to the camp, thinking it abandoned, and fell asleep in the empty cabins we found. It had felt like a fairy tale, Goldilocks and the Three Bears, stumbling upon a story and entering into it.

This feels the same, in a strange way, but instead of a fairy tale we've fallen into a nightmare, and I have to be strong enough to help my daughter climb out.

As we approach the main cabin, Jack slows, and I stand next to him. There are lights on, and a few people have gathered in a knot outside. I can hear raised voices.

"This isn't what we agreed on," a woman says in a high, thin voice, and it takes me a second to recognize it as Patti's. "We're meant to be protected, but right now it feels like the danger is on the inside!"

"Hush." It's Adam, the doctor who cared for Daniel as he approached death. "Patti, don't go mouthing off now."

"Do you really support Wade?" Patti shrieks. "Adam, he just fired a *gun*."

"We don't know who fired that gun—"

"Really?" Patti flashes back. "Who else is armed here, Adam? *Who?*"

Who, I am wondering numbly, is Wade?

"Patti..." Adam sounds tired.

"If Mattie gets hurt," Patti warns, "or if she *dies*, God forbid, I will never forgive myself or any of you for letting that man into our camp, no matter what Vicky says."

I draw my breath in sharply and Jack grabs my arm to stay me. I don't realize I've lurched forward, as if I was about to run into the main cabin.

"Wait," he whispers, and I nod jerkily. *If Mattie dies...*

What is going on here? And how can I save my daughter?

"That's enough," a woman says, and it takes me a second to realize it's Vicky. She sounds so different—angry, in a cold and distant way. "I won't have any of you speaking against Wade. He's done so much for us. And Mattie has caused us so much trouble! If we have North Dakota coming down on us like a load of bricks, you all know why."

I glance at Jack, the whites of our eyes gleaming in the dark. We are the sum total of that *load of bricks*.

"Maybe that wouldn't be a bad thing," Patti mutters as Vicky stalks off. I watch her stride away into the darkness, her long hair streaming behind her, and I glance again at Jack.

"We need to follow her," I mouth urgently, and he nods.

The others drift back into the main cabin as we keep to the shadows nearer the lake, which is no more than a swath of moonlit darkness, and follow Vicky to one of the cabins I don't remember being inhabited during my time at this place.

Clearly distraught, she wrenches open the front door as we hang back.

"Wade!" she cries, and I hear a man swear.

Jack and I both start forward. We stand in the doorway of the cabin, watching the tableau unfold from a distance—Mattie huddled in the corner of a bedroom, her face pale, her hands to her mouth; a man I don't recognize staring levelly at Nicole, who has a pistol pointed at his heart. Vicky is standing off to the side, looking shocked.

It feels as if a whisper or twitch could send everyone spinning into disaster—or even death. Jack puts his hand on my arm, willing me back even though everything in me longs to sprint toward my daughter. I have a gun, I think wildly, I can use it. Use it on this man who has so clearly been threatening my daughter. Use it to kill him. Why shouldn't I? I've done it before; I know full well that I could do it again, especially for Mattie.

My fingers grapple for the gun, but then still as the man speaks.

"You going to shoot that thing again?" the man—Wade, I assume—drawls. "Or are we gonna stand here all day playing chicken?"

"I might have missed once," Nicole replies coldly, "but I have five more bullets in this gun, and you only have two kneecaps, so..."

I almost smile at that, because the dark cynicism is so like the woman I remember—the woman I could almost, but not quite, call a friend.

"And you know what, honey?" Wade replies in the same drawling voice. His hair is pulled back in a dirty blond ponytail and his eyes are narrowed, his thin lips pursed. On a normal day, in a normal *world*, I wouldn't even notice him, and now he holds my daughter's life in his hands.

"I don't believe you can do it," he states with a smirk. "You missed once already. Went *way* wide, but maybe you were just nervous. But even if you have the aim..." He pauses, the smirk curving his mouth as his eyes glint with derision. "You don't have the balls."

Nicole stares at him for a second, and with a hitched breath I see Vicky has drawn her own gun to aim at Nicole. My fingers curl around the handle of the pistol tucked into my waistband. Do *I* have the balls to shoot this man? Shoot *Vicky*, someone I once called a friend?

"You know what?" Nicole says, mimicking Wade's drawling voice. "I don't need balls." She pulls the trigger, and Wade screams.

I scream, and Jack claps a hand to my mouth, pulling me tightly toward him, his arm wrapped around my ribcage, as Wade crumples to the ground, blood streaming from his shattered knee. From behind the hands clapped over her mouth, Mattie whimpers.

"You *bitch*!" Vicky cries and raises her gun to point it at Nicole's head.

Nicole spins around, pistol in hand, just as Jack pushes me from him in one forceful movement, and in no longer than it takes for me to blink, whips the rifle from his chest and aims it at Vicky.

"Stop right there," he roars out and Vicky turns to face him, her face white, her eyes wild. It only takes her a second to grasp the full picture—Jack, in full military mode, and me, standing behind.

Then she lets out a ragged cry of rage as she points her pistol at Jack—and he shoots her straight in the chest. The heart.

It feels like time stills. Stops, and we're all frozen in this gruesome and macabre tableau. Then Vicky falls, blood blooming bright on her chest, and Mattie cries *"Mom!"*

I rush to her as Nicole gazes down at Vicky with something like pity on her face and Jack soberly reholsters his rifle before bending down to crouch by her.

"Mom," Mattie sobs again, and I put my arms around her, pulling her close, so very grateful my girl is alive. Then we both instinctively turn to Vicky, and I flinch at the sight of her—her

blood-soaked chest, pink spittle foaming at her lips as the last of life's light fades from her eyes. I take a step toward her, and her fading gaze meets mine.

"Vicky..." I say helplessly. I don't know what else I can say. I have no idea what happened here at Red Cedar Lake, but just over a month ago, this woman was my friend, and she promised to take care of my daughter.

My arm tightens around Mattie. Vicky stares at me, her gaze unfocused, for another few seconds before her stare turns vacant and empty. Mattie lets out a sob as she buries her head in my chest and I glance from Vicky, who is clearly dead, to the man—Wade—who is barely conscious, his knee a blood-soaked, shattered mess.

In an instant, I feel the shock hit me like an electric jolt, and my knees buckle. I stumble to the bed with Mattie and we sit there, our arms wrapped around each other, as Jack kneels by Wade and Nicole holsters her pistol.

"I was wondering when you'd get here," she remarks, and I try to summon a laugh and find I can't. I'm too exhausted, too overwhelmed, too utterly spent.

"Where did you get that gun?" Mattie asks, and Nicole raises her eyebrows.

"I've always had it."

"You could have told me!" Mattie sounds surprisingly resentful, again making me wonder just what's happened here. "It might have made a difference."

Nicole's brows arch higher. "Five bullets and a pretty pearl handle?" she drawls. "I don't think so. I was biding my time, Mattie. I didn't want anything to happen to you, but..." A shudder escapes her, revealing the frightened woman beneath the reserved exterior she usually manages so well. "I had to be careful."

I shake my head slowly, still overwhelmed. "What *has* been going on here?" I ask in a wavery voice. I gaze at Vicky's body, and then Wade, who has passed out from the pain, his face waxy and white, and I shake my head, because I'm not sure I want to know.

And maybe Mattie doesn't want to tell me, because my daughter just hugs me tight, her face buried in my shoulder, and right now that is all I want. All I need.

THIRTY-EIGHT
ALEX

We stay at Red Cedar Lake for three days to provide statements to the local military, who launch an investigation into Vicky's death and Wade's injury. Apparently they already had Red Cedar Lake on their radar. It's a surreal time, being back where my family found sanctuary and my husband died. Mattie doesn't want to talk about anything, and I don't push her to.

We spend hours sitting in the Adirondack chairs by the lake, simply enjoy the sight of sunlight on the water as the spring sunshine warms our faces and souls. Eventually, the black flies force us indoors, and we curl up on the sofa in the main cabin, cocooned in our silence, as if it can both heal and protect us.

Eventually, the story comes out in jagged bursts—how Vicky started to change, Wade's arrival, the breakup with Kyle, the looming sense of danger and the constant fear.

My heart aches with a particularly fierce mother guilt. "I should have realized something was going on, the first time you talked to me on the radio," I tell Mattie, and she shakes her head.

"Why would you? I'd told you I wanted this. That I was old enough to choose it." Her face crumples, reminding me that sixteen is not an adult, not even in an apocalypse. "I don't think I was," she whispers, and I hug her again. There have been a lot of hugs over the last few days, each one its own form of quiet healing. I've missed my daughter, and my daughter has missed me, more even than I realized.

It's strange to be back at the lake, and I'm not sure how to deal with any of the other residents. Are they my friends? Once I might have said so, even if I never knew them very well. But after some of the things Mattie has told me, how no one was willing to defend or help her, except for Nicole... I'm not angry at them, but I avoid them, and I sense that they are avoiding me too. Even Kyle, who I used to know so well, seems like a stranger, although when he meets my gaze at dinner he seems abashed, and I wonder how much he regrets.

Never mind the people here, however; it's the memories I can't avoid. I picture Sam and Kyle fishing by the lake, Daniel calling encouragement from above, his voice weakening by the day. I force myself to stand in the living room of what was once our cabin, but which Mattie told me Vicky and Wade took over, and where Daniel told our children he was going to die.

I can see his tired smile, the pain in his eyes he tried to hide, the sense of his own failure that never left him, even when it should have. I should have helped much more with that, but the guilt I feel now is nothing but the echo of an old emotion, because of course it's far too late.

Daniel is gone. I said my goodbyes. I visited his grave. But as I stand at the dock and look out at the shimmering water, the trees so dark and impenetrable on the other side, I feel a sense of uncertainty about my own future. I left this place for Watford City with so much hope, even if it was such a hard-won thing, but I'm struggling to hold on to it now. And yet what else does the future hold? Where else could we go?

Eventually, we are free to leave—Jack, Mattie, Phoebe, and I, to head back to North Dakota. Kyle has chosen to stay at Red Cedar Lake; he and Mattie had already broken up, and their goodbye was stiff, almost indifferent. I felt duty-bound by our history, despite his and Mattie's breakup, to offer a ride, but he refused. It saddened me, the ending of another relationship. It took me a while to become fond of Kyle, but I did, and I hope he is able to thrive here, even if I can't expend any more energy on this place.

When we're given the all-clear, I go find Nicole. I haven't spoken to her much over the last few days. We were close once, in an uncertain sort of way, but I feel the distance between us now.

"So you're going?" Nicole says as I enter her cabin. She's standing by the fireplace, her cashmere cardigan swathing her thin frame, her blond hair pulled back in a messy bun. She looks fragile, her skin almost transparent, violet bruises under her eyes. "I guess it's all worked out in the end." Her voice is brittle, and I can't tell if she's angry or hurt or afraid.

"I suppose," I reply, although it hardly feels like a happy ending. Several days on I'm still reeling from Vicky's death, which seems both tragic and needless. Mattie explained to me how she'd come under Wade's control, but also how she couldn't bear to lose this community. Like me, she wanted to go back to the past, but she certainly chose a terrible way to try to do it.

Nicole lifts her chin to give me a challenging stare, one I recognize, because she's never been an easy person to like. "Are you angry with me?" she asks.

"For what?"

"For... for not protecting Mattie more." Her voice breaks, and to my shock I realize she's weeping, her head lowered, her shoulders bowed.

"Oh Nicole..." Any residual anger, or hurt really, I might have felt disappears in an instant.

I come forward to put my arms around her, and, another shock, she lets me. "You risked your *life* to protect her," I tell her. "Why would I be angry?"

"I should have done more," Nicole weeps against my shoulder. "She wanted to leave, back when Vicky would still have let her, and I wouldn't go with her. I was too scared. I've always been too scared."

"You've had a lot to be scared about," I murmur. An abusive

husband, a billionaire in that wretched hellhole of a bunker who assaulted her... Nicole may have once led a charmed life, but not recently, and I can't blame her for not being willing to risk even more, especially when she has her own son to think about. "Will you come to North Dakota?" I ask.

Nicole sighs and steps back as she wipes her eyes. "I don't know if I can handle another change, but for Ben's sake, I think we'll have to. We can't stay here, not after everything."

The community at Red Cedar Lake, I know, will continue on, without Vicky or Wade. What that will look like I don't know, and I'm not particularly interested in finding out. I just want to leave this place and return to my family—to Ruby, Sam, and Mattie, all of us together.

After that... I don't know what the future holds, but I hope we can figure it out together.

We leave the next morning—a bright May day, all blue sky and sparkling sunlight, the air crisp but warm. Mattie has accepted Jack's presence with a guarded friendliness; I see her glance between him and me, and I know she's wondering what there is between us, as I am. I suppose you can't have someone save your life without wondering what they might mean to you.

Now, however, is not the time to answer or even think about that question. We've been gone for five days, and I'm conscious that Sam and Ruby have been left on their own. I radioed Sam from Red Cedar Lake to assure him we were all okay, Mattie included, but I still feel a visceral ache to get back to both him and Ruby. To get our lives back, whatever they might look like now, and begin to rebuild our family.

Over the last few days, Jack has been busy coordinating with the local military; Red Cedar Lake is going to be under their jurisdiction, although I don't know what that even means. As in North Dakota, the government here is taking more control.

Jack did apologize for killing Vicky; he knew I counted her as a friend, but I knew he did what he had to, and I was grateful. Beyond that, though, we didn't talk about anything else, anything about *us*. I don't think either of us wanted or were ready to talk, and sometimes I wondered if there was anything to talk about.

There isn't, in any case, much of a chance in a car with a sixteen- and five-year-old. Phoebe sticks to Mattie's side; Mattie told me how Vicky had separated them, another aspect of the whole sad story that I find so troubling and bizarre.

We drive west through sun-dappled forests toward Sudbury, and this time, now I'm not so terrified for my daughter, I notice more signs of civilization—a man pushing a plow, cows in a field, a sign for medical services in Sudbury.

The city is being operated by the military, with a sign on the main road through town warning us of a security checkpoint which only residents of the city may pass through. It seems North Dakota isn't the only place with borders.

We drive around it on Route 17 and we pass several military vehicles, as well as a man driving a horse and wagon. The sun is high in the sky as we head west toward Lake Superior, and I see more signs of this new world stumbling to life—working farms, a school with children running in its playground, another town with a security checkpoint.

Mattie looks around at it all with wide eyes; she hasn't left Red Cedar Lake, save for the one trip with Wade she told me about, in nearly six months. We spend the night in the car at a derelict rest stop on Route 94, after a dinner of bottled water, beef jerky, and protein bars, all provided by Jack.

I have so much to thank him for, and I don't even know how to begin. I tell myself our conversations can come later, after I've seen to my family. I still don't know what those conversations will look like, what I want them to look like.

By the time we arrive back in Watford City we have been gone for an entire week. After being so terrified for Mattie, I now turn my terror to Ruby. How has she coped this last week? How has Sam coped, managing her?

As soon as I open the door, I find out. Ruby hurls herself toward me, hugging me tightly, before turning to Mattie, and then Sam comes in, looking tired but relieved, and somehow we are all hugging and crying because we are all together, and we are finally safe.

Later, when I am tidying up the kitchen—Sam manned the fort but did not keep it particularly clean—and Mattie and Ruby are curled up on the sofa together, like the long-lost friends they never really were before, Sam finds me.

"What was it like there?" he asks in a low voice. "I've heard about some of these places being taken over by these prepper guys. They can be seriously hardcore."

"Yeah, well." I scrub at a particularly hardened bit of rice in a pan. "That's pretty much what it was like, from what I've been able to gather. I don't think Mattie wants to talk about it much." I turn to him. "How has Ruby been?"

He shrugs. "Okay. Not as angry as she has been, you know? Just... quiet. And sad. She had a couple of meltdowns, but they were manageable."

I nod slowly. "Thanks, Sam, for being there for her."

Sam pauses and I tense, because I sense something more coming from him. "Andy's asked me to work at Minot," he tells me. "They're starting a kind of apprenticeship for college kids—you work during the day, and then you can take your classes at night. I wouldn't be fighting—it's in civil engineering. Rebuilding, like you said you wanted to do." I'm not sure, but I think I hear a faint note of accusation in his tone, the implication that I'm the one who has changed while he has not, and I know he's right.

I *have* changed. I just don't know what it means for me or my future. *Our* future, as a family.

"So you'd live at Minot?" I ask, and he nods.

"Yeah, starting next week."

Next *week*. "And you want to do this," I confirm, even though it's obvious.

Sam nods again.

I know this is all part of being a parent—letting your children grow up, letting them go. Even in an apocalypse. And so I force a smile as I tell my son, "Well, that sounds like an exciting plan."

He looks surprised, like he expected me to fight it, and maybe I once would have. "You mean I can go?"

"Sam, you're nearly twenty years old. You need to live your life as you see fit. And it does seem like a good opportunity."

He smiles, a look of incredulous relief breaking over his face, and while I feel glad for his excitement, I can't help but feel that the very second I got my family together again, we are already breaking apart.

THIRTY-NINE
MATTIE

Three days after she comes home, Mattie enrolls in the high school. Her mom insisted it would help her adjust, and that at almost seventeen, she should be in eleventh grade, making friends, having opportunities.

Mattie feels like her mother is speaking in a foreign language, one that has faded from use, like Latin or Sanskrit. The words still exist, but no one actually speaks them. And Watford City feels like a toy town to her, or a stage. She can't quite believe that everyone here is *real*, cosplaying as normal people living normal lives. Watford City has schools, stores, a library, a medical center, a park. People walk to work and guys her age hang around street corners, shooting the breeze, at least until nine p.m. which is the curfew for anyone under eighteen—just one of the many cracks in the façade of this place that prove it's not real.

Still, she agrees to go to high school, because what else is she going to do? Phoebe has been enrolled in kindergarten, and being assigned some menial job in this town doesn't feel like a future Mattie wants, not yet, anyway. Hanging around their depressing little house doesn't feel like it either.

And yet school is worse. How, in a matter of months, have teenagers like her, who have seen their lives completely blown apart, suddenly become so stupidly *normal*? They gossip about mean teachers and cute boys and who is dating whom. There's already a popular girl in her class who sashays around, smugly secure in her position; somehow she's managed to hold on to her Hollister jeans and Nike sweatshirts and sneakers, while everyone else is dressed like they fished their clothes out of a donation bag from Goodwill, which is essentially what they've done.

Mattie can't summon the energy to dislike her; she realizes she finds her pathetic. She finds this whole place pathetic, which she knows is a self-righteous and judgemental way to think, but she can't stop herself.

They're all like robots who have been programmed to revert to their factory settings. She could be in a dystopian novel, she thinks, the badass girl who is the only one who dares to question anything, except of course she doesn't.

She goes to class, and she does her homework, and she stays completely quiet, because if she ever was badass, and she's not sure she was, she doesn't know how to be that girl anymore.

She finds herself thinking about Red Cedar Lake—missing the smooth stretch of water, the lonely hoot of an owl, the way the dawn light crept over the horizon. She also misses the people, more than she thought she would. Nicole, who has yet to arrive in North Dakota, and Kyle, whom she realizes she didn't treat very well but still doesn't want to see again. She misses Patti, who felt like a mother, and Vicky, who she can't stop thinking of as a friend, even after all that happened.

Sometimes she wonders if she dreamed the whole thing. At other times she wonders if Vicky really did have a point after all—she wasn't as grateful as she should have been, for the security and sustenance the community provided. Not having to take care of Phoebe all the time is, Mattie is ashamed to admit even to herself, something of a relief. Even though she's not enjoying high school, she appreciates the weight of responsibility that has slid from her shoulders.

As the days pass, life falls into a normal pattern, even if it doesn't feel like it. Sam leaves for Minot, full of optimism and determination. Her mom goes back to work. Ruby is evaluated by a psychologist and diagnosed with intermittent explosive disorder, caused by trauma, which Sam joked to Mattie sounded like diarrhea. It made her smile, but she feels sad for Ruby, who's clearly struggling so much, in a way Mattie has never seen before.

Ruby starts going to a psychologist for therapy twice a week and has been prescribed anti-anxiety medication, which seems to help, but Mattie's mom told her it's going to be a long road to recovery... for all of them, she said meaningfully, and Mattie knew she was hinting that maybe she should go to therapy too, but she doesn't want to.

She already thinks too much about what happened. She doesn't need to talk to some stranger about it. And yet as the days pass, she feels a restlessness inside her, along with a sadness. She can't summon the energy or even the desire to try to fit in, to make this life *work*, even though she knows her mom is desperate for her to be happy, to put the past behind her. But can anyone ever do that, especially when the past is such a bloated thing, full of trouble and sorrow and grief and regret?

And yet she has moments of almost doing it, or at least seeming to. She and Ruby play Monopoly, arguing over Park Place the way they used to—Mattie insisting that two oranges for a dark blue is more than fair, Ruby doggedly holding on to her property. She helps her mom make dinner, peeling potatoes or stirring beans—the diet in North Dakota is mainly rice and beans; her mom jokes that the US Army must have an almost unlimited supply of both.

Sam comes home for the weekend and is as annoying as ever—farting on the sofa, teasing Mattie about her freckles, leaving his dirty socks on the floor. Her mom pretends to be exasperated by it all, but Mattie knows she is heartened by these signs of normalcy. They have become precious.

Mattie has thought about asking her mom about Jack Wyatt, who saved her life and seems to care about her mom. He's been to dinner twice but seemed ill at ease despite trying not to be, and

Mattie doesn't want to know what might be going on with him and her mom. As the weeks pass, she doesn't see him again and she realizes she's glad. She might owe him her life, but she doesn't want him involved in it—or her mother's.

And as the weeks pass, there are other signs of normalcy, not just in their family, but in the world. Fields are being planted. More land is being reclaimed. The high school is putting on a play; the medical center is offering the normal childhood vaccines. Everyone gets cellphones.

Mattie holds hers like an artifact from an ancient age. She can call and text people, but who would she message, and what would she say? The phone is preloaded with an array of apps—calculator, camera, maps. There is no social media, and her mom jokes that at least one good thing has come out of all this.

"All this" being a nuclear holocaust, but whatever.

Sometimes, like Ruby, Mattie has flashes of anger, but she generally manages to control them, at least from the outside. Inside she feels as if everything is wound tightly, ready to snap, but it never does. Not yet, anyway.

At other times, she feels flat and empty, like she cannot rouse herself to care about anything, not even Phoebe, who has been the source of her strength for so long. She is astute enough, she believes, to recognize that these reactions are common and expected, that after experiencing so much trauma and instability, she has finally come to a place where she feels safe, and that gives her brain and body permission to experience all the emotions she has held at bay for so long.

She recognizes this, but the knowledge does not make her feel better.

May blooms into June, and the days become hot, the nights still chilly. Her mother buys herbs for their little patio, plants them with painstaking diligence. She goes to the library and gets out books; she shops with those weird blue tickets for treats from the grocery store—a jar of jam, a Hershey bar, a banana.

She's still working for the newspaper, and Mattie reads it every week, trying to summon interest in all the good things that are happening both in Watford City and further afield.

Apparently, there is a whole *other* United States in Texas, with a military government which is operating the oil wells. North Dakota is in negotiations to unite with Texas, which sounds like something out of a history book. Mattie supposes they'll unite, one day. The North Dakota settlement has expanded to all of eastern Montana, parts of South Dakota and Wyoming, and the northwest corner of Minnesota.

They have a president, of sorts—some guy who was in Congress who looks haggard but friendly. In July, a bus service between all the settlements is offered, with a pass you have to apply for. Her mom thinks this is great news, but Mattie cannot see the point of traveling to Williston or New Town, which will be exactly like Watford City, with the same low brick buildings and wooden store fronts, the endless vista of prairie and badlands, and nothing else.

Her mother waits in line for a pass, proudly brandishing a yellow piece of laminated plastic upon her return, but Mattie can't care about any of it.

Finally, two months after they returned from Red Cedar Lake, her mother decides to talk to her. It's a Thursday afternoon, and Ruby is at her therapy appointment. Her mom left work early to take her, and when she comes back to the house Mattie can feel some sense of purpose emanating from her, and she has to steel herself.

"Mattie," her mom says, her tone gentle but firm, and Mattie thinks, *Here we go*. "I don't feel like you're happy here," she continues. "Like you've settled."

Mattie shrugs; she has no other reply.

"I know life in Watford City is far from perfect," her mom continues, her tone quiet. "It's small and simple and sometimes it can feel pretty restrictive. I..." She pauses as she briefly closes her eyes. "I can't always imagine a future here myself."

"You can't?" Somehow Mattie is surprised. "You seem like you can."

"Do I?" Her mom smiles wryly. "Well, I guess I'm trying. I'm trying very hard. But... I'm not sure how hard I should *have* to try, you know?" She sighs. "But maybe that's just naïve. Maybe trying hard is the point."

Mattie shrugs again; she still has nothing to say. She almost wishes she did.

"If you could go or do anything," her mom asks after a minute, "where would you go? What would you do?"

Mattie can't help but feel this is the stupidest question her mother has ever asked her. "Nowhere," she says. "And nothing. Because I can't... I can't go back."

She feels her eyes fill with tears and she tries to blink them back.

"We can't go back," her mom agrees, and Mattie sees, to her surprise, that her eyes are full of tears as well. "We can't go back to Connecticut, or Red Cedar Lake, or a life with..." Her voice wobbles now. "With Dad. I so wish we could."

"I miss him," Mattie whispers, like a confession.

Her mom nods as a tear slips down her cheek. "I miss him too. So much."

A shuddery sigh escapes Mattie, and then something in her bends, just a little, enough for her to lurch over and put her arms around her mom. Her mom holds her tightly, and it takes Mattie a moment to realize she is comforting her mother as much as her mother is comforting her.

Neither of them speaks as they hold each other, and then eventually they ease back, both of them wiping their eyes.

"We can't go back," her mom resumes, her voice sounding stronger. "Not in that way. But... we can go back in another way, maybe. I've been thinking about it a lot and I have no idea if it will work, but... I think I want to try. And now that there's freedom of movement, with more opening up every day, we actually *could*."

Mattie has no idea what her mom is talking about. "Where would we go?" she asks.

Her mother smiles, her eyes still shining with tears. "Home," she says simply.

FORTY

ALEX

I tried to make it work. God knows how I tried. I went to work, and I made dinner, and I read books, and I potted plants. I did everything I could to make this little life in Watford City enough, but with every small action I could feel that it wasn't.

That it might never be... not for me, not for Mattie, who is still so clearly struggling, and not for Ruby, who is doing better but still going through the motions.

Only Sam seems to have blossomed at Minot, working in civil engineering, sporting camo fatigues. At first he came home every weekend, but then it became every other, and now in mid-July we haven't seen him for a month. I know it's normal, it's the way of parents and children everywhere, and I've made peace with it.

But if he can find his place, his way, then so can the rest of us. Just not here.

I thought Jack would make a difference, and he almost did. After we came back from Red Cedar Lake, we moved gingerly around one another, not quite sure where we stood, or if we stood anywhere. I went back to the newspaper and Bruce told me, exultantly, that we no longer had a brief from HQ. We could report what news we liked, how we liked, and I knew that was up to Jack.

It gave Bruce a new sense of purpose and energy, his weary cynicism flaking away like old paint. But as for me, I found it didn't make the difference I expected it to.

Because the funny thing was, once given that freedom, I found there were lots of positive things to write about after all. When offered the opportunity to investigate, I found my suspicion softened into a more pliable and reasonable thing. I still tried to cover both sides of the story, but without the fierce criticism I might have once felt duty-bound to provide. And while I still enjoyed my job, I didn't feel that sense of purpose I needed. Something was still missing.

In any case, there really were encouraging developments every day; the world was opening up just as Jack said it would, and it was such a *relief*. Every day there was news about new areas for development, new trade agreements with other countries, new opportunities and possibilities in a world that was finally, finally starting to heal.

Yet none of it changed how I felt about Watford City, our little life here. That it wasn't enough, or maybe that it wasn't right. Or maybe *I* wasn't right. Whatever it was, something continued to jar, like a constant clanging inside me, and I didn't think I was the only one who felt it.

But part of me *wanted* Jack to make a difference and hoped that he would. He came to dinner twice, just as a friend, although Mattie eyed him narrowly when he stepped through the door. At one of the town socials we stood and chatted and even laughed, but it felt forced, like we were strangers pretending to be friends, and I don't think either of us really understood why.

Still, we persevered in this dance of friendship that maybe could become something else, until Jack finally confronted me.

"Alex." His voice was low, with that familiarity I had begun to count on. He'd asked me to go for a walk; the evening was balmy, the sun just starting to sink as we strolled down Main Street toward the park where we'd once found Ruby. I think I knew what he was going to say, at least the nature of it, before he said it.

"I feel like we missed each other, somehow," he told me. "Without either of us ever saying anything."

I was silent for a few moments as we walked, absorbing the truth of his statement. "I don't know how," I finally said, "but that's how it feels to me too." I risked a glance at him, and saw how thoughtful he looked, as well as sad.

"Is it just too soon," he asked, "for both of us?"

"Maybe." I knew that was part of it; Daniel still took up so many of my thoughts. But there was something else too. Something I couldn't get over. "But it's more than that, Jack," I told him. "I'll never be able to repay you for getting Mattie back to me. And for all the other things you've done that have been so kind. But..." I swallowed hard and then pressed on. "I can't be a part of this world, this rebuilding, in the same way you can. Like I told you before, I don't believe in it the way you do."

Frustration sparked his eyes as he shook his head. "Is this just because of Ekalaka?"

It wasn't, but there was still a question I had to ask, an answer I needed to know. "Did you know that I might be shot at?" I asked him. "Was that the *point*?" Once, it would have infuriated me. Now I realized I didn't care either way, but I still wanted to know the truth.

"You think I would have put your life in danger?" he demanded.

I kept his gaze evenly. "Just a little danger."

He sighed, a sound of frustration, but he didn't deny it. "The truth is, I don't know," he said at last. "I suppose I accepted that there was *some* risk. I wanted to prove something to you. To myself. That what we're doing is right and good, because it *is*." He turned to me, and there was a zealous light in his eyes that I understood and almost envied, but which I didn't share. "If that makes me a bad person, then so be it, Alex. I don't regret it."

"I'm not mad," I told him after a moment. "And I don't blame you for anything. I even understand your reasoning, but I don't share it." I blew out a breath, unsure how to articulate what I felt to myself, never mind to Jack. "I just don't feel like I belong here," I told him. "Maybe I will one day. But... in order to go forward, I need to go back."

He frowned, his face filled with confusion. "*Back...*"

I nodded, the decision firming inside me, settling in a way that felt right. "Yes, back. Back to my home."

Jack stared at me, his forehead furrowed, his lips pursed. "I understand about wanting to go back and take stock of what's left," he said. "I've thought of doing the same. Heading back to our little cabin... we buried our daughter there. I buried my wife." He sighed, closing his eyes briefly. "But I don't know that it would do any good. It wouldn't change anything. We still have to go forward."

"Eventually," I agreed. "But I think that looks different for me."

He opened his eyes and stared at me. "Go back," he said. "And then see where you are. And who knows?" He spread his hands, managing a small, sad smile. "Maybe one day..."

He let that thought trail off, and I nodded slowly. "Maybe one day," I agreed, because I felt that, at least, was something I could believe. There's a lot of scope with "maybe."

"I'll miss you," Jack said, and I stepped forward to put my arms around him, breathing in his scent that had become familiar, if not dear. His arms closed around me, and I rested my head on his shoulder. It was a goodbye, but for how long? Neither of us knew.

By the time Mattie, Ruby, Phoebe, and I leave in September, the world is like an oyster that has opened to reveal its precious pearl. Roads are clear, gas is available, stores have food. Pockets of civilization are open to the public and travel is allowed. Renegades still roam, but they are a low-grade threat rather than a constant and ever-present danger.

There are still constraints—eleven p.m. curfews for travel, limited food available, swaths of the country that are unlivable, with stark black-and-white signs forbidding anyone from going further, and barbed-wire fences scarring the land, telling us where it is safe.

There's even a mail service; Tom wrote me, having been released from prison and reunited with his family. They're farming a small plot of land in Minnesota, a new beginning for them all. Nicole also wrote me, from Wyoming, where she and Ben have settled, in a little town in the mountains. She sounded happy, or at least happier. I was glad for her, although I wondered if we would ever see each other again; the letter felt like a farewell.

And here is another farewell, although I don't know how final. A military bus takes us to Mackinaw City, where we buy a used car; for the last two months I've been paid in actual money, and it feels both strange and satisfying to use it now. We drive east, past farms whose metal roofs glint in the sunlight and towns offering farmers' markets and fall fairs, both of which still feel like miracles. Nearly two years after the first bomb fell, the world *is* starting to feel almost normal.

The road to the cottage is overgrown with weeds and brambles, even a few small saplings that have determinedly sprouted toward the sky. Several times during the quarter-mile journey, I have to get out of the car to clear the road. All I have is a pocketknife, so it's slow-going, painstaking work, cutting through the saplings and the bigger weeds.

Mattie and Ruby get out too, beating down the weeds, determined to be part of this. We're like the prince in *Sleeping Beauty*, hacking our way through the woods to find the castle forgotten by time... but will any of it be left?

And then we come around the bend and there it is—my parents' cottage, burned to the ground after it was attacked, a choice I made deliberately but which I've sometimes regretted. Why destroy the thing you love, just so someone else can't have it, even someone evil?

And yet... it's *not* burned down, not nearly as much as I'd assumed, all this time. We left when it was still on fire, but now, although the roof has gone and the walls are a collapsed shell, the foundation and some of the innards still remain.

"*Mom*," Mattie says wonderingly. "I thought there wouldn't be anything left."

We all climb out of the car, Mattie holding Phoebe's hand, Ruby striding through the long grass. We step through the front door, which is half-rotted and hanging from its hinges but miraculously not burned. We walk through the mudroom to the kitchen, which is the most damaged since that's where the fire started. I'd thrown bullets into the wood stove, but I guess they didn't do as much damage as we'd either feared or hoped, because the living room, minus the roof, is almost intact, the chimney of the huge stone fireplace I've always loved pointing straight up to the bright September sky.

Even the furniture is there, although it's obviously ruined—soggy and smoke-stained and rotting. My dad's old wicker chair is no more than a pile of broken twigs. I stoop down in the mess and find the bugle made from a deer antler that used to hang above the fireplace. My dad would blow it every morning, a wakeup call whether we wanted it or not.

A broken sound escapes me, something between a laugh and a sob. I can't believe we're here, and I can't believe so much is left, when we thought it was all gone. It feels like a miracle.

Of course, the cottage is still a ruin. To rebuild it will take more resources and skill than Mattie, Ruby, or I have or most likely could ever learn. And yet it still feels possible, and more than that, so much more than that, it feels *right*.

This is where we belong. Maybe not forever, but certainly for now.

I glance at Mattie, and from her tremulous smile, I know she feels the same way. I turn to Ruby, who is crouching down near some purple flowers. "Fireweed," she says as she cups a blossom. "It grows where things have been burned, and it draws out infection."

There is something so fitting about that, like something wounded is being drawn out of *us*, simply by being here again. And I am so glad to see my daughter finding her love once again, remembering the plants she studied and picked and prepared.

I step through the living room to the edge of the deck, which has fallen through and is no longer safe to walk on. From here I survey the lake, a shimmering oval of blue, reflecting the clear perfection of the sky. A loon, its wings outstretched, sails elegantly onto the water, landing with graceful ease.

Mattie comes to stand beside me, holding Phoebe by the hand.

"Can we do it?" she asks, and I let out a shaky laugh.

"I don't know."

"I think we can," she insists.

I stare at the lake, and I think of my parents, who built this place with their bare hands and loved it more than I ever could. I think of Daniel, of Kerry, both of them gone, of Sam, over a thousand miles away. I think of all I've lost and what I still might have to gain, here among the ruins and the weeds.

There are a dozen arguments I could make about why we shouldn't bother trying to rebuild the cottage; how we don't have the building materials or the skills, and what kind of life can we really have here anyway, out in the sticks?

But I don't say any of it, because somehow none of it matters, even if maybe it should.

"Rubes?" I call back, a smile in my voice. "What do you think?"

"Yes," she states firmly, and I laugh, because somehow we all know the answer even when I didn't really ask the question.

"Yes," I agree, and the word, the knowledge, settles inside me in a way that makes me feel rooted and strong. "Yes," I say as I put my arms around my girls, all three of them. "Yes, we can."

I don't know what the future holds—whether we'll stay here or even be able to rebuild this place, or whether we'll go back to Watford City or somewhere else, now that the world has opened up. I don't know if I'll ever see Jack Wyatt again, although part of me feels that I will, maybe one day.

None of that matters now, because here, under this crisp September sky, with the sun shining down on all of us, I know we have finally found the right place to be, to live.

We are home.

A LETTER FROM THE AUTHOR

Dear reader,

Huge thanks for reading *Where the Dawn Finds Us*. I hope you were hooked on Alex and her family's journey. If you want to join other readers in hearing all about my new releases and bonus content, you can sign up here:

www.stormpublishing.co/kate-hewitt

If you enjoyed this book and could spare a few moments to leave a review that would be hugely appreciated. Even a short review can make all the difference in encouraging a reader to discover my books for the first time. Thank you so much!

Writing this book has been a huge labor of love for me, and the ending was particularly fitting, as my family and I have recently taken on our cottage in Canada that Alex's family's is based on. There are exciting times ahead for all of us!

Thanks again for being part of this amazing journey with me and I hope you'll stay in touch—I have so many more stories and ideas to entertain you with!

Kate Hewitt

KEEP IN TOUCH WITH THE AUTHOR

www.kate-hewitt.com

- instagram.com/katehewitt1
- facebook.com/KateHewittAuthor
- x.com/author_kate
- linkedin.com/in/kate-hewitt-38b44521a

ACKNOWLEDGEMENTS

Thanks so much to Oliver and Kathryn, who have been so supportive of this trilogy and all it represents. I don't know that I would have had the courage to try writing something so different without their encouragement! Thank you also to the wonderful team at Storm who have brought this series to light, and lastly to my family, who have all shared the wonder of our cottage with me. For my mom and dad, who first had the dream, and shared it with me and my siblings, and then for my own children, who will take it to the next generation. I am so grateful to keep it going, and this story has certainly been a part of that!

Made in United States
North Haven, CT
06 December 2025